Someone to Talk to

~Someone to Talk to~

Silke Chambers

Someone to Talk to

ISBN-13: 9798418976475

"Gracious words are as a honeycomb—
sweet to the soul, and healing to the bones."
Proverbs 16:24 NIV

1~Spring 2012

Ow!" Charity ducked as the Scrabble game tumbled onto her head and clattered on the closet floor, scattering the little wooden tiles around her feet. Rushing to get ready for the RN pinning ceremony, she had dislodged the game from the closet shelf when reaching up for her black shoes.

As she knelt to clean up the spilled pieces, her older stepson, Jeremy, strode into the room. Partially dressed in his favorite formal outfit, he tucked the black shirt tail into his black pants and said, "You okay? I heard you yell."

"I'm okay. I just dropped something out of the closet. Go and finish getting ready, and make sure Zach is, too."

"He's trying to squeeze into his pants."

"From the Middle School Formal? They don't fit anymore?"

On cue, Zach entered, wearing dress pants an inch too short. "These are too tight." He walked around the room, penguin-like, to demonstrate. "And they hurt my stomach."

She sighed. There hadn't been time to take the boys shopping lately—just another thing she neglected in her rush to finish nursing school. "See if you fit into a pair of your brother's old pants," she said. Zach began for Jeremy's room, across the hall.

"He can't wear them. I'm saving them," Jeremy said, following him. "Hey, Zach!"

"Jeremy, help him!" Charity called after him. "I have to get dressed too."

She carefully gathered the game tiles and slipped them into the velvet drawstring bag. Closing the box, she slid her hand over its well-worn cover, repaired several times with masking tape. It had been her mother's game—fragile, like her mother's last days.

Handling the game just now brought back memories—about her mother's illness and death, and her father's death shortly after. Life's other happenings—graduating high school, marrying, attending nursing school—had supplanted those events. The memories surfaced once again while cleaning up the game. The times playing Scrabble with her mother, before the illness took her away, were precious. The neurologist said handling the game pieces would help preserve her mother's manual dexterity a little longer, so it became a nightly ritual for them to play at least one round of the game.

Recalling the task at hand—getting her family and herself to the pinning ceremony—she quickly slid the box back onto the shelf and removed a finely knit black sweater and swingy plaid skirt from the closet. She bent down to pick up the shoes. Taking a last look at the game up on the shelf, she closed the closet door. Unexpectedly, a tear sprang to her eye.

"You about ready, Chair?" It was Jeff, coming up the stairs to find her.

She swiped the tear away on her bathrobe sleeve and turned to look at her husband as he entered, handsome in his brown suit. "A few minutes and I'll be ready. Make sure the boys are dressed. Zach was having a problem."

"Hmm. Will do," he said, closing the bedroom door behind him.

Charity donned her sweater and skirt. She sat on the bed and began pulling up shear black stockings. As she stood to get them all the way up, her toe kicked a wooden letter tile, one she missed when cleaning up the game. It was a blank square on which the letter 'U' was written in black marker. She picked up the tile and rubbed it with her finger. *Mom wrote that on there—to give 'Q' a better chance.* She placed it on her dresser next to a popsicle-stick-framed Christmas card portraying the Nativity, a project Zach made in Sunday School several years ago.

Another tear trickled from her eye, and she could feel her nose getting red. Unexpectedly sentimental, repressed memories sprang to her consciousness: a picture of her mother's peaceful face, freed from the body that betrayed her, the tormented expression her father wore that day he missed work, and she found him collapsed in the basement.

What did he die of? What should I have done differently? She asked herself for the umpteenth time.

She shook her head and glanced at the cell phone on her dresser. The pinning ceremony was this evening, and it would take a half hour to drive to Kent. She stepped into her bathroom and washed her face with cool water to tame the redness of emotion from her skin. As she spent a few moments on her hair and makeup, she could hear Jeff calling for the boys to get in the car. She slipped her feet into the shoes and joined them.

◆◆◆

Charity sat on stage with the twenty-four other Kent State University class of 2012 nursing graduates. Her best friend, Josephine Ortego sat next to her. A "nontraditional" student, like her, Josephine became more than just a study partner or occasional carpool ride to class. She and Jo really connected, and were each other's sounding board while being stretched too thin working on their nursing degrees along with all the other responsibilities mothers have.

When Josephine's name was called, Charity gave her hand a squeeze. Josephine smiled at her and stepped forward to be met by her four children. Charity beamed.

Josephine's older daughter placed the nurse pin on her lapel and gave her a hug. The other three children all joined in a group hug with their mother, then went together to their seats in the audience.

As her other classmates' names were called, Charity looked over the audience to where her family was sitting. She could see Zach raise his arm in a wave, and Jeremy nudging him with a disapproving glance. Jeff smiled a little uncertainly beneath his bushy moustache, his expression more confident as she smiled back. She imagined her parents being there, too, sitting with her family, proud of her.

Becoming a nurse was her mother's dream. However, since she married right out of high school and had two children in quick succession, the closest she got to that goal was working in their family doctor's office two days a week. And then, when she developed the illness—Charity's father always called it *the illness*, refusing to acknowledge it by its real name—her hope was for Charity to go into nursing after high school. Charity's heart felt tight wishing her mother could be present to witness her finally fulfill that dream.

It was her turn. "Charity Cristy, RN," was announced.

She grinned widely as she was joined by her husband and stepsons on the platform. Jeff reached for her hand. Zach dragged behind, stumbling over the cuffs of Jeremy's old pants as he mounted the stairs. He tripped as he reached out to the dean of the nursing school for the nurse pin. Charity winced as the dean caught him and placed the pin in his hand. He fidgeted with the clasp, a tie-tack back, something he had not seen before. Jeff snatched it from him, quickly removed the clasp, and gave it back to Zach. Charity leaned down, waiting to be 'pinned'.

Zach peered at the tie-tack back in one hand and the pin, shaped like a tiny shield with a nail-like protrusion sticking out of the back, in the other. He shrugged, and thrust it through Charity's sweater and into her collarbone.

She jumped back, clamped her lips to avoid crying out, and pressed her fingertips over the puncture. She looked up and glimpsed Josephine in the second row of the audience, hand to her mouth, suppressing a smile. Glancing back at her family, she caught Jeremy's eye roll and Zach's look of mortification as he handed the pin to his father. Jeff gently worked it through Charity's sweater, pressing the clasp in place.

"Thank you," she whispered.

Jeff smiled and kissed her cheek.

Led by Jeremy, they stepped to their reserved seats in the auditorium, a row behind Josephine, Charity still applying pressure to her injury. Josephine turned around and produced a bandaid; she was always prepared for emergencies.

Charity squeezed her friend's shoulder and murmured, "Can you believe we're done?" Josephine gave her a broad smile.

Later, on the drive home, Zach said, "You're not still bleeding, are you mom?"

"No, I think the bleeding's stopped," she said, smiling at her son next to her in the back seat. She examined the skin under her sweater beneath where the pin was affixed, close to the neckline, and removed the bandaid. The puncture mark was barely visible.

She laughed. "We learned in nursing school that all bleeding stops eventually."

Zach shifted in his seat. Suddenly enlightened, his still immature voice squeaked as he exclaimed. "Mom, I didn't make you bleed that much!"

Jeremy, driving on a permit, was behind the wheel, his father riding shotgun. "Next time I'll put the pin on," Jeremy said with a nod into the rearview mirror. He deftly spun the steering wheel of the Blazer one-handed and turned onto their street, Poplar. As he completed the turn, he grazed the passenger side wheel along the curb.

"Watch that," Jeff said. "Keep both hands on the wheel, pal."

"I *know*, Dad. It's just a bump."

Charity glanced at her husband, whose face was grim. "Listen to your father," she said.

Jeremy made an impatient sound as he pulled into the driveway.

Choosing to ignore his insolence, Charity said, "Some of my class are moving up to Akron. They're hiring a lot of nurses there, being a bigger city and all. There's more hospitals."

Jeff turned to look at her. "Surely there will be a job opening in town. Maybe at Quarry Gen."

Like everyone else, he used the familiar nickname of Quarry Run General Hospital, part of NEOHOS, the Northeast Ohio Hospital System. It was located in the downtown area, south of the village proper. This part of town was paved with brick sidewalks and boasted a Bargain Retail, two or three churches, a cheese factory, and a three-story government building. The pottery and a few other businesses were boarded up, testament of some hard times in Quarry Run's recent past.

"I don't want to move." Zach said. He opened his door as the car came to a stop and hopped onto the drive.

"Me neither." Charity said, getting out behind Zach. "I've lived here all my life, like you. I'm sure to find a job close by."

Charity had married Jeff Cristy ten years ago, when his sons were three and six years old. She firmly believed in stability for her stepsons and didn't want to uproot them from their hometown now.

Besides, she loved the village of Quarry Run, named after the numerous limestone quarries in northeast Ohio which provided a living for early inhabitants. In addition to the stone quarries, many acres of farmland, dairy farms, and grass-fed beef surrounded it. There were small communities of Amish, with their guarded ways and simple lifestyles. Their plain black buggies could occasionally be seen drawn by sturdy horses along country lanes.

The 2500-some inhabitants of Quarry Run were mostly descendants of quarry workers or farmers and had a keen pride in their town. Charity's great-grandfather worked in limestone and was an early settler, taking part in the formation of village government and serving on the council for many years.

Charity reached for Jeff's hand as they stepped away from the car and past the daffodil borders gracing the front walk. He released her hand and reached around her shoulders, giving them a squeeze. "I can't believe you're finally done," he said.

She leaned against him as they followed the boys into the house. "Mm-hm," she murmured. "Me too."

~2~

The summer after graduation was an arduous time of studying for the state nursing exam and cramming during the Fourth of July festivities. Jeff and Zach were involved in the afternoon parade through town, riding a float sponsored by Jeff's workplace, Country Springs Water. Jeremy volunteered to pass out bottles of the company's water to those watching from lawn chairs or beds of pick-up trucks.

Dropping off her guys downtown in the cheese factory parking lot, Charity admired the bunting and flags decorating each home and business along the parade route. The parade would proceed north, along route 93, past Barney's restaurant, and end at Limestone Place, a shopping plaza built last year on the verge of a posh housing development, constructed on land that used to grow wheat and corn. The plaza included several shops and boutiques, a café with outdoor seating, and a spacious grassy park surrounded by neatly clipped box hedges. The cheerful splashing sound of the fountain helped drown out the traffic noise from the state route that was just a cornfield away. A cook-out was scheduled in the park for those participating in the parade.

Coming home, Charity got down to the business of studying for the exam. She felt sorry for herself for having to stay home from the parade and cookout, nursing a cup of herbal tea as she read and re-read the notes she took at a review class, absorbing very little. What was she thinking, scheduling her test on July fifth?

As twilight approached, she tossed down her notes and grabbed her keys. She would meet them early, as a surprise, and watch the fireworks with them. It was the least she could do. Spending the remainder of the holiday with her family was more important than cramming a few more pages of notes into her already full brain. Relaxing with them at sunset to watch the fireworks over the plaza was just the distraction she needed. Maybe there would even be some leftover picnic food.

She approached her guys from behind.

"Hey, Mom," Zach exclaimed, jumping up from the blanket they sat on. She wrapped her arms around him.

Jeff handed her a foil-wrapped hotdog. "I saved this for you."

She grinned and took a generous bite, mustard dripping on her chin.

"Done studying?" he said.

"Mm-hm." She took a big swallow. "I can't learn anymore."

"The fireworks should start in about ten minutes," Jeremy said. They all sat down on the blanket to wait for the show.

The next day she travelled to the testing center in Canton, bundles of notes and travel cup of coffee in hand. She glossed over the notes in the parking lot and left them in her car, entering the building with just her ID, keys, and coffee. Two and a half hours and ninety-three questions later, the computer stopped, programmed to calculate the percentage of questions answered correctly or incorrectly using an impossible algorithm. No one ever knew if stopping early was better than stopping later.

For that reason, she felt ambivalent about her success and checked her email twice daily over the next three weeks for the results. Just before dinner on July 30th, she was rewarded for her diligence with a passing grade on the state exam.

She kept the news to herself for now, barely able to suppress her smile, waiting for the best time to announce her triumph. Passing the plate of warm pancakes and sausage links around the kitchen table (breakfast for dinner was one of their favorites), her grin spread across her face as she remembered the terse words of the email: National Council Licensure Examination-RN, for Ohio: *passed.*

She spooned sliced strawberries onto her short stack and added maple syrup. Placing the syrup bottle back in the middle of the table, she gazed around at her guys, all staring at her.

"What?" she said.

"What's with the big smile?" Jeff said, a grin playing on his lips.

Jeremy nodded toward the laptop, kept on a kitchen counter. "Did you get an email?"

She nodded.

"And?" Jeff said, eyebrows raised.

She shrugged, her grin taking over her face again. "I passed!"

They congratulated her all at once: Jeremy reached over and squeezed her shoulder, "Good job, mom."

Jeff leaned in and kissed her. "I can't believe it," he said, shaking his head.

Zach raced around the table and threw his arms around her, squeezing tight for a moment. When he released her he said, "Let's get sundaes at Barney's to celebrate!"

Now that school was behind her, Charity hoped she would have time to do more things with the boys. Everything but the most essential tasks or activities had been neglected as she completed that final semester, clinicals, and a forty-hour preceptorship. Deep cleaning needed done, Jeremy still needed several more driving hours before he could get his license, and Zach was down to just a few items of clothing that fit.

Perhaps she could get back to a few hobbies that had been set aside, as well. She would love to get out her art things again and start on another painting, or return to a knitted afghan that was only half done.

And then there was Jeff. Working extra shifts to help pay college bills, he ended the day being as tired as she. Their relationship had become rote, monotonous, days ending with them both collapsing into bed, sleeping back-to-back. Occasional lovemaking was hurried and desperate, ending in a rush to get a few hours of sleep before starting daily life again. She felt like they had to get to know each other all over.

◆◆◆

To celebrate passing the nursing exam, Charity and Jeff decided to take the boys on a long-overdue vacation. They borrowed Charity's sister Nadine's camper, a luxurious vehicle that slept six comfortably, and drove north, to Presque Isle, on Lake Erie.

The week spent camping, swimming, and relaxing recharged everyone's batteries. Zach wanted to cook supper over a campfire that first night. As it had rained the whole way to the campground, everything was too wet to get a fire started, and they had to make do with sandwiches and potato salad. The next day the sun shone, and after spending the day in leisure activities around the campsite, Jeremy utilized skills he learned in Boy Scouts to get a fire blazing.

A partially burnt hot dog with mustard and chopped onions was Charity's favorite combination. Zach and Jeff experimented with other condiments while Jeremy ate his plain.

After supper Jeremy visited the neighboring campsite, presumably to play with the dog tied to the side steps. Later, Charity, seated next to Jeff in a lawn chair around the fire pit, noticed Jeremy with the dog's owner, a cute girl with hair the color of gold where the firelight played on it.

"Jeff," Charity said, gazing past her knitting.

He was deep in his monthly Civil War magazine.

"Jeff!"

He looked up. "Hm?"

"Look." She pointed to the next door campsite, where Jeremy lazed beneath an awning, bare-chested, showing off his abs. He was having an animated conversation with the blonde girl, who sat, rapt, at his feet.

"Mm-hm."

Charity grinned. "Cute, isn't it?"

"Hmph," Jeff muttered, and returned to reading.

Hmph, indeed! That boy is growing up before our very eyes.

Having lost count on the row she was knitting, she pulled it out to the beginning of the row and started over, peering at it closely in the fading firelight.

The rest of the week continued to be balmy and sunny, and they spent the next three afternoons at the beach swimming and picnicking. The third day Charity wasn't in the mood for squeezing into her one-piece again. Rather than buy a new bathing suit, she determined to lose those ten pounds or so that she gained on a poor diet during that last year of nursing school.

Dressed in capris and a tee shirt, she parked her chair beneath a cluster of small trees that grew along the far end of the beach. The filtered rays of the sun warmed her skin and she prepared for a few hours of relaxation while Jeff and the boys took to the water again.

Watching her guys play in the water and hearing the sound of other families having a good time, her body relaxed in the lawn chair and her hands stilled on the knitting needles. School was done. No more attending classes all day and cramming for tests. No more feeling guilty over neglecting her family to attend clinicals. She did look forward to using her new skills and determined to look for a job after vacation.

She reached up for a strand of hair and twirled it through her fingers. Closing her eyes, she listened to the waves lap the stony shore, and gave in to her thoughts.

The joyful laughter of children running to the water brought back memories of past visits to the beach, Charity's parents toting her and Nadine to the water in matching bathing suits. Their father would let them bury him up to his neck in the sand, and then would rise, zombie-like, and chase them, screaming and laughing, into their mother's arms. In those days before 'selfies', they managed to snap pictures of themselves close together, perhaps with the top of one head cut off, or only catching their four faces from the nose up, showing a china blue sky with cotton ball clouds. Her mother displayed the photos on a bulletin board at home. They all looked so happy.

That was before *the illness.*

It was during the summer following Charity's freshman year that her mother, Lilly, was diagnosed with ALS, Lou Gehrig's disease. She was thirty-nine years old. Back then Charity practically lived in hospitals—mainly Akron General, and later, Cleveland Clinic, as doctors attempted to diagnose her mother's unusual neurologic disorder.

Charity liked staying with her mother in the hospitals. The nurses made sure she had a comfortable recliner and always ordered an extra plate for her at mealtimes. Charity took it all in—observing phlebotomists draw blood samples, listening to doctors explaining test and imaging results, and taking notes of the neurologist's findings.

Her father depended on her to learn as much as she could since he worked six days a week at the grocery store he managed, and could only visit on the weekends. Once she had nothing to report to him—it was a day of delays and the neurologist had an emergency consult that kept him from coming. Charity's father was incensed, and accused her of not being aware enough to take accurate notes. How can we make sure they are doing everything they can for Mom if you don't pay attention? He had said.

For the remainder of her hospital stay, four more days, she made sure to take detailed notes even about the most ordinary things, such as when the linen was changed. When he came on the weekend, he reviewed the notebook and was satisfied.

Nadine visited often, but couldn't stay the night, as she was attending community college on a fast track to get her paralegal degree. So it was just her and her mother, and the sounds and smells of the hospital.

Charity's thoughts fast-forwarded one year later, when their mother became bedbound, and she and Nadine took turns helping her with personal care—bathing, dressing, fixing her hair. There was so much to learn. The first few weeks the home care nurses taught them how to help her turn in bed to avoid bedsores, how to use a bedpan, and what foods would provide optimal nutrition and protein. Their father lifted her into the comfy chair in their bedroom so she could watch the birds through the window, and sat next to her to tell her about his day. At dusk, he carried her back to bed, tucking in the blanket around her shoulders the way she liked.

As the illness progressed her mother was dependent on a ventilator for breathing and a feeding tube for nutrition. She could no longer leave the bed—a hospital bed, now. Their marital bed had been put in storage. Charity's father moved to the basement family room, originally to allow more room for her care in their bedroom. He remained there, Charity now realized, due to the deep depression he had sunk into, unable to cope with the worsening condition of his wife.

His brief visits with her became less and less frequent until finally he hardly even looked in on her. Just couldn't bear to see her that way, helpless and frail.

Charity's musing was interrupted by a frisbee nearly careening with her head, bringing her thoughts back to the present. She reached up to where it landed in the tangle of branches above her and looked about for its owner.

"Here, mom!" Jeremy waved a hand in her direction.

Charity shielded her eyes and tossed it to her son. It wobbled in the breeze and fell at the feet of, not her son, but the blonde girl from the neighboring campsite. She giggled and tossed it to Jeremy, her terrier chasing it joyously.

Shading her eyes and gazing out to the water, she observed Jeff and Zach trudging her way, dragging beach towels in the sand. She bagged up her knitting and shuffled through the sand to the cooler, set on a weather-worn picnic table. As she unpacked lunch, her thoughts ping-ponged back to days with her parents at the beach, then to what she was thinking about just now: the progression of her mother's illness and how it affected her father. His pranks and carefree laughter of her younger years were by that time a distant memory, replaced by the constant dispirited expression of loss.

"Hi, Mom," Zach said as he reached their picnic spot. Reaching into a bag of potato chips, he crammed a handful into his mouth.

Jeff threw his legs over the bench of the picnic table and took a slug of bottled iced tea. Before long Jeremy and the blonde girl joined them. Charity produced sandwiches and drinks for everyone, tucking her memories away for now and enjoying this lighthearted time with her family.

~3~

After the vacation week, they returned Nadine's camper and arrived home two weeks before Labor Day. Charity finally got down to the business of looking for a job.

Charity's friend from nursing school, Josephine Ortego, was hired at Hill 'n Dale Retirement Home that summer, soon after passing her state exam. She told Charity about her job over coffee at their favorite hang-out, the outdoor patio at The Coffee Cave, in Limestone Place.

"It's really just a nursing home, not a 'retirement home' like you'd picture, with a masseuse and spa and valet parking," Josephine said. "I like it, though. It's set in what used to be farmland, and there's still a working dairy next door. Sometimes the cows come right up to the fence at the parking lot. The people I work with are real friendly and I'm getting used to the patients—I mean, 'residents'." She spread her toasted raisin bagel generously with cream cheese.

Charity lifted her pen from her napkin, pausing in the doodle she was drawing. "'Residents'?"

"Yeah, we're supposed to call them 'customers' or 'residents'. I just can't manage the 'customers' thing. They live there, they aren't buying time-share. Anyway, since a lot of them aren't really sick, just need a lot of help, 'residents' is a good word to use."

"Sounds like a nice place. Did you apply anywhere else? I have to be honest—I haven't heard from any of the jobs I applied for yet."

"I did apply at Quarry Gen first, but there weren't any openings. So I took the first thing I could get." Josephine paused. "Don't get me wrong, I do like it there. And I was glad to get day-shift. With *mi mama* living with us, it works out better. I really need to be home at night."

Charity nodded. She finished her doodle of a muffin by drawing a smile face, then set her cup on it to keep it from blowing away in the afternoon breeze. They sat at a round table shaded by a large umbrella. A waist-high brick wall bedecked with seasonal flowers shielded café goers from the noise and smell of cars in the parking lot.

Josephine chewed a bite of her bagel. She wiped the excess cream cheese from her lip and licked it off her finger. "There are a couple of positions open for night-shift. They're looking for two or three aides and an RN. You should apply."

"I've applied for all day-shift positions. I don't know about working nights, but I have to get something soon. Jeremy will be graduating high school in two years and we have to save up for him going to college. He wants to go to Notre Dame."

"That's good. Expensive. But good. He should go to college." She shook her head. "George could have gone this year. He's even smart enough to get a scholarship, but he wants to get a full-time job instead. He won't listen to me."

"He doesn't want to go to college?"

"He says he wants to help me out at home. The bills are piling up with *mi mama's* doctor visits, my nursing school loans, and Natalie's therapy." Josephine's youngest daughter attended special classes on Saturdays for children with Autism and Asperger's.

"Maybe he'll decide to go in a year or two," Charity said as she got up and went inside for a coffee refill. Dropping a splash of cream into the cup, she enjoyed the swirly pattern it made as it surfaced, and mused if one could have a fortune told by the design it made, like reading tea leaves. Maybe it would give her advice about taking a night-shift job.

Stirring her coffee, she thought about working the night shift. She always considered herself a “morning person” and enjoyed getting up with the sun. It gave her a jump on the day and prepared her to take care of her family who would be arising soon. She got used to a certain routine over the past four years of nursing school: having a first cup of coffee by herself while saying her morning prayers, catching the early news show, preparing a simple breakfast for her family before leaving for classes or clinicals. She hoped to continue a similar schedule.

Stepping past the coffee shop fireplace on her way out the door, Charity noted autumn decorations already in place. A garland of fall leaves was draped across the mantle, and a scarecrow with a cheesy grin was seated up there next to a brilliant yellow mum. A little early for autumn, maybe, but it would not be long before the maple trees that were so abundant in town would be showing their true colors in shades of red and orange.

She took her seat across from Josephine. “I just don’t know about the night-shift. I like to be up early to get breakfast for my family and make their lunches. I wouldn’t want to stop doing that.”

“You could still do all that right when you get home, and then sleep after they go to school or work,” Josephine said. “If it doesn’t work out, you could keep looking. You should call about the position. You need a job. It would be stupid to pass it up.”

Josephine liked to give advice, and sometimes her recommendations came out sounding harsh. Probably the result of raising four children on her own. After the youngest child was born, her husband traveled back to their home village in Puerto Rico to visit his family. He never returned. Josephine did not offer any more details, and Charity supposed her occasional lapse in tolerance was a result of managing her large family by herself.

"You're right. And it's not like I never had to stay up late to take care of someone," Charity said.

"Your mom?" Josephine asked.

Charity nodded. "That last year I was her primary caregiver, and she died just before I started my senior year. I'll never forget finding her that morning—her face looked so peaceful and happy." She smiled at the thought. It was good her mother passed when she did, and in the way she did. Rather than struggle against death, she gave in to it, releasing herself from the prison her body had become.

Josephine reached out and touched her hand.

Charity looked up at the sky, full of the billowy clouds of autumn. "Sometimes I picture her in heaven, baking brownies for the angels or relaxing in a meadow with her pet lion, a flock of birds pecking the ground around her."

"That's a nice way to think about it."

Charity pressed her lips together and sighed. By the time her mother passed away, Nadine had already moved out, having finished community college. She had been hired as a paralegal in a large law firm and planned to marry one of her bosses. "My dad died shortly after," Charity continued, "so I had to live with my sister in Akron till I graduated high school."

"I don't remember you telling me that. What did he die of?"

"I wish I knew. Just a broken heart, I guess. At least that's what my sister used to tell me. Now, of course, I realize it was probably something else. My hope is that as I learn more as a nurse, I might figure out what was wrong with him. Maybe figure out why he died." *And hopefully learn it wasn't my fault.*

"There are no records?"

"Maybe. At one time. But things weren't computerized back then. It's all on paper. I even asked my brother-in-law, since he's an attorney. He said health care facilities aren't required to keep records longer than seven years. So that was the end of it."

She took a final sip of coffee and said abruptly, "I just don't know why he died."

Josephine squeezed her hand. "It's okay."

"After high school, I moved back to Quarry Run as soon as I could. Big city life isn't for me."

"Is that when you started college?"

"No. No money. I couldn't bear to move back to my own house, so Nadine helped me sell it to give me some money to live on. I got a cheap apartment above the pottery downtown and worked for Home Helpers, assisting the elderly, clear up till I met Jeff."

After a moment, Josephine said, "Do you want the phone number to call Hill 'n Dale? You really should apply. Just think—we would see each other almost every day. That should make you want the job, if nothing else." She grinned and rummaged in her voluminous bag for a pen. She jotted down the phone number and pushed the slip of paper toward Charity.

"That is the best reason ever." Charity took the paper and promised to make the call.

Driving down her street Charity waved at a woman she got used to seeing around the neighborhood, named Laura. She lived on Dogwood Lane, and took her 'daily constitutional', as she put it to Charity one day, to keep fit. At her age, she said, one must constantly work at it. Charity had noticed the woman's lean figure and knew she probably did many other things to stay so healthy.

After supper Charity called Hill 'n Dale from her landline. She endured four or five 'menus' before finally reaching a real person, only to be told she had to apply online, on the retirement home's website. *When did everything become so impersonal?*

She spent her evening at the kitchen table attempting to navigate the retirement home website on the laptop. Obtaining some help from Jeremy, she filled out the online application form for the night shift RN position and clicked 'submit'.

Joining Jeff in the family room, Charity sat next to him on the couch and lowered the volume on the TV. "I applied for a job at Hill 'n Dale."

Jeff raised an eyebrow.

"It's for night-shift."

"Night-shift?"

"Mm-hm. Josephine thought I might get it."

"Hmph. Josephine." He fiddled with the remote. "She thinks you should work nights? Is that what she works?"

"No, she has to be home at night to take care of her mother." Charity rested her head on his shoulder, nudging it a little. He responded by lifting his arm and wrapping it around her. Her body relaxed into the space between them.

"I just hope you get enough sleep. It might be hard for you."

"That's true. But Jo said I can still do everything I am used to doing, I just have to sleep at different times. I'll make breakfast for you and the boys when I get home and sleep while you are at work or school. Then I can always get a nap after dinner if I need to." She grasped his hand which was draped around her. "I'll make it work."

She turned up the volume on the show, "Cooking with the Stars". It was one of the few TV programs they liked watching together. Tonight, several B-level movie stars were attempting to cook the perfect poached egg.

Jeff looked at her. "You don't have to make it work alone. We'll help you."

Leaning into his shoulder, she smiled. "That sounds good."

To her delight, Charity was called the very next day by the Hill 'n Dale director of nurses and asked to come in. After a cursory interview, she was hired. Driving home, she got the distinct feeling that she was the only applicant for the job. She hoped that wasn't a bad omen. However, the truth was she was unemployed, in debt with nursing school loans, and had no RN experience. She was just grateful to get a job.

Orientation was to be on day shift for the first two weeks, then she was to spend a week training with the night shift RN she was replacing. That nurse was moving to Akron at the end of the month to work in a state prison. Quite a change.

◆◆◆

Before starting her new job, Charity and Josephine made plans to go to the uniform outlet in nearby Canton to purchase the required cranberry colored scrubs. Apparently, the Hill 'n Dale staff voted on a new uniform color that year and 'cranberry' won out over 'seafoam', 'mustard yellow', and 'avocado'.

Charity arrived at the uniform store ahead of Josephine and perused the circular racks of uniforms in all different styles and colors. She looked at the cranberry scrub sets and jackets. The higher-priced uniforms were made of a lovely soft fabric that would 'give', and also wear well. They had interesting features like multiple pockets and contrasting color trim. The cheaper sets, made of a stiffer fabric, were sturdy, but plain, with simple patch pockets. She deliberated about spending less money for more scrub sets or purchasing just a few sets of the more expensive ones, realizing she would then have to do wash more often. Such decisions. She chose a few different styles and brands and searched for the dressing room.

Trying on clothes in stores was always a time of frustration for Charity. She usually avoided looking at herself in full-length mirrors, but in the changing room, it couldn't be helped. She grimaced at the pale rolls of flesh she hid from the sun, too self-conscious about the extra weight to wear more revealing clothes, like shorts or a cami or a two-piece. Those extra pounds just lingered around her belly and thighs, like houseguests who overstay their welcome. She was tired of trying to get rid of them.

Quickly donning one of the uniform sets, she appreciated the way the warm-up jacket hid the extra weight. The scrubs made of the stretchy material were the most comfortable, the waistband of the pants giving firm support around her middle. They were costly, but she hadn't spent money on new clothes for herself in . . . ? She did not know how long. It was a good investment, she would tell Jeff. A conservative spender, Jeff may have to be convinced of the benefit of paying nearly a hundred dollars for each scrub set.

She was just about to change clothes when she caught sight of herself in the full-length mirror, looking so professional in the uniform. She stood straight and tall and turned to view herself from all angles, observing how she actually looked like a nurse at last.

She thought about her mother working at the doctor's office and how professional she looked in the teal green uniform sets she wore. She would bring Charity pens and notepads the drug reps gave them. Charity loved using the sturdy, comfortable click pens in her schoolwork, proud of how they represented her mother's occupation at the doctor's office.

And now here she was, *looking* like a nurse. And *feeling* like a nurse. Envisioning herself doing what nurses do—talking to doctors, administering medications to residents, learning about their medical histories.

She looked up. *I'm doing it, Mom. I'm really a nurse.*

She couldn't wait to get started.

While she was trying on another uniform she heard Josephine calling to her. Exiting the dressing room, she did a twirl in the scrub set.

"Is that the one you're getting?" Josephine said.

"I don't know." She reached for the price tag. "These are expensive. I could only afford two sets for now."

Josephine nodded firmly. "You should get those. It would be foolish to get something you don't really want just because it's cheaper. And besides, you look good in them."

"Thanks. They do feel comfy. And it's a good investment."

"You're right. You'll save money in the end, because they wash well and will last longer."

"Exactly!" She re-entered the changing room and undressed.

Charity put her glasses back on after donning her own clothes again. The new look she adopted after graduation included dyed light-brown hair, which effectively hid the grey streaks, cut into a fresh bobbed style, and new brushed-chrome rimmed glasses. She picked up her selections and exited the changing room.

Josephine walked toward the front of the store with her. "Sorry I'm late. Natalie was having an issue with me leaving. She's usually good as long as Maria reads her a book. But we couldn't find the specific book she wanted. Jesus, Mary, and Joseph! She threw a fit." She adjusted her tote bag on her shoulder. "Anyway, we finally found the book under the couch, and she calmed down."

"That's tough. I would have understood if you couldn't come."

"No, she has to learn to adapt to change. With her Asperger's, it's hard. But if we always give in, she won't learn." She leafed through a clothing rack with solid color jackets. "George is really good with her. He's usually home when I have to leave the house, but he was out at a job interview this afternoon. He hasn't been able to find work since he graduated high school this year."

"It's hard. There aren't many jobs in this town. I worry my boys will want to move away once they are done with school."

Josephine was quiet, her hand paused on a clothing hanger. "He said if he can't find work he's gonna go in the army. It makes me so worried. Especially for Manny. Since their father left, George has been a sort of father figure to him."

Charity squeezed her arm. “Maybe he’ll get this job. Do you know where it is?”

“Country Springs. They’re hiring temps.”

“That’s where Jeff works! I can have him put in a good word for your son. I’m sure he will remember George from helping out with the youth group at church.”

Josephine brightened. “Would he do that?

“Of course.”

“There were a lot of applicants, it would help if he had a reference by someone who already works there.” She selected two warm-up jackets in XXL from the rack and moved to the check out with Charity. A curvy, plus-sized woman, Josephine always seemed comfortable with her build. Her best feature was gorgeous chestnut hair that she wore down her back in charming ringlets.

Charity bought a warm-up jacket, two sets of uniforms, a good pair of white athletic shoes and bandage scissors. She felt prepared to face her new job, both in body and spirit.

“Is there anything I need to know about work before I go in tomorrow?” Charity asked her friend as they stepped to the parking lot.

“Don’t be late. In fact, you should come early. At change of shift the night-turn nurses are always in a hurry to leave right at seven thirty in the morning, so come before seven so they can give you report on the patients—I mean, ‘residents’ before they leave.”

“Alrighty! I’m just glad you’ll be there when I start my training.”

“And I’ll see you at shift change once you are on nights.”

“Good luck to George on getting the job,” Charity said as she hugged her friend goodbye.

Watching her drive away in her mini-van, she admired the well-organized manner in which Josephine coordinated all the responsibilities in her life. Raising four school-aged kids in addition to taking care of her mother and holding down a part-time job at the cheese factory was demanding enough. Josephine had been able to do all this while also managing to graduate from nursing school in the top ten percent of her class. She hoped now that school was over life would be a little easier for her friend.

~4~

Driving into the employee parking lot at Hill 'n Dale Retirement Home, Charity grinned to observe several black and white cows near the perimeter fence, chewing lazily with eyes half closed. Exiting the car, the pungent scent of country air greeted her. She never minded that smell—it took her back to the days riding in the old car they had when she was a child, during weekly trips to farm markets to get fresh produce. Driving with windows down, her father sped past beef and dairy farms, the odor of manure a tell-tale sign of cows ahead. Nadine would wrinkle her nose at the smell, but Charity knew it also meant they were close to the farm markets that sold strawberries, honey, and Amish-made jam and pastries She looked forward to it.

Her father passed the time by encouraging her and Nadine to join in a rousing chorus of "Ninety-nine bottles of beer on the wall." Their mother insisted he temper the words to "Ninety-nine bottles of Coke on the wall", but when she couldn't come along, because she was working at the doctor's office or deep in some project at home, he switched back to "Ninety-nine bottles of beer on the wall", to the girls' delight.

The tranquil cows, slow and deliberate, taking their time to eat and to chew, were part of the pastoral scene that calmed Charity's first-day jitters as she walked across the parking lot to her new job.

She strode to the sprawling single-story building, sided in dove grey with a black shingled roof, and stepped onto the portico. Moving past earthenware planters containing brightly colored annuals, she passed through the front entry in her new uniform and shoes, doing her best to appear self-confident despite the apprehension in her heart. Would she have enough skill to take care of real patients? During clinicals and preceptorship she always had someone with her, guiding her, preventing errors. But this . . . this was the real thing. Her skills as a nurse and caregiver would be exposed—good or bad, flawless care or mistakes.

Susan Morgan, the Nurse Manager who was to be training her, was off her first day at a continuing education seminar. The nurse who was filling in was usually only there on Saturdays and Sundays, which were less busy. Not used to all the normally occurring weekday activity, she was unable to give much attention to training Charity.

Charity essentially followed her around, trying to be helpful. After lunch the fill-in manager seemed at a loss of what to do with her. Feeling in the way, Charity left the nurses' station and made rounds, introducing herself to residents and keeping busy by assisting them with bathroom help, laying down for a nap, or just sitting with them for a few minutes of conversation.

This kind of personal care was something she was very familiar with and brought her back to the times she helped her mother in the last stages of the illness. Brushing her mother's thick hair and applying a little makeup to brighten the pallor of her face always made her mother feel better, in spirit if not in body. And the smile she gave Charity after such ministrations heartened her, bringing back the former, confident person that had been her mother.

Striding along the corridor, Charity encountered a woman named Sophie, with wild curly hair. Seated in her wheelchair, she backed into her room using her one good leg, crashing into her dresser and upsetting everything on it.

"Whoa!" said Charity, picking up a hairbrush and a few bottles of lotion. "Do you need some help?"

Sophie pivoted to face her bed. "I was trying to get a nap in before dinner." She scooted to the edge of the wheelchair and pulled herself onto her bed. Charity helped get her legs up and covered her with an afghan.

She sat beside the bed and picked up a book from the nightstand cluttered with paperbacks. "Is this a good book?" It was a cheap romance novel, a god-like figure on the cover wrapping muscular arms around a waif of a woman.

Sophie grinned. "Why don't you read it to me? You can pick up where my great-niece left off yesterday."

Charity nodded. Opening it to the bookmarked page two thirds through, she began reading. "Jaxon hefted the flagstones and laid them side by side on the gravel base. 'Is this how you like it, ma'am?' he asked the lady of the house.

She peered through the back door. 'I like it any way you do,' she teased. Her skimpy robe slid off one shoulder.

He cleared his throat and shook his golden locks out of his face. His sweaty chest glistened. 'And how would that be?'

She could see the evidence of his desire for her growing. 'Why don't you come and see? My husband won't be home till tomorrow,' she cooed alluringly, holding the back door open.

Jaxon stepped into the cool interior of the marble mansion, gazing expectantly at the woman, who dropped her robe to the floor. He reached for her."

Charity could see where this was headed, and was loath to read anything that churlish to an elderly person. Although, who was she to judge what this resident might enjoy? About to continue the saga, she glanced up and noticed Sophie lying with eyes closed, upper dentures loose in her mouth. Carefully removing them, she placed them in a denture cup and swirled a splash of water in it. Stepping toward the door, she caught the reflection of the window in a mirror, next to the door. She turned and stepped to the window, looking across the parking lot toward the cows once again.

The trips to the country were the first things she remembered changing as the illness took hold in their lives. Her father had been promoted manager of his store just before Charity's mother was diagnosed, which gave him first dibs on fruit and veg near the sell-by date at a price reduction. The farm-market trips ended as Charity's own time was taken over helping her mother, who depended on her more and more that first year, when she began to lose her mobility and started using a wheelchair. She taught her daughters how to cook simple meals and gave them quick tips for housekeeping. Her mother's sister, Aunt Beatrice, came over once a week to help clean, tidy the flower beds, and cook dinner.

At the sound of Josephine's voice Charity turned from the window.

"I been looking all over for you," Josephine said. "You should be at the nurse's station by now. I have to give report."

"Oops. Sorry. I'm coming."

"It's a lot to get used to, I know. But we try to be prompt so everyone can leave on time."

Charity followed to join the rest of the staff in the nurses' station, and tried to focus on Josephine's shift report.

Still stuck in her memories, however, she was thinking about a time riding with her father to his store to pick up groceries for Aunt Bee, who was missing a few items to make dinner one night.

Trying for levity, she started up a chorus of "Ninety-nine bottles of beer on the wall, ninety-nine bottles of—" and was interrupted by her father.

"Not now, Charity. It's not funny anymore."

After report, Charity and the day-shift staff made their way to the locker room. This false start with the interim nurse-manager was not exactly Charity's impression of what her first day as an RN would be. She wanted to *do* something—assess someone, give an injection, talk to a doctor. She aired her frustration to Josephine in the locker room. "I feel like I learned nothing at all today."

"It's not always like that," Josephine said. "When Susan's here, everything runs a lot smoother. It was a bad idea for you to start on the one day she's not here. You can start fresh tomorrow."

"So today was a waste."

She touched Charity's arm. "No, no—you shouldn't look at it that way. Nursing care is more than just performing tasks. Didn't you get to know some of the residents and staff?"

"Yes, I did. I met Sophie, that resident with long curly hair. She's in a wheelchair. You know which one I mean?"

"Oh, yeah! Sophie. I love Sophie. She's just wild the way she gets around in that wheelchair, and with only one good leg, too. Used to ride a motorcycle. A Harley." Josephine opened her locker. "Did she get you to read to her?"

"Well . . . yes. I mean—"

"Ha-ha! We've all had our turn reading her those trashy novels. I guess it's the most excitement she gets any more." Josephine closed her locker door after retrieving her lunch bag and other things, shoving them into a massive vinyl tote bag."

They exited the building and walked to their cars.

"I'm glad to get out on time," Charity said. "I wasn't able to clean up the kitchen from breakfast or get anything out for dinner."

"Your husband should take you out tonight to celebrate your first day as a nurse," Josephine said, taking out a large bunch of keys.

"That sounds good. After I get the kitchen cleaned we can go to Chef Mario's, in the plaza, maybe sit outside. I can have a large frou-frou coffee drink with whipped cream."

"That's right! See you tomorrow."

~5~

Josephine was right about things running smoother when Nurse Manager Susan Morgan was there. She introduced Charity to Susan during morning report, held in the main nurses' station, where the two units of Hill 'n Dale met.

Susan held out a hand to Charity. "Glad to have you join our team," she said, giving Charity a firm handshake.

Charity began with, "I'm happy to meet—"

She was unable to finish because Susan's attention was caught by a resident in a wheelchair, pawing at her from across the counter. She leaned in to listen to the woman's request.

"Dorothy," Susan called out to the Health Care Associate crossing the hall, laden with an armful of linens. Dorothy turned and faced Susan, who was holding onto the hand of the resident before her.

Voice lowered, Susan said, "Mrs. Patterson needs bathroom assistance. You have time now, don't you?"

Dorothy unloaded her burden of linens onto a handy side table and said, smiling at Mrs. Patterson, "Sure, I have time, sugar. How 'bout I help you back to your room? You can use your own bathroom."

"Thank you," Susan said. She turned back to Charity. "Sorry. A constant source of anxiety for our residents is loss of dignity. We try to meet their personal needs as quickly and privately as possible." Susan sat in an office chair and Josephine,

Charity, and the other nurses and HCAs all seated themselves in chairs facing each other.

The night-shift RN gave a brief but comprehensive report on the residents of both the Garden Hall and the Reflecting-Pool Hall, affectionately known as the 'Pool Hall' by the employees. Susan remained quiet throughout the report.

Once completed, she consulted the notes she had jotted on her clipboard and began giving instructions to the staff. "Garden Hall residents will have to eat in their rooms for lunch today, as the dining room carpet is being cleaned at that time. Josephine, make sure Mr. Thomas has the packed lunch his daughter left for him when he goes to dialysis today. The ambulette people forgot it last week."

Josephine nodded her head. "I'll be sure he has it."

She addressed the HCA seated across from her, "Matty. I promised Mrs. Ramos you would let her have a hot soak in the tub today. Her arthritis was acting up last night after a visit with her little great-granddaughter, and she says a hot bath always helps."

Matty grinned. "Her granddaughter left some lilac scented bath salts when she left yesterday. She figured she would be needing them soon."

Susan rose from her office chair and gave a single nod to Matty. "Thanks for doing that." She swept the group with a glance. "You've all met Charity Cristy, our new night-shift RN?" She inclined her head toward Charity.

Josephine grinned. Matty stepped forward and greeted Charity with a friendly, "Welcome aboard." The Practical Nurses and other Health Care Associates nodded or smiled in greeting as they passed by, mobilizing to get their work done.

LPN's stocked med carts and wheeled them to the dining rooms to administer meds best given with a meal. HCA's pushed trolleys loaded with linens to the rooms of bed-bound residents to attend to their personal needs and help reposition those who were unable to move on their own.

Being in the midst of this activity, Charity felt a flood of excitement go through her. *This is nursing! And it's about to start!* She draped her stethoscope around her neck and filled her uniform pocket with writing implements.

Susan Morgan beckoned her to follow along, herself already halfway down the corridor. Josephine smiled at Charity as she fled down the hall, trying to keep up with Susan.

Susan's method of teaching was to give a running narrative of what she was doing and why. She pulled some information from the fax machine at the far end of the Pool Hall where there was a mini-nurses' station—two wall-mounted computers and the fax machine on a stand.

Susan leafed through the papers. "Looks like we have a new admission coming this morning." Looking at Charity, she said, "The RNs and LPNs team up with admissions, doing a thorough skin check and noting any anomalies, such as bruises or skin tears. We will do a medication reconciliation and consult with our house doctor. Then we will fax that med list to the pharmacy. By this afternoon dietary, physical therapy, and the activities director will be waiting to have their turn to assess the new resident."

Without warning, Susan took off down the hall again, Charity in her wake. Calling over her shoulder, Susan said, "I wanted to check on Edith DeMattis. In report this morning, we heard she had a weight gain of nine pounds from last week. She's 229 now"

Charity caught up and strode side by side with Susan, working out in her mind some intelligent observation or comment she could say that might make a favorable impression on her new boss.

Susan continued. "Night shift does the weekly weights every Tuesday morning. A sudden weight gain usually indicates fluid accumulation, either in the form of ascites or edema. Mrs. DeMattis has congestive heart failure, so we will do a thorough exam to determine where the fluid is. She might need to be transferred to Quarry Gen."

Out of breath when they arrived at Mrs. E. DeMattis' room, Charity said, "She should lose weight, and be put on a low-salt diet." This would be a good opportunity to teach the resident about common CHF risk factors.

Susan paused and looked at Charity, giving a single nod. "Correct. But at her age, and level of activity, she won't be able to lose weight. And as far as the low sodium, it's her right to eat as much bacon as she wants for breakfast, no matter how bad it is for her." Susan knocked on the door before entering Mrs. E. DeMattis' room.

Charity remained close behind, feeling slightly deflated. How could the health of residents be restored if they weren't taught what was making them worse? Chronic health conditions may be improved, and life expectancy lengthened.

After assessing Mrs. E. DeMattis, Susan placed a call to Dr. Domicile, the house doctor. He ordered a diuretic, changed a blood pressure medication, and asked for a weekly blood potassium level to be drawn.

Shortly thereafter an ambulance arrived bringing the new resident to the retirement home.

By lunchtime the new resident was all settled in his room, Charity having observed the entire detailed admissions procedure. Anxious to actually take part in nursing care, she gladly performed the skin assessment with the LPN. Under Susan's watchfulness she placed the call to Dr. Domicile notifying him of the new resident's arrival and obtaining admission orders.

At the end of the day, Charity was exhausted by the volume of instruction she received from Susan and sat, stupefied, on an office chair during shift report. Susan just seemed further energized by it all and was seen striding purposefully to her car after work, arms laden with binders and a laptop bag which promised additional work at home.

At the kitchen table that evening, Charity recounted the day's events to her husband and sons. "I don't know if I will ever be able to keep up with the workload. Susan—she's the manager—worked non-stop all day, and even took some papers to go through at home."

"Maybe night-shift won't be as busy," Jeff said, helping himself to another slice of pizza.

"I hope not." She slid the mushrooms off her pizza with a fork. The rest of the family liked them, and rather than ordering a separate pizza, she conceded to simply removing the offending fungi from her slice.

Jeremy reached over and forked her mushrooms, placing them in his mouth with a grin.

"You'll just have to get used to working again," Jeff said, reaching for the iced tea pitcher. "You can do it."

Charity squinted her eyes. It's true, she had quit her job at Home Helpers shortly after marrying Jeff, but she did *work*—how else did the house get cleaned, or the kids fed, or the million other things that a household needed get done?

"You mean I'll have to get used to working away from home."

Jeff looked up at her. "Hm?"

"I mean, I have always worked here. For all of you."

Jeff froze. He slid a look at Jeremy, to his side.

Charity continued. "I might need a little help in that department. Okay?"

Jeff and Jeremy nodded. "Will do," they said in unison.

Zach shoved another slice of pizza into his mouth.

"I see your belly feels better," Charity said. He was prone to frequent stomach upsets. Usually a dose of pink bismuth and a trip to the toilet made him feel better.

"Huh? Oh, yeah. I had a big poop after school."

"Ugh!" Jeremy rolled his eyes.

Zach flinched at his brother's disapproval. After chewing for a moment in silence, he turned to Charity and said, "Since you're working nights, Mom, can I sleep over Damion's?" His best friend in middle school lived in the house directly behind them, and they loved spending hours competing at video games.

She looked at Zach, then at Jeff, who shook his head. "Every night?" she asked Zach.

"Yeah. That way you don't have to make my breakfast in the morning, you know, when you are all tired from being up all night."

She smiled. "Nice try, Zachy. No, you may not sleep over at Damion's every night I work. I can go to bed after you boys leave for school."

"Sorry, pal," Jeff said. He reached around Zach's shoulders and pulled him close. "I'll make breakfast when mom's working, how's that sound?" Zach grinned up at him. Jeff stretched out his other arm to bring Jeremy into his embrace, but his older son stiffened and slid his chair back.

"I can get something to eat in the school cafeteria. I get there early enough," he said as he strode out of the kitchen.

Zach squirmed out of Jeff's arm. "I can, too," he said, and followed his brother up the stairs.

Jeff gazed after the boys, his eyes cinched.

Charity reached across the table and touched his hand. "It's hard to see them grow up."

Jeff sighed. "I'm obsolete, it seems."

"Not to me." She gave his hand a squeeze.

Jeff gathered the paper plates and napkins in a stack and stood up to dispose of them in the trash can next to the side door. He turned to Charity. "I wanted you to know the Civil War club meeting is tomorrow. I won't be home for supper."

Charity put the iced tea back in the fridge and began rinsing out the glasses. "Do you want me to come? I'm off tomorrow night." He had asked her to attend a few times over the past years, but studying for school had precluded her from coming.

"That's okay."

She turned off the water. *Is that a yes or a no?* "Okay?"

"Zach's coming with me this time."

"He is? How'd you talk him into that?"

Jeff grinned. "I told him we usually have sword fights at the meetings. And pizza."

"Sword fights?"

"Well . . . we have swords. And we talk about battles. Fights. It's close."

"Sword fights and pizza. You don't mind pizza two nights in a row?"

"No."

"Well . . . I'll come next time, then." She wanted to find a way to connect with Jeff better, find that togetherness they used to have but lost during the last few years of frantic activity while she finished nursing school. Maybe getting involved with something he enjoys would be helpful.

"Hmm. No. It's okay." Jeff stepped to the doorway between the kitchen and the back entrance to the family room.

Charity reached out and touched his arm. "What do you mean? You don't want me to come?"

He moved away. "It's not that. It's just . . . It's nothing." He retreated to the family room and settled in his recliner to read the newspaper.

Charity felt confused. What was this—Jeff not wanting her to go to the meeting. It was okay for Zach to go but not her?

She was still worried about how night-shift was going to affect her family, and determined to continue doing things to keep them connected, no matter how much the boys were growing and changing. Gathering together at least once daily at supper was one of her priorities. Showing more interest in her sons' and husband's outside activities was another goal.

If he didn't want her to go to the club meetings, she would have to find another way to connect with him, and better ways of communicating.

~6~

Charity's first week of training kept her so busy in mind and body, she didn't have much time to think about missing the Civil War Enthusiasts meeting, and was glad Zach went somewhere with his dad. He ended up enjoying it and set the bronze medal they gave him in a special place in his room.

Passing by his bedroom, Charity saw him showing it to Damion the next day. "This medal was only given to those who were *honorably* discharged."

"Cool," said Damion, as he peered at the engraved inscription. "*With malice toward none with charity for all*," he read, his voice reverent.

Zach took it back and, after buffing it with his tee-shirt, placed it back on the shelf of his bookcase, next to his guitar hero trophy, straightening the blue and white ribbon by which it was hung.

Charity made a goal of meeting every resident of Hill 'n Dale, all forty-eight of them, during her first week. She was soon able to greet many of them by name as she made her way through the rooms at the beginning of the shift. She enjoyed hearing them return her greeting and tried to spend some time reading to them, listening to their stories, or playing a game in between her own duties.

At the end of the second week of orientation, Susan had a mountain of work to do for the annual Joint Commission inspection. She freed Charity to spend time socializing with the residents, while she attacked her paperwork with vigor.

Charity wandered into the common room to find someone to talk to. It was a lovely room, separated from the dining halls on each side by pairs of French doors. Sage colored walls were complemented by ivory curtains with satin rope ties, and goldenrod club chairs. The large picture window bowed outward, facing the street. Later, when Charity worked the night-shift, she habitually looked for the electric candles illuminating each pane as she drove in.

Moving past a heavy bookcase filled with donated reading material, she observed Sophie dozing in her wheelchair before a TV airing afternoon soaps. She picked up the paperback that had fallen at her feet and placed it on the side table. A couple of women sat in a well-lit corner sharing a newspaper. A group was at the game table, one of them unpacking the Scrabble game.

Charity joined them. “Mind if I play?”

Tony, a burly Italian with a comb-over, gave her a wink. “We’d love some young blood at our game, right Ned?”

“It’s ‘Ed’,” he retorted. Turning to Charity, he straightened his bowtie and tipped his head in a little bow. “I’d be delighted to have you at our little game.”

Charity grinned and took an empty seat.

“You’re the new one, aren’t you?” Tony said.

She nodded. “I came two weeks ago.”

Elise squinted her eyes in a smile. “Welcome! We’re just getting started.” She slid the game box toward Charity. “We always choose eight letters, not seven. Makes the game go faster.”

Tony laughed. “Right. Who knows how much time we have left.”

Charity chose eight letters from the box and placed them in her wooden rack.

Elise started with the word EXILE.

"Good one," Charity said. She thought for a moment, then played LEMON.

Tony quickly placed the letter A on the X.

Ed peered at his letters. He reorganized then in his rack a few times. He chose a letter, then put it back.

"Ned!" said Tony. "The clock's ticking."

"It's 'Ed'! And I'm thinking." Finally, he played the word UNIQUE.

"Nice," said Charity. "My mom drew a U on one of the blanks of our game when I was growing up. She thought it made it easier to play the Q if there was an extra U."

Tony winked at her and turned around one of his tiles. "We lost the Z last month, so I marked on this one." It was a blank with the letter Z written on it in a shaky hand.

The game progressed companionably, and was won by Ed, no surprise. Elise was a close second. Charity walked her to the door of her room, charmed by the tiny woman, so full of life, before joining the rest of the staff for report.

It was grey and raining as she took the interstate home that morning. Leaves were changing, and wheatfields had that lonely look, cut down to stubble. Charity's thoughts wandered back to the Scrabble game. Playing the game was a family tradition while she was growing up, and had united the four of them nightly after supper. Her father loved trying to sneak in a misspelled word, to see if anyone would notice. When challenged, he would say it was the 'old English' spelling.

As the illness stole her mother's fine-motor ability, Charity helped her place her letters on the board. Her father quit playing when her mother took to the hospital bed.

Funny, how something as ordinary as a board game can generate memories.

She thought about the last time she played the game with her mother. It was day before she died.

It had been a warm night in mid-August. The cardinal's evening song and the rhythmic sound of crickets were heard through the open window.

Charity lounged in the hospital bed, pressed against her mother's slight frame, playing their nightly game of Scrabble. It kept them busy from the time she gave her mother the two cans of nutrition through the feeding tube, until it was time for lights out.

As she reached for the bottle of sub-lingual morphine drops, her mother made a grunting noise—she had something to say. Charity moved the letter board back across her bed in an upright position in its stand. It was the same communication device they used for the Scrabble game. Placing the chopstick between her mother's teeth, she watched as her mother pointed to the letters and phrases on the board.

She pointed at the letters T, then A, then K.

"'Take'?" Charity said.

She pointed at "YES" on the board.

Then C-A-R-E.

Charity smiled. "'Care'. Okay, mom. I'll take care." She reached for the letter board, but her mother grunted, so she left it in place.

O-F-D-A-D

"*Take care of dad.* Is that what you want to say?"

She pointed at "YES". Her eyes were alight.

Charity hugged her mother, avoiding the breathing tube protruding from her neck and the hose connecting it to the ventilator. "I will. Of course I will." She placed the morphine drops under her tongue and tucked the fleece blanket around her shoulders. Taking a last look at her mother, eyes closed and lips relaxed and pale, she turned out the light.

Take care of Dad? Charity's interactions with her father since her mother required the hospital bed and ventilator had been very few. He kept to himself in the basement family room, doing who-knows-what. Gone was the carefree man who loved to play pranks on his daughters and could be relied on to make the most mundane event seem like a holiday. He had withdrawn into a dark closet of despair which Charity couldn't enter. In addition, she fought with her own feelings—resentful that he never offered to help with her mother's care. Other than leaving bags of groceries every few days, he did little to help with housekeeping. Good thing her mother had arranged for auto-pay for utilities and other monthly bills, and Aunt Bee continued to be available whenever needed. Other than that, with her sister living in Akron now, it all fell on her.

Take care of Dad? She would do it, for her mother's sake.

The next morning when Charity came into her mother's room, bright with the summer sun and alive with birdsong, her mother's skin was grey, her lips blue and curved into a gentle smile.

"Mom?" she had said. She touched her hand. It was cold. She nudged her shoulder, then shook it gently. No response.

A chill went through her and she glanced around, searching for direction. What to do? She looked at her mother's face again and leaned closer to her, hesitating a little, and finally placing her head on her mother's chest, listening. All she could hear was the continued woosh of air into the lungs as the ventilator labored on. In-out, in-out.

Bent over the machine, her hand paused on the power button. She had never touched it, as the ventilator was in constant use since her mother began needing it, almost three months ago. But she wanted to be sure. She wanted to ascertain there was no heartbeat. She had to know.

Abruptly, she pressed the button. The room was still. A moment of panic seized her as she watched her mother's chest not rise after a few seconds.

She leaned over and listened at her chest again, gently laying her head against the cotton nightgown.

Nothing.

Her heart was stilled and her spirit gone, slipped out the open window during the night.

Continuing her drive home, Charity's mind was on her mother's charge to "take care of dad". After the funeral service and visits by Nadine and other well-wishers, it was just her and her father, awkward in the new dynamic that didn't include her mother to care for. She kept to herself the next few days, watching a lot of TV, not knowing what to do. She planned to sort through her mother's things, eventually, but not now. Her father languished in the basement. Her own grief and feelings of bitterness toward him for neglecting her mother kept her from taking part in his life. Where they might have comforted one another, Charity withdrew inward, as did he.

~7~

Autumn, Charity's favorite season, was in full color in mid-October—Maple trees in reds and yellows, and pumpkin and sunflower fields a kaleidoscope of hues. Great round bales of golden wheat were still seen in some fields. Locally grown sweet corn was a favorite of her family's and showed up at meals at least two days a week to accompany grilled meats.

Potted mums in yellow, rust, and orange lined the portico of Hill 'n Dale and bundles of corn stalks graced the doorway where Charity entered, pulling her light jacket around herself against the night air. After two weeks of orientation on day-shift, and a month working nights, she was accustomed to the routine of dropping off her lunch in the employee lounge fridge and visiting her locker to leave her purse and jacket. After a few friendly greetings, she and the rest of the night-shift staff—two LPNs and three or four aides—made their way to the main nurses' station for report a few minutes before eleven.

The early morning hours were busiest, as residents were assisted with baths and getting dressed in time to gather together for breakfast. They were walked or wheeled to the dining halls and escorted to heavy oak chairs around tables covered with linen cloths. Classic art prints hung on the wood-paneled walls at wheelchair height. Soft orchestra music or Sinatra was played on the CD player, all to give one the idea that you are anywhere but a nursing home.

Charity shared the early morning med pass with the day-shift LPN, wheeling her cart to the dining room where many of her patients were gathered. It was the last task of her shift, and she usually worked overtime, staying after morning report to finish dispensing the medications that made up the biggest med pass of the day.

It was not just a matter of distributing pills—many residents had to have a blood pressure or glucometer check before receiving certain medications. Some required medications crushed or in liquid form. A few took pills one at a time, with a generous swallow of water between each. It was a laborious task.

She enjoyed her interactions with Elise, of the Scrabble game, and poured her an early cup of coffee—four creams and two sugars—as she waited for her meal.

"Thank you, Charity," said the spry 88-year-old as she reached for the cup. She looked up, her shiny white hair cut in a boyish style brushed away from her face. "You know I love my morning coffee." Her gray eyes squinted as she smiled.

After breakfast, she liked to joke with Charity when receiving her pills. "Well, here is my dessert," she would say before swallowing all five pills at once with a last sip of coffee.

Walking her back to her room after breakfast one morning, Charity eyed a faded photograph in a gilt frame on her dresser.

Elise chuckled. "You like that?" She picked up the frame and pointed to the figures on the photo. "That's me! Probably didn't think I'd dress like that."

Looking closer, Charity observed a much younger Elise in a skimpy show outfit, posing with . . . "Is that Danny Kaye?"

Elise nodded vigorously. "Yep! He and I did shows for the troops during the second world war almost every night, dancing and singing. And sometimes during the day we would go to the hospitals." She paused and shook her head. "Those boys suffered so much—some with blown off legs or arms. We just did what we could to cheer them up, hoping they would get well enough to go home."

◆◆◆

Later that week, while hurrying to finish the med pass, Charity approached Elise and offered her a paper cup of pills.

Elise looked up at her.

Charity rattled the pills in the little cup. "I brought you your dessert, Elise."

Elise took the cup in her left hand and stared it. She looked up again, her expression blank. Charity noticed that the coffee she had placed before her earlier was untouched and her breakfast tray still had most of the food remaining. Something was wrong.

Matty, the HCA working in the dining room that morning, said to Charity, "She's been down in the dumps all morning. They had a hard time getting her out of bed and she's just been playing with her food. I don't think she ate three real bites."

Elise didn't say a word, just looked at Matty with a muddled expression. Her usually bright smile was absent, replaced by a tell-tale right-sided facial droop, and she allowed her right arm to drop to her side.

"Looks like she may have had a stroke," Charity said to Matty. "Was she this bad when she got up?"

"Dorothy helped her out of bed and got her dressed this morning. All she said was that Elise seemed real weak. They had to change her bed once overnight, too. That's unusual—she always rings for bathroom help during the night."

Charity regarded Elise for a moment, who gazed about helplessly, the pills spilled in her lap. Her heart broke at the bewildered expression and the mouth attempting to form words. She reached down and touched Elise's shoulder. "Matty will help you back to bed now, okay?"

Matty scooted a handy wheelchair next to Elise's chair and they both helped her transfer into it. Carefully propelling the wheelchair, Matty took Elise to her room.

After relaying this change in status to Susan, Charity placed a call to Dr. Domicile and Hannah, her great-niece who lived in Chicago. Hannah was out and a message was left on her voicemail to call the nurse's station.

Dr. Domicile called back and discontinued Elise's aspirin. He checked her code status—DNR, Do Not Resuscitate, meaning unless the family requests that tests are done and treatments initiated, she would be 'comfort measures' only.

He agreed it sounded like a stroke and said she may recover her speech and eating ability, or she may not; it was a fifty-fifty chance. As much as he knew, this was the first stroke she had. Charity left work later than usual, hoping for the best for Elise.

Charity was putting away her painting things that evening in preparation to take her nap before work. She had finally started the watercolor of an autumn still-life: sunflowers, dried seed pods, and wheat stalks in a rustic pottery jug. Returning to this hobby, a much needed me-time activity, reminded her of her mother, as it had been one of her favorite activities.

Her mother had adorned the family home with many examples of her creativity. Colorful landscapes were displayed in several rooms. A large painting of a pitcher of lemonade, surrounded by cut lemons and cheerful sprigs of mint, had hung on the second floor landing, near Charity's childhood bedroom. The melting ice and juicy lemon slices always gave her a craving for the refreshing drink as she walked by. *Whatever happened to all those pictures?* Expressions of her mother's sparkling personality, Charity hoped they were taken by family members before the house was sold.

She rinsed the brushes, shook most of the water out of them, and rolled them back and forth rapidly between flattened hands to expel the rest of the water. Covering the unfinished piece with a pillowcase, she placed the easel in the corner of the spare room and closed the door behind her, relaxed enough now to take her nap.

As she entered her bedroom, Josephine called.

After a few minutes of small talk, Josephine said, "Elise's great-niece, Hannah finally called back. I guess she goes to work early and didn't get the message until her lunch break. Susan explained everything to her, and Hannah agreed to comfort measures. She didn't want to have her aunt transferred to the hospital for a CT scan and other tests just to confirm what we already know."

"That was kind of her. I wish more people thought that way," Charity said.

"Me too. Elise did actually seem better in the afternoon. She was trying to joke around with Ben, you know, that new HCA. He was helping her to bed for a nap and she said, 'Don't you get fresh with me!' in kind of a slurred voice. But Ben said you could definitely understand her."

"That's good. Dr. Domicile said she may get her speaking and eating ability back."

Josephine finished with, "Tomorrow speech therapy will be doing a swallow study, so we'll see."

"Alrighty, Jo. Well, it's almost nine, so I'm gonna lay down for an hour before going to work. You're on tomorrow, right?"

"Yep."

"Then I'll see you in the morning." She placed her cell phone on the nightstand and turned out the lamp.

At that moment, the bedroom door opened and the overhead light shot on as Jeff strode in. She threw the covers over her head.

"Sorry," said Jeff. He turned the switch off and lowered his voice. "Just putting this away." He placed his hat on the dresser. It was a wool replica of a union soldier's cap, complete with crossed golden muskets on the front.

"How was the meeting?"

He turned back from the doorway. "Good."

Charity sat up in bed and turned on the bedside lamp. "Did Zach go?"

He nodded. "If he goes next time he gets a hat."

"Nice. He's enjoying it. I heard him tell Damion all about the last meeting." She peered out into the hall. "Where's Jeremy?"

"His girlfriend picked him up."

"What girlfriend?"

"McKayla."

"The girl from homecoming last week, with the purple hair?"

"Mm-hm."

"She seems nice. Except for the hair."

Jeff chuckled. "Well, I'd better let you sleep."

"Thanks. Make sure I get up in an hour?"

"At ten?"

She nodded and turned out the lamp as he gently closed the bedroom door.

◆◆◆

The following day speech therapy performed the swallow study and Elise was deemed appropriate for a pureed diet with thickened drinks. This was necessary so she would not choke on 'thin' fluid draining down her windpipe. A special thickening agent was to be mixed with all drinks to create a 'honey-like' consistency. All food would be pureed in a blender; this helped to avoid pocketing of food in her cheeks, a real problem when loss of sensation has occurred following a stroke.

Elise did not tolerate the new diet well. She ate barely half of her meals, and eating was a huge effort. She was uncoordinated handling the utensils with her left hand, and just the act of chewing and swallowing was exhausting. Usually, a staff member would sit with her and help her eat, spooning the pureed food into her mouth, making sure she swallowed, and offering the thickened drink between bites.

After finishing the morning med pass, Charity started staying over even later than usual to help Elise eat. She warmed her breakfast in the dining room microwave and brought it to the table, taking a seat next to her. Dipping a spoon into the pile of mashed pancake, she offered it.

Elise smirked, clutched the spoon with her left hand, and aimed for her mouth. Missing completely, she smashed the pureed food on her chin and dropped most of it on her lap.

Charity's throat got tight. She had a flash of remembrance of trying to get her mother to eat, spooning in soup or pudding or mashed potatoes. Her problem was swallowing, an advanced sign of the illness. She gagged on the food and sometimes retched it back up.

It was sad that Elise, who lived independently all her life, now had to rely on others to help her do the most basic tasks. It was a loss of dignity to have others feed and dress you. Gone was the lively, intelligent individual, greeting Charity every morning as she entered the dining hall. She was replaced by someone helpless and vulnerable.

Holding her hand out for the spoon, Charity said, "Let me help you."

Elise pressed her lips together and gave her the spoon. Resigned, she opened her mouth for a bite of scrambled eggs, like a little bird, and allowed herself to be fed. A sip of thickened apple juice was given in between bites.

When Charity offered the cup of thick coffee, Elise held up her hand and shook her head. One of the few pleasures she had in life, a good cup of hot coffee, had necessarily been taken from her.

Despite the efforts at getting Elise to eat, she started losing weight. Two weeks later she was down eight pounds.

At the end of the shift that morning, Charity overheard Susan Morgan on the phone giving Elise's great-niece, Hannah, a progress report.

"There are a couple of options Elise has at this point," Susan said into the telephone. "We can have a feeding tube inserted into her stomach surgically and feed her special liquid nourishment that comes in a can, about four or five cans per day. She could also get all her water and medications that way. Even though she is a DNR status, feeding is considered a comfort measure and the feeding tube would be appropriate."

Charity leaned nearer to hear the niece's response on the telephone, but a disapproving look by Susan shot in her direction halted her efforts.

Susan continued, "Alternatively, we could try a serving of fortified pudding with each meal. It's made for people with swallowing problems. Has the same nutrition as Ensure, but in pudding form, so it's easier to swallow. Remember, though, that the feeding tube is always an option."

A feeding tube. Charity left the nurses' station and made her way to the locker room thinking about it. When her mother could no longer eat, she had a feeding tube inserted those last three months of the illness. It had been up to Charity to manage, after a bit of training by the home care nurses, and it was one of the last things she did for her mother before she died. A feeding tube might help Elise maintain her weight until she improves enough to eat better on her own. It might be worth trying. Even though she knew Susan already discussed this with Hannah, Charity thought she would bring it up to her tomorrow morning.

Finishing her duties a few minutes early the next day gave Charity time to talk to Susan before joining the rest of the staff for report. She found her in her office pulling some pages from a fax machine.

"Excuse me. Can I come in?"

Susan waved her in and Charity made room for herself on the settee against a wall, moving aside several brown envelopes stuffed with papers before sitting down. She waited till she had Susan's attention.

"I wanted to talk to you about Elise," Charity said. "Is there a possibility she might get a feeding tube? My mother used one the last year of her illness, and—"

Susan held out a hand. "I discussed it with her niece. She wants to hold off for now."

Charity sighed. It was problematic talking to Susan, who was so good at her job she rarely sought or took another's advice. But she wanted to try once more. "But my mother—"

"—Don't you think I know my patients? Elise isn't your mother. It won't work for her, and Hannah, her niece—her *power of attorney*—refuses to try it." *End of discussion*, was implied, though not said.

Charity slunk out of the office, disappointed she couldn't make a better case for trying the feeding tube, a solution she knew would ensure proper nutrition and hydration. It wasn't fair Hannah was allowed to make that decision. It should at least be discussed with Elise, and explained to her, so she could decide for herself. But Hannah was the POA, and that's that.

Joining the rest of the day-shift staff in the main nurses' station, Charity began her report.

~8~

The new admission at the retirement home that day was an African American gentleman named Oliver—Ollie, for short. His diagnosis was severe lower back pain from two fractured lumbar vertebrae occurring from a fall. This was one of many falls at home which led the family to realize he needed around the clock care. He was settled in a room with another resident, one who was bedbound, non-verbal, and required total care.

Charity introduced herself to Ollie in the dining room the next morning. It was his first breakfast at Hill 'n Dale. He struggled to his feet and extended a hand. "Pleased to make your acquaintance," he said in a deep, throaty voice.

"Same here," she said, smiling and taking in his appearance. Ollie dressed as formally as he spoke, in suit-coat and tie. His graying hair and generous moustache were neatly groomed.

She placed the little cup with Ollie's pain medication on the table in front of him as he sat back down. "Here's your pain medication. I hope you feel better."

As she spoke, she saw Ollie steal a glance at Elise, seated to his side.

"Ollie," she said. "This is Elise. Elise, Ollie."

Ollie gave a little bow and shook her hand, his right into Elise's left, as her right hand remained immobile in her lap.

"Ma'am," he said.

She answered her new acquaintance with a wide, lopsided grin.

Charity noticed that Elise perked up when she was around Ollie. He paid attention to her and spoke to her in that velvety voice of his, telling her stories or commenting on the events of the day. Over the next few days Elise began to talk more. Being engaged in conversation with Ollie helped her speech improve—she slurred her words less and worked hard at enunciating. The nurses and HCAs joked among themselves about Elise's new "boyfriend", but they were truly glad that someone was showing her extra attention.

After Ollie was done with his meal, he would often be seen spooning pureed food or fortified pudding into Elise's mouth. Charity began crushing her morning pills into a coarse powder and mixing them with some of her pureed breakfast so Ollie could give them to her. She still couldn't finish her meals, but seemed to enjoy them more with his company.

Ollie began complaining that the pain pills weren't helping him and there were one or two days he couldn't get out of bed in time for breakfast because his back hurt him so much. A prescription was obtained for oxycodone, which controlled his pain better. Charity began giving him one routinely every morning with the early med pass, at 5 AM, hoping it would help him make it to the dining room. Most days the pain would be relieved enough for him to join Elise and the others for breakfast.

Ollie and Elise continued to form a friendly relationship. Josephine told Charity that they attended music presentations together and played dominos or worked on puzzles in the common room. He often waited for her while she was getting physical therapy or speech therapy, and wheeled her back to her room when finished.

Nevertheless, Elise slowly continued to decline. She lost more weight and a month later seemed more frail than ever. Even with Ollie's help and patience, she ate less and less with each meal.

That weekend, as the nursing staff distributed the few midnight medications and HCA's completed first rounds of the night shift, that was when it happened.

Dorothy approached Charity in the darkened hallway. She pulled her aside and said quietly, "I don't think Miss Elise is breathin'."

"Not breathing?" Charity said, placing the pill packet she was holding back into the med cart. She followed Dorothy down the Pool Hall corridor to Elise's room, almost at the end.

Matty was already there, rubbing her hands together, gazing at the motionless body of Elise. "We just came in to do her 'every two hour' check," she said.

Charity stepped closer to the bed and slipped back the comforter. She observed Elise's chest not rising to take a breath, the gray cast of her skin, her lifeless eyes. She stroked her forearm and hand, unmoving and stiff. Elise had been dead for a while. Using her stethoscope, Charity listened for heart sounds and checked for breathing, both absent. It was just a ritual, done for the benefit of the HCAs. She knew her spirit was in another place.

She also knew she had to be strong, and not betray how she really felt—her heart in her throat and just wanting to collapse right there on the floor beside the bed and weep over the loss of this resident. This friend. As a nurse, she had a job to do, which included respect for this woman who gave in to death, and to treat her body with dignity.

Like when her mother died.

The hospice nurse who came the morning her mother died handled everything. She bathed her body, humming a calming melody as Charity watched from the comfy chair, her legs tucked beneath her and a blanket clutched around her shoulders, an occasional tear escaping from her eye. The nurse changed the pillowcase and top sheet, smoothing it over her body, and bundled the ventilator and other home care equipment into a dark corner of the room.

When her father came in, the nurse ushered Charity out of the room to allow him privacy. As they waited in the hall, Charity heard the despair in her father's voice as he repeated her name, along with great, wet sobs.

In the presence of the hospice nurse Charity felt a child again, in need of comfort, instead of the eighteen-year-old who single-handedly cared for her mother for the past year. Her sorrow poured out from deep within as the nurse held her close, allowing her to weep into her shoulder until there were no tears left. Finally, her father opened the bedroom door and they all stood in the dimness of the little hall, a little dazed from the expenditure of so much emotional energy.

At length, the hospice nurse said, "Death comes to give relief when one can no longer bear to live."

Charity placed her stethoscope around her shoulders and glanced up at Dorothy and Matty. "Yes, she has passed. She no longer has to fight to live. I think we should wake Ollie. He should know."

Matty slipped out the doorway. Dorothy remained to help Charity wash Elise's body and change the linens.

Dipping a cloth into the basin of warm water, Charity asked, "Did you notice a change earlier?"

Dorothy paused. "Tonight's one of my twelves, so I started at 7 PM. After report I helped Elise to bed. She was extra sleepy—couldn't keep her eyes open. I don't think she had much for dinner, so I tried to get her to eat some of that key lime yogurt she likes. But she kept fallin' asleep." Dorothy reached down and straightened a wrinkle from her pillow. "I wish I knew it was my last chance to say anything to her."

Charity wiped Elise's arms and upper body with warm water. She eased the washcloth over her sheer eyelids and dabbed at her formerly cheerful pink lips, now pale in death. She combed her bright white bangs over her forehead.

Dorothy finished tucking the fresh linens around Elise as Matty came back. She held the door for Ollie, clad in a silk dressing gown. He moved his walker through the door and, gazing on Elise's still form across the room, pushed the walker aside and shuffled to the bed. He clasped her hand, his large hand such a contrast to her small one.

It felt like church. Like a ritual, seeing Ollie holding her hand, eyes closed, lips moving silently. The woman who was Elise, who with spirited enthusiasm cheered the hearts of hurting soldiers, and was a lively addition to the retirement home, was gone. She was at peace.

Observing Ollie brought tears to Charity's eyes, and she could see Dorothy and Matty were also sniffling. "I'm so sorry," Charity said, touching Ollie's shoulder.

He released Elise's hand and looked at Charity. "Don't be sorry. It's what she wanted."

He reached down and stroked her hair, moving the whisps away from her eyes and caressing her cheek with his thumb. "I'm gonna miss her. I didn't know her long, but she was a good friend."

At a loss, he took a step back and turned toward the door. Matty handed him his walker, and he slowly stepped out into the hall, murmuring, "Yep, really gonna miss her."

~9~

Charity dimmed the lights in the room as she left with Dorothy and Matty. She took a seat in the nurses' station and made phone calls to the funeral home and Hannah. She planned to call Dr. Domicile around 7 AM, just to let him know. There was no need to call him in the middle of the night. He could do nothing now.

The phone call to Hannah went right to voicemail. Charity was reluctant to leave that kind of message, so she just tried calling back. This time Hannah answered with a sleepy, "Hello?"

Charity braced herself. "I'm so sorry, Hannah. We found your aunt has passed away during the night."

Hannah was silent for a moment. "Was she? I mean . . . did she have any pain?"

"No, I don't think so. No. She appears to have gone quietly, in her sleep."

Hannah let out a sigh. "That's good. I mean, if it was her time, I'm glad it was peaceful."

Charity and Hannah talked for another minute. The great-niece was relieved to learn Elise had made pre-need arrangements and that she would be picked up by the funeral home that morning. She would book a flight to be present for her interment and collect her belongings from her room.

Charity continued her early morning duties, her mind not really on the job. Despite understanding Elise's death was a result of 'failure to thrive', a condition that often follows a stroke, she had a hard time accepting it. She had kept hoping Elise would turn a corner and start eating more, hoping her swallowing function would improve or the physical therapy would help her regain the use of her right hand.

Was there anything else she could have done to help her? To help her eat better, gain weight. Maybe she should have had the feeding tube inserted. She should have talked to Elise about it, suggested she try it. A brief surge of resentment rose in her heart against Susan for shutting her down when she talked to her about it, a month ago.

In nursing school, they were taught to look for something else to try when the current treatment was ineffective, and it disturbed her that she had not found the right way to save Elise.

Josephine and the rest of the day-shift staff were arriving, so Charity prepared her report, the most important thing she would relay being Elise's death.

Josephine remained in the nurses' station after report, absorbing the unwelcome news. "I'm so sorry you had to take care of all that," she said to Charity. "The thing I will miss most is the way she squinted her eyes when she smiled. It was so cute."

Charity nodded. "It was cute. She was cute, and sweet. It will be strange, not seeing her every morning." She then turned to Susan to inform her of the steps she had taken and calls she made. Susan offered to call Dr. Domicile so Charity could move on with the morning med pass.

"It always leaves a hole in my heart when one of my people dies," Susan said.

Thrown by Susan's uncharacteristic bit of sentiment, Charity proceeded to her morning work.

Entering the dining hall a little late, Charity rushed through her task, trying not to look at Elise's vacant seat. Ollie, also, was absent. Conversations with other residents were stilted, her mind still on the events of the night.

The mood among the staff was somber, as one of their favorite residents was gone.

Charity drove home with a heart full of sorrow, slushy snowflakes that fell from a grey sky matching her mood. She entered the house to Jeff and the boys getting ready for church. He was in the kitchen, pouring coffee.

He offered her a mug. “The boys are getting dressed. We should leave soon since I have to usher today.”

She wrapped her hands around the coffee, glad for its warmth. “I don’t think I’ll make it to church today. It was a rough morning.” The service started at 10AM, and it was almost 9:30 now.

“Hmm.”

“One of my patients died over night.”

Jeff sat across from her at the kitchen table. He placed a hand on hers. “Was she old?”

Charity withdrew her hand. “What does that matter?”

He sat back in his chair. “I mean, she didn’t have long to live, right?”

“She was eighty-eight. She could have lived longer. Some people live to a hundred, or more. Look at Betty White. She’s about ninety, and still acting.”

“But if she was in a nursing home, she must have been sick.”

“She didn’t have any children, so just didn’t have anywhere else to live. But she was healthy, and a lot of fun. I really liked her.” Charity took a sip of her coffee, then set the mug down. “She had a stroke about a month ago.

“Hm. Not really healthy then.”

“Not now. But she used to be.”

He nodded, his mouth in an exaggerated frown. “I s’pose it’s for the best, then.”

“Best? How could you say that? It would have been best for her to recover, to get better.”

Just then, Zach lurched into the room, shoving his arms into his parka. "Are we going?"

Jeff thrust his chair back and stood up, glaring at Charity. "What do you want me to say?"

Charity shook her head, looking down at her mug. "I don't know."

"You okay, mom?" Zach said, touching her arm.

She rose and stepped to the kitchen entry. "I'm alright. Just tired. I can't go with you guys today. Say a prayer for me at church, okay, Zachy?"

Her mind was still on what Jeff said as she listed up the stairs. She felt disconnected. He just didn't get her. Conversations with Jeff were brief and revolved around the logistics of life—where the boys needed to be driven, work schedules, bills. Talking about anything involving emotions or feelings—*the heart*—usually prompted an impatient response.

Early in their relationship she tried talking to him about her parents' deaths. Jeff's response was a brief mention of his own mother's passing away after Jeremy was born. His mother had left the family and married someone else when he was ten. Never close with her, it had been a nuisance to be involved in calling hours, stand in line for all those people, having to respond appropriately to their expressions of sympathy, when he was tired from being up all night with a cranky baby. That was what he remembered about it—how it inconvenienced him. And then he changed the subject. She quit bringing it up.

She slipped beneath the covers, asleep in a few seconds, weary in body and spirit.

◆◆◆

A day later, to Charity's surprise, Ollie was up and dressed by five fifteen, even before she could give him his pain pill. In fact, he had not needed it the day before, either. He seemed a little lost, however, not having Elise as his dining companion. Throughout the day he spent more time in his room, talking to the non-verbal resident that was his roommate.

Two days later was when Charity heard it.

Ollie had returned to his room after breakfast. Charity wheeled her med cart near Ollie's doorway and was having a hard time preparing the roommate's pills to give via feeding tube, due to the pill-crusher having gone missing. She stood in the hallway, attempting to grind the pills into a powder with the back of a spoon, when she heard talking. Remaining in the hall near the doorway, she heard Ollie have a one-sided conversation with his roommate.

"I just couldn't see her endin' up this way. You know, *like you.* She would have hated having a feedin' tube in her. It's not what she wanted. You understand why I had to do it, don't you?"

A chill shot through Charity and she immediately envisioned Ollie with Elise, feeding her in the dining hall. Feeding her pureed food, crushed pills hidden within the spoonfuls. Could he have—?

Taking a deep breath, she entered the room to attend to the roommate. She instilled the medication into the feeding tube and irrigated it with water. Using the positioning wedge and slide sheet, she turned him onto his other side, arranging his arms and legs to prevent pressure areas.

After these ministrations, she faced Ollie, seated on his bed. "Morning."

He gave a nod, his eyes downcast.

"How are you doing?"

He shrugged a shoulder. "Okay . . . you know."

"I know." She reached out to touch his hand before stepping out of the room, her mind a jumble of emotions.

~10~

Having to stay overtime at work day after day limited the time Charity was able to spend with her family. They were usually gone by the time she dragged herself into the house, encountering the usual mess—cereal bowls with milk drying in them, half-drunk mugs of coffee, damp towels mildewing on the bathroom floor. Gone was her plan to make breakfast for them after work and send them off merrily, nutritious lunches in hand, before she lay down to sleep. Being the perfect homemaker just didn't seem possible as a night-shift nurse, and getting enough sleep during the day was becoming a challenge.

She brought it up to Jeff the Saturday before Thanksgiving as they drove to visit Papa, his father, who resided at Northern Woods. Jeff had gone by himself most of the past two months, and she felt it was her duty to visit as the holidays approached. Despite working all night, she changed her clothes and accompanied Jeff to the nursing home.

"The boys disappeared this morning again before I came home from work," she said. "They left the house a mess."

Jeff drove the car into the parking lot.

She turned to him. "Where did they go?"

"Zach went to Damion's and Jeremy is playing basketball with his friends at school."

Walking to the front entrance of Northern Woods, Charity said, "So why couldn't they at least pick up after themselves before they left the house? *You're* home—make them clean up. It shouldn't all be up to me. I'm tired enough when I come home, and then I have to pick up after them, and you, and plan for dinner, and try to get some sleep, and visit your dad . . . and . . ."

She turned to him. "You said you'd help me." She clamped her mouth shut and inhaled deeply to suppress the tears of frustration she felt coming. A few snuck through, despite her efforts.

Jeff grasped her hand and led her to a bench by the front door. "I *will* help you, but you don't have to do all that. I'm not worried if the house isn't always picked up." He placed a placating arm around her shoulders.

She shrugged his arm away. Searching in her purse she found a napkin to wipe her face and blow her nose. "But *I am.* I like to keep the house clean, but I just can't do it by myself. Why don't you see that?"

He kept quiet. More visitors were coming, and some of them were looking at her. He stood up. "We'll talk about it later," he said, tugging at her arm.

Charity stepped into the visitor bathroom as soon as they entered the building. She peered at her face, swollen and red.

She didn't want to be like that—irritable and demanding—and never expected the lack of sleep to affect her so much. It was true, her family would have to step up and help with household chores, something she never demanded of them before. But this working five nights a week, and overtime every morning, this would have to stop. She had talked to Susan about getting out at her scheduled time, but the best she could offer was, "Work faster. If you quit chit-chatting with everyone, you would get out on time."

Charity knew she could cut down on the time by foregoing the little snatches of conversation she included with the pills she dispensed, but couldn't see herself just shoving a handful of pills at the residents without a few kind words. The loved talking to her, and they lit up when she brought them their meds, often detaining her with their stories. It made a normally routine task enjoyable.

No—there was no other way. As much as she was getting used to working at Hill ‘n Dale, she would have to look for another job with better hours just to keep her sanity.

She also realized that, despite enjoying the work, she would be better fulfilled if she had the chance to reach patients before their illnesses became chronic. With some well-placed teaching, some of those with diabetes or heart failure, like Mrs. E. DeMattis, might enjoy improved health and a longer life.

~11~

Monday morning provided the opportunity Charity needed. The local news playing on the common room television highlighted a story featuring a newly refurbished medical-surgical unit at Quarry Run General Hospital. This unit originally housed Labor & Delivery, which had been moved to a larger hospital in the NEOHOS system, in Canton, earlier in the year. The grand opening was planned for the first week of December, and the newscaster remarked they were still seeking to fill four or five positions for nurses or aides.

Charity met up with Josephine in the locker room at change of shift and surreptitiously described the job openings she heard about on the news story. They had talked before about checking job opportunities at the hospital, both of them feeling they would prefer to work there, with better benefits, better pay, and more regular hours.

Josephine closed her locker. "We should apply. Let's go after report, around three thirty."

Charity thought for a moment. "Alrighty. Once I get some sleep, I can get the boys off the bus and meet you back here. I'll call you if something comes up." She followed Josephine to the employee lounge.

"I just hope all the day-shift jobs haven't been taken. I still have to be home at night for *mi mama*; my kids really aren't old enough to handle her by themselves." Josephine emptied the last of the Bunn coffee pot into her mug, wrinkling her nose at the burnt-tar odor.

"That coffee was on all night," Charity said.

"Hmph. You can tell." She stirred three packets of sugar into it to tame the strong flavor. "My sister, Rosa, stays at my house during the day, but there's no one else to stay with her at night."

"How's your mom been doing?"

"Well, she has good days and bad days. Yesterday she kept calling me Genevieve, my oldest sister's name. Jesus, Mary, and Joseph, it freaked me out! Genny died in a car accident five years ago. I told her, 'It's me—Josephine.' She said, 'Nah, you were always better looking than her, and not as fat.' What can I say to that?"

Charity smiled, "Just remember, she really doesn't know what she is saying."

"I know. I try to remember that."

"When Jeff's dad first went to Northern Woods he was confused, too, and sometimes lashed out at Jeff. But once they got his diabetes under control he really improved."

"Does he have dementia?"

"No. Just neuropathy from the diabetes. And he's practically blind, too. But his last A1C was around seven."

"That's pretty good."

"Mm-hm. We try to visit him as a family at least once a month. Jeff goes more often."

They walked to the nurse's station together and sat in a semi-circle of office chairs. Charity updated the staff on any problems that occurred overnight. She also reminded them of doctor's appointments two of the residents had that morning, and one having dialysis. Ambulettes had been arranged to take them to their destinations and family members were notified.

Following report, Charity finished the med pass and headed home, late as usual. She promised Josephine she would see her later that day. She had finally made the first step to a more manageable work schedule, and hoped it would lessen the stress level at home. Just making the decision to apply for another job improved her outlook, and she felt a little less weary as she drove home.

They met as planned that afternoon and followed each other to the hospital. They made their way to the recruitment office on the second floor and inquired about the postings for the new med-surg unit. Seated before computers, they logged onto the hospital website to fill out the online application. Josephine could still only take a day time position but Charity clicked both the 'day' and 'night' boxes, just hoping she could get her foot in the hospital door.

Charity wasn't sure how Josephine felt about applying for work elsewhere, but *she* felt a bit disloyal. What about all those wonderful residents she had gotten to know and love, like Ollie, Sophie, and Tony? Is it fair to abandon them to another job just for convenience? The position for which she was applying was four nights a week, instead of five, and eight hours each shift. Working fewer nights and shorter shifts would make it worthwhile to change jobs, giving her an extra night to sleep and an extra day to accomplish household tasks and spend time with her family.

If Hill 'n Dale had been more accommodating about her schedule, she might have decided to stay. Conflicted, she forged onward and submitted the application.

Josephine thought to bring her nursing license and made a photocopy for the office; Charity promised the secretary she would bring hers the next day. Stepping out of the recruitment office, Charity said, "Let's check out the cafeteria."

Josephine had worked straight through lunch that day, so she readily agreed.

Traveling the long main hall, Charity said, "How's George doing at Country Springs?"

"It's a good job, though right now he's a temp in quality control. I pray something permanent opens up. By the way, tell Jeff 'thanks' for giving him a good reference. I'm sure it helped him get hired."

"I'll tell him," she said. "Although we aren't really talking."

Josephine slid her a sideways glance.

Charity sighed. "It's my fault. We were visiting his dad after work on Saturday, and I had a melt-down. I don't like visiting my father-in-law. He's crotchety and always has something to complain about. And I was tired from working. Everything was just piling up."

"You shouldn't go anywhere after work. Just go home and sleep."

"You're right. I yelled at Jeff in the parking lot, about him leaving the house a mess that morning, and all the things they expect me to do, no matter how much sleep I *don't* get. He tried to get me to calm down, but he just doesn't get it. He thinks it's helpful that he doesn't expect the house to be clean, or everything in its place. But I like it to be that way, for my own satisfaction. It's restful to be in a well-organized environment. It's making me crazy that I don't have time or energy to do it all." She quieted her voice. "I left the nursing home and waited for him in the car. I didn't even go in to visit Papa."

Josephine stopped in the hall. She shook her head. "What you're doing wrong is not making them help you more. Maria always makes breakfast for us and packs the lunches for her and Manuel and Natalie. Sometimes she even packs me a lunch. And George cleans up the kitchen after supper. They all help out with chores on the weekend. Even Natalie."

"I should have trained them better."

"It's not too late."

"I'm trying to lay low, to patch things up with Jeff. Now isn't the best time to start hard-lining them."

Turning into the cafeteria, Charity was charmed by the energizing atmosphere of the room. Seating was done in apricot, light gray, and leafy green. Great drums fashioned in fabric the same shade of green were suspended from the ceiling, offering muted lighting easy on the eyes.

Charity selected a cup of coffee and a cranberry-walnut muffin while Josephine waited in line for the day's dinner entrée, broasted chicken, rice, and steamed broccoli. A slice of coconut cream pie completed her meal.

They sat in comfortable benches at a corner booth. As she bit into her muffin, Charity glanced around the cafeteria. At that moment, she realized what else was missing in her job at Hill 'n Dale. A little excitement. The cafeteria felt charged with activity, as groups of nurses in navy blue scrubs strode to tables for a well-earned lunch break, physicians carrying pagers hurried to one place or another, and overhead the occasional Rapid Response Required was announced.

It would be nice to be part of the exciting activity.

Josephine ate the first several bites of her meal without stopping. "I know it's just cafeteria food, but it's so nice to eat something I didn't have to cook."

Charity nodded, her mouth full of muffin.

Josephine sat for a moment looking at her plate. "You know, you asked about *mi mama* this morning. Talk about cooking—I have a hard time getting her to eat *anything* I cook. She's losing weight and stays in bed most of the time. All she wants to eat is potato chips or pretzels. But I can't let her eat anything that salty because of her blood pressure."

Charity felt a pang of sympathy. "That's hard. It's hard enough to make kids eat."

Josephine nodded. "I keep thinking about Elise. How she passed in her sleep last week. That would be a good way to go. I hope that's how *mi mama* goes when it's her time."

"That's the key, isn't it. When it's her time to go."

"Well, yeah, of course. She's not there yet." She slowly worked her way through the slice of pie.

Charity took a sip of coffee and finished the last bite of her muffin. She was thinking about Elise. About how she died. Was it her time? Or did she have help? A little nudge in that direction, perhaps.

She looked at Josephine. "What do you think about 'helping' someone along the way. To die peacefully, that is. Do you think that's ever okay?"

"You mean to assist someone to die?"

Charity nodded.

She shook her head firmly. "Well, no, then. That's up to the good Lord. No one should ever help someone commit suicide. Or, you ever hear of a 'mercy killing'? That's wrong, too. Like I said, it's up to God." She narrowed her eyes. "Why? Did you hear of that happening to someone?"

Charity stirred her coffee. "Hmm . . . Maybe." She looked up and hesitated. "There's . . . there's a possibility someone may have given her something to help her sleep. Or . . . or die. A narcotic, maybe."

"You mean Elise?"

"Mm-hm,"

"Was it an accident? Charity, if you gave her a sleeping pill and she ended up dying, that's not your fault."

Charity shook her head. "No, nothing like that." *How to say it?* "I mean . . . I think someone else, another resident, slipped her something."

Josephine cinched her eyebrows as she thought a moment. "Ollie?"

"I *think* maybe. I can't prove it." She took a last sip of coffee. "I don't know if I would want to."

"He shouldn't have done that. It wasn't up to him."

Quickly, Charity said, "Like I said, I don't really know."

"If it was him. How could he have gotten it?"

Charity sighed. She closed her eyes for a moment. She could trust her friend. It had been on her mind for days and she had to say something. “My fault . . . maybe. He was getting oxycodone for his back pain. I always gave it to him first thing in the morning, before he got dressed. Sometimes he would be in the bathroom, and I would leave it for him while I crushed the roommate’s pills to give in his feeding tube. I don’t know if Ollie always took it before I left the room. You know how it is in the morning—so many meds. We don’t have enough time as it is.”

Josephine nodded.

“Maybe he didn’t take them. Maybe he was saving them.” Charity wrestled with her story. She did not want to incriminate anyone but did have reasonable cause to believe this is what happened. “A few days after Elise died, Matty found the pill crusher in Ollie’s room, on the windowsill. I told her I probably forgot it there when I gave the roommate his meds. But now I don’t know.”

“You think he crushed the oxy’s and gave them to Elise?”

Charity gave a slight nod. “And, I overheard him talking to the roommate. He essentially confessed it all to him!”

“Hm.” Josephine sat silent for a moment. In halting words she said, “I guess, what I would say is, it’s not something you could prove. She’s already buried. The doctor didn’t think anything was suspicious. And maybe, just maybe, she was spared some suffering. A lingering death.”

“That’s what I keep trying to tell myself.”

“I think the good Lord would understand. He probably likes having her with Him now.” Josephine grasped Charity’s hand across the table. “Don’t blame yourself.”

“You’re right.” She gave a somber nod.

As they both got up from the table, the sense of relief Charity hoped to feel by bringing the situation out into the open wasn’t there. Her heart was just as heavy as when she first brought it up, still having not resolved the matter.

Josephine gathered the trash onto the tray and emptied it before exiting the cafeteria, parting with Charity in the parking lot.

"Let me know if you hear anything from recruitment," Charity said.

"You too," said Josephine as she stepped into her mini-van.

Charity drove home still bothered about what the whole Elise incident—an ethical dilemma for which nursing school did not prepare her. She thought by unloading on someone she would feel better. What Josephine said made sense. Elise was slowly dying anyway, and was likely spared additional suffering. But the sanctity of life!

Her mother came to mind. Charity recalled the promise of each morning—another day to cherish being with her, until that last sputtering flame of life was extinguished, and all that was left was a whisp of smoke rising from the brittle wick, the candle left a stump of melted wax.

She would have given so much to have her mother with her a little longer. Stopped at a traffic light, she was overcome with a longing to have her here even now. Not in the condition she had been in at the end—unable to move, breathe on her own, or even communicate well. But in a healthier state. Sound and vigorous. Brimming with creativity, instead of crippled by the neurologic sickness. She thought about how this time of year her mother would have been busy designing her and Nadine's Halloween costumes. Later, after hosting Thanksgiving dinner, she would busy herself creating hand-made Christmas cards, complete with the latest photo of them four posing by the Christmas tree.

She looked at the passenger seat and imagined her seated there, smiling at her and talking about her latest craft store purchase as they drove somewhere to have lunch together.

The illness stole all of that. It robbed Charity of her high school years as she spent them caring for her ailing mother. It robbed her of a mother who could have helped her celebrate the milestones of life: getting married, becoming an instant mother herself, graduating college. A fount of good advice when it came to raising those boys, a shoulder to cry on during times of discord between her and Jeff. The illness robbed her of a mother who might have been with her still.

And that's why it bothered her so much, Elise's dying, and the fishy circumstances around it. If her suspicions were true, her final days were stolen, possibly leaving some work undone, or depriving someone of her company and wisdom.

~12~

The next day proved the usual chaotic jumble of household tasks to accomplish between sleeping and work. Thanksgiving was coming up in a few days, and Charity didn't even feel up to celebrating. With general housecleaning neglected until a day off, her home was in an uncommon state of disorganization: the dishwasher needed emptied, and filled again, as dirty dishes crowded the sink, the pile of bills on the kitchen counter had to be attended to, and she was pretty sure the clothes in the washer had never made it to the dryer, which meant they had to be washed again. Good thing they were going to Nadine's for the holiday.

Her interactions with the boys lately were fraught with irritability. They were typical adolescents, absentminded and forgetful, but was it too much to expect them to hang up damp towels after showering and put dirty clothes in the hamper? Shouldn't she be able to count on them to carry backpacks and school books to their rooms instead of letting them accumulate on the steps, or communicate with her better when they needed rides to places after school? She was tired of reminding them, and the lack of sleep made her patience slim.

Jeff was working an extra shift at Country Springs that night; he wasn't coming home till after 11 PM. Charity would be gone by that time, so she wouldn't see him the whole day. Her only contact with him had been the note he placed by the coffee maker before leaving for work early that morning. Written on the back of an old envelope, it said, "Let's get breakfast at Barney's tomorrow. I have the morning off. Jeff." *Hmm. 'Jeff'. Who else would it be?*

Chiding herself for being annoyed, she was glad he wanted to take her to breakfast. Apparently, he did not hold their falling-out last week against her.

Charity's five hours of sleep that morning was interrupted several times by the downstairs phone ringing, Jehovah's Witnesses at the door, and the city road crew and their noisy dump trucks filling potholes in the street. She let the boys in the front door when the bus dropped them off and planned to get another hour or so of sleep before preparing dinner for them (frozen chicken nuggets and mac-n-cheese. A gourmet feast in two boxes).

Her unceasing fatigue had stolen any creativity she had for cooking. Most meals were laden with salt and carbs, and, instead of losing weight, she had gained five additional pounds in the past two months. Her new uniforms were getting tight. It was impossible to diet when always tired.

Jeremy placed his backpack on the stairs and entered the kitchen. He opened a box of cereal and began eating it by the handful, alternatively drinking large swallows of milk, bypassing a bowl and spoon. Charity paused at the doorway to observe him. She noticed how tall he was getting as he leaned against the kitchen counter, raising the milk jug to his mouth with strapping arms. The soft, childish face was growing manly, complete with a hint of a beard along the sharp jawline. He wore his dark curly hair short and took to sweeping it back with gel or mousse.

She sometimes wondered about him, quiet like his father. He liked to collect things—old school papers, outgrown clothes—he even had a box of birthday cards dating from his grade school years. Without any hobbies or real interests outside of school, he didn't seem to fit into any definite role. She hoped the few friends he had provided enough of a social outlet, and was glad he took to playing basketball with them on the weekends.

"I'm taking a short nap before dinner, boys," Charity said as she turned toward the stairs.

Jeremy looked up. "You have to take me driving tonight. I just need a few more hours to get my license, and my permit expires next week." The last time he and McKayla went out on a date, she drove. Charity heard him complain to his father that he should be the one picking her up for dates.

Zach strode into the kitchen and snatched the box of cereal from Jeremy. "And I need you take me to the library. I have to get a book on Abraham Lincoln for history class."

"Can't you just pull up something on-line? Or see if Dad has something on his bookshelf?"

"Naw. She wants a book from the *library*."

Grrr—what's wrong with a teacher who wants students to actually come up with a library book. Doesn't she know what century this is? "Well . . . tonight isn't good for the library, Zachy, how about tomorrow?"

"It's due tomorrow. And I have to have a costume for the eighth grade reenactment, too. I'm a soldier. You have to make me a costume tonight."

"Zach! When was this assigned?"

"When was it assigned? Um . . . about two weeks ago I think. But I've been busy, and yesterday I had a bellyache, and had to lay down, and . . ." Zach faded into his lame excuse.

"I can't make you a costume tonight. Can't you just wear your hat from Civil War club?"

"My hat? That's a *union* hat. I'm supposed to be a *confederate* soldier."

Thinking quickly, she suggested, "You could always wear Jeremy's old Boy Scout uniform. And tear up an old white sheet and wrap your arms and head with it and go as a wounded soldier. Use a red marker to draw blood stains on the sheet. And I guess I'll drop you off at the library when I take Jeremy driving.

We'll have dinner when we get home." If Jeff was home, he could play taxi driver for the boys, but tonight it all fell on her.

She continued her lecture. "In the future, Zach, you have to work on these projects before they're due. Don't wait till the night before. You had two weeks! You should have been doing something on it over the weekend, or last week."

The blank expression on Zach's face was sufficient to make Charity stop her tirade. She knew nothing else would be absorbed.

"Come on, boys. Let's go now so I can at least sleep after dinner." Snatching the keys from the hook by the side kitchen door she tossed them to Jeremy. "You drive."

Coming back home from their outings, she encountered Laura taking her evening walk, charming in her gray wool coat and red beret. Charity paused to greet the elderly woman as the boys walked up the front steps.

"You look tired," Laura said, reaching for Charity's arm.

Charity nodded. "I am. It's working all these nights. I thought it would work out, sleeping when they guys were at school or at work, but I'm always tired."

"Sleeping at night is more restful. It's more natural."

"That's the truth. I sleep like a log on my nights off."

Laura stepped away. "Take care of yourself. You can't do any good for them if you're run down."

"You're right." She watched Laura stride away and realized she knew very little about this neighbor from the next street over, despite seeing her at her walk a few times a week. Her words of wisdom rang true, however. If she didn't hear from Quarry Gen about the job, she purposed to continue looking for something that would give her more time to take care of herself.

Charity followed the boys into the house to prepare dinner. Sitting down and eating together whenever possible was important, even if it was only chicken nuggets and macaroni and cheese. After cleaning the kitchen, she lay down for two hours and almost slept through her alarm to get up to go to work.

Driving to work, her eyes closed at every traffic stop. She put her window down to let in a blast of cool air and pulled into a drive-through for coffee. The events of that evening were on her mind as she parked her car and trudged into the building. She didn't want to be impatient with the boys, or Jeff. In a rare communicative moment, he asked her recently if she was depressed, stating, "You don't laugh with us anymore." It stung.

After change of shift report, Charity began rounds in her usual manner. Her lethargy slowly passed as caffeine from the coffee entered her bloodstream. She tread lightly through the dimly lit halls and peered into each room. Most of her charges were asleep, having been assisted to bed a few hours ago by diligent LPNs or HCAs. Charity enjoyed the quiet and peacefulness. In four or five hours daily activity will be starting—assisting residents with baths and getting dressed. Going to the dining room for breakfast. Some of them would be uncooperative, resisting help or arguing about getting out of bed at all. But for the next few hours, at least, there should be calm.

A few of the rooms contained the night owls, patients who never could get used to going to bed so early. Subsequently, they were allowed to sleep late in the morning, their breakfast trays warmed up and brought to them in their rooms.

Charity heard the TV playing in Tony Leoni's room and peeked through the slightly open door. Tony sat hunch-shouldered in a battered recliner he had brought from home. His hair continued to be a luxuriant dark brown, even at his age, with most of it settling, as if by gravity, just above his ears. A few whisps were combed over to cover his otherwise bald pate. As usual, he was up late, watching sports on a cable channel.

Charity knocked gently on Tony's door. "Who is it?" he answered, in a sing-song voice.

“Who else would it be?” she said as she entered, smiling at him.

He picked up a plate of fudge from his nightstand. “How about a treat?” he said with a wink.

She took a piece and popped it into her mouth. “Delicious!”

“Dorothy brought me this. Said it was left in the lounge by a drug rep.” He partook of another piece of the fudge before setting the plate back down next to a framed photo of his wife, Margaret.

Tony had been a fixture as a visitor to Hill ‘n Dale when Margaret was living there. He was still living independently, driving to the Retirement Home daily to visit her, often bringing pizza or donuts for the staff.

After she passed away, Tony’s blood sugar became uncontrolled. He was therefore admitted to Quarry Gen for three days to help regulate his blood glucose and adjust his insulin regimen, then transferred to Hill ‘n Dale, presumably for the short term. The plan was for physical therapy to strengthen his legs, affected by diabetic neuropathy. He had been there for nearly three months and had become a favorite of Charity’s.

“Did I ever tell you about my wife winning first place at the fair for her fudge?” he asked, grinning up at Charity. Tony’s favorite topic of conversation still revolved around his wife. He turned the TV volume down with the remote.

“No, Tony, you never told me that one.” She took a seat on an afghan on his bed. As he started the story, she gathered the newspaper pages scattered on the bed and folded them into a neat bunch.

“Ha ha! Well, she was a great baker, and she was also good at canning peaches and pears in the fall. She had just baked a pie using her canned peaches and had it all wrapped up, ready for me to take to the Stark county fair. She entered baked goods every year—pies, cookies, cakes—and usually won some prizes.

"Just as I was about to leave with the pie, our neighbor brought a plate of fudge over. She met me in the driveway as I was getting to my car. I told her thank you and said I would put it in the house when I got home. I drove to the fairgrounds; both plates were in the back seat, the pie and the fudge. Both were covered with foil."

Tony paused and peered at Charity, a grin playing on his lips. "Of course you know what happened. I took the plate with the fudge into the fair instead of the pie! Margie was really upset when I came back home and we uncovered the plate holding the pie. She couldn't understand how I could have confused the two. Well, I told her to a man, they all look alike when they're covered up. Anyway, when she won first place with the fudge, we did the only honest thing. We gave the prize money and the ribbon to our neighbor. They gave two dollars for first prize in that day. They insisted on splitting it with us. I think we all went out to get ice cream. It was enough money for all of us to get cones. Margie wasn't so mad then."

"I'll bet," Charity said. "I love to get ice cream out. My Aunt Bee used to take my sister and I to Isaly's in downtown Akron. These days we like to go for sundaes at Barney's restaurant."

Tony shifted in his recliner. "I've never been there. Is the food good?"

"Food is so-so. The service is good and breakfast is usually a safe bet. In fact, Jeff and I are going there for breakfast this morning, after I get off work."

"He's a lucky man," Tony said with a wink.

Charity reached over and patted Tony's hand. "By the way, did your neighbor ever enter her fudge in the fair again?"

"No, that's what was so funny. I didn't tell you the best part. She had bought the fudge at a bake sale at church the day before and wanted to share it with us. We don't even know who made it."

“No kidding?” she said, smiling broadly. “That’s a great story, Tony,” She rose to leave. “Why don’t you get to bed now, okay? I’ll have Dorothy come in and help you. And don’t eat too much of that fudge. Your blood sugar will be way up by morning.”

Tony reached the remote on top of his nightstand and turned off the TV, leaving the room darkened. Moonlight shone through the slats of the window blind. He reached up to her, took her face in his hands and gave her a wet smooch on the cheek. “You’ve become my favorite, you know?”

Charity straightened up, wiped her cheek with the back of her hand, and said, “Don’t tell, but you’ve always been mine, too.” She was glad he couldn’t see the tear edging its way from the corner of her eye as she stepped into the hall.

Completing rounds, she thought about Tony and Margaret, and their long marriage. From the many stories Tony told, it was obvious they had a real bond. She understood him, and he appreciated her.

With Jeff, lately, there seemed to be no connection. He just didn’t get her. She wondered what thing she could do or say to create a better relationship between them, get him to understand her better. What would it take?

~13~

Early morning pre-Thanksgiving shoppers were already out crowding the main streets and Route 93 when Charity left work. Cold-hardened snowflakes dotted her windshield as she drove past Limestone Place on the way home to pick up her husband for their breakfast date at Barney's.

She envisioned the diner with a packed parking lot, breakfast being their most popular meal. The restaurant was originally built on the premises of an old railway station which became obsolete when several limestone quarries nearby closed. The brick façade of the train station was used as the restaurant's frontage, its clock tower rising above the entry door.

Charity remembered when it was first opened and how her parents took her and Nadine there when they were children. The restaurant offered small toys with each kid's meal back then, and her father liked to sneak the prizes from the table when she and her sister weren't looking. After a frantic search for the coveted object, he would "find" it—perhaps hidden by his coat draped on the bench or in the space behind him where he sat—producing it with a conjuring air. Nadine was onto him after a few times, and snatched the toys from him, ruining his little game, and Charity's enjoyment in it.

Jeff was just donning his fall jacket when Charity stepped through the front door. "Thought I'd rake the rest of those leaves," he said. He had already raked the yard three times that month. It was a concern of his to have all the leaves removed from the grass before any snow accumulation. This morning's scattered flakes lent urgency to this task.

"Let's go now, before I collapse and don't want to go. You can rake later." She handed Jeff the keys and followed him to her car. Reclining the seat, she closed her eyes for the five-minute drive to Barney's. He gently shook her awake after parking the car.

The odors of strong coffee and frying bacon greeted them as they entered the restaurant. They walked by the counter, mostly 'regulars' seated on the stools. Occasional friendly or off-color remarks were made to the waitresses, who laughingly answered them in kind.

Their favorite spot, a booth by the window, was available. They made themselves comfortable on the duct-taped vinyl seats as the waitress brought mugs and poured coffee.

"Cream's on the table," she said, indicating a tiny ceramic pitcher near the salt and pepper and sugar. The breakfast menu was displayed there, as well—a greasy cardstock sheet printed on both sides offering any combination of waffles, eggs, breakfast meats, and potatoes imaginable.

Charity wrapped her hands around her steaming mug and inhaled. She swirled some cream into it before taking a sip. Perfect—strong and hot.

Jeff preferred his black. He sucked up a sip and inhaled quickly.

She looked up at him. "You okay?"

"Hmm? Just a little hot."

"It's nice you wanted to get breakfast. Thanks for taking the time off."

Jeff nodded. "They're having the temps work extra hours this week, to give the regular staff a break for Thanksgiving."

"Is George working?"

"George?"

"Josephine's son."

"Mm-hm. I saw him yesterday."

"And?"

"He was working."

She made an impatient gesture. "I mean, is he working Thanksgiving?"

"Don't know." He gazed out the window.

"Are you going to see your dad tomorrow?"

"Saturday," Jeff said. He was watching a backhoe at a construction site across the street.

"Will they give him a proper Thanksgiving meal?"

"I s'pose."

She remained silent, facing him with flinty eyes. This one-sided conversation was chafing.

He turned back to her and winced, feeling the vexation in her gaze. "What?"

"Well—do they cook whole turkeys? Or is it the processed kind? And do they include all the fixings? Talk to me!"

"They, um . . . they do their best. Last year he said it was a good meal, except he didn't like the gelled cranberry sauce."

"What does he like, cranberry relish?"

"Is that the chunky kind?"

Charity nodded. "It has real cranberries in it."

"That's what he likes."

They sat silently as they waited for the waitress to come back and take their order, Charity too exhausted to start any more conversation. Determined to be pleasant and not argumentative, she was just getting more and more irritated by his barren responses.

It was better during their early years together—raising two small boys took most of their time and attention, and the lapses in communication weren't as obvious, as now. Few were the times they had together back then, just the two of them, without one son or the other needing something.

Going to nursing school created a whole new kind of busy. As the boys became more independent in their middle school years, Charity was grateful they needed her a little less for ordinary care—they could make a snack for themselves and could usually be depended on to shower regularly. It freed her to pursue the nursing degree with less distractions. At that time, she was glad Jeff was a man of few demands when it came to interaction with her. He was happy to spend the evenings seated in the living room, magazine or book in his lap, as she sat nearby studying for an exam. The hours spent at the laptop—writing papers, creating care plans, or researching diseases—would have been disrupted had Jeff been of a more vocal bent. And she enjoyed the feeling of companionship as he sat in the same room quietly reading.

Things were different now. She had settled into a routine of work and home life, and wanted to really get to know her husband of eleven years. It was not fair really, that now his taciturn nature irritated her. But sometimes the quiet evenings in the living room emphasized the loneliness in her heart, as she knitted, watching a TV show, and he continued to sit quietly, book open in his lap.

The waitress came back and filled their coffee mugs. Dangling the coffee pot and holding her pad in the same hand, she stood with her pen ready.

"Number three," Jeff said. "Scrambled. Country toast."

Charity looked up at her. "Same for me. Except, no toast. Can I substitute a waffle? With strawberry topping?"

The waitress nodded. "Whipped cream, too?"

She gave a guilty smile. "Yes please."

The waitress departed and Charity glanced out past a few greasy smudges on the window. "I wonder what they're building across the street." The work site was surrounded by a temporary chain link fence. Backhoes were digging deep trenches as dump trucks removed the debris. Sturdy I-beams rose from a cement pad.

"It's gonna be a Mr. Speedy gas station. S'posed to be open 24 hours."

She started a doodle on her napkin: the words "Mr. Speedy" in balloon letters. *Mr. Speedy—wonder why it's not Mrs. Speedy?* She looked at him. "How do you know that?"

"Antony."

Jeff's brother, Antony, worked in construction. Presumably, he was part of this project.

"Oh. Is he working on it?"

"No."

"No?"

Jeff shook his head. He sipped coffee and watched the work site across the street.

Charity accepted a coffee warm-up and added a splash of cream. "So . . . how does he know?"

He shrugged a shoulder. "Not sure."

She waited for a moment, but no more information was forthcoming. This was too much work. She finished filling in the balloon letters of "Mr. Speedy" on her doodle while waiting for breakfast. After downing her meal, she rode home with Jeff in silence.

Lying in bed, she set her cell phone alarm to 3 PM, shortly before the boys would be getting home from school. Her last thought before going to sleep was: *So why does he even want to spend time with me? He can't even talk to me. How do I break through, get him to open up?*

~14~

A week after Charity and Josephine applied for the new jobs, Charity received a phone call from Quarry Gen. The voicemail message invited her to call back to set up an interview.

After returning the phone call, she immediately called her friend Josephine, hoping to find her at home. Josephine said she didn't get a call from recruitment, and Charity suggested she call if she doesn't hear from them in a couple days.

Josephine wished her good luck at the interview, finishing with, "I hope you get the job."

Charity was able to schedule the interview for the next afternoon. Jeff agreed to come home early to be there when the boys came home from school.

Dressing up was a bit of a problem. Beside nursing uniforms, and jeans and tee-shirts, she had very little in the way of casual/chic or even mildly dressy that fit her and had not gone out of style five years ago. With a little bit of creativity, she threw a suitable outfit together. She wore a plain white blouse with the knee-length tartan skirt she had bought for the Pinning Ceremony. Dressing the blouse up with one of her husband's narrow ties updated the look. Using her nurse pin as a tie tack was a nice touch. She slipped on the black mules given to her by her sister, Nadine. Nadine always overbuys and Charity sometimes benefitted by this. Although they were completely different sizes in clothes, they wore the same shoe size. Besides the nursing shoes, Charity hadn't bought shoes for herself in years.

She spritzed a little spray-gel into her bobbed hair and gave it a tousle, creating a care-free look away from her face, and applied a little foundation and blush powder. Finishing with peach colored lip gloss she had since high school, she felt ready to face the public.

Updating her resume in the computer, Charity printed three copies and placed them in a manila folder, along with her nursing license and CPR certification card. She drove to the end of Poplar, and turned right onto the main street, Quarry Run Road.

Their neighborhood featured different varieties of trees as street names. Dogwood Lane, where Laura lived, was the next street over. Then there were the usual Oak and Elm Streets. Maple Drive, Cottonwood, and Buckeye Avenue filled in the rest. Her sons, when they were younger, thought their street name was 'Popular', and Charity enjoyed hearing them explain this to others, reasoning that since it was the Best Street, it was also the most Popular. And why was it the best? Because they lived on it, that's why!

Turning left on Rt. 93, she drove past Barney's Restaurant, the parking lot packed with the lunch crowd. The recent breakfast date with Jeff came to mind, and she winced at how dissatisfying it was, trying to get him to open up. He had gone back to raking leaves when they got home, appearing to prefer the solitude of that activity.

Last night Charity asked him to practice with her using some of the questions she thought may be asked at her interview, like, 'what is your biggest strength?' or, 'name two of your weaknesses'. The last one was problematic. It's difficult to identify your own shortcomings.

Seeing her struggle, Jeff offered, "You could say you have trouble with being organized."

Her puzzled look prompted him to continue. "Because . . . you know . . . it's hard for you to keep up on the cleaning."

Only a significant effort at self-control had made her able to disregard what he said. Was this his idea of being helpful? Donning her thicker skin, she said, "I'm sure I can come up with something," and continued with the practice questions.

After driving ten more minutes she arrived at the Quarry Gen visitor parking lot. She made her way to the fourth floor to meet with the nurse manager of the unit, Joyce Foster. She knocked on the office door and nudged it open.

"Come in, come in," Joyce Foster said, holding out a hand. "I'm Joyce."

Charity shook her hand. "I'm Charity Cristy. Nice to meet you."

Joyce indicated an armless chair in front of her desk. "Sit down. Coffee?" A woman of few words, she nonetheless conveyed great warmth in those words.

"Coffee's fine. Thanks," Charity answered, sitting in the indicated chair. She smoothed her manila folder on her lap.

"I only have basic K-cups. That okay?"

"Sure. With cream?"

As Joyce worked her way to the corner of the room to start up the coffee machine, Charity had a chance to observe her potential new boss. Dark straight hair lay over her shoulders in a classic style. Small gold hoops complemented her brown skin. Her simple white scrub jacket had neat, tell-tale creases where an iron passed over it.

"So, you graduated from Kent State earlier this year?" she said, her back still turned.

"Yes . . . in May."

Joyce turned around and handed Charity the coffee and a powdered creamer packet. "That's my alma mater, too. Good nursing school."

Charity nodded, smiling.

Joyce sat down behind her desk with her own mug. "First, a little about me. I started with this unit when it opened earlier this month. I've also worked on other floors in this hospital too, either as a floor nurse or manager."

Charity noticed that despite Joyce's neat personal appearance, her office was cluttered with stacks of papers on the desk and floor, and a trash can filled with take-out food containers, indication of a busy work schedule. A few photos in cheap frames crowded one corner of the desk, displaying what was probably her daughter in different stages of growing up.

Joyce continued. "Now, tell me about you."

Charity took a sip of coffee from her mug, smiling at the caption 'Nurses call the shots' written on it. She set it on the desk next to the photo frames and began with: "Well, I started nursing school about five years ago, when my sons were younger, they are fourteen and seventeen now." She faltered, not sure what to say next. Her heartbeat quickened and she could feel her face flush.

"Takes a lot of initiative to go back to school, and with children, too!" Joyce sat back in her chair, at ease and taking her time. "Tell me—what pushed you to do it?"

"My husband encouraged me. And . . . my mom. I took care of her when I was in high school."

Joyce tilted her head and raised an eyebrow.

Feeling she needed to explain, now that she brought it up, Charity said, "She was diagnosed with ALS and died just before my senior year. She always told me I would make a good nurse."

Joyce murmured a sympathetic word.

Charity took a deep inhale. "After taking care of my mom, going into health care was what I wanted to do. I worked for Home Helpers for a few years, and once our sons were old enough to be a little independent, we thought it was a good time for me to go to nursing school. The extra income will help pay for the boys' college. Jeff—that's my husband—supported me all the way."

She took a sip of coffee and continued, her confidence growing. "When I graduated, I wanted to work in this hospital, but they weren't hiring then, so I got a job at Hill 'n Dale—you know, the nursing home—in September. I've learned a lot working there, and really enjoy it. But it's five nights a week. And I always have to stay over at least an hour in the morning to finish the work. I decided to look for a job with better hours."

"The job that's available is four nights a week, all eight hours," Joyce said. "We try to consider people's personal lives when we make out the schedule. Our staff has the chance to request days off or pick up extra hours. And there is no mandating. It works out well for us."

Charity felt her heart swell. She really wanted this job. This manager was reasonable and kind. And the schedule would give her more time at home, an extra night to sleep, and maybe lower the stress level all around.

"Besides the schedule, are there any other reasons?" Joyce asked.

Charity pressed her lips together, thinking. "Well . . . I've been at the retirement home for almost four months now. Realistically, most of the residents are probably going to be living at Hill 'n Dale the rest of their lives. Or some other nursing home. Some of them don't have very long to live. We try to avoid uncomfortable or invasive treatments and let them live out their lives in relative comfort."

"Extended-care nurses are doing a very important work," Joyce interjected.

"Thank you. I don't have the attitude that we don't . . ." She paused, collecting her thoughts, hoping she was conveying her feelings adequately. "I just wanted to have the opportunity to help people before they got to that point, when there is still a chance to change bad habits and teach a healthier lifestyle."

Joyce nodded, smiling.

She felt encouraged. “So many of my patients have emphysema, congestive heart failure, or diabetes. I think better patient education and more aggressive health care when these people are younger could prolong and improve their lives.”

“I agree,” Joyce said, with emphasis.

“The ones with emphysema or COPD want to continue smoking, despite the fact that they need oxygen just to walk to the bathroom. We have to let them go outside to smoke, it’s their right. I always worry that they’re going to try to smoke while their oxygen is on! I also have a patient with CHF who insists on eating four slices of bacon with breakfast each morning. We fight with her all the time about it, but we can’t refuse her to have it.” Charity smiled.

At that moment she knew the answer to Joyce’s question. “That’s the main reason I wanted to work here. To learn more and to pass on what I learn to my patients. Maybe that will improve the quality and length of their life.”

“Very good points. You will learn a lot here. Patient and family education is a key priority on the med-surg unit.”

As the interview went on, Charity continued to feel more comfortable and at ease. Ten minutes later, Joyce concluded the interview and promised to call her in a few days.

~15~

Driving home from the hospital, Charity grinned broadly and couldn't wait to tell Jeff how well the interview went. She drove up the driveway and sprinted to the front door.

She strode into the front entry to a scene of activity and chaos. Making her way around cardboard boxes littering the family room, she found the Christmas tree had been set up in the front window.

Jeff rounded the corner from the basement doorway. Seeing Charity, his face beamed. "What do you think?"

"Very nice," she said, gazing at the tree and ropes of garland hanging out of boxes. She smiled at her husband, his neck and shoulders draped with strands of colored lights. Since Thanksgiving dinner at Nadine's last week, she had wanted to start decorating the house for the holidays, but did not have the time or energy. This was a welcome surprise.

"This is cute," she said, touching the twinkling lights he wore.

He began unwinding the strands of lights, ducking his head from under them. "They're tangled, but at least they still work."

"I think this is the last box of decorations," Zach said, entering the room bearing a large plastic tote. He looked up and said, "Hey, Mom! When did you get home?"

"Just now. I see you and Dad have been busy." She grasped the tote and placed it on the floor by the coffee table.

"We wanted to surprise you." He began unpacking Nativity Scene figures. "Dad said we have to help you more."

She glanced at Jeff, behind her. "Thank you," she said, reaching out and squeezing his arm. Turning back, she said to Zach, "Be careful with those." She pulled Joseph out of the tote, unwinding him from tissue paper and peering at his arm, repaired last year with glue. She set him on the coffee table.

She looked around. "Where's Jeremy?"

"Out with *McKayla*," Zach said with an eye-roll.

"She picked him up?"

"He took my car," Jeff said. Jeremy had finally gotten his drivers' license a week ago.

Charity stopped. "Surely he asked you first."

"Sort of."

She gave him a surprised look, eyebrows raised.

"More like told me."

"What do you mean?"

"He said he promised his girlfriend he would drive on their next date. So I had to let him use my car."

She shook her head. "Next he'll be wanting his own car."

"He'll have to get a job first, so he can afford a down payment on a newer one. I called our insurance man so he can use our cars till then."

"Can I put these under the tree?" Zach asked, gathering up the Nativity Scene figures.

Charity sat on the couch. "Let's put them back on the table, Zachy. We have to finish the tree first." She held out her hands as Zach gave them to her.

Holding the figures, she remembered when her mother painted them. It was in the years before the illness stole her ability to hold a paintbrush, or eating utensils, or even Charity's hand.

Endeavoring to diagnose her mother's problem had been difficult in the beginning. Was it just clumsiness that made her stumble often or drop things at home? She struggled while making Charity's ninth grade spring formal dress. It had a flouncy skirt covered with sequins sewn on by hand. Charity knew her mother spent hours completing the task, doing most of it when she wasn't home, or at night after she went to bed, perhaps to hide the fact she had difficulty holding the sewing needle by then.

It was when her mother dropped her mug of tea they knew something was seriously wrong. She liked to have tea after dinner while watching TV, seated on the couch with Charity's father. Charity usually lounged on a bean-bag nearby.

One evening her father said, "Lilly, what you do that for?" He dabbed at his wet pant leg with a tissue.

"What?"

He picked up the dripping mug from between them on the couch and held it up.

Confused, she looked at her hand—upright, and fingers still pinched as if holding the mug. "What happened? Did I drop it?"

At her doctor's appointments all that summer she was worked-up for MS, Guillain Barre, and other neurologic diseases. She had Cat scans and MRI's searching for evidence of a stroke. Finally, the neurologist at Cleveland Clinic determined that by the results of the Electromyography, and the way it was progressing, it was amyotrophic lateral sclerosis: ALS.

"My mother painted these." Charity said to Zach, brushing a finger along Mary's light blue gown.

"Your mother?" he said. He picked up a camel and examined it.

"She had a lot of talent."

Zach smiled. "Like you."

Charity looked at her son, her heart full of love. He was the sensitive one, and often had a kind word to say.

"Let's leave them here till the tree is all done, okay?" She placed Mary down next to the other figures.

At that moment, Jeremy blustered through the front door, followed by a petite, sprightly thing with purple hair—McKayla.

Charity watched him carry two pizza boxes from Chef Mario's to the dining room, then turn to face them. "You remember McKayla." It was more of a statement, rather than a question.

Charity advanced. "So nice to see you again. You looked lovely on homecoming."

The girl wrapped one arm around Jeremy's back and placed the other hand on his chest. "Hmm. I'm just glad Jerry remembered to get a matching vest."

Charity turned and gave Jeff a look. *Jerry?*

She turned back. "Right, the lavender one. To match your dress, and . . . and . . ."

Shaking her locks, the girl giggled. "My hair. I just had it done that day. It took two hours to get the black bleached out and this color applied. I didn't like the first shade they used, so they had to mix a whole new color just for me."

Jeremy disentangled himself from McKayla and said, "Who wants pizza?"

Charity stepped into the kitchen and reached for paper plates and napkins. Jeff was right behind her, and grabbed several cans of soft drinks from the fridge. She caught his disdainful look as they went back into the dining room. "Be nice," she whispered.

He raised his eyebrows. "I am," he murmured, and began distributing drinks.

After dinner, Zach, Jeremy, and McKayla finished decorating the Christmas tree. Charity brewed a cup of herbal tea and sat in the kitchen with Jeff, who was nibbling on a leftover slice of pizza.

"I had my interview today." She stirred a spoonful of honey into her tea.

Jeff looked up. "How'd it go?"

"Good, I think. Thanks for helping me prepare yesterday."

"Don't worry if you don't get it. There's other jobs."

"What do you mean?"

"I don't want you to be disappointed."

"You don't think I'll get it?"

"No—"

"No?" Her voice rose a smidge.

"I mean, 'No', it's not that I think you won't get it."

She set down her mug. "What, then?"

"Never mind." He chewed moodily.

She sipped her tea, a soothing blend of chamomile and lavender. This conversation was pointless, and was heading into dangerous, nitpicking territory.

Keeping her voice even, she said, "I know I may not get it. But I hope I do. One of the main reasons I want this job is the hours will be better for me, which will be better for all of us. It's still night-shift, but only four, instead of five nights a week. I'll get an extra night to sleep and won't have to work over as much. So I can see you more. And do more things together. That's why I hope to get it. For *us*."

He got up and put his paper plate in the trash. Kissing the top of her head, he said, "Then I hope you do, too." As an afterthought, he added, "Good luck."

◆◆◆

With Thanksgiving behind, a massive Christmas tree was moved into the reception area at Hill 'n Dale during the week. The colors of blue and silver were featured on the tree in large shiny balls and glittery bows. Here and there, a bright pink ball could be seen, competing with the more traditional colors, probably the idea of an innovative decorator hired for the season. The tree was illuminated with a multitude of tiny white lights. An evergreen garland with silver and blue ribbon, and a few pink balls, graced the mantle of the large gas-log fireplace in the lobby. Stockings hanging from the mantle and a faux-fur tree skirt completed the festive look.

The only thing missing was a Nativity Scene. In these modern times of political correctness, it was thought best to omit it. Strange, Charity thought. It was His birthday, after all. Otherwise there wouldn't even be Christmas.

She enjoyed taking breaks in the pleasant atmosphere of the lobby when only the Christmas tree lights were on. She turned on the gas logs and sat in a fireside chair, coffee in hand. Reaching for a strand of hair, she let it slip around her fingers, and pictured the bustle of activity that would take place that morning. For now, however, she could take five minutes to sip coffee and absorb the beauty of this space.

After her coffee break she walked the darkened halls, checking on her charges. She peered into Sophie's room, noting the ceramic tabletop tree on her dresser, all lit up with tiny colorful bulbs. Many of the residents had cute and kitschy holiday decorations in their rooms, placed there by family members or friends. Holiday wreaths dressed up several doors. Even Ollie's door had a pine wreath with an old-fashioned velvet bow.

Josephine and a few other staff members took to adopting those residents who had no one to decorate their rooms. They placed something festive—a strand of colored lights or a poinsettia plant—in those rooms, just to make sure they didn't feel forgotten.

Charity moved along the Pool Hall corridor and noticed Tony was still up, as usual. She knocked on the door and entered his room. He had a white wreath on the door decorated with candy canes and striped ribbon.

"Have a candy cane," Tony offered, indicating the wreath. "My granddaughter sent that today."

She pulled one from the wreath and sat on Tony's bed, removing the crinkly cellophane.

He lowered the TV volume with the remote. “Have you heard from the hospital yet?”

Tony had overheard her and Josephine talking about waiting to hear from Quarry Gen about the jobs they applied for. Later, he sidled up to her in the hall and asked about it. At that time, she simply said, “We’ll see.”

“I . . . um . . . I haven’t heard anything definite yet.”

“You’ll get the job.” He lowered his voice. “Now, I hope you know I don’t want to see you leave. But you should do what’s right for you and your family.”

“I’m trying to.” Charity paused. She straightened the pictures of Margaret on Tony’s dresser, then turned to him. “I promise if I leave, I won’t forget you. I’ll come to visit.”

Tony answered with a grin and a wink. Charity smiled and exited the room, lost in her thoughts. *I’ll miss this. I hope I’m not making a mistake by trying to get another job.*

Turning at the end of the corridor, she walked back to the central area near the nurses’ station and crossed into the common room. She was charmed at the ‘old world’ theme with which it was decorated. A Christmas tree in the corner bedecked with plaid ribbon and small, old fashioned St. Nicholas’s contained little cards tucked within the branches. It was the Resident Tree, and each card named one resident and three or four gift ideas. There were very few cards left, which made Charity feel good. She hoped each one would receive some special gift on Christmas. She picked a card and placed it in her scrub jacket pocket. The name on it was “Ollie”.

~16~

Charity opened her eyes Friday afternoon to her cell phone alarming. She gazed up at the ceiling, willing herself awake. Stretching, she sat on the edge of the bed and looked around her room. Painted in an 80's version of 'clay', with a darker tone beneath the wainscoting, it was a comfortable, if dated, room. When they bought the house before their second anniversary, they had great plans to change this or that—wall colors, floor coverings, bathroom fixtures. Somehow the daily cares of life got in the way and, besides painting the boys' bedrooms and changing window coverings, they did very little to change the house's original appearance.

She donned her bathrobe and stepped to the window. Moving the curtains aside, she could see the bare branches of the front yard tree were covered in a layer of snow, and there was about two inches on the ground. The down-comforter sky promised more snow later.

Showered and dressed, she strode down the steps, turned into the kitchen, and began cleaning the table, rinsing dishes, and loading the dishwasher. What to make for dinner? She opened the refrigerator and gazed in absently.

The phone rang. Passing into the rear of the family room, she reached for the phone just as it stopped ringing. Glancing down at the answering machine, she noted its red light was blinking from previous messages. Charity sat on Jeff's recliner and began clearing the messages.

She skipped the ones left by telemarketers and a pre-recorded message letting her know they owed fines at the library (no surprise). She then listened to a message left by someone from Quarry Run Middle School. The message asked Zach Cristy's parents to call the attendance department.

The attendance department? She knew Zach went to school that day. He had taken his lunch from the fridge and his backpack was gone from its usual place on the steps. Maybe he was late. She wouldn't know, as she didn't get home from work till after the boys left for the day.

While considering this, the phone rang again. She picked it up and was delighted to hear from the unit manager of Four South, Joyce Foster.

"Ready to work here?" Joyce asked, with her typical word economy.

"Yes!" Charity was unable to contain her delight. "When do I start?"

They worked out the details; Charity would be giving the Retirement Home two weeks' notice and then begin training at the hospital. She had a letter of resignation already composed, and decided to print it out after dinner and run it over to Hill 'n Dale that very night. No reason to put it off, and perhaps she could avoid having to give it to Susan in person.

After her conversation with Joyce, Charity was sure this was the right move for her. The excitement she felt about starting this job was different from the apprehension of beginning work at Hill 'n Dale. She could already feel the tension of overly long work hours ease. Her mind whirled with plans for that extra day off: deep cleaning projects, new recipes to try, coffee dates with Josephine. Or Jeff. Yes. She would have more time to spend with her husband. She would like that. And so would he.

Working at the hospital would give her the chance to make a difference in people's lives by educating them on ways to improve their health. At Hill 'n Dale, Susan discouraged most attempts at changing unhealthy habits, standing behind her attestation that "it's their right" to continue them. What a difference it will be to help someone heal, overcome a harmful habit, or improve their health in some way by giving a well-timed word of advice or teaching.

She also hoped to learn more about acute health problems and diseases since the medical-surgical floor should have patients with a variety of ailments. Perhaps she will obtain some clue to what illness took her father so quickly. Part of her didn't want to find out—what if it was something she should have known about? Something she could have helped, but didn't? But then maybe she would discover it was nothing she could have done anything about. Maybe she would be cleared of any wrongdoing, and for failing to take care of him.

Loathe to ruin her good mood by investigating the call from the attendance department of the middle school, Charity's sense of responsibility and curiosity won out. How bad could it be?

She took a few steps from Jeff's library nook to the couch to make the call. This room had always been her favorite. Extending the entire depth of the house, it had been two separate rooms, a living room and an office, when the house was built. The previous owners had removed the separating wall, creating this larger space. Jeff's recliner and bookshelves comprised the rear, and the front opened to a bay window looking out to the street. The couch and two accent chairs formed a grouping around a coffee table in the center of the room.

She took a deep breath and dialed the middle school.

Mrs. Picaune, from the attendance department, answered the phone. "Zach was tardy once last week, and he was tardy twice this week. Is there a problem with his transportation to school?"

"He always takes the bus," Charity said. "He gets it at the corner at 7:30. Maybe it was late."

"He was on time today, but the busses weren't tardy all three of those other days. Students who are tardy three times must serve Saturday detention. We will expect him at 7 AM sharp tomorrow."

As Charity hung up with Mrs. Picaune, she felt an intense dislike for the exacting, annoying woman. *"Tardy—tardy—tardy." Why does she have to say "tardy" so many times?*

At that moment, Zach dragged himself into the entryway. As the bus sloshed away, he stomped the snow from his feet on the doormat and hung up his coat.

"Hey, Mom," he said, dropping his backpack near the stairs.

Plopping onto the couch next to Charity, he swept his dark hair out of his eyes, picked up the remote, and selected a cop show rerun on the TV, mounted on the opposite wall.

She reached for the remote in his hand and lowered the volume. "Hey, Zach, I got a call from school today. They said you've been late three times in the last two weeks. You have to serve Saturday detention tomorrow. Has the bus been getting to your stop on time?"

He gave her a sidelong glance. "Today it was late."

"Okay, but supposedly you were on time today. Why were you late all those other days?"

He was focused on a new video game commercial on TV.

"Zach!"

He turned to her and flashed a sheepish grin. "Sorry. Why was I late? So . . . Sometimes I miss the bus and have to walk to school. Or if I'm quick enough, I can pick it up on Maple Avenue, at Damion's stop. Yesterday Dad took me to school on his way to work, but I was still late." He shoved his shoes off, still tied, and propped his feet on the coffee table.

"Why don't you just get to the corner stop on time? You only have to walk up four houses. Jeremy's bus comes a half hour earlier and he seems to make it."

He rubbed his belly. “I had a stomachache yesterday. That’s why I missed the bus. And one day last week.”

She sat up and faced him. “Why am I just finding out about this now? How often does this happen?”

“How often? Only about once a week, sometimes more.”

“Zachy! You should have told me. Dad should have told me.”

He shrugged. “It’s no big deal. He gave me the pink medicine and I felt better. Then he took me to school.”

“Do you feel okay now?”

Zach stood up. “I’m fine. Just hungry. Are there any cookies?”

Charity went to the kitchen with him to fix him a snack. She handed him a tall glass of milk and said, “Make sure you’re up early tomorrow. Detention starts at seven.”

Zach groaned and snatched a handful of cookies.

“Hey, don’t complain. You think I like getting up early on my day off?”

He flipped the bangs from his eyes. “Sorry, mom.”

She gave him a sideways hug, his shoulders nearly reaching hers. “It’s okay. But we have to figure out what’s wrong with your belly, too. I’ll get you an appointment with Dr. Stoudt.”

The next morning Charity rose early with Zach and drove him to Saturday detention. They picked up carry-out breakfast sandwiches on the way, and he finished his as he walked into the school. When she returned home, Jeff let her in, still dressed in his shorts and tee-shirt, and followed her to the kitchen. He poured a cup of coffee and opened the carton of his breakfast sandwich. “Thanks for getting this,” he said with a grin.

She shot him a tight-lipped look.

“What?” Jeff said. He took a sip of coffee.

Sitting at the table with him, she said, "I heard Zach was sick this week. He had one of his bellyaches and almost stayed home from school."

"He felt better, so I drove him."

"I need to know when he's sick. You should have told me."

"But he felt better."

She sighed. "There's something wrong. Kids don't always have bellyaches like that. He's been getting them at least once a week. *I'm* a nurse. Don't you think you should have told me?"

He nodded. "I s'pose. Next time I will. Okay?"

That would have to suffice. Men just can't be depended on to cover all the details. They ate in silence for a few minutes. The combination of eggs, cheese, and English muffins, washed down with stimulating cups of coffee, was a hearty but not overly filling meal. She enjoyed the companionship of breakfast and, ready to start a few projects for the day, stood up and topped off her coffee at the kitchen counter.

Having dealt with the uncomfortable topic of Zach's tardiness, Charity's mind jumped to her good news. "Oh," she said, spinning to face Jeff. "I meant to tell you, I got a call from Quarry Gen yesterday. They said I can start next month." She had crawled into bed early the previous night, before Jeff came home from the late shift.

Jeff raised his eyebrows. "So you got the job?"

"You sound surprised."

He rose and crossed the room, placing his arms around her waist. "No. Of course not. I'm glad for you."

She returned his embrace, pressing into the old cotton tee he slept in. She always found his sleepy, before-shower scent comforting. Backing away, she said, "I'll be off for Christmas and New Years. The next orientation class doesn't start till January."

He smiled. "That's great. We could do some things together, with the boys. You won't be sleeping all the time."

She winced. She didn't sleep *all* the time.

She opened the dishwasher and placed her mug in the top basket. "Where's Jeremy?"

"Upstairs. He came home late from his date with McKayla."

She called for Jeremy to come down and have breakfast, then dialed the number for Dr. Stoudt's; he was open half a day on Saturdays. She was able to get an appointment for next Wednesday, after school.

Then she called Josephine. Multitasking, she balanced the phone on her shoulder as she closed the dishwasher and turned it on. "Hey, glad to catch you at home," she said to Josephine, "I didn't see you at work yesterday morning, and didn't know if you were off today."

"It's my first weekend off in over a month. I've been picking up extra since that LPN quit. Making some extra money for Christmas."

"You'll be glad you did it come payday."

"Yeah. But I don't like missing church so much."

"I saw George bring your kids to Sunday School last week. It was my turn to teach, and I had Maria and Manuel in my class."

"He's good about that. I don't know what I would do without him. But we plan to attend church together tomorrow."

Charity wiped the kitchen table with a dishrag, and draped it over the sink. "How much longer will you have to work those extra days? I thought we were hiring."

"Susan's interviewing a few nurses Monday, so I'm keeping my fingers crossed. What's up with you?"

Unable to contain her grin or the joy in her voice, Charity said, "Well . . . I got the job."

"I knew you would! When do you start?"

"After Christmas. I took my two-week notice to Susan's office last night. I didn't think she'd still be there, and wanted to leave it in her mail slot. But she was working late."

"Oops. How'd she take it?"

"Like you'd expect. She said, 'You think working in a hospital will be easier?' and snatched the letter from my hand before I could answer. I wanted to tell her I can't go on working that many hours anymore. Things are getting neglected. I have to make dentist appointments for all of us, and I need my annual check-up. And Zach has to go to the doctor's next week. I just don't have time for anything."

"Is Zach okay?"

Charity sat down at the table and took a sip of her leftover coffee. "He's been having these bellyaches—about once a week. Sometimes he's late for school because of it. I didn't realize how bad they were getting."

They concluded their conversation after a few minutes with Josephine asking Charity to keep her updated on her son's problem. She gathered the dirty kitchen towels and stepped down the basement steps to put in a load of laundry.

◆◆◆

Charity took Zach to see Dr. Stoudt after school on Wednesday. He had been their pediatrician for several years, after taking over the practice from his father, old Dr. Stoudt. Jeremy had moved on to a general practitioner, but Zach just turned fourteen that summer and was still young enough to remain with him.

Charity sat in the updated waiting room, complete with a flat-screen TV and leatherette club chairs, while Zach had his appointment. She watched two youngsters play house in the corner of the room near a painted wood kitchenette. One was stirring a large pot on the range as the other filled it with plastic fruit.

After examining him, Dr. Stoudt invited Charity to come into the exam room, with Zach's 'okay'. "I feel Zach is dealing with irritable bowel syndrome, IBS," he said. "It is something we see in about ten percent of teens, and is sometimes related to stress or anxiety."

Zach glanced at his mother, then back at Dr. Stoudt. "Anxiety? I don't have anxiety."

Charity peered at him. "Do you know what that means?"

"Means you're always worried about something. Damion's mom has anxiety. He told me. And she's *always* worried."

Dr. Stoudt nodded. "It can also be aggravated by foods you eat, like greasy, or fried foods, caffeine, or milk products. Or sometimes just eating too big a meal. Do you sometimes get a crampy belly after eating any of those things, or after a big meal?"

Zach looked up and thought for a moment.

Charity said, "Greasy foods, maybe. Right, Zach? Like fried chicken or French fries?"

"French fries? Mm-hm. Or those corn dogs they sell in the school cafeteria. They're so good. But I ate one last week and had a bellyache the rest of the day."

"Right," Dr. Stoudt said. "You'll have to stay away from those things. And make sure you are eating fresh foods, like salads or apples, so you go to the bathroom every day."

"Is coffee okay?" Trying to mimic his big brother, Zach had started drinking coffee at breakfast, instead of his usual chocolate milk.

Dr. Stoudt shook his head. "No, that has a lot of caffeine. And, instead of using pink bismuth, I'll prescribe an antispasmodic pill for when you get those bellyaches. Docs you have any trouble swallowing pills?"

"No. I can swallow pills just fine," Zach said.

"Let me know if the pills don't relieve the symptoms," Dr. Stoudt said as he opened the exam room door.

Charity took the co-pay at the receptionist counter and drove to the pharmacy to fill the script for the antispasmodic medicine, Spaz-no. They decided to keep them in the kitchen cupboard, and Zach promised to tell her whenever he needed one.

She glanced at her younger son, his arm draped out the passenger window, the breeze drifting his hair across his forehead. She felt a catch in her throat. He was growing up, and looking more like Jeff than ever. She was about his age when her mother began having symptoms of the illness. It was about that time the loss of feeling in her hands and legs pushed her to visit their family doctor, who sent her to specialists at Akron General. Charity dutifully accompanied her on all her doctor and hospital visits, so much more mature than her years, she now realized.

~17~

Charity's last two weeks at Hill 'n Dale passed quickly. She waited until her last shift to say goodbye to the many friends she made working there, both staff members and residents. Josephine brought two dozen donuts from the Coffee Cave that morning to give Charity a proper send-off.

Susan Morgan stopped in the staff lounge to say goodbye. "I really hoped you would change your mind and stay," she said brusquely.

Charity was taken aback by this statement. What to say? She stood up and raised the box from Coffee Cave, holding it out to Susan. "Donut?"

"No," She said, pressing her lips together firmly. She spun on a heel and left the room.

Charity looked up to see Josephine watching her, eyes filled with mirth. Charity raised an eyebrow. "Alrighty. I guess it's good she didn't want me to leave." The two laughed at the awkward exchange with the nurse manager. It takes all kinds.

"Probably miffed she would have to train someone again," Josephine said as she sat back down at the table. She chose a donut covered in cream cheese icing and took a generous bite. She scooped up a fingerful of icing and popped it into her mouth. "You shouldn't waste time worrying about her. You're doing the right thing."

Charity finished her double chocolate donut and sipped tepid coffee. She had been nursing this cup of coffee since morning report. She turned to Josephine. "When do we give the Resident Tree gifts? I mean, should I just leave it by the tree?"

"Do you have it with you?"

Charity reached down and brought out a hunter green gift bag. It was decorated with a stenciled burgundy reindeer. Green and burgundy tissue paper popped up out of the bag. "It's for Ollie."

"You should go see him today. It's nicer to give it in person, and he might like to say goodbye."

Leaving the boxes of donuts open in the staff lounge, Charity stepped into the Garden Hall passageway and walked to Ollie's room. She expected to find him there, as he usually returned to his room after breakfast.

Ollie was standing at his closet, back to the doorway, sorting through his clothes on hangers. He was dressed in pressed trousers, a dry-cleaned white shirt, and festive red and green plaid vest. Charity cleared her throat as she entered.

He turned around and smiled with recognition, carefully stepping toward her using a carved wooden cane. It presented a much more elegant picture than the chrome legged walker with neon yellow tennis balls for feet. He was still expected to use it when walking the halls, but in the privacy of his room, he used the cane.

Charity approached holding out the gift bag.

"What's this?" he asked.

"It's a Christmas gift. I picked your name from the Resident Tree."

Taking a step toward the bed, he sat down next to the neatly arranged pillows. Charity sat next to him. He pulled the tissue out of the bag and carefully set it aside. He removed the gift, a pair of faux-leather slippers.

"That's nice!" he said in his rich baritone. He gazed down at the slippers, held before him in both hands. Charity noted his old slippers were placed side-by-side under his bed. They were a tired looking pair in navy blue fabric. She hoped he would like the new, spiffy pair of slippers she bought him.

She pulled a square box wrapped in tissue out of the bag and handed it to him.

"This too?"

She smiled and nodded.

Ollie gently untaped the wrapping from the package and opened it. He unrolled a long scarf, knit in black and gray stripes, and immediately wound it around his neck. "How does it look?"

"Real fine," Charity said.

"Did you make this?"

She nodded. It was one of her favorite things, presenting her hand-made items as gifts. She relished the enjoyment they brought people. This scarf was something she had started last year, originally meaning it as a Christmas gift for Jeremy. Since she never finished it, she thought about it after picking Ollie's name from the Resident tree, and decided it would look good on him. Knitting the last few rows and adding fringe, she was conflicted, still having that nettling doubt in her mind. Striving to be objective, she boxed and wrapped it, picturing the joy it would bring to Ollie—Elise's friend—and decided to give it to him in memory of her.

He removed the scarf and folded it reverently. "That's one of the nicest gifts I ever had. Thank you, Charity." He placed his large hand on hers.

"You know today's my last day."

He gave out a heavy sigh. "I heard that. Matty was talkin' about you leaving this morning."

"I'm starting at Quarry Gen next month."

He sat quietly for a moment, stroking the folded scarf in his lap. "I remember you was one of the first nurses I met when I moved in here."

Charity smiled. "Mm-hm. I remember that day. I introduced you to Elise. She gave you the biggest smile when she met you."

He nodded. "She was a good friend. I felt sorry for her, not being able to eat right 'n all." His voice cracked. He sniffed and wiped his nose with a cloth handkerchief he produced from the vest pocket. "I hope I did the right thing."

Charity's attention perked up. *'The right thing.' Could this mean . . . ?*

"Why? What did you do?" she asked gently.

He turned to her and sighed. "What I told her. When she couldn't eat right, and her niece talked to her about puttin' a feeding tube in. She asked me what she should do." Ollie pointed at the now empty bed across the room. His roommate had passed away recently after an emergency transfer to the hospital. He never returned to the retirement home.

"I told her she didn't want to end up like him. I said I would help her eat, and not to have the feedin' tube put in."

"You told her that?"

Ollie looked at Charity with misty eyes. "You think I did the right thing?"

She squeezed his hand. Her mother's last days came to mind. Her mother had made it clear she did not wish to have any more nutrition given that way, through the tube. Back then, it broke Charity's heart not to give the tube feeding, so she kept it up, not strong enough to see her mother waste away more than she already had. She felt it was *something* she could do to keep her mother with her just a little longer. Her mother closed her eyes, resigned, as she poured it in.

But now Charity understood. It was one of the last forms of control a person can have—whether or not to eat. Perhaps Elise ate less and less as a way to have her way, make it *her* decision, since many of her abilities were taken by the stroke.

"I think you did the right thing," Charity said. "Sometimes it is a good idea to place a feeding tube. For some people. But she wasn't going to recover fully. And it would have just dragged out the end."

Ollie nodded.

"Plus, it was a kindness for her to make that decision for herself, and not have it forced against her will."

She rose from the bed and Ollie walked her to the door. After a brief hug and wishes of Merry Christmas, she left his room and made her way to her locker to collect the rest of her belongings. She had already said goodbye to Tony Leoni last night. It was an emotional encounter, with both of them trying to be cheerful; there were a few tears at the end. She said the rest of her goodbyes as she left. But her mind wasn't really on those interactions. Her mind was on Ollie. On what he did. And what he didn't do.

She finally felt at peace knowing the worst Ollie did was to give a friend some advice, and not, as she thought, help that friend into the afterlife. Additionally, Elise *was* included in the decision about the feeding tube, after all. Charity didn't have to think any longer that she should have brought it up to her. Didn't have to feel she had done Elise a disservice by not offering its use. Elise had already made up her mind.

Her heart light, she unlocked her car and turned to face the building of Hill 'n Dale Retirement Home. The building was surrounded in a carpet of three inches of snow. A few crackly brown leaves trembled on nearly bare branches, awaiting their descent to the earth. Large pine wreaths graced the doors leading into the front lobby, decorated with extravagant bows in blue, silver, and pink.

She turned to her car, at the edge of the small employee parking lot, and smiled at the black and white cow reaching over the fence to long grasses poking from the snow.

"Goodbye," she murmured. She tossed her bags into the back seat and drove home, a satisfied smile on her face.

~18~

Having the week before Christmas off, with no work or school to distract her, was a gift. Charity used the time to do some baking and finish decorating the house. She lugged the rest of the bins up from the basement and withdrew pine roping, gold ribbon, and strands of white lights. Untangling the lights and straightening the lengths of ribbon was a tedious job. Once done, she applied a festive touch to the stairway banister, rising from the entryway, and across the bookcases that graced the back wall of the family room, behind Jeff's recliner.

Jeff strode into the room, sporting his Union soldier cap. "Zach and I are going to the club Christmas party tonight, remember."

She finished tucking a strand of lights into a corner of the bookcase and said, "Is he ready?"

"He's looking for his hat."

At that moment, Zach strode in, cap in one hand and medal in the other. "Ready, Dad?"

Jeff reached for Zach's cap and plunked it on his head. "Sure, pal. Let's go."

Mostly over being excluded from the Civil War club meetings, Charity felt that perhaps it was good Zach had this one distinct thing with his father. It seemed to be bringing them closer together.

There was a special tradition her own father had kept up with just her—taking her out to buy her mother's Christmas gifts.

He said she was better at picking them out than Nadine, and they had fun searching high and low for the perfect gift, usually going to the shopping plazas in Canton for better selections. They would go to dinner then, just them two, at a nicer restaurant, with linen tablecloths and large, single-sided menus.

It was difficult choosing the right gift during the illness. The Christmas she spent in a wheelchair they selected a pair of fluffy light blue slippers and coordinating bathrobe. Then they found a set of thirty artist-grade felt-tipped markers, thinking they would be easier to use than a paintbrush. Excited, her mother soon unpacked the markers and attempted to sketch on a pad of thick paper. They kept slipping from her fingers, despite her efforts to grip them firmly. Watching her struggle, Charity regretted choosing the gift, one that emphasized her mother's disability in such a conspicuous manner.

"See, Charity, she *can't* use them," her father had said.

Charity tilted her head as she looked at him. "But, Dad, you helped me—"

The look he gave her, lips pressed together disapprovingly, stopped her.

"No matter," her mother said, in her halting speech. "I'm just . . . having an . . . off day."

She put the paper and markers aside "for another time".

Charity went to her room that night blaming herself for not realizing the extent the illness had reached. Additionally, her father's reprimand stung, and she suffered a few tears because of it.

Making her way past this year's Christmas tree she paused, and straightened a wooden rocking horse hung by a red cord. The Christmas tree, all bedecked with ornaments and glitter, livened up the room, and lifted her mood any time she looked at it.

Her mother's last year, Charity had set up the tree in the front room, but never had time to decorate it. Demands of eleventh grade and taking care of her mother sucked up any spare time she had. The tree sat there, dark and joyless, until summertime. By then it was getting dusty, so she packed it up and placed the box in the corner of the room.

If she had finished decorating it, it would have been a source of joy to her, and maybe even to her father. It might have given him a reason to spend his evenings in the front room, instead of the basement family room he had moved to. It might have made him want to visit with her mother more. But she didn't finish it, and her father, in his depressed state, just quit taking part in holidays anymore.

Stepping back she took in the tree as a whole, and was cheered by it once again. What a nice thing for Jeff to do this year—set it up and initiate decorating. Just putting on the lights was always such an arduous task, and he did it without her asking. And what he had said to Zach, "we have to help you more", made her smile as she turned and moved through the entry.

She stepped into the dining room and covered the table with a red cloth. The centerpiece, an advent wreath with four white candles in brass holders, had already been used the past three weeks. The fourth candle would be lit this Sunday, and on Christmas Eve the large center one, as well, while they ate a simple dinner after Christmas Eve service.

When evening fell, she reached into the corner cabinet of the family room and withdrew a snow globe, setting it on the drum table in the front window, next to the tree. There was a turn-key underneath, and it played several Christmas songs when wound. It was a gift from Jeff at their first Christmas together.

Focusing on the scene within the glass globe—a grouping of miniature houses on a snowy slope—she was charmed once again by the detail of tiny villagers sledding among tiny fir trees. It was a thoughtful gift, something she wouldn't have purchased for herself. It showed Jeff's insight of what would make her happy those years ago. Anymore, he didn't know what to buy for her, and she found it was better to just tell him outright rather than let him guess. A few of the surprises weren't very welcome—there was the year of the vacuum cleaner . . .

Charity wound the snow globe and gave it a shake. She sat back in a velvet armchair and gazed out of the front window as snow fell in delicate flakes, coating all surfaces with a sparkling layer. A few children were still out across the street, finishing a snowman with a lumpy head. After a few moments they all turned toward their door, called in from the cold.

Laura strolled by on the sidewalk in a long coat and her usual red beret. She turned and waved in the direction of Charity's house. Charity stepped toward the window and waved back, answered by Laura's smile.

Sitting back in the armchair, she picked up her mug of tea and sipped on it while "Jingle Bells" tinkled merrily from the snow globe. This has been a good day—a day of leisurely decorating the house to welcome the celebration of Christ's birth. How fortunate they were to have one another, and their health, and this house, and all these nice things that help set aside a certain time each year for this occasion.

The next day Charity attacked Christmas baking, mixing up several batches of sugar cookie dough and gingerbread. On break from school, Zach enthusiastically assisted in brushing icing and dropping sprinkles on cookies shaped like snowflakes, Christmas trees, and stars.

A purchased kolache nut roll and poppyseed roll were sliced and arranged on a platter along with the cut-outs and gingerbread drops.

Jeff entered through the side kitchen door after work. "Smells good," he said, kissing Charity's flour-dusted cheek.

She held out a platter. "You can eat these, but don't eat the ones in the fridge. They are to take when we go to Nadine's for brunch tomorrow."

Jeff nodded and chose a gingerbread cookie.

The timer dinged. Charity reached into the oven to pull out a last tray of cookies and placed it on the formica counter. “We should get to her house around eleven.”

“Will do,” Jeff said as he mounted the stairs to get in the shower. Charity left the oven on and placed the shepherd’s pie she had prepared earlier in it, setting the timer for 40 minutes.

~19~

They arrived at Nadine's Christmas Eve morning, and Jeff was immediately drawn into the office by her husband, Kirkwood. He closed the door against the child, Dane who, at age six, had the annoying habit of needing frequent attention. The men could be heard through the door talking in confidential tones.

Zach always enjoyed playing with his young cousin and went with him to his room, which featured a treehouse bed and wooden railway table. His huge collection of Legos were spilled on the floor and the boys immediately began building something.

"We'll put your cookies on this," Nadine said to Charity, producing a crystal platter.

"Alrighty," she said, and added it to the many desserts and brunch items already on the oversized dining table. Her cookies looked lost among the cheesecakes, sausage balls, Belgian waffles, and pots of warming syrup and fruit compote.

Nadine's cook, Anne, was just entering through the swinging doors bearing a large bowl of fluffy scrambled eggs. "That's the last of it, besides the glazed bacon. I'll bring that out as soon as it's done."

Nadine bustled around re-arranging the food on the table and giving orders to Anne.

Jeremy had made himself at home in a massive recliner in the den, switching channels on the wall sized TV, three pug dogs in attendance. Charity joined him there to keep out of the way. It was a soothing room, paneled in rich oak, a large fireplace with glowing gas logs at one end. She relaxed on the couch next to a chubby pug dog who kept nudging her hand, demanding cuddles, and absently watched the football game Jeremy had chosen.

Gazing around the room, she admired the tastefully placed Christmas decorations. Real pine boughs and holly with red berries adorned the mantlepiece, similar to the elaborate wreath on the front door. She looked closer and observed the urn with her parent's cremains, combined, among the holly. The urn was in its usual place, but today it was graced with photos of their parents in their youth.

She disentangled herself from the pug and moved across the room. Nice her sister thought to create a remembrance of their parents in this way, with the photos, one of them posing on their wedding day, another a snapshot in bathing suits on a summer day. Peering at the urn, she read, "Lilly and James—together again" engraved on a tiny brass plaque. She traced the words on the plaque and her throat caught. Was this all that was left of them? A jar full of burnt remains? No, it was not. Certain of an afterlife, she knew they were together in Heaven, bodies whole. Happy once again.

Happy . . . not despondent and heartbroken like her father was those last days. Why didn't she realize what he was going through? His relationship with her mother was different than hers. They were lovers, soulmates, friends. It was a different kind of loss. And, as much as she didn't understand his sorrow, he must have not understood hers.

Could his depression have been a causative factor in his death? Or was there some other illness she wasn't aware of? Again, she remembered the drinking, and recalled the scent of booze on his breath the infrequent times she encountered him in the kitchen. She should have noticed more. Should have paid attention to how much he drank. Should have taken better care of him.

Interrupting her thoughts, Dane charged into the den followed by Zach. “Aunt Charity, Mommy says time to eat.”

Jeremy and the pugs followed the boys to the dining room.

Charity touched the urn and murmured, “Sorry Mom. Sorry, Dad,” before turning toward the door. She stepped down the hall and summoned her husband and brother-in-law to the table.

Linking her arm with Jeff’s, she leaned against him as they walked to the dining room, feeling downcast from her memories. Kirkwood, taking his seat at the head of the table, continued his monologue to Jeff about investments.

She sat next to Jeff and tried to shake herself from her mood. She took a sip of champagne.

He reached for his glass and she caught a pungent whiff from his jacket sleeve. “Cigars?”

He grimaced. “I tried one, but it made me cough,” he whispered to her. “I guess I inhaled.”

“You’re not supposed to inhale?”

“I don’t know. I left it on the ashtray.”

Jeremy passed a dish of sausage balls to his father. Using the tiny silver tongs, he placed a few onto his plate, and handed it to Charity. Food continued to be passed around until everyone’s plates were piled high. Kirkwood said a blessing that would make any Methodist minister proud, and they all dug in.

Pine scented candles and softly playing holiday tunes added to the ambiance. Charity’s mood improved in the festive atmosphere. She looked around the table and observed her sons talking to Nadine, as she questioned them about their school activities. Kirk continued making the occasional comment to Jeff, who made cordial, nonspecific remarks in return.

Picking up a fork and spearing a sausage ball, Charity noticed the dishes were embellished with gold and silver snowflakes. They looked familiar. “Where did you get this china?” she asked Nadine.

"Aunt Bee. She used to collect it at the grocery store."

Charity nodded. "I remember you had to spend a certain amount and you would get another piece to add to the collection. She was lucky to have collected all this."

"She didn't," Nadine said, and nodded toward Kirk. "He found a website that sells replacement china and bought enough to complete the set this year. We even have a soup tureen and turkey platter."

Charity was glad her sister still had enough of her blue-collar roots that she didn't mind using grocery store china. "Aunt Bee will be glad to see it in use. Is she coming over later?"

"Tomorrow, for Christmas breakfast."

"Hm. I thought she'd be here today. I didn't know if I should plan to have her come to our house, or if I would even see her over the holidays, because she didn't answer my phone calls."

"She doesn't answer mine either," Nadine said. "She just wrote in her Christmas card that she wouldn't see us today because her garden club had an outing."

"Christmas Eve?"

Nadine shrugged. "She wrote that she would come here Christmas morning. That's how I know she's coming."

After the visit, Nadine sent Charity and her family home with elaborately wrapped gifts for everyone, leftover food packed in Charity's container that originally held her cookies, and three boxes of almost brand new shoes for her. Nadine had to make room for the ones she just bought to match new, updated outfits.

Driving home, Jeff was quieter than usual. Charity said, "I appreciate you talking with Kirk. I know you two don't have much in common."

He drove in silence for a couple blocks. Finally, he said, "Today it was investments. He wanted me to buy gold. It's something he started doing this year."

"How much is gold?" Zach asked from the back seat.

"A lot! I think we have enough saved to buy maybe a fourth of a gold bar. Maybe not even that much," Jeff said.

Charity looked pained. She knew Jeff had a self-conscious streak when confronted with people of wealth. "Did you tell him that?"

"No."

"So you told him you'd buy some?"

"No."

She sighed. "What did you say?"

He turned to her. "I said I'd talk it over with you."

She nodded. "Okay, we talked about it."

"That's what I say." He turned into the driveway, pressed the garage door opener, and pulled in.

Christmas Eve ended peacefully. After the church service they came home to a dinner of homemade wedding soup and salad in the candle-lit dining room. Then they exchanged gifts around the tree.

Charity was excited to give Jeff the coffee table book on guns and cannon used during the Civil War, along with a tiny metal mounted soldier to add to his collection of figurines. He kept them locked in a glass case on a bookshelf as Zach and Jeremy used to take them out and play "army men" with them when they were little. At $25-$50 apiece, he wasn't willing to let them be used like toys.

He sat back on the couch and peered at the figure. "Look. The buttons on his uniform are painted gold, and so is the horse's bridle."

Charity grinned. Still a boy at heart.

Jeff offered Charity her gift, wrapped in shiny red paper.

She smiled. "It's nice you wrapped it. Even though I know what it is."

"Maybe you do. Maybe you don't."

She gave him a bemused look and unwrapped the set of paints and pad of watercolor paper. Just what she asked for.

"Look inside the paper."

Riffling the pages, an envelope dropped out. Charity opened the rich, lined envelope and withdrew a card with the words "Lenore's Day Spa" embossed on it in extravagant font. It was a gift of a day of their extra-deluxe treatments: mani-pedi, therapeutic massage, and choice of waxing, facial, or hair styling.

She held it up. "Ooo. This is nice."

"It was Jeremy's idea." Jeff nodded toward their son.

"It's what McKayla wanted for Christmas," Jeremy said. "I told Dad you might like it, too."

"You can go together, Mom," Zach said.

Aghast, Jeremy shook his head rapidly.

She laughed. "I'll want to go alone. Have some *me* time." Still seated on the floor, she turned to Jeff and looked up at him. "That was very thoughtful. Thank you."

Jeff's moustache turned up in a smile as he passed out gifts to the boys.

Later in the evening, he settled in his chair with his new Civil War book. The boys went up to bed by midnight bearing armfuls of new jeans, hoodies, and video games.

Charity rearranged the Nativity scene beneath the tree—two shepherds had been knocked over by gift boxes, and Baby Jesus had fallen out of the manger.

Backing up a step from the Christmas tree, she looked up from the Nativity scene at some of the ornaments on the tree. There was Zach's handprint in plaster from kindergarten, painted to more-or-less resemble a reindeer. Jeremy had created toothpick stars in Sunday school when he was eight. They looked like asterisks covered in gold glitter and there were still three or four of them left to hang on the tree.

A precious ornament took up a place of honor near the apex of the tree—a ceramic disk on which a tiny blanket-swathed form was painted. "Charity's first Christmas" was printed below the figure—her mother's work. It was hung by a fading pink ribbon.

Glancing down at the Nativity scene figures once more, and satisfied with their placement, she stepped into the kitchen to make tea in her new mug, a gift from Zach that had MOM inscribed over the word WOW on both sides. A sweet sentiment.

Returning to the family room, she approached Jeff in the library corner where he sat in his recliner, surrounded by bookcases bedecked in pine roping and white lights, and held out a plate. “Want a cookie?” He took a cut-out snowflake.

She sat on the couch with her tea and cookies and flipped channels on the TV, her legs tucked beneath her and covered with a knit throw she had just finished. She hoped “It’s a Wonderful Life” was playing on some channel. It was not. Settling on “Elf”, she bit into a cookie.

“You don’t mind, do you?” Jeff said from across the room.

She looked at him. “Mind?”

“About the gold bars.”

“What about them?”

He sighed. “That we can’t afford them.”

Charity smiled. “I don’t want gold bars. And I’m not worried that we don’t have that much money saved. Nadine always wanted more. And marrying an attorney ensured she would have it.” She took a sip of tea. “I hope you know I’m not like that. I’m happy with our house, and the boys. And you.”

Jeff nodded. He looked down, gazing absently at the book open in his lap.

She took a careful sip of her hot tea, observing Jeff across the room, engrossed in his reading. Once again, his mind was elsewhere and had to be reeled in.

“How’s the book?” Charity said, hoping to reach him, wherever he was.

He looked up at her. “And I am happy with you, too,” he said, his expression earnest.

Charity smiled and inhaled her lavender tea. Jeff, a man of few words, nonetheless sometimes came through. The unexpected gift of a day at the spa was a genuine attempt at giving her something she would enjoy. He made an effort. He took Jeremy's advice and spent time going to the spa and purchasing the gift card, and hiding it in the pad of paper, as a surprise. Maybe she should appreciate those little things more, and not let his occasional verbal offences or lack of communication skills bother her so much.

After all, he did bear the unwelcome advice of Kirkwood with grace and made polite conversation at the dining table. He even helped clear the brunch dishes and brought her a cup of coffee for her cookies.

Nadine once told Charity she thought Jeff was quaint. Quaint? She was almost insulted. Quaint usually meant old fashioned or outdated, although her sister probably didn't mean it that way. Or maybe she did. No matter. Charity admitted to herself that he could be a fuddy-duddy sometimes, preferring his well-worn corduroys and evenings reading in his old recliner to more exciting pursuits.

In her mind, though, she felt this meant he was comfortable enough with their partnership that he didn't have to put on airs or try to be something he's not. And that is something she valued in a relationship. It was honest. And real.

~20~

The call from Antony, Jeff's brother, came late the next morning as Charity was cleaning the kitchen after breakfast. She had made a holiday breakfast of homemade waffles with whipped cream and fruit topping, a tradition she started when the boys were young. Wiping the waffle iron, she stored it in a rarely-used cupboard until next year.

The landline rang as she loaded the dishwasher. It was Antony.

"I thought I'd come see my big brother for Christmas."

Charity faltered. "We, um, we didn't plan anything special for dinner."

"I'll bring Chinese food. They don't celebrate, you see, so they're always open."

She wasn't sure about this, and thought it was an unfair stereotype. Surely there were some Christian Chinese who celebrated the Lord's birth. "Hold on." She took the phone to Jeff. Holding her hand over the mouthpiece, she said, "It's your brother. He wants to come for dinner."

Jeff took the phone and had a brief conversation. He came into the kitchen and said, "He's gonna bring Chinese food. Apparently they—"

"—I know. They don't celebrate Christmas." She draped the dish towel over the edge of the sink and turned to him. "So he's coming? Just him?"

"Well . . . he's bringing someone. His girlfriend. Sunny."

"Sunny?"

"Mm-hm." He retreated into his library nook.

Antony wasn't exactly the person she wanted to see on Christmas. There was always some drama with him, and an underlying sense of discord between him and Jeff. She didn't want to host dinner for this problematic family member, and had hoped to start a painting project that night with her new paints. Maybe the girlfriend, Sunny, would offer some diversion. Hopefully it would be a short, peaceful dinner, and she could follow her own pursuits later.

Additionally, they had planned to go to Northern Woods to visit Papa that afternoon. They would have to go earlier than later now, and cut the visit short to accommodate Antony coming over. She realized, to her surprise, she was actually looking forward to seeing Papa that day and enjoyed putting together a plate of cookies to take to him. Perhaps she was feeling more relaxed since being off work for a week. Knowing her next job wouldn't be as demanding also had her in a better frame of mind, anticipating more sleep and that extra day off. She called upstairs to the boys to be ready for the visit soon.

Visits with Papa were a combination of him retelling old stories and offering life lessons to Zach and Jeremy. This time he also talked about the passing of another of his friends from the steel works in Canton, and complained about the meals, the staff, and his failed eyesight. Listening to those fishing shows he liked on TV wasn't the same as seeing the action of the anglers fighting to catch saltwater fish in the Atlantic, or fly fishing in trout streams. It was one of the last enjoyments taken away from him in his ninety years.

Before leaving, Charity placed the cookies on his night table. She informed the nurse on duty that they were leaving so she could attend to Papa's personal needs and help him lay down for a nap before supper. She did enjoy the visit with Papa, despite his complaints. As they left, he complimented the cookies and said she smelled good. She made sure to give him a warm hug goodbye.

When they returned home in mid-afternoon, Charity decided on a short nap, and lay in her darkened room before yet another social experience.

After an hour she woke abruptly to the doorbell ringing. She oriented herself to the time—4 PM—and changed out of her sweater, deciding on a drapey tunic that fell loose over her hips. 'Celebrate first, diet later', she had chosen as her 2013 New Year's resolution. 'Later' would be some time next year.

As she ran a brush through her hair she could hear Jeremy pounding down the steps to greet the arrivals. Following him down to the entryway, she observed Antony talking to Jeff, paper bags of food in hand.

In a shiny dress shirt and polyester trousers, Antony stood next to Sunny, who was enshrouded in a long stadium jacket. He extracted his hand from hers and approached Charity, kissing her on each cheek. "Feliz Navidad!"

"You too, Antony. Thanks for bringing food." She peered at the girl. "Is this Sunny?"

Antony reached for her and tugged her his way.

"Merry Christmas. Glad you could come," Charity said to her.

Sunny shook her head to allow the hood to fall back, exposing a startling array of long golden hair. Now that her face was no longer shadowed by the stadium jacket hood, Charity could see her green eyes and high cheekbones. "Thanks," she said, her lips in a pout.

"She's shy," Antony said, placing an arm around her.

"Alrighty, then. We can set the food in the dining room," Charity said, mobilizing. "Jeremy, clear your schoolwork from the table. I'll get some plates and forks." She looked around the room. "Where's Zach?"

"Damion's," said Jeremy. "He wanted to show him his new video game."

“Still there? He went there right after we came back from Dad’s,” Jeff said. “Give him a call, Jer. It’s a holiday. He should be with his family.”

Jeremy called Zach at Damion’s. He then gathered his notebooks and set them on the bottom step to be taken up later. Jeff retrieved cans of beer and soda from the fridge and Charity set the table. Antony, proud of being father of the feast, conveyed the cartons of food into the dining room with ceremony and placed them around the advent centerpiece. Sunny, useless, trod behind him and sat on a chair, lost in her coat, her chin propped up in her hand. She looked bored, and still hadn’t said much.

Dishing out helpings of stir-fried rice, teriyaki steak, and sweet and sour chicken, Charity’s tastebuds watered in anticipation of the delicious food.

The side kitchen door slammed shut as Zach bounded into the house. He ran through the kitchen and raced up the stairs.

“Zach!” Jeff boomed after his son.

Zach returned, penitent. He gazed around the dining room. “Oh, hi, Uncle Ant. I didn’t know you were here.” He hung his coat in the entry and took an empty chair.

Jeff glared at Zach, who slunk down in his seat.

Conversation was sparse. Antony spent a few minutes telling Jeff about his success working at King’s Klassic Kars, a job he began after quitting construction that autumn. Having spruced up his look for the new job, he now sported a tapered hairstyle that looked a little bit fake, slicked back with some kind of product.

Jeff had little to say to Antony, and their conversation fizzled. There was a sense of friction between them as Antony shot furtive glances at Jeff, and Jeff kept his eyes on his plate.

Charity looked around the table. Zach had already taken second helpings.

“Better slow down there, Zachy,” she said. “Don’t eat too much.” His belly-aches had become less frequent, and she didn’t want a recurrence of that complaint to ruin his holiday.

"Just this, and I'll be done," Zach said.

"Hm." She glanced at Jeremy. "Is McKayla coming over today?"

He looked up. "She's with her dad. It's his holiday with her."

"Does he live around here?"

"No."

"Where does he live?"

"He flies her to his place in West Palm Beach."

"Cool!" said Zach. "Maybe you could go sometime, and then I—"

"—I don't want to go there."

"Doesn't she want you to come?" Zach asked.

Jeremy put down his fork. "She only goes because it's court-ordered. Her dad has a different girlfriend each time she goes, and the last one was about her age and tried to become her BFF. No thanks. Too much tragedy for me." He nodded sagely, and returned to his meal.

A long silence stretched among them as they all ate. Jeff chewed quietly. Antony deftly handled his chopsticks, alternating bite sized pieces of steak and vegetables. Sunny toyed with a tiny pile of white rice, nibbling at it, grain by grain. Charity peered across the table at Sunny's left hand, curved around a glass of soda. A gold band bedecked with large diamonds was conspicuous on the ring finger. Glancing up, she caught Charity gazing at it and quickly slid her hand in her lap.

Charity focused on her face. "You like Chinese food, Sunny?" She hoped to smooth the awkward moment.

The girl shrugged.

Antony gestured toward her with a chopstick. "Sure she does. Don't you, Sun?"

The doorbell rang.

Thank God! Charity slid her chair back.

Jeff placed his fork down. "I'll go." He strode to the front door.

The door closed with a firm thud and Jeff turned into the dining room, Aunt Bee in tow.

Charity sprang up. "Aunt Bee!" She wrapped her arms around her aunt. "I didn't know you were coming. I thought you were going to Nadine's today."

Jeff helped her remove her old-fashioned coat and hang it in the entryway before taking his seat again.

"I *was* there this *morning*, but Sparky doesn't get along with her dogs, so I had to leave *early*." Her little terrier had a notoriously bad temper.

Charity looked behind Aunt Bee. "You didn't bring . . . ?"

"No. He was *worn out*. I left him home."

"Well, I'm glad you're here. You're just in time to eat."

"Now, Charity, I don't want to be a *bother*. I took a taxi. He's waiting for me. I just wanted to bring these *presents*." She raised up two large paper bags by their handles. They were stuffed with festively wrapped packages.

Charity took them from her and said, "You didn't have to do that. But I'm glad you're here." She looked around the table. "Please stay. This is Jeff's brother, Antony. And . . ."

"Sunny," Antony said. Sunny looked up from swirling a chopstick through her rice. Antony rose and reached over the table for Aunt Bee's hand, giving it a gallant kiss.

"Oh!" she exclaimed.

Charity rolled her eyes. "Anyway, I'll send the taxi away. Jeff can take you home after dinner." She placed the gifts beneath the tree.

Aunt Bee began to protest, but Charity pulled out a chair next to Zach.

"Hey, Aunt Bee," Zach said, glad for a friendly face.

"Hey, Jeremy." She squinched his cheek.

"I'm Zach."

She narrowed her eyes. "Zach?" She looked around the table and waved at Jeff. "Oh, there's Jeremy."

Jeremy, seated across the table from his dad, said. "Aunt Bee. Over here."

She glanced at him.

"I'm Jeremy."

Shaking her head, she said, "Oh, well. It doesn't matter. I brought you boys something."

"We can open them after dinner," Charity said, not anxious to unwrap the random items that usually made up Aunt Bee's 'gifts'. She had a huge heart, and derived much pleasure in giving gifts, but Charity sometimes wondered what inspired her selections. On her last birthday Charity received a shoebox stuffed with an assortment of used CD's (Aunt Bee was a garage sale queen), porcelain sugar bowl without the lid, and a Ronco vegetable chopper, still in the box. Who could tell what this year's treasures hold?

Charity fetched an extra plate and silverware and served Aunt Bee portions from each of the paper cartons. Setting the plate before Aunt Bee, Charity glanced across the table to see Antony having a secretive conversation with Jeremy. Jeremy had his hand over his mouth, concealing a wide smile. Catching his attention, she raised an eyebrow in a questioning look. He quickly re-focused on his plate and shoveled in a forkful of fried rice.

Glancing at Jeff, she saw him gazing at Antony through squinted eyes. Whatever scheme Antony and Jeremy were plotting was yet to unfold. Hopefully it wouldn't disrupt the peaceful evening.

Aunt Bee reached for her fork and began telling Charity about the bus trip to Pittsburgh with her garden club yesterday while everyone else finished their meal. Charity was glad for the distraction to the uncomfortable atmosphere in the room.

As the guests retired to the family room, Jeff helped Charity clear the table. He rinsed while Charity placed the dishes into the dishwasher.

"What's with you and Antony?" she asked.

"What do you mean?"

"You could at least talk to him."

He handed her a stack of plates. "I have nothing to say to him."

"Well, it makes it awkward for everyone."

He sighed. "I'll try to be civil."

He shut off the water and wiped his hands on a dish towel. She closed the dishwasher. As he turned toward the family room doorway, she whispered, "I think his girlfriend is married."

"I wouldn't be surprised," he said, stepping toward his recliner.

Charity gathered a few mugs together on a tray to serve coffee.

Lounging in post-Chinese food lethargy, Charity sat on one end of the couch, her knitting in her lap. She watched Antony and Sunny, in each other's arms near the wall-mounted TV, shuffling to the music of Michael Bublé singing Christmas songs. Eventually Antony broke away and took a seat at the other end of the couch. Sunny continued moving side to side, her stadium jacket swaying to the music, silvery eyelids closed, in her own world.

"Sun," Antony called out. He patted his hand on the cushion next to him.

Looking at him through half-closed eyes, she sauntered to the couch and into his arms.

Despite Antony and Sunny not requiring any further attention at this time, Charity wished they had left after eating. She was ill at ease whenever having visitors, and felt she still had to be 'on' as long as they were there, rather than merely being comfortable in her own home. She wanted to get into her jammies, go up to the spare room, and start her new painting. It would be improper to do that with guests over, even if it was just Jeff's brother.

Trying to relax, she picked up her knitting and continued the scarf meant as a gift for Josephine. It was worked in yarn that was chestnut brown with tiny flecks of black and white throughout. Despite being a little late for Christmas, she planned to give it to her friend during their next coffee date.

Jeff turned his attention to the holiday edition of the paper, which he shared with Aunt Bee. She brought a dining chair into the library nook, next to his recliner, and pulled out the comics and obituaries.

Zach and Jeremy dutifully played with the gifts Aunt Bee brought. Always forgetting their ages—to her they remained perpetually as children—she brought an almost complete set of toy trains for Zach, and a plastic spaceship with space ranger action figures for Jeremy. She beamed at them over her newspaper as they arranged the figures and trains on the floor near the Christmas tree. Zach, still childlike at heart, actually enjoyed himself, placing the space rangers into the train cars, and attacking it with the spaceship.

Fidgety, Jeremy kept glancing at Antony, dozing on the couch with Sunny. He finally reached for the remote and switched the TV to football, settling into one of the accent chairs by the couch. Zach stayed on the floor near the tree.

The phone ringing broke the sleepy mood.

Aunt Bee picked it up and handed it to Jeff. Charity couldn't hear the conversation, just Jeff's occasional 'Mm-hm', and the final, "I'll be right there." She shot him a look as he hung up.

"My dad fell," he said.

"What happened?" asked Aunt Bee.

Charity's eyes got big. "When?"

"Today." He rose from the recliner and strode to the entryway.

Charity stood up and grasped his arm. "Jeff, what's going on?" It was frustrating, the little he deigned to communicate sometimes.

Antony was awake by now and, observing something happening, stood up, leaving Sunny to slouch into the couch, still asleep. “What’s wrong?”

Jeff looked at Charity, then at Antony. “Dad fell. He got out of his wheelchair on his own. They found him crawling through the doorway of his room.”

Zach snickered. “Papa was crawling?”

Jeremy shot Zach a look and said, “Is he okay? Was he hurt?”

“Yes, and No,” Jeff said. “At least they don’t think so. He’s on his way to Quarry Gen.”

“Wasn’t there an alarm on his chair?” Charity said. “To let the staff know when he gets up? I’m sure it was on when we left.”

“S’posed to be.” Jeff plucked his coat from a hook and slid it on. “I have to go meet him at the hospital.”

“I’ll get my coat,” Charity said.

He turned around and placed a hand on her shoulder. “You don’t have to. I’ll call you when I get there.”

Antony was looking reticent, glancing at the sleeping Sunny, and then back at Jeff. “I would come with you, really I would, Bro. But . . .” He nodded toward his girlfriend.

Jeff looked at Antony through dark eyes. “It’s okay, *Bro*. We don’t all have to go.” He opened the front door. Whirling around, he glared at Antony, “What’s that car in the drive? The one with the *big red bow*?”

Antony retreated a step. “It’s just . . . it’s a gift for Jeremy.” He turned to face Jeremy. “For my favorite nephew!” Fishing into his pants pocket, he pulled out a set of keys. Tossing them to him, he said, “Merry Christmas!”

Jeremy and Zach rushed to the front door. Jeremy grasped the doorknob and swung the door wide. He gazed at the old Buick Century, dusted with snow and gleaming in the brightness of the front door lantern, the dent in the rear door barely noticeable. He turned back to Antony, speechless.

Antony followed him out the door. "There it is. Go ahead, open it!" The boys raced past Jeff to the car.

Charity watched as Jeff strode off the front steps and clutched at Antony's arm, spinning him around. "We have to talk about this. You know I didn't want you to—"

Antony yanked his arm from Jeff's hold. "Relax! He likes it. Don't you, Jer?"

"It's great, Uncle Ant!" he said, sitting in the driver's seat. "Look, Dad, cloth seats. And a CD player." He grasped the steering wheel and worked it back and forth.

Jeff turned back to the doorway, to Charity. His face was dark. "He had no right . . ."

Charity reached for his hand and made soothing noises. "I know." She gave him his keys. "But now you have to check on your dad. We'll talk about it when you get home."

Antony and Sunny made their departure shortly after Jeff left for the hospital, driving away in a scuffed Chevy Cavalier with a magnetic car dealer plate on the back. Jeremy wasted no time in making the maiden journey of his new car by driving Aunt Bee home; Zach bounced into the back seat to go along.

After they left, Charity called the night shift nurse manager at Northern Woods and voiced her disapproval at the lack of concern for her father-in-law's safety. She knew she was being one of *those* family members—critical of long-term health care workers, acting like they could take better care of their loved ones. So why didn't they? Charity had dealt with people like them at Hill 'n Dale. Nonetheless, with the experience she gained working there she knew it was possible to keep residents safe if devices such as alarms were activated, and residents were checked on frequently. Nurses and HCAs were responsible for those in their charge, for their safety and well-being. They had a duty of care. There were the odd times accidents still happened. Accidents—events that cannot be helped. But many times even those could be avoided if safety protocol was observed.

Now, at nearly eleven o'clock, the boys had returned and gone up to bed. Jeff was about due home. He phoned a few times to update Charity on Papa's progress—CT scan of the head, hip x-rays, and blood work all were negative. In the medical world, negative is positive. He was also given an infusion of dextrose to correct his low blood glucose before being allowed to leave in an ambulette back to Northern Woods.

"Did his blood sugar improve?" Charity asked.

"They did a finger-stick, and it was ninety-seven after the IV glucose."

"Hmm. It must have been pretty low, then. Maybe that's why he fell."

Jeff was silent.

"You still there?"

"Mm-hm. I was just thinking," Jeff said. "Maybe . . . maybe I shouldn't have put him there."

"At Northern Woods? It's his first incident in four years. Believe me, that's not too bad."

"I know. But he still complains a lot. He's never happy."

"You did the right thing. We couldn't take care of him, with him going blind. No one could stay with him all the time. It really is safer this way."

There was a pause, and Charity could hear talking in the room. "I have to go," Jeff said. "The doctor's here to discharge him."

"Make sure to ask the doctor if his insulin should be changed."

"Will do."

"See you soon."

Charity set the teakettle on the stove and waited for it to boil. She poured it into a mug and sat with elbows propped on the kitchen table, dunking the teabag up and down, thinking about the times her mother spent in hospitals and rehab facilities. She often stayed with her, lugging a backpack of school books and homework. She wanted to be available whenever her mother needed bathroom assistance or help back to bed. She was in a wheelchair by then and couldn't do the transfers on her own, her arms weakening and her hand grasp feeble.

They continued playing their nightly game of Scrabble and sometimes worked on a puzzle to pass the time. Painstaking as these activities were, the occupational therapist encouraged them as a way to exercise her small muscles.

The remembrance of her mother made her heart feel tight. Her mother knew she wasn't going to live long, with the way the illness was progressing. The nights spent in the hospital, her mother having trouble sleeping, lent themselves to heart-to-heart talks between mother and daughter, discussing Charity's plans, her mother giving advice in her halting speech. It was then she told Charity what a good nurse she would be, and that she hoped she would make that her life's work.

Thinking about her mother just now, she realized how much she missed her. Missed the joyful holidays, so unlike the fiasco of tonight. The evening with Antony and Sunny had not been how she wanted Christmas to end. Why did Antony have to barge in on their peaceful day? Jeff shouldn't have let him come; should have stood up to him, inviting himself over. And then he had the nerve to bring that clunker of a car for Jeremy. It was probably one he couldn't sell, so he figured he'd pawn it off on him. It was a good thing Jeff had to go to the hospital to attend to Papa right then, or he might have had more than just a verbal argument with his brother.

Christmastime as a child was memorable—with her mother's handcrafted decorations and cooking, and her father's excitement in giving unexpected gifts to her and Nadine. Once, when she was about eight, it was an unbelievably soft fur capelet. She begged for the impractical garment when taken on a trip to the Canton mall, and was told she already had a winter coat. How she screamed in joy when she unwrapped it. Another time it was a pony. A real pony! Borrowed for a week from an Amish friend of her father's, she and Nadine spent the entire week after

Christmas in the backyard riding it and taking care of it. Charity smiled at the memory.

Recounting those happy times made her melancholy, missing her mother and father even more, especially considering this evening, fraught with misunderstanding and tension. In the intimacy of the darkened kitchen she allowed her sadness to escape from where she kept it locked, in the secret places of her heart.

That last Christmas came to mind—the tree that was set up but never decorated as her mother's illness took over all her time. Her mother's illness, and her father not helping her at all. No wonder she wasn't so keen to insinuate herself into his world right after she died. Until she remembered her promise to her mother, that is, and tried to keep it.

She stirred her tea, inhaling the aroma of lavender as she wrapped her hands around the warm mug. Her thoughts drifted to this and that, and as the warm tea drained down her throat she started to feel its soothing effects on her spirit.

At 11:30, Jeff trudged through the doorway and slumped into the chair across the table.

Charity rose from her seat and dabbed at her eyes with a napkin. "Tea?" she asked.

Jeff nodded. He didn't often drink it, but she knew a cup of herbal tea would be soothing after this day charged with unease.

Charity couldn't understand why there was a pervading sense of disquiet Jeff and his brother, but sometimes it was palpable. It didn't help that he deliberately went against Jeff's wishes about the car for Jeremy.

Charity poured boiling water from the kettle over a lavender-vanilla teabag, added a drop of honey, and placed it before her husband. He stirred it slowly. She sat quietly with him in the darkened kitchen, the dim bulb over the sink offering gentle light, watching him wrestle with what he wanted to say.

Being reserved was especially problematic when it came to things that needed discussed.

Jeff leaned over his mug. “Antony . . . Antony shouldn’t have done that.”

She closed her eyes and nodded.

“He shouldn’t have given that car to Jeremy. He knew better. I told him how I feel about it last week. He asked me if he could get him a car, and I told him no. I don’t want Jeremy driving a junk car that’ll break down.”

“You told him that?”

Jeff nodded.

She knew what he meant. It was a matter of respect, that his brother not go against his wishes for his son. She reached out and touched his hand. “Don’t let it get to you. He just wanted to do something nice.”

Jeff sighed and shook his head. “You don’t understand. He tries to one-up me, and it’s not the first time. I just don’t want Jeremy looking up to him. He’s not someone to admire.”

“Don’t take it personally. Jeremy was just excited. You know, his *first car*. I know you wanted to be the one to help him get it; help him take out a loan to get a newer car. It would be the better way to go—”

“It’s not just that. He had no right.”

Charity thought for a moment. How to approach this? Jeff’s usually even temperament was sometimes disturbed by periods of moodiness that were hard to break through.

“You could make him give it back.”

He pressed his lips together and sighed. “That would make me look like a real jerk. My brother would love that.” He took a sip of tea. “I guess he keeps the car.”

“Think of it as a chance for increased maturity and responsibility for Jeremy. He can drive himself to school, get a job. He will have to pay for insurance, and gas, after all.”

“True.”

"Figure out how much he will owe on our joint policy and collect that from him monthly."

He nodded. "He'll learn a gift like that usually comes with strings attached."

After a last sip of tea, she said, "How's Papa?"

"Okay."

She gazed at him in silence. When he glanced her way, she raised her eyebrows expectantly.

He sat back in his seat. "That is . . . a little sore, that's all. He thought it was a lot of bother making him go to the hospital."

"What did he say?"

"The aide that came with him said he argued about going. Even cussed at them."

She chuckled.

Jeff thought for a moment. "I guess it comes down to respect. He wanted his wishes considered, too." He rose and placed his mug in the sink. "I'm a little like my father that way."
Charity nodded and followed him up the stairs, pausing to turn off the Christmas tree on the way.

~21~

Charity started her new job in the new year with two weeks of computer classes and hospital orientation. By the time her neighbors had taken down their outdoor Christmas decorations she began the night-shift orientation on the Four South medical/surgical unit. She felt proud and a little bit small as she stepped onto the unit in her new navy blue scrubs.

Settling before a computer after shift-to-shift report, Charity looked to her side as another nurse took a chair.

She turned to her with a friendly smile. "Hi. My name's Charity. This is my first night."

The other nurse flipped copper bangs out of her eyes and said, "I'm Miranda, but you can call me Randi. Welcome to the unit." She sipped ice water from a styrofoam cup.

"They don't mind us having drinks at the nurses' station?"

"They do. But I'm in my second month, and drinking ice water helps with my nausea."

"Oh! When are you due?"

"End of August, if I counted right."

Charity observed her preceptor signaling her from the corridor "I'd better go."

Miranda said, "Come get me anytime you need anything. On night shift we try to help each other more. Fewer resources, you know."

"Thank you," Charity said, getting up to join her preceptor.

The following Sunday, Charity caught up with Josephine as church was letting out and updated her on her new job. "It's a lot to learn. It's only been a week, but I love it. I love teaching my patients and getting to know the doctors. And my new co-workers are great." She lowered her voice and glanced around. "Except for this 'Theda'. She's one of those old school nurses who still wears a nurse cap. She's a little harsh."

"Will you have to work with her often?"

"She's day-shift. So, no. Thank God."

Josephine chuckled.

They walked toward the exit, following Jeff and the boys. Josephine's children caught up to them at the door.

"Are you getting more sleep?" Josephine asked.

"I am," Charity said. "I can't believe what a difference one extra night off means. Plus I get home in time to make breakfast for the guys, right Jeff?"

Jeff glanced back. "Hm?"

"I'm getting home much earlier now, right?"

He nodded and opened the exit door for her. "Although I have learned to make breakfast."

Charity cinched her eyes. "True, but now that I'm home earlier, I can do it."

"S'pose so," Jeff said, starting for the parking lot to get the car.

Charity gave Josephine a questioning look.

Josephine chuckled and nodded. "He appreciates it."

"I hope so," Charity said, gathering her coat around her in the winter air. The sun was high in a bright blue sky, recently fallen snow cushioning all sound.

Zach and Manuel started a conversation about a new video game system they both coveted. Maria skipped her way through the cars to get in the driver's seat, her excitement at being a new driver showing in her springy step. Natalie kept close to her mother, holding her hand, and peering out shyly from behind her large form as they waited for Maria to bring the mini-van around.

"I'm just glad *I* don't have to go through training right now," Josephine said. "It's enough taking care of *mi mama*. Her dementia is getting worse, and my sister Rosa can't handle her anymore. We had to hire an aide."

Charity nodded, "Too bad."

"That's were George is, now. Home with *mi mama*. The aide doesn't come on Sundays." She pulled her scarf around her neck. "I love this scarf you made for me."

Charity grinned, pleased. "I had fun making it. And it looks good on you."

"It's really—"

"I'm gonna take off, too." Jeremy announced, pulling his car keys from his pocket. "McKayla needs to go shopping."

Charity gave him a look. "Jeremy. Don't interrupt." She turned to Josephine. "Sorry."

Josephine waved away her apology. "It's okay. We have to go home, too. This one still takes a nap." She held up her and Natalie's clasped hands. Natalie suppressed a yawn.

Maria pulled the mini-van right behind Jeff driving his car, and everyone piled in. "Let's get coffee soon. Let me know how the new job's going," Josephine said.

"I'll call you," Charity said.

◆◆◆

After six weeks of training side by side with one of the other RN's, Charity began working on her own with a moderate sense of self-confidence.

She took her place before a computer in the nurses' station early one morning, preparing to check on bloodwork results of one of her patients.

"Oh, no, here they come," Miranda said.

"Who?" Charity asked, looking around and hiding her nearly finished cup of coffee behind the computer screen.

Miranda grimaced. "Medical students and new first-year residents. They start to invade the nurse's station around this time of year. They'll take over for about an hour—it drives me crazy!" She picked up her ice water. "We'd better scatter."

As announced, several medical students, residents, and Dr. Chole, the fourth year resident in charge of the newbies, all in white coats, strode onto the unit. It was like a scene from *Scrubs*. They sat themselves before every computer in the nurse's station.

Charity caught up with Miranda in the med room. Miranda was laden with a plastic basket containing a glucometer, alcohol wipes, and three souffle cups with individually blister-packed pills.

"Don't forget room 19 might need morphine this morning. Isn't he a fresh post-op?" Miranda told Charity. Miranda had been working at Quarry Gen for about three years, on different units. One of the few Licensed Practical Nurses remaining in the hospital, she transferred to the new unit when it opened. The rules governing what LPNs were allowed and not allowed to do still confused Charity. IV injectables, such as morphine, were among the meds given only by RNs. She appreciated the reminder about the pain med for room 19.

"Thanks, Randi. I'll check on him." Charity logged into the medication dispensing machine. "I wanted to ask you, too, what you thought about giving a blood pressure medication to the patient in room 7. Her systolic BP has been low all night. She's due for HCTZ this morning."

"Is she getting fluids? Or drinking enough?"

"She's on a continuous IV drip. And she voided twice overnight."

Miranda considered this. "Hm. She's not dry, then. Maybe she just gets too many BP meds."

"She does get an evening BP med, as well as two in the morning. She's barely ninety pounds. Maybe it's too much."

Miranda gathered her supplies and stepped to the med room door. "I'd hold the med," she said. "The day-shift charge nurse can call her doctor and see if he wants to change the dose."

"Alrighty," said Charity.

After passing the morning meds and administering IV morphine to the patient in room 19, Charity made her way back to the nurses' station. She logged onto a computer and noted the name of room 7's primary care physician. She wanted to pass the info along to day-shift so they could call about the blood pressure medication.

As Charity was about to sign off the e-chart, she heard a voice behind her. "Hey. Do ya'll mind if I check Mr. Johnston's chest x-ray?"

Charity turned and quickly scanned the resident bending over her. His badge said 'Dr. N. Kennedy, PGY1'. Miranda had told her that meant 'post-graduate year 1', therefore, a first year resident. His wavy hair fell casually over his broad forehead. He looked at Charity, lips pressed together, eyebrows raised.

"Sure. I'm already logged on. I can pull it up for you." Charity replied. She brought up that patient's most recent radiograph results on the computer screen. "I was his nurse overnight. He's still coughing, but his lung sounds are much clearer and his pulse oximeter has been in the mid nineties. On room air."

"Thanks a lot. I appreciate the info." He took a seat next to Charity and peered down into the computer screen, reviewing the radiograph result. After a moment he said, "By the way, my name's Neil," and extended a hand.

Charity shook his hand. "Good to meet you. I'm Charity."

He sat back in the chair, legs thrust out before him. "A good name for a nurse."

"I've heard that before. I do try to live up to it."

"Have you worked here long?"

"No. I was at Hill 'n Dale before here." Seeing his puzzled expression, she added, "It's a nursing home in town. I worked there right after I graduated nursing school last year. I just started working here in January."

"I just started today."

A cluster of residents strolled by the nurses' station.

He rose from his seat and said, "Well, I'd better go see my patient before Dr. Chole catches me socializing. See y'all later."

A rush of heat sped through her as she watched the rangy first year resident stride away, his gait graceful and confident. She shook her head and attempted to focus on her work. This was interrupted by overhearing Dr. Chole scold one of his charges in a loud voice. She glimpsed him across the corridor, waving his hands at a penitent resident.

Charity had heard several say that chief resident Dr. Chole, with his imperious nature, usually didn't speak to the nurses, except maybe to ask them to print a report or borrow their stethoscope. The perpetual scowl he wore indicated either pants that were too tight or a superiority complex. Maybe both. Or maybe the responsibility he shouldered—the actions and decisions of unseasoned doctors—was overwhelming, constantly ensuring patients' safety and correcting mistakes. Damage control was stressful.

Charity, at 38, was older than many of the residents and felt that they overlooked a vast store of knowledge and insight by not communicating with nurses better. She heard that with each year of residency, some of them became more and more distant and superior. Others, however, valued the information the nurses provided and were eager to discuss options. She was happy to have a chance to communicate with this first year resident, Neil, hoping that, early on, he would learn to appreciate nurses' observations.

Charity met with Miranda after their shift was over at 7:35 that morning. Teri Green, another RN on their unit, joined them. The three made their way to the cafeteria and purchased final cups of coffee or soft drinks before driving home. They found an unoccupied round table and settled in stackable leaf-green chairs.

"I don't know how we do it, working nights. I don't think I'll ever get used to it," Charity said, yawning. She listlessly stirred her coffee and took a nibble of her muffin.

"I've always been a night owl," Miranda said. "Even when I'm off, I sometimes stay up all night and go to sleep when Olivia's in school and Mitch is at work."

"I'm still not used to it," said Teri. "But it's only been a few months. I used to sleep till dinnertime, but then my mom would worry I'm not eating enough. She started waking me up for lunch, and then I would lay back down. But lately I'm not able to sleep after lunch anymore. I thought about taking a sleeping pill, but I don't want to get too used to it. So now I drink a cup of herbal tea before I lay down. It has all sorts of antioxidants in it. Sometimes I drink chamomile. But usually lavender tea. It smells so nice." Teri took a sip of coffee and looked at her two coworkers. "Ya know what I mean?"

Charity's eyes were big. *Mean? About what?* "Whatever helps you sleep, I guess."

At 25, Teri was the youngest nurse on the unit. She graduated from nursing school last year, same as Charity. Being new to the coffee drinking habit, she stirred in three creamers and three sugars to better tolerate the taste. Charity observed that her tawny skin looked the same as the coffee with all that creamer in it. Her nearly black hair was an arrangement of short corkscrew curls that sprang out from her head in an energetic style that Charity envied. *Her* hair never did anything that interesting.

Continuing her train of thought, Teri said, "Sometimes I do a half hour on my treadmill after lunch and that makes me tired enough to sleep. I have a treadmill in my room. I use it a lot because I'm training for the marathon this month. It's on St. Patrick's day and two of my cousins are entering, too. They ran a marathon in Akron last fall. I didn't do that one because I had a sprained ankle that week. Remember when I sprained my ankle last fall?"

Charity shook her head. She could picture her spraining her ankle however, the way she bounced from here to there, with such verve. She was bound to make a misstep at some time.

Miranda said, "I remember. You said you tripped over your dog or something."

Teri shook her head. "My cat, not my dog. She was on the steps and I was going up and she was going down and I was carrying something. I think it was a load of laundry. Or maybe some library books. Or it may have been—"

"I'm ready for another pop." Miranda said, rising abruptly. "Charity? Don't you need a refill?"

Charity rose to her feet. She lifted her half-full coffee cup. "Yep. I'm out."

"I really can't take another of her stories," Miranda said as she filled her cup with crushed ice and topped it off with cola. "That girl can talk. She drives me crazy!"

Charity nodded, refilling her cup with coffee. "How have you been feeling lately, Randi? Still having morning sickness?"

"No. That's over now that I'm in my second trimester. This week's problem is heartburn. I'm eating tums like candy and have to sleep in the recliner. It drives me up a wall."

They took the long way going back to their table. "This is definitely a 'two-coffee morning'. I didn't get a break all night," Charity said.

"I quit drinking coffee back when I was pregnant with Olivia. After six years I still can't stand the taste." Miranda said, sitting back down next to Teri, who was busy texting someone on her phone.

It was hard to picture Miranda with children. A middle-class diva with a voluptuous build, milky white skin, and hair the color of a new penny, she seemed more the type to spend her time on Caribbean cruises or trips to Atlantic City rather than being a homemaker. But the truth was that Miranda and her husband, Mitch, lived a modest lifestyle in the upstairs apartment of a four-plex. Her biggest vice was spending money on cheap makeup, costume jewelry, and frequent visits to the salon to keep her hair in the stylish bob that complemented her larger build.

Miranda crunched on ice. "For some reason, this pregnancy doesn't have me as tired as the other one. I get about three hours' sleep in the lazy-boy. My husband's grandma said that was because this next baby will be bull-headed and hard to manage."

Teri looked up from her cell phone. "I've never heard of that."

"Really? Well, she'll probably be the death of me!"

"You know it's a girl?" Charity asked.

"Mitch's grandmother told me. She's kind of a gypsy. My husband's family came over from Romania, and his granddad Americanized his last name, Ivanokov, to Vanek when they immigrated. His grandma still can't give up the old ways. She believes she has powers and can tell the future. She did some kind of test on my stomach and said it would be another girl."

Teri put her cell phone down and examined her fingernails, painted sparkly gold. She produced a file from her cross-body bag and worked on a nail tip that had broken. "What kind of test did she do? Was it the one with the quarter taped to a string? I saw something like that on a cable show. It was a show about ghosts, or supernatural, you know, phenomena, or something like that. The host was some sort of ghost-buster you could hire if you thought your house was haunted, ya know what I mean? He had all this equipment that he would set up—speakers, microphones, video recorders." She stashed the nail file back into her bag. "You don't actually believe that, do you? "

Miranda looked at Charity, who shrugged her shoulders, confused.

"Believe what?" Miranda said.

"The test your grandmother did."

"My husband's grandmother? Nah. I just play along to humor her. I really do like her. Don't want her to give me some kind of curse!" She took another mouthful of ice.

"You should have that checked," Teri said.

"What?"

"That ice. Crunching on ice can mean you're anemic."

"Did you know that?" Miranda asked Charity.

Charity shook her head.

Teri returned to her cell phone. Carelessly, she added, "It's the iron that's low."

"Guess I'd better have it checked," Miranda said, rising from her seat. "You guys coming? It's almost eight."

Teri collected her belongings and pushed her seat back.

"I'm gonna finish this coffee." Charity said, propping her chin in her hand. "I'll see you tonight."

After Miranda and Teri left, a group of white-coated residents and medical students carried trays past Charity and seated themselves at a long table in the corner. Ravenous, they dove into breakfasts of scrambled eggs, French toast sticks, and black coffee.

Charity noticed the medical resident she met earlier, Dr. Neil Kennedy, arriving after the rest of the group. All the chairs at their table were filled and he looked around for a place to sit, holding his tray aloft.

She signaled him, "You can sit here, if you want."

He nodded and sat down across from her. He rested his elbows on the table, leaned into his shoulders, and took a careful sip of steaming black coffee.

"Thanks," he said, his voice deep and breathy. "Nice of them to save me a seat."

"I guess it's first come, first served. Being a teaching hospital, it gets a little competitive around here," Charity said.

"I've noticed that. I'm from Yellow Creek, Carolina. It's a small town down the road a bit from Charleston. People aren't as aggressive there," Neil said. At that, Charity finally was able to place his accent: a gentle, southern drawl, where 'I' came out like 'ah'. Very pleasant, a little like the Appalachian accent she was used to hearing, but less twangy.

"Is that where you went to med school?"

"I did my pre-med at North Carolina State, then moved to Ohio for medical school. My residency for the NEOHOS system starts here, at Quarry Gen, and then I'll be finishing in Canton in two years, doing labor and delivery. I figured this hospital would bring me some good opportunities, being a little smaller." He dipped a French toast stick into syrup and bit it in half.

Charity swallowed her last sip of coffee. "It should. Quarry Gen is smaller, but we always have good patient satisfaction ratings. We just remodeled the four surgery suites last month, and we're building a helipad later this year. That way complicated cases can be flown to Akron or Cleveland right from here."

As they talked, Charity forgot her fatigue in the stimulating conversation. She focused on his words, his voice. She found his earnest manner refreshing, and she was captivated by his expressive brown eyes.

Being new to the area, he asked her where to go for a meal out. "Chef Mario's, in the Limestone Place shopping plaza, is nice Italian restaurant," Charity said. "There's also a bar called The Golden Nugget, south of the village, on route 21. They're supposed to have great burgers. So does Barney's."

"Are there any coffee places?"

"There's the Coffee Cave. It's in the plaza too. They have good coffee and pastries."

"We had a place like that in Yellow Creek. My wife and I used to go there on the weekends. It was locally owned, and they let me display some of my work there, to sell."

She gave him a puzzled look, her head tilted to the side.

"My photography. I take black and white photos. Mainly landscapes, and sometimes—" He was interrupted by a signal from one of the other residents getting up from their table. "I'd better go." He said, picking up his tray. "It was real nice talking with you."

Charity watched as he joined his colleagues, placing a hand on a shoulder of one of them. Had they been talking for a half hour? She had to look again at the large clock on the wall, and confirm that it did say 8:30. The enjoyable conversation made the time fly by.

◆◆◆

The next morning, as she was finishing her computer charting, Charity was approached by a day-shift nurse. It was Theda. Her nurse cap was pulled low over steel grey bangs.

She consulted her clipboard. "When you gave me report on room 4, you didn't tell me about the bedsore on his left hip. Is he being turned every two hours?"

Charity looked up and flinched from the accusing look of her flinty eyes. "I . . . I told you Nikki and I turned him at six, right before report. He has a foam wedge as a turning aid."

"Hmph. And what about the wound. Is there a wound care consult?"

"Yes. A dressing order is in place. It was changed yesterday."

Theda thought a moment. Charity squirmed, feeling like she was in the principal's office, wishing she could just go.

"Well! Let's hope dietary is on the case. He should be taking high protein supplements to promote healing." Theda began walking off, triumphant.

"Not to contradict," Charity said, feeling she must tread lightly. Theda turned back. "But he is also a dialysis patient. It's a fine line, you know, about the protein."

"Hmph," she said again, and marched away.

Her shift over, Charity logged off the computer and was greeted by Dr. Neil Kennedy entering the nurses' station. "Hey, Charity."

She gave him a tired smile, charmed by the way he said her name, like, 'Cheerity'. "How can you be so wide awake this early in the morning? I'm ready to fall over. I need some coffee!"

"I just got here, that's why. On my clinical days I get up at 4 AM. Usually, I go home around suppertime, or whenever I'm done. Believe me, I'm not that energetic in the evening. And I usually have two or three cokes with supper to keep me going."

"Well, I'd better get out of your way . . ."

Neil raised his eyebrows and gave a nod. "Meet me for coffee?"

"Um . . . sure. I should be down there in a few minutes."

~22~

Over the next few weeks, Charity made a habit of meeting Neil in the cafeteria when her shift ended. She appreciated the way he really talked to her. They talked about her watercolor paintings and his hobby of photography. He showed her several of his works on his cell phone—photos depicting the tall pines of North Carolina covered with a dusting of snow, and landscapes with the Blue Ridge Mountains in the distance.

"See this one?" He swiped his finger on his phone. The photo was of a farmland after harvest, great rounds of wheat in the background. The shadows indicated sunset, and from the bent position of a few still-standing stalks of wheat, Charity could imagine a stiff breeze blowing across the barren field.

"It's nice. And looks . . . familiar," she said.

"It's just west of here, past route 21. I took it last fall when Becky and I drove up to look for a house."

She took his cell phone in her hand and peered at it. "I love that. Reminds me of the times my father took us for rides in the country when I was young."

"Does he still like to go?"

She hesitated. "He . . . um. He passed away years ago, when I was in high school." She handed him back his phone. "My mother died first, and then he died two weeks later."

"I'm real sorry."

She looked down. "Thank you."

"Were they . . . were they sick long?"

She nodded. "My mother was. She died of ALS. My father's death was kind of sudden. I never knew what he died of." She toyed with her coffee cup. "It was a long time ago."

Feeling his eyes on her she glanced up and was startled at the depth of emotion in them.

"Some hurts never go away."

Did he just say that?

A buzzing came from Neil's lab jacket. He pulled out his pager and glanced at it. "Sorry. I'd better go. Summons from Dr. Chole."

"I have to go, too." Charity watched Neil get up, give her a nod, and leave the cafeteria through the doors to the main hall.

At once fatigued, she dragged herself out of her chair and stumbled to the outside exit, thinking about her relationship with Neil. Not *relationship*, really. Just *friendship*. It was harmless, right? Making friends with this handsome doctor. This colleague. It was professional. They discussed patients' diagnoses and test results, hospital gossip, and occasionally their own off-hours activities or plans.

She didn't think about Neil on her drive home. She didn't daydream about the way he looked at her without blinking, waiting eagerly for her response. About his infrequent barely-there smile, and the way he raked his fingers through his hair.

Except maybe when stopped at traffic lights. Or when cruising the short stretch of freeway. Or as she pulled into her driveway, pausing a few moments before getting out of the car. Maybe then he came to mind.

Such were her thoughts when she let herself into the house that morning, and found Jeff seated on the couch sipping a cup of coffee, the TV on a news channel. "I poured this for you a while ago," he said, indicating another mug on the coffee table. "Thought you got off at seven."

Charity deposited her purse and keys on the hall tree in the entryway. "Seven-thirty, usually."

"It's nine," he said.

Her heart skipped a beat and she thought quick. "I had breakfast, with . . . with my friend. You know, Miranda, the one I told you about." She sat down and took a sip of cold coffee. "I sometimes do that after work—have something to eat in the cafeteria."

"Hmph. Thought you were able to have breakfast with us now that you're working this new job." He crossed his legs and switched channels with the remote.

"I did yesterday."

"You didn't work."

She turned to him. "Aren't you working today?"

"Called in sick." He sat forward and reached behind himself to massage his lower back. "Woke up with a sore back."

"From moving that furniture yesterday?" Jeff had spent the evening cleaning the garage, a task he had started over the weekend. He hauled out the lawn furniture, which included a heavy glass-topped wrought iron table. Jeremy helped him carry it to the backyard patio.

He nodded.

"I can make you some eggs," she said, rising from the couch. "Or toast. What do you want?" Penitent for spending time with Neil while her husband was waiting for her at home, she wanted to do something to ease her conscience.

He looked up at her. "Sure. Toast would be fine." He lifted his mug. "And do you mind a refill, please?"

She smiled at his cheesy grin. "Of course. Better leave me a good tip." She moved to the kitchen to prepare a light breakfast for her husband.

Placing the plate and mug before him on the coffee table, she sat back down and relaxed into the soft cushions of the couch.

Jeff spread butter on his toast. "Jeremy's car had a flat tire this morning."

She gave him a surprised look.

"He had to change it before school."

"Did you help him?"

"I stood out there with him. Told him how to do it."

Charity glimpsed a definite smirk on Jeff's face. "You love that, don't you?"

Jeff's smirk expanded into a grin. "I s'pose."

"It's not nice, you know."

"What?"

"*You* know."

Jeff chewed on toast.

"Well?" she said.

He turned to her. "That I'm glad Antony's piece of junk car he gave to my son isn't the dream ride Jeremy thought it was? You bet."

As he finished his breakfast, Charity figured it was fair. Maybe it would be a blessing in disguise, in a way. It did bring father and son together this morning, and could be a connecting point for them, a reason for Jeremy to look up to him, a chance to realize Dad can still show him a few things, despite him being all grown up.

She rubbed his back as he leaned forward, and watched the weather report with him, feeling comfortable in his presence and glad he dropped the issue about her coming home late. At the next commercial, she kissed him on the cheek and stood up to go to bed.

"G'night," he said.

She paused. "Hope you feel better. Take some Tylenol."

He nodded, and she went up the steps to their bedroom. Removing her uniform and getting into her nightie, the remorse hit her. How was she to know Jeff would be home, waiting for her? She didn't know he called off work. And what about that fib, telling him she had breakfast with Miranda? She didn't want him to know what she was really doing—except, what was she really doing? Just having a meal with a friend, like she said. Just not *that* friend.

Maybe she should limit the time she spent with Neil, so she could still be home for her family in the mornings, since it seemed Jeff expected it now. She could spend more time with Neil on the weekends, when her guys slept in. If she was careful she could manage it.

~23~

Springtime at Quarry Run burst forth with a sudden growth of luxurious grass and flowers of every color. It was such a welcome event after the depressing months of winter, all grey and wet and cold.

It was Charity's weekend off and she looked forward to spending it with her family. Jeff's job at Country Springs required him to work one weekend a month; she was always pleased when their weekends off coincided, like this time, and tried to make the most of it.

She prepared an Italian meal Saturday night—spaghetti with meat sauce and a bibb lettuce salad. Her mother had taught her the simple, three-ingredient recipe, and it was a favorite of her family. Stirring the ground sirloin in the skillet until browned, and adding the jar of sauce, she recalled the first time she made this dish on her own: a week after her mother passed. She had thought to make a nice meal for herself and her father.

Her mother's funeral was over, Nadine took the cremains with her, and life settled down into a new sort of rhythm. Although her father continued to live in the basement family room, Charity wanted to follow through with her promise to her mother, to take care of Dad.

For a few days she struggled with feelings of resentment toward him for abandoning them in her mother's last days. But finally, she just felt lonely, and wanted to have a meal together, like they used to.

Her father was late from work that night. She had set the table with matching plates, silverware, napkins, and the 'nice' glasses. The sauce was still in the skillet on the stove, hot pasta in a bowl on the table.

She sat at the table, nibbling garlic bread, thinking up a plan to take care of her dad. She would try to make a nice meal every Sunday, and during the week they could have leftovers or carry-out. But they would eat together, at the table, and talk about their day. Thoughts of how she would decorate the table to match the seasons took over. Her mother had a closet full of candles, centerpieces, and table linen appropriate for all times of the year. Later this week she would bring out the pumpkin spice candles and rust colored tablecloth, it was almost September, after all.

Engrossed in these plans, she sprang up when her father finally strode into the back door bearing a usual bag of take-out food, and headed for the basement.

"I made us a meal," she said, gazing proudly at her creation. She wiped her hands on the apron she wore—her mother's ruffled apron—and tucked her hair behind her ears.

He took a step back into the kitchen and watched as she dished up the pasta onto a plate and covered it with meat sauce, adding a sprinkle of cheese with a flourish. She placed it on the table at his spot and pulled out his chair.

He approached and picked up the plate and a fork. He said, "Thanks. It looks good," and stepped back to the basement door with the food.

"I thought . . ."

He looked at her, eyebrows raised.

"I thought we could eat together. You know . . . like we used to."

He paused, looking at the floor. Glancing up at her, he had said, "It's not that I don't want to, Charity. I just have a lot of paperwork to do." He opened the door, then turned back again. "Next time, okay?"

She was still thinking about her father as she served the spaghetti meal to Jeff and the boys. She had been so hurt when her father rebuffed her back then, it was several days before she recovered.

Tonight, sitting with her family in the candle-lit dining room, she watched them talk to each other in between bites of spaghetti and garlic bread. Jeremy asked his father when he could help him change the oil in the Century. Zach brought up the Civil War Enthusiasts club, saying Damion might like to come to a meeting. After these topics were discussed, the room was quiet again, with just the sounds of eating.

"You like it?" Charity asked as she passed the basket of garlic bread.

Jeremy nodded, chewing a large mouthful of food.

"It's fantastic!" Zach said, grinning. He took a slice of garlic bread.

"Jeff?"

He swallowed, and said, nodding, "It's nice. Glad you had time to cook us a meal."

"What do you mean?"

He looked at her, his eyes rounded.

The time working at Quarry Gen had been much easier than the three and a half months she worked at Hill 'n Dale in a lot of ways. She spent her extra day off on deep cleaning, meal prep, or connecting with her friends. Once she even surprised Jeff at work and took him to lunch. It was good to have more time to do things. She wasn't sure what Jeff meant about having time to cook them a meal. "I always have time," she said.

Jeff put down his fork. "I know. But sometimes you're tired, or sleeping."

"Has there ever been a time I didn't have something for you to eat?" she said, her voice raising in register.

"No. That's not what I meant."

A tense silence ensued. Jeff glanced at the boys as he reached for another piece of garlic bread. They nibbled at their meals, stealing glances at each other.

Charity closed her eyes and leaned her forehead in her hand. Her thoughts back in her parents' kitchen, she again envisioned her father picking up the plate and opening the basement door. She once again felt the hurt of his rejection. Maybe why she was extra sensitive just now.

Jeff touched her hand. "You okay?"

She looked up into the concerned eyes of her husband and nodded. "Yeah. I was just thinking about my father. I made this same meal for him a week before he died."

"Mm-hm."

"I remembered about it while I was cooking," she said. *Some hurts never go away.* "It still hurts. I still miss him."

He paused a second. "Of course. I'm sure you do."

Charity gave him a sad smile, her lips pressed together. "Thank you."

Glancing at the boys, she said, "There's cherry cheesecake from the Coffee Cave for dessert. Any takers?"

A collective cheer was a positive sign of their approval.

After church the next morning Charity had a brief conversation with Josephine before going to Northern Woods with Jeff to visit Papa. They brought him an Easter lily to celebrate the coming holiday.

The strong scent of the plant offended him so much he crabbed, "Get that out of here, it smells like a funeral home." They donated it to the front desk on the way out.

Sitting by herself at the kitchen table early Monday morning, Charity cherished the time alone, Jeff at work and the boys at school. She nursed a cup of coffee as she said her morning prayers. Mentioning her husband's name, she thought back to when she met Jeff Cristy, almost twelve years ago.

She was still living above the pottery and used to see him at the grocery store on the weekends. His build tended toward ‘hefty’ and his salt and pepper hair and mustache made him look like a retired cop. It was cute the way he toted the two young sons, aged about two and four, to pick out the week’s groceries. She sometimes spoke to the boys. It’s funny how kids and dogs often help break the ice when adults are meeting each other.

She had an awkward encounter with him in the early summer, just after turning 26, as she carried her groceries to her car, parked next to his. He was loading up his trunk. She said to the older boy, “What’s mom making for dinner tonight?”

Jeff intercepted. “Sorry,” he said, “Their mom passed away last year. She had cancer.”

Shamefaced, Charity had replied, “I’m . . . I’m so sorry.” Not knowing what else to say, she placed the bags in her car and left the parking lot. *Nice! He’ll never want to speak to me again.*

The next Friday she went back to the grocery store to pick up a container of dried Thyme, a spice she rarely used but was called for in a new recipe she was trying. When she returned to her car there was a store receipt tucked in her windshield wiper, with a note written on the back. “Call me if you want to get coffee, or something. The boys are at their grandparents this weekend. Jeff”

She whirled around. Was he still in the parking lot? Watching her? She looked all over but didn’t see him anywhere. Hurriedly, she got into her car and turned onto the street for home, her heart thumping wildly and a broad grin on her face.

Before Jeff, Charity had dated two men, one seriously, one not so much, since moving back to Quarry Run after high school. One of the nurses who worked for Home Helpers used to take her out on the weekends after work. It was a casual relationship. Several coffee dates and a few kisses later he moved north to work at Akron Children’s Hospital. She was losing interest, anyway, and wished him well.

The other man she dated worked in the pottery below her apartment. After playing house together in Charity's hot upstairs apartment, he purchased a used RV and planned to start his own pottery, creating artistic pieces and selling them from his mobile home as he journeyed around the country. Charity wasn't ready to leave town again to travel with him like a pair of Bohemians and had to break it off.

Getting to know Jeff, however, wasn't like dating the other men. After the trip home from the grocery store that day, Charity immediately called him, hoping not to appear too eager. She was attracted to the self-possessed man, careful with his children as he helped them into the back seat, and couldn't sleep that night for thinking of how he, too, sounded enthusiastic as they set up a time to get together.

For their first date he picked her up dressed in pressed slacks and a new oxford cloth shirt, still with the tell-tale creases from the package. The dinner at the restaurant in Akron lasted three hours as they spent more time talking than eating. Or maybe she spent a lot of time talking. Having lived alone for the better part of the last six years, she was anxious for communication, and he was a willing listener.

Several more dinner or coffee dates over the next months resulted in them getting engaged in the tiny sitting room of her apartment on a muggy summer night. He got down on one knee! The ring had been his mother's. She looked at it now, caressing it lightly with her forefinger, remembering the crack in Jeff's voice, and how he cleared his throat, as he asked her to spend the rest of her life with him.

They wed in the prayer room at Prince of Peace Church, attended by his small sons in miniature tuxedos. Aunt Bee, Nadine and Kirkwood, and Papa also attended. A week later was 9-11 . . . She was glad to be comforted by her new husband in the wake of one of the country's worst hours.

Jeff had also been a rock of support to Charity when she decided to go to nursing school, often taking the boys to the park or the library on the weekends to allow her more time for studying.

The Civil War Enthusiasts club and church were his main social outlets, as he preferred staying home most nights. Problem was, they had run out of things to talk about, and Charity found his inept responses annoying. Like what he said at dinner Saturday—"Glad you had time to cook." She still didn't know what that meant.

When she talked to Neil . . .

Her conversations with the resident made her feel valued and understood. He made intelligent comments when she showed him photos of her paintings on her phone, and was able to critique them in a thoughtful way. He enjoyed sharing his black and white photography with her, especially the award-winning landscapes. He always had something to say, and their coffee mornings flew by.

As she lay down for a nap Monday evening and drifted off to sleep, she thought about seeing him the next morning after her shift ended, and fell asleep with a smile.

~24~

Later that week Charity had another unwitting encounter with Theda. Just before change of shift, she dashed into the locker room for a moment to retrieve some money for the annual Easter Basket drive for underprivileged children. Closing her locker, she heard Theda talking to another day-shift nurse. She observed her from behind a bank of lockers.

Adjusting her nurse hat before the mirror, Theda said, "Hope I don't have to endure report by that *Charity* this morning."

There was a mumbled reply by the coworker.

"Well, because she's so new. Thinks she knows more that we do, with her *computer knowledge* and *apps*. I'll bet she would be lost having to interpret a doctor's handwritten order."

"I for one am glad those days are behind us," said the other nurse. "Remember how many mistakes were made because we couldn't read the writing?"

"Hmph. I never made any."

It was time for Charity to return to the unit, and she held her head high as she strode purposefully past Theda and out the door. She heard Theda's quick intake of breath as she walked by.

Returning to her floor, Charity gave bedside report to the RN taking over her five patients that morning, thankful it wasn't Theda. Then she and Miranda clocked out and walked to the locker room.

Slipping into her jacket, Miranda said, "How about breakfast today? Mitch is home with Olivia, and I'm off tonight."

"Sure," Charity said, opening her locker. "A few minutes, anyway."

"I was thinking more like going to the Coffee Cave this morning. You're off tonight, too, right? So you don't have to go home and sleep right away."

"Mm-hm."

"I meant to ask you earlier, but—"

"—I know, there just wasn't time," Charity said. It had been an unusually busy shift.

"Come on," Miranda said, "We haven't caught up in ages."

Charity opened her locker, tossed in her pens and stethoscope, and retrieved her jacket. "I don't really have that much time today."

"You told me that last week, and then I saw you take the elevator to the cafeteria."

"Well—how about next week. When are you off again?"

Miranda whirled on her. "You know, Charity, you drive me crazy. We haven't gotten together in forever, and now you're putting me off again. Trust me. I know what's going on."

Charity slammed her locker. "What do you mean—'what's going on'?"

Miranda pointed a finger. "Probably having breakfast with Dr. Kennedy again. Am I right? What else are you two doing? And what would your husband think?" She picked up her belongings and strode out of the locker room without a backward glance.

Charity didn't follow her.

After a moment or two, Charity slunk out of the locker room and took the elevator to the second floor. She picked up a coffee and muffin in the cafeteria and sat at a table, mulling over her friend's objection. Miranda was correct. She did plan on meeting Neil for breakfast in about fifteen minutes, when he got his break. Since it's Saturday, she would have a little more time to spend with him before having to go home. She didn't want to give that up.

Anyway, what right does Miranda have determining who she should meet up with? She should have given her more notice if she wanted to spend all morning at a restaurant to catch up. It's just inconsiderate.

Charity's heart gave an irregular beat as Neil strode into the cafeteria. He gazed around the room, looking for her. She smiled in response to his nod in her direction.

"Hey", he said in greeting, and placed his tray on the table.

They exchanged pleasantries, and sipped coffee companionably.

Taking another bite of her muffin, Charity approached another favorite topic of discussion—their patients' diagnoses. They both enjoyed the professional give-and-take. Today she asked him about Rhabdomyolysis, something she was unfamiliar with.

"Rhabdo is caused by damaged muscle tissue leaking proteins and electrolytes into the blood, which can damage the heart or kidneys," Neil said. "You see it in crushing injuries and bad falls."

"This patient I have with Rhabdo was trying out some new exercise equipment he had purchased, and apparently overdid it. A couple days later he couldn't get out of bed and his urine looked like tea. He's on IV fluids and they're watching his creatinine level. If it doesn't go down he might need dialysis."

Neil leaned back, his elbow hooked over the back of his chair. "I'm not surprised. People have to start gradually on any exercise program."

This enjoyable exchange continued for a few minutes. After a short period of silence while they finished their meals, he said, "My wife's just bored whenever I try to talk about my work."

Charity knew Neil's wife was unhappy with living up north. He had told her about how much she misses her family and the various things she complains about, including money being tight and how he doesn't have time to make repairs in the drafty old farmhouse they purchased. She felt a tinge of misgiving when he talked to her about his wife, but felt it was beneficial to him to air those complaints, instead of keeping them inside. And she was willing to be a sounding board.

He continued. "Our agreement was, when I was done with med school, she could go back to college. She's looking into starting this fall."

"What does she want to study?" Charity said. She was drawing a figure of a cat on her napkin. It was a cartoony doodle she drew often, inspired by a stray cat she used to feed when she was about fifteen or sixteen

"She either wants to be a dental hygienist or x-ray tech," he said.

"It seems like a fair arrangement." She added a few whiskers to her doodle and held it up.

He peered at it. "Cute. But . . . don't cats have four toes on their feet, not three?"

She shrugged. It was a cartoon, after all. "My husband had to work extra shifts when I went back to school. Sometimes you have to make sacrifices like that."

Neil leaned over his coffee cup, inhaling the steam. He glanced up at her beneath muddy-brown hair. "See, you understand. Now that I've graduated, things should get much easier. I wish Becky was more like you."

It was an awkward moment. Charity glanced around the cafeteria, seeking a distraction. She caught sight of Theda leaving the room and rolled her eyes.

Neil noticed. "What?"

She was glad to change the subject. “Oh, it’s just this day-shift nurse I’m having trouble with. She thinks because I’m new here I don’t know anything.” She took a last sip of coffee. “I know I have a lot to learn, and she does have much more experience. I am willing to take advice, but it’s beyond that with her. She just likes to find fault.”

“Who is it?”

“Who is it?” Should she tell? She didn’t want to incriminate another coworker, but she could trust Neil. “Theda.”

“Theda?”

She nodded.

“Older? Wears a nurse cap?”

“Mm-hm.”

“Not surprised. She gets in arguments with the residents all the time. Even Dr. Chole. Always thinks she knows better than us.” Offhandedly, he added, “You’re already a better nurse than she is.”

Charity suddenly felt like a fifth grader on a first crush, and had an urgent need to refill her cup.

He’s just being nice, saying what he said. But the pleasure of the compliment made her feel warm all over.

While returning to her seat, she observed Neil from across the cafeteria. She admired the way his lab coat draped over his broad shoulders. As he bit into a slice of toast, she observed his generous lips and strong chin. The angle of his jaw. She always liked a strongly-featured face.

Her heart flip-flopped in response to his glance when she returned to her seat. She had given up ever thinking she would actually see him smile, always so serious. But that look he gave her. That look. Hungry for rapport. For connection.

“Getting enough coffee?”

Charity crumpled up her napkin with the doodle on it and stood up. “Yeah. But I’d better go. Jeff wanted me to meet him for lunch later today, and I still have to sleep a little before that.”

"I'd better go, too. See ya'll tomorrow?" His eyes were expectant.

She was loathe to disappoint, but a remote sense of discretion raised a note of warning. She smiled that one-sided smile she used when apologizing. "Sorry, I'm off tonight, so I won't be here tomorrow morning. I work the rest of the week, though. I'll catch up with you later."

Picking up her purse and keys, she retreated. She was regretful for making Miranda mad and was becoming uncomfortable with how her relationship with Neil was developing. She wasn't sure of his feelings toward her, but she knew the pleasure she felt at seeing him, talking with him, and hearing his complimentary words, wasn't entirely innocent. It was an affair of the heart.

~25~

Easter came with the usual events at church during Holy Week. On Maundy Thursday there was a potluck dinner that ended with a meaningful foot-washing ceremony. Jeff urged his sons to participate, and they begrudgingly washed his and Charity's feet. She and Jeff took their turns washing their sons' feet. The ceremony reminded Charity of was the many times she washed patients' feet, old and gnarly, which probably more closely resembled the disciples' feet that Jesus washed at the Last Supper. This act of Christ's selflessness was a fitting illustration of how we should be servants of one another.

Drying his own feet thoroughly, Jeremy quickly slipped on his socks and shoes. He glanced around to make sure his youth group friends didn't see, and appeared relieved to observe most of the families were still busy completing the ritual. Zach enjoyed soaking his feet in the soapy warm water and was the last to get his shoes back on.

After Easter Sunday service they visited Papa at Northern Woods. Charity tried to be more faithful in visiting Papa with Jeff, ever since the melt-down in the parking lot, and went with him most Saturdays she didn't have to work. On holidays, the boys went along, too.

Zach was antsy from being in his new suit all day. He pulled his shirttail out, unbuttoned his jacket, and got comfortable in Papa's recliner, flipping channels on the TV.

"Turn that down," Papa scolded from his wheelchair. "I can't hear your brother talk."

"Sorry," Zach said, lowering the volume.

Jeremy continued his conversation with Papa. "My girlfriend's name is McKayla."

"Layla?"

"Mc-KAY-lah."

"Is she pretty?"

Jeremy grinned and nodded.

"Jeremy," Charity said, nodding toward Papa, who was still waiting to hear his answer.

"Sorry, Papa. Yes. She is pretty. She's a cheerleader," Jeremy said, a little too loud.

"You don't have to shout. Nothing wrong with my ears."

"Sorry."

Papa reached out a hand and pawed Jeremy's knee. "It's okay. Just be careful of those cheerleaders. They always go after the football players. Do you play football?"

"No, Papa. But she's not like—"

"They're all like that. Better get yourself an ordinary girl. One who can cook."

"I'm not marrying her."

Jeff broke in. "Dad. It's okay. They're just going out."

"Out where?"

Charity tried to change the subject. "I like the view from your window." The flower beds were alive with spring bulbs—daffodils, lilies, and hyacinths.

"What view? What does it matter how nice it is? I can't see it."

Jeff shot her a withering look. "She knows, Dad. She didn't mean anything."

The TV cop show was the only sound for a moment—screeching tires and gunfire. Then a nurse came in, bearing a tray. "I brought your lunch." Noticing his company, she added, "Oops! Want me to bring it back later?"

Jeff, Charity, and Jeremy all shot up. "No," Jeff said. "It's okay. We were leaving."

"Already?" Papa said. "You just got here."

Jeff leaned over to kiss his cheek. "I'll stop by later this week, Dad. Boys, say goodbye to Papa."

Zach slid out of the recliner and he and Jeremy shook Papa's outstretched hand.

"Love you, Papa," Charity said, and kissed his cheek. "Enjoy your lunch."

He found her hand and held it tight. "Come back soon. It gets lonely in my room all day."

"I will, Papa. I will."

Walking through the parking lot to the car, Charity's thoughts were on those words, "It gets lonely". Was that how her father felt, living in the basement? Did he feel like no one cared for him? She should have been more attentive, but she was busy doing everything for her mother—attending to her personal needs, giving her the liquid nutrition and medication in the feeding tube, cleaning her room, keeping her company.

It was finally that last week, the one after the spaghetti dinner she made for her father, which he took to eat downstairs, that she planned to do a better job at caring for him, like her mother asked.

Brooding till the middle of the week at how carelessly he had put her off that day, she finally decided to try again. Shopping for groceries, she purchased sausage links, pancake mix, and syrup. She knew how to make pancakes. And breakfast for dinner was always a treat. Maybe while they ate she could bring up her mother, try to commiserate with him and talk about how much they both missed her.

Rummaging in the closet that evening, she found the autumn decorations and withdrew a tablecloth the color of apple cider, and the pumpkin spice candle. She decorated the table like her mother used to, and would serve the Sunday dinner on the nice dishes.

Had she known how little time they had together, she would have tried harder, not waited a whole week before another attempt at having a meal together, been more persistent in trying to communicate. Maybe whatever sickness caused his death would have become evident, and they could have done something. She could have called her mother's doctor and made sure her father went to see him. She could have tried to help him.

But she didn't know how limited their days were. She thought there was plenty of time.

~26~

A week of torrential rains heralded summer, followed by a vigorous bloom of wildflowers—daisies, buttercups, and violets. Charity loved the changing seasons in the Midwest. The lengthening days of summer invited outdoor living and working. She and Jeff usually devoted this season to large household projects like power-washing the house, laying a brick walk, or painting the wood-sided detached garage. This year they finished the backyard patio area, installing a low brick wall around the cement slab. They also looked into building a pergola with an attached wooden swing. This was still in the works.

Jeremy started a job at Bargain Retail for the summer, stocking shelves and unloading trucks. He fell into bed exhausted most nights, and spent the weekends with McKayla.

July 26 was the annual gathering of the northeast Ohio Civil War Enthusiasts clubs. They met in Salineville to commemorate the northernmost military action between the Union and Confederate armies. It involved a mock battle and lots of food. Zach couldn't sleep the night before for the excitement of it. Earlier in the year he had finally gotten his uniform, and hoped he would be allowed to participate in the battle.

Charity and Jeff were both scheduled the same week off in August and planned for a family vacation. This vacation was long overdue. During the years Charity was in nursing school they couldn't afford to go anywhere and had to make do with local fairs and festivals. The boys always had a good time as long as the trip included carnival rides and fair food—elephant ears being Zach's favorite, and greasy fries doused with vinegar, Jeremy's. The trip to Presque Isle last year didn't count as a real vacation in Charity's estimation. To be a real vacation, one had to go out of state, or at least drive more than two or three hours.

Since Jeremy wasn't able to go on the vacation—he wasn't eligible for time off from work yet—Zach opted to stay home, too.

"Can I sleep over Damion's?" Zach asked at breakfast. Charity had gotten home from work in time to make scrambled eggs and bacon this morning. Jeff already had the coffee brewing.

"Sure, pal." "No way." Jeff and Charity said at the same time.

Zach looked at Jeff with questioning eyes.

Charity nodded in Jeff's direction. "Your call."

"One night, okay?" He held up one finger.

"One night? Thanks, Dad."

Jeff got up from the table. "See you guys tonight," he said to Jeremy and Zach. "And you, too." He gave Charity a kiss on the cheek.

"Once I get up I'll look into making those reservations online, see what hotels are available," Charity said to him.

"Make sure there's a free breakfast."

She nodded, and he stepped out the side kitchen door to go to work.

Charity cleared the kitchen table of dishes and poured a last cup of coffee. "What do you plan to do at Damion's while we're gone?" she asked Zach.

"He got that new game system for his birthday, and we're gonna stay up all night playing Warrior Kings."

Jeremy slid back his chair. "I've got to be going, now, too. I start at nine." He took a final swig of black coffee.

"Do you like your new job?" Zach asked.

"It's . . . it's adequate. McKayla likes to go out to dinner, and the car needs tires."

Zach rolled his eyes. "Glad I don't have a girlfriend."

"You will, some day," Charity said, catching Zach in a sideways hug as he started for the stairs.

She got up from sleeping in the early afternoon. It was harder to sleep in the summer, with nice weather and the neighbor's activities beckoning her outdoors. She opened the room-darkening blinds Jeff had installed in their bedroom and stepped into her shower.

Before preparing dinner she looked up hotel availabilities for their vacation week. She also called Aunt Bee and prevailed on her to stay with the boys that week, instructing her on Zach's dietary needs to avoid spells of IBS. Determining there were enough Spaz-no pills in the kitchen cupboard, she felt more prepared for their week away.

A couple's getaway—hopefully a time to reconnect and reach a better understanding of each other. The impasses lately, the disagreements and bickering, had her wary. She hoped there would be opportunities for communication and better appreciation of each other's points of view and opinions. Maybe he would open up more, and she could learn what he was really like, deep inside. Maybe that would encourage him to understand her better. It was worth a try. And being away from work, and Neil, would help her to focus on him instead.

Charity got together with Teri and Miranda over coffee the next morning. Ever since Miranda yelled at her in the locker room, she tried to make more time for her. They got together about once a week all that summer.

"So you're off all next week?" Miranda said.

"I am! We're going on our first real vacation in over ten years," Charity said.

"Really?" Miranda crunched a mouthful of ice. She tossed her head to flip her bangs out of her face. This month her hair was a razor cut short style with long bangs that swooped sideways over her head. "I think my last vacation was our honeymoon, four years ago. We went to the Outer Banks."

"Where'd you stay?"

She looked up and gazed at the ceiling. "Umm, it was a real kitschy place. Olivia had a good time, too. I wish I could remember . . ."

Teri had been texting on her cell phone, seemingly not part of the conversation taking place. Without warning, she said, "I went to the Outer Banks a couple times. My aunt lives in Norfolk, Virginia. So usually we went to Virginia Beach. But sometimes it was the Outer Banks. They had this festival near the beach one year and there were all these rides. My cousins dared me to ride the Ferris wheel, even though they know I have a fear of heights. Or, not really a fear, it's just my stomach gets all queasy, ya know what I mean? And I think I'm gonna throw up. And I told my cousins that, and they thought it would be funny to see me get sick. But then my aunt told them to just go on the ride by themselves. But then Leyla, she's the bossy one, Leyla said—" She took another deep breath.

Taking her chance, Charity cut in. "Maybe we will go there. We still haven't decided. What's there to do?" She looked pointedly at Miranda as Teri continued her story, unconcerned they weren't really listening.

Taking the hint, Miranda said, "Lots of things: shop, eat really good seafood, walk on the beach . . . ." Her voice faded for a moment, then her eyes met Charity's. "Now I remember! It was called Pirate's Cove. It was a cheap one-floor motel. There was a large pirate ship on the front lawn for kids to play on. Olivia loved it but kept getting stuck in the crow's nest. Mitch had to get her out. She was only two but already was always getting into trouble."

Teri's voice faded as she answered a text on her phone.

"Sounds like fun. I'll try to find it if we go there. Jeff usually likes staying in name-brand places that offer a free breakfast. Not much for adventure, that one. I'm just glad he agreed to go. And, it's just us two!"

"Ooo!" Miranda said with a suggestive wink.

Charity chuckled. "*And* I'm real glad to get away from that *Theda* for a week. She always tries to get me on something at change of shift. Yesterday I forgot to clear an IV pump. Wouldn't you know, she noticed. And it wasn't enough for her to tell me about it. No way. She had to give me a five minute dissertation on the importance of accurate intake and output documentation. I mean, I know it's important to report fluid intake, but she could have charted it herself, without lecturing me about it."

Miranda shook her head. "She drives me crazy."

Teri looked up from her phone. "You know, she's leaving."

"Leaving?" Charity and Miranda said together.

She took a deep breath. "Nikki told me." Nikki was the Health Care Associate usually scheduled on the night-shift. She was often privy to classified information just by keeping a low profile and being observant.

Teri continued. "Theda got in an argument with Joyce. It was over taking breaks. She said she never takes breaks, that it wasn't how they did it when she first started working as a nurse, and she didn't agree with it now. She told Joyce she didn't think nurses should take breaks at all. Just maybe a ten minute lunch. Although I know some nights are so busy we just don't have time, with admissions, and our patients not sleeping and all. But I always try. I usually take a lunch around two and a short break right after passing my five o'clock meds, in the lounge, just for a cup of coffee, ya know what I mean?"

Miranda peered at Teri. "Hold on—how did Nikki know all this?"

"She . . . um . . . she happened to be by Joyce's office, wiping down her blood pressure monitor, and the door was open."

"What did Joyce say to Theda?" Charity asked, her face eager.

Teri glanced at Miranda, and then said to Charity, "She said the nurses and HCAs all deserved their breaks and full lunch times, and that Theda shouldn't refuse to take care of someone else's patients when they're on break. I guess that's how it all started. Someone told Joyce that Theda refused to watch their patients while they were at lunch, so Joyce asked Theda about it."

"Where is she going?" Charity said. She nudged Teri, who had returned to her phone. "Is she retiring?"

"I don't know. I just saw her name scratched off next month's schedule." They were silent for a moment, absorbing the welcome news.

Charity sighed. Her heart felt lighter knowing this unpleasant and critical coworker wouldn't be there to give report to in the morning anymore. Some people cause a dismal atmosphere just by being there, with their negativity and demands. Those people communicate their displeasure clearly. It could be just a look, or tone of voice, or a cupboard door slammed too loudly. But there's no mistaking their meaning. It was something that always lay heavy on her mind, the thought of having to deal with her. She was glad she didn't have to endure a whole shift of that behavior, and felt the day-shift nurses must be ecstatic about Theda leaving.

~27~

The following week Charity and Jeff drove twelve hours to a tiny rented beach cottage in Nag's Head, in the Outer Banks. It was cheaper than a hotel, and they could cook some meals themselves, so Jeff was all for it. The cottage opened onto its own private stretch of beach. It was separated from neighboring properties by a length of slat fencing entangled with bunches of tall seagrass and spreading nopal cacti. The drive had been exhausting and, after stopping at a small store for some groceries, they were glad for the comfortable bed to collapse into.

The first morning they woke to the crash of waves on the shore and heavy rain falling. The sky was several shades of gray, from great swirling clouds of charcoal pouring water onto the sea, to patches of lighter gray illuminated by a sun trying to break through. The top of the slatted fence nearly touched the sand, sliced by the wind. An occasional dark shape leapt out of the water, joyful in the tumult. A whale? Or dolphin? They gazed out the window at the storm, sharing fresh coffee and donuts.

The seclusion forced by the violent weather afforded an opportunity for conversation. Still facing the roiling sea through the kitchenette window, it was as if the fount of discussion that had been trapped in the cares of daily life had finally broken free, like the drenching rain from the clouds.

They talked about projects still left at home—the pergola, replanting the lawn borders, and remodeling the kitchen, which still had the original cupboards from when the house was built in the 40s. This led to a discussion about Jeff's brother Antony, and his new venture of flipping houses. Evidently used car sales were down.

They discussed plans for their sons—Jeremy was still counting on going to Notre Dame next autumn to study engineering, and Zach? Just about to enter high school, they weren't sure what interests he would have, besides playing video games and the Civil War club.

They talked about Papa.

"He wants me to visit every day," Jeff said. "I can't do that."

"Maybe call every day?"

"I should. Sometimes I forget to call him all week, and then it's time to visit again."

"We could take turns, I could go see him on my day off during the week, and you could go on the weekend."

"You wouldn't mind?"

She turned to face the window, observing a single beam of sunlight breaking through the clouds, turning the edges cotton candy pink. "He told me he was lonely."

"When did he say that?"

"At Easter." She sipped her coffee. "It reminded me of how my dad must have felt, living downstairs all alone."

"You said he chose to do that."

"Hm. I know. But it's still sad."

Jeff fidgeted with his mug, and dabbed at his plate, picking up a few stray crumbs of donut.

Charity stood and reached for the coffee pot, splitting the remains into their two mugs. "Why now call your dad now?"

Jeff nodded and reached for his phone.

"Make sure you let me talk to him, too."

The next day was spent on the beach. Still overcast, it was warm and breezy, creating moderate sized waves that washed up on their legs as they sat in the sand. Charity collected a few shells and Jeff eventually retreated back to his lounge, far enough from the spray of waves that his book wouldn't get wet. Charity joined him there later and picked up her knitting. The afghan for Miranda's baby wasn't going to knit itself. She was due this month.

They cooked a simple supper of baked salmon and rice that night. After their meal they took the rest of the wine to the tiny back porch and sat beneath a string of low wattage lightbulbs. An occasional pelican was seen resting on nearly motionless water, its long bill nestled in its back. The moon shone a path of silver light on the surface, and a multitude of stars speckled the water like the flashes of bic lighters at a concert. Tomorrow should be glorious. They had planned to finally leave the cottage and do some sight-seeing.

Seated in a folding chair, the sand of the beach just beyond her feet and the salt-scented air of the sea in her nostrils, Charity scrolled through the calendar on her phone, noting a few appointments she had made. It was then she remembered what day it was.

It was August 16, the anniversary of her mother's death.

"Remind me to check the oil in the Blazer tomorrow before we go anywhere. After that long drive here, it might need topped up." Jeff said.

She remained silent, clutching her cell phone.

He turned to her. "Chair."

She scuffed her foot on the bare wood floor. "Sure. I'll remind you."

After several quiet moments, he reached out and touched her arm. "You're not talking. What's wrong?"

She turned to him, her eyes moist. "It's been twenty years, today, since my mom died."

"Twenty years?"

"Today. August 16."

It was an uncomfortable topic. Jeff was never good with death, or condolences, or funerals. "You go for the family, not for the person who died," he would say. His meaning was, if you didn't really know the survivors, it didn't make any sense to go. *They*, your friend, wouldn't know if you went. It was different with relatives, of course, but Charity still had to urge him to go to calling hours on those occasions.

"It has been *twenty years*, after all," he said, raising an eyebrow.

What does that mean?

Turning back to the sea, he added, "I guess it still bothers you."

She didn't expect much, but his insensitivity hit a nerve. What does it matter? Twenty years, or a day? Grieving for a parent can sometimes take a lifetime. And the memories return when least expected, and then you have to deal with them.

"You wouldn't understand." She slid back her chair, strode into the cottage, and retreated to bed.

She reclined back against the pillows finishing her wine. She knew she should be getting over it by now. And, honestly, there were some years she didn't even remember the anniversary. Years of getting married, raising boys, going to nursing school. But lately . . . it's been on her mind often. Being a nurse and working in the hospital constantly reminded her of her mother's many days and nights in hospitals and how she suffered in the end, unable to move, eventually just willing herself dead.

She remembered how wretched she felt after the *two* funerals, returning to the empty house. The hospice people finally removed the home care equipment and hospital bed. Charity closed her mother's bedroom door and the basement door and never opened them again.

It wasn't something Jeff understood, her grieving this much after so long. He got over things. He moved on.

When she told Neil . . . *"Some hurts never go away."*

She shook her head and took some cleansing breaths, focusing on the air filling her lungs, and then exhaling completely. Curling up beneath the covers, she tried to empty her mind of thought so she could sleep. The lonely cry of a single seagull came to her through the window.

A moment later, she heard the creak of the bedroom door. Jeff padded across the floor and crawled in next to her. Tentatively, he wrapped his arms around her from behind. He said into her hair, "I'm sorry. It was a stupid thing to say."

She gave it a few minutes, not wanting to be too easily mollified. The breeze through the screen freshened the room, gauzy curtains fluttering against the windowsill. A slice of moonbeam illuminated the bed covering, a cotton quilt in washed out colors. She fingered the frayed edge. Finally, she said, "Yes. It was."

He caressed her cheek, wiping a stray tear. "I'm really sorry."

Being held was a comfort, and she leaned back against the familiar bulk of his body. He tightened his embrace. She placed her hand over his, interlacing their fingers.

She could tell he wanted something. And, truth was, she wanted it too. Of course she could remain frigid, hold a grudge. Maybe tomorrow she would give in. Make sure he was really sorry, first, and then slowly come around, on *her* terms. She tried to focus on the sound of waves lapping the shore rhythmically, and the occasional splash of a fish leaping out of the water.

He was nuzzling into her neck, reaching for—

A flash of heat sped across her middle.

Her desire taking over, she shifted her body around to face him, his mouth searching for hers in the darkness, and finding it. She responded by moving against his body, clutching his back, and losing herself in the curves of his arms, legs, and thighs.

◆◆◆

The following day they toured the Cape Hatteras lighthouse and aquarium. Jeff was developing a new appreciation for sea life and was fascinated with the sea turtle sanctuary and rehab center at the aquarium. They listened to a talk on conservation efforts being made to reduce plastic waste in the ocean, and purchased a souvenir photo of them in front of a full scale model of a sunken ship.

At the aquarium gift shop Charity chose tee-shirts for the boys and a coffee mug for Aunt Bee. She searched the 'named' mugs for her aunt's name, Beatrice, and didn't find it, so she selected one decorated with images of brightly colored seashells. She also chose an aluminum travel cup for Papa—it would keep his coffee warm and avoid spills.

Charity was used to not finding her own name on gift items. She could usually find Zach and Jeff, and occasionally Jeremy. Searching among the mugs, she found one with 'Neil' emblazoned on it, along with a whale with a toothy grin. She picked it up and smiled intimately, thinking about the handsome resident, and their last breakfast together.

He had been away for a five-day trip to South Carolina. When he returned last week, he told her all about visits with his family and participating in an artisan's fair in his hometown, where he sold several framed black and white photographs. She told him she would be on vacation for the following week. He said he would miss her.

Glancing back at her husband, immersed in a coffee table book on sea turtles, she quickly set the mug back. Despite last night's misstep, they were starting to communicate on some uncomplicated level.

She left the mug display and joined him at the book table.

"Do you know these leatherback sea turtles have been around since the dinosaurs?" He pointed to a glossy photo of one of these in glistening water.

She slipped her arm through his. "So you found a new interest. Does this mean the Civil War Enthusiasts will lose a member?"

He turned to her and smiled. “Zach would kill me. He’s really getting into it.”

She tilted her head. “I’m glad. It’s good you two are doing that together.” She took the book from his hand and added it to her purchases at the cashier counter.

While driving around from place to place at the Outer Banks, Charity kept her eyes peeled for the Pirate’s Cove motel. She thought it would be fun to have Jeff take a picture of her in the pirate ship.

Unfortunately, when they found it, the motel was in ruins as a result of Hurricane Sandy, in 2012. She walked around the miserable building. It was sunlit inside through the nearly absent roof.

Jeff watched her from beside the car. “Don’t go too close,” he called out.

Charity looked back from in front of faded caution tape. “Alrighty. I’ll be careful,” she said.

She stepped over the caution tape and across a cracked cement walkway, approaching the main door. Peeling paint hung in strips of faded blue and green. A brittle note that said “No $ to rebuild Thanx for the memorys” was thumbtacked to the door.

Charity turned around and, peering over waist-high grasses, could just make out the foundation of what was probably the pirate ship. She trudged through the dry grass and climbed up. Jeff strode to the edge of the grass and shielded his eyes from the sun.

“Take my picture,” Charity said. She posed leaning against what probably used to be the mainmast. She flexed a bicep. “Aargh!”

Jeff took the picture with his cell. “Come on, then. Don’t want you getting hurt.”

Returning to the car together, Charity texted the picture to Miranda. “This is all that’s left of Pirate Cove. See you next week.”

Next week. She immediately thought of Neil, and telling him she would see him next week. Glancing at Jeff, in the driver's seat, she tried to work out in her head what she would tell him when she returned. "Sorry, Neil, I can't see you anymore" sounded just too much like a break-up, when, to his mind (she thought) they really were 'just friends'. He treated her as a colleague, and as a friend, never displaying any more intimate feeling. Her secret infatuation really was *just hers*. She knew spending less time with him personally, and keeping it professional—a simple greeting at the nurses' station or query about a difficult case, for example—was part of the solution.

~28~

The last morning of the vacation Charity woke alone in bed. There was a note in Jeff's recognizable scrawl on his pillow, written on a paper napkin: "gone for breakfast. Be back soon. Jeff".

Charity took a leisurely shower and rubbed her hair with a towel. Best let it finish drying in the sun on the beach. She slipped into a cotton sundress and heated a cup of coffee in the microwave. It was yesterday's brew, but still tasted fresh. The book she bought yesterday, a self-published paperback on the history of the Outer Banks, was just the thing to take to the beach this morning. Soon, she was settled in a beach chair by the water, book in one hand and coffee in the other.

She was halfway through chapter two when she heard Jeff calling to her. "Chair!" he said, rounding the cottage and treading across the sand. He held two white paper bags aloft.

"There's a muffin for you, and I got this." He pulled out a dinner-plate sized cinnamon roll slathered in white icing, and displayed it with a broad smile.

"Wow! Have fun with that." She bit into the cranberry muffin. It was moist and tender, and she could detect seasonings of orange and ginger. It was nice of him to remember her favorite breakfast food. "Where'd you get this? It's really good," she said while chewing.

He made it through one round of cinnamon roll on his way to the delectable center, where most of the cinnamon lie. "From that bakery two blocks over."

"What's it like inside?" She remembered they drove past it, but had not gone in.

He pulled two paper cups of coffee with lids out of the second bag and nestled them in the sand. "What do you mean?"

"What do they sell?"

"Muffins, these huge cinnamon rolls. Other stuff."

"Did you get the coffee there too?"

He nodded, chewing on cinnamon roll.

Hearing a raucous noise above, she looked up. By now seagulls had noticed the breakfasting humans on the beach and had begun to circle, waiting for handouts. Despite signs warning against feeding wildlife, it was obvious these birds were used to having scraps fed to them. One seagull landed several paces away and bounced toward them on gnarly feet. Jeff tossed it a fragment of cinnamon roll.

The sun was getting high. Charity was done with her coffee and wanted a cold drink. She closed her book and said, "Do we still have that lemonade in the fridge? . . . Jeff?"

He was texting on his phone, shielding it from the bright sun.

"Jeff."

He looked up at her, and held up the phone. "Sorry. It's Jeremy."

"Is he okay?"

"Problems with McKayla."

"What problems?"

"She, um . . . she wants to move back with her dad."

"In Florida?"

"Is that where he lives?"

"Mm-hm."

Jeff continued texting as Charity stood up.

He looked up from his phone. "Where are you going?"

"To get something cold to drink." She gathered up her book and coffee mug and started picking her way back to the house among the driftwood and seashells.

She turned back. "Why does she want to move back with her dad?"

Jeff blinked in the sun as he looked at her. "It's complicated."

She advanced and held out her hand. "Can I see your phone?"

Turning so the phone was in her shadow, she scrolled through several screens of conversation. "Jeff!"

"Huh?"

"She's accusing him of mistreating her?" She pointed to the phone. "What's this about him leaving her at the plaza and making her get a ride home?" There was a break in the thread that didn't explain the situation.

"He called me yesterday and told me about it."

"Yesterday? What did he say?"

"His car broke down."

She took a step and looked down at him, still seated in the sand. "What else?"

"It was the battery."

"The battery?"

He nodded.

She glanced up to the sky. Again, dragging it out of him. This was too much. And it was about Jeremy.

He stood up and reached for his phone, which she held out of his reach. "What happened? Tell me."

He snatched his phone and shoved it into his back pocket. "The car battery was dead. He got a jump start in the parking lot of the plaza, and then drove to Bargain Retail to buy a new battery."

"And McKayla?"

"He forgot she was waiting for him in front of Chef Mario's."

"He forgot?"

"When he remembered, after buying the battery, she was already gone."

"Did he call her then? Did he apologize?"

"He didn't say."

Charity looked up and gazed over the waves. She saw a fish leap out of the water in the distance, and a pelican go in for a dive, and resurface. The sky was azure, with one lonely puff of cloud.

At that moment Charity felt lonely. This vacation . . . the first few days they had lots to talk about. She felt close to him, and there was a tenuous connection. Yesterday, and today, it was back to searching for things to say, and forcing conversation out of him. It wasn't fixed, this problem between them. He still didn't get her.

She felt her throat catch, and squeezed her eyes shut.

He noticed, and reached for her hand. "It's okay. She wasn't the right girl for him anyway."

She slid him a look and jerked away from his touch. "That's not why I'm upset."

He drew back.

"You don't understand, do you? He told you this yesterday. Yesterday. Why am I just learning about this now?"

"It's not that big a problem. I talked to him."

"But I'm his mom. I should know these things. You should tell me."

"I just did." His voice was getting testy.

She rolled her eyes. "I had to drag it out of you." Her voiced raised in register.

He pressed his lips together and raised his chin.

"You don't communicate," she threw at him, whirling back and stomping to the cottage.

"You don't make it easy," he tossed back.

She turned at the back door. "What?"

He advanced, his eyes dark. "You. Don't. Make. It. Easy."

"What do you mean? When did you ever offer to discuss anything with me on your own? I always have to start every conversation."

"Maybe . . . maybe if you didn't act like I always say the wrong thing I would talk to you more."

"So what. If there's something going on with the boys, I should know. You should tell me. That has nothing to do with whether you say the wrong thing. That's just good parenting."

Out-argued, he sulked back to the beach.

Back in the cottage, she looked through the kitchenette window and saw him standing, facing the water, his arms folded. She overreacted, she knew. It wasn't a big deal, Jeremy and McKayla's problem. But that wasn't the crux of the issue. It was, again, Jeff's difficulty with communication, and not understanding her need of it. It affected everything and caused everything: the loneliness in her heart, the continued, and renewed, grieving over her parents' deaths because she couldn't talk to him about it, her ability to enjoy spending one-on-one time with her husband. Even the reason she became 'involved' with Neil.

She placed her mug and the other dishes into the dishwasher and started it up. Glancing around, she remembered they would have to clean the cottage, as check-out was today at 1 PM. She picked up the small trash can and strode around the cottage, filling it with carry-out containers and drink bottles. Snatching up other small bits of trash, she found the napkin with Jeff's note: "gone for breakfast . . .". She crumpled it and tossed it out.

What a fun drive it will be going home. Maybe she'll sit in the back seat and read her book. Or finish the afghan for Miranda. Maybe she'll call Josephine. Yes, she would have to call her. Sometime when she could talk to her in private. She needed someone to tell her what to do, tell her how to manage this ongoing conflict with Jeff. She was miserable, and she was making him miserable, too.

When Jeff finally entered the cottage she handed him the broom. "Here, I packed our stuff already. You can sweep while I wipe down the bathroom." She snatched the bakery trash he brought in and placed it in the can. Wordlessly, he took up the broom and got to work.

She drove the first leg through North Carolina. Passing the tall pines along the roadside got her thinking about Neil, and how he probably drove this very highway on his trips back and forth to his home state. It made her feel closer to him, somehow.

Jeff busied himself with his book and phone. He made occasional remarks about the passing countryside, but gave up when she didn't respond. He took over driving when they reached Virginia.

She sprawled in the back seat and closed her eyes. This vacation was a disaster. Rather than bringing them closer together, she felt farther from him than ever. He just didn't get her; the continuing problem with communication, *miscommunication*, was proof. All she wanted was for him to take her into his confidence, to discuss problems with her, or to hear her out when she was upset. His solution was to clam up even further because, according to him, she made him feel like he says the wrong things all the time. Well . . . a lot of times he does say the wrong thing.

She must have fallen asleep, because when she woke up the sky was a blanket of stars and Jeff was getting off the exit for Charleston, West Virginia.

Looking at her in the rearview, he said, "Thought we'd get some dinner. It's almost nine."

"Good idea," she said. She was hungry, and her funk was lessened a little having had a nap.

"Pizza?"

Pizza sounded good.

Seated at the restaurant table, Charity said, "I better call Aunt Bee to let her know our ETA."

Jeff nodded as Charity pulled out her phone.

"She can stay, if she wants," he said.

"What do you mean?"

"At our place for a while. Her neighborhood is getting rough. Maybe she should think about moving."

Aunt Bee lived in an old Firestone neighborhood south of Akron, a twenty minute drive away. When she was in her forties she started seeing a man who worked at the tire plant, and they dated for several years. When Larry died, he willed the house to her, since he had no other relatives, and she lived there ever since. Eventually, Firestone merged with Bridgestone, and much of the work was outsourced or moved to other countries. The Firestone neighborhoods no longer housed plant workers, and many were sold as rentals, or became dilapidated as elderly homeowners were unable to keep up with repairs.

Jeff had offered to replace the broken screens and missing porch floorboards, but Aunt Bee was always just 'too busy'. When he suggested he come to fix the upstairs toilet, her response was, "It's just *me*. I can only use one toilet, and the downstairs one works just *fine*."

The truth was, she was a collector, and guarded her piles of junk mail, numerous knick-knacks, and old clothes against meddling from outsiders.

"You're right." Charity said. "I didn't realize it, but when I talked to her yesterday she seemed kind of muddled. She had cooked oatmeal for the boys for supper, and asked why we didn't have any eggs."

"Oatmeal for supper?"

"I think she thought it was breakfast time. And there were eggs in the fridge. Remember we got some at the grocery store before we left on vacation?"

“Her mind’s going. She’ll have to go to a nursing home.”

Charity shook her head. “She’s not that bad. She’s still with-it most of the time. And gets around good. She might be okay in a senior apartment.” She picked up her phone and tapped the contact icon for their home landline, waiting for Aunt Bee to answer.

By the time they pulled into the driveway at 2 AM, Charity was leaning on her husband for support up the front stoop, grateful for his strength in being able to drive those long dark hours home.

As they stumbled into the house, they were surprised to find the back of the living room lit up and Aunt Bee sleeping in Jeff’s recliner, the TV on and Sparky in her lap. Charity gently tapped her arm. Sparky gave a half-hearted growl.

Aunt Bee peered at her, momentarily confused. “Lilly?”

Charity glanced at Jeff, then back at her aunt. “Aunt Bee, it’s me, Charity. We’re home.”

She looked at the phone in her hand, then back at Charity. More fully awake, she held up the phone and said, “Oh, Charity. They called from that place . . . that place where . . .” She looked at Jeff. “Where your father is.”

Jeff strode forward. “Northern Woods?”

Aunt Bee nodded. “He . . . he had a heart attack.”

Charity shot a look at Jeff and knelt before her aunt, trying to remain calm. “Did they take him to the hospital?”

She pressed her lips together for a few seconds, thinking. “I told them you were on your way home, and . . . .”

“Give me the phone,” Jeff said, snatching it from her hand. He pressed the speed dial button for Northern Woods.

Aunt Bee looked at Charity, penitent. “I’m sorry I couldn’t remember your phone number to call you.”

She patted her aunt’s hand. “It’s okay.” She stood up on tiptoes, close to Jeff, listening to the phone conversation. Once he rang off, he led the way to the car again.

Charity called out, "Don't wait up, Aunt Bee. Not sure when we will be back."

Entering the darkened nursing home, Charity and Jeff were guided to Papa's room by the night-shift nurse.

"I'm so sorry," she said, touching Charity's sleeve.

She nodded and gave a sad smile. Jeff stole to his father's bedside.

The smooth top sheet covering Papa, and the neatly combed hair indicated after-death care had been performed by diligent staff members. He looked so peaceful there, a man giving in to the return to his Maker, healthy and seeing once again.

Driving home in the quietest hour of the night, Charity said, "I wonder why they didn't call us on the cell phone."

Jeff pulled into the Mr. Speedy drive-through and ordered coffee for both of them.

She wanted to say something comforting, to take the sting out of the sudden loss. Trying to set aside the arguments of the past week, she hoped to come up with suitable words of consolation. "I know it's a shock for you, but it's better he didn't linger. He wouldn't want that."

She took the cup of coffee he offered and sipped carefully.

He drove silently through the side streets, devoid of other vehicles.

"We'll have to call your brother." She peered at him over the plastic lid. "Jeff."

"What?"

She touched his hand. "Are you okay?"

He pulled into the driveway, parked, and turned to her. "There's so much I should have told him."

She nodded, her lips pressed together.

"Now I won't have the chance."

His words and his downcast expression pointed to remorse, something Charity understood. She remembered that feeling when her father was taken to the hospital. It surged when he finally died after those two days, hooked up to all kinds of machines. And lately it continued to taunt her, filling her heart with blame.

The words Papa said to her, about being lonely, also grieved her. She hoped he had enjoyed their last visits, and wished they had spent more time with him. Her own father had been lonely, too. And she had been too absorbed in her own grief back then to notice.

"You were a good son," she said, squeezing his hand. "You took all the responsibility, and made the tough decisions, even though it made him mad sometimes."

There were many more words that needed said, but being so tired from driving home from vacation, and dealing with the emotionally exhausting events of the night, neither had the strength. It would have to wait for another time.

~29~

Antony sat with Jeff, Charity, and their sons in the front row of the church at Papa's funeral service. Nadine and her family sat behind them with Aunt Bee. Also attending were some of Papa's friends from the mill, and a cluster of nurses and aides from Northern Woods. Miranda and Teri arrived a little late and sat together in the last pew. Charity glanced back at her friends and noticed Josephine had arrived, as well, and stood against the back wall.

Josephine gave her a little wave. Charity smiled at her and nodded, glad she came. Papa's funeral arrangements and clearing his stuff out of Northern Woods kept Charity busy all week, and she only had time to leave Josephine a brief voice-mail message.

As the organ music drew to a close, Charity felt the seat begin to shake. Jeff looked at her, and they both glanced back, catching Dane kicking the pew again. Nadine mouthed, "Sorry" and nudged Kirkwood, who grabbed for the boy's knees. Aunt Bee, on his other side, reached into her handbag and pulled out a set of bingo markers and an old Reader's Digest. Dane kept quiet the rest of the service, coloring the pages fluorescent yellow, green, and orange.

The pastor kept the eulogy short and personal—Papa had been a member of the church for many years, and he knew him well. He talked about his love of fishing and the times they went angling together. He mentioned his strong work ethic and devotion to family and community.

As the pastor talked, Charity admired how lovely the church front looked, bedecked with flower arrangements from some who didn't attend. The Civil War Enthusiasts sent a large wreath, and there was a peace lily from Northern Woods. A unique display of English ivy and dried seed pods sprayed silver caught her eye. Squinting her eyes, trying to read the card as the pastor finished the eulogy, she could discern "Neil" on it. Miranda must have told him. A shiver went through her and she reached for Jeff's hand.

She hadn't seen Neil since she came back from vacation. The four allotted bereavement days she had off work saw her till the end of the week, till today's funeral. Once again observing the arrangement Neil sent, she was touched he had thought of her. She missed their stimulating conversations over coffee. Despite promising herself to end their get-togethers, the stressful week made her long for them even more.

There still had not been a satisfactory resolution to the impasse in communication she and Jeff were struggling with, having set it aside to help him deal with his father's death. Despite knowing it was her duty to be there for him, and she was willing to perform that role, the irony of the situation was not lost to her. How would he feel if she made light of his grieving?

After the eulogy, Jeremy stepped behind the podium and did a reading from the Bible. He spoke firmly, but there was a tremble in his voice at one line in Ecclesiastes chapter three, ". . . a time to be born, and a time to die." Jeff squeezed Charity's hand. The boys would miss their Papa. And it was a good thing, too. Means they had a relationship with him, after all.

She did, too, when she finally let herself. The past summer, visiting him weekly with Jeff, she came to appreciate and understand him better. It also gave her a window into Jeff's personality. Papa was an enigma, like her husband. Usually a man of few words, he listened to TV and radio, or just sat silently in his room, waiting.

Sometimes, however, the most unexpected thing would produce a sentimental response.

A new nurse named Ellie attended him one Saturday as they were visiting. She brought his lunch and afternoon meds.

"Ellie?" he had said. "Did you say your name is Ellie?"

She nodded. Then said, a little loudly, "Yes, Mr. Cristy. It's Ellie."

"Ya don't have to shout."

"Sorry, Mr. Cristy."

He held out a hand, searching. She came nearer and touched it.

"No. It's okay. It's just . . . My wife's name was Ellen. I used to call her Ellie."

"Ellen's a pretty name. Was she pretty, Mr. Cristy?"

Papa had reached up to swipe beneath his eye. "She was as pretty as her name."

Charity glanced at Jeff during this exchange. He raised his eyebrows and pressed his lips together.

Placing the meds into Papa's hand, Ellie said, "How long since she died?"

Snapping out of his reverie, he pointed in Jeff's direction and said, "What do I care? She left me when he was ten years old."

Following the brief grave-side ceremony behind the church, the family went to Chef Mario's for the mercy luncheon. They personally invited the others who attended the service, as well. The small banquet room at the restaurant had adequate seating for the family and the twelve others who joined them.

The family style meal—bowls of salad, pasta, and meatballs in sauce, all in the middle of the three tables—was accompanied by baskets of homemade crusty garlic bread and the chef's selection of red wine.

As Antony passed the food to Jeff, he said, "They should have called me that night Dad died. I could have gone there right away, instead of waiting till you came home from vacation."

Jeff selected a piece of garlic bread and handed the basket to Charity. "I suppose you could have done something, too," he said with a sidelong look.

"I might have. Or at least have an ambulance take him to Quarry Gen. Maybe they could have saved him."

Jeff remained silent.

"It would have been better than doing nothing," Antony said.

Charity saw the dark look on Jeff's face and the way his nostrils flared. As he opened his mouth to respond, she touched his hand and leaned toward Antony. "We were listed as his contacts. That's why they called us. When they found him that night, he had already passed. There was nothing they could do. The autopsy showed a ruptured aortic aneurysm."

"I thought it was a *heart attack*," Aunt Bee said from across the table.

"That's what the nurse thought. But she didn't really know," Charity said. "In either case, heart attack or aneurysm, death can come suddenly."

Jeff glanced at her, a wounded look in his eyes.

She sighed. "I'm sorry. I didn't mean it that way. I'm sure he went peacefully, in his sleep."

"Why didn't they know?" Antony said.

"What?" Charity said.

"His aneurysm. They should have known about it. What's wrong with those people? They're supposed to be treating his health problems."

"They took good care of him," Jeff said, his voice even. "Maybe if you had visited you would have known that."

Antony glared at him.

Charity put her fork down. She glanced at Jeff, then at Antony. "It's an uncommon problem, and easily misdiagnosed.

The chest pain it causes can feel like you're having a heart attack."

"What causes it?" Jeremy said.

"An aneurysm is a weakening of the walls of an artery. Sometimes the layers of the artery wall dissect—come apart. That can lead to the artery actually leaking blood, which is probably what happened to Papa. There are surgeries to fix it, but it's risky."

"So?" said Antony. "When it leaks, how long does it take? Hours? Weeks? How long was it going on?"

Charity steeled herself. "I don't know. There's no way of knowing how long it was going on. Keeping his blood pressure under control is one way of guarding the aneurysm from getting worse, although sometimes it still does. I know he was on two or three BP meds."

"Stubborn," Jeff said. "He probably refused to take them."

Listening intently to the discussion, Zach said, "Was there a lot of blood?"

Quick to answer, Charity said, "No, Zachy. The bleeding is internal. Inside the body. You don't see it."

Antony kept silent the rest of the meal. Charity figured he knew he neglected Papa while at Northern Woods, and was like so many family members who are absent for day-to-day care of a loved one, but like to swoop in when there is a crisis, attempting to appear the hero. But it just makes them look shallow.

As the luncheon concluded, Charity and Jeff stopped at the other tables to have a few words with Papa's two friends from the mill and the staff from Northern Woods. They then visited briefly with Nadine and family, and Charity's friends.

"I'm glad you two came," Charity said to Miranda and Teri, reaching down and giving them both a hug.

Josephine stood and embraced both Charity and Jeff. "I'm sorry about your father."

Jeff nodded.

"I remember him at church years ago, singing in the choir."

"You do?" Charity said.

"George was just a toddler when we started going to Prince of Peace. Your father always had a beautiful voice."

Jeff nodded again. "Thank you."

Charity gave her friend one more hug before she and Jeff returned to their table, gathered their sons and Aunt Bee, and departed.

Jeff drove in silence. Charity stole glances at him and observed the tightness of his neck, the way he held his lips pressed together, his frequent sharp exhalations through flared nostrils.

"Jeff," Charity said.

Nothing.

She touched his arm. "Jeff."

He glanced at her. At a red light, he turned to her and said, "Antony had a lot of nerve saying he should have been called the night Dad died. As if he ever visited, or brought him clothes, or put up with him complaining about the living arrangements." In his outrage, it all came pouring out.

He continued as he drove the rest of the way home. "It was *me*. *I* took care of things. *I* tolerated the unpleasant visits, him making me feel guilty each time I came. Complaining about being there. Antony never took him anywhere, or offered to let him live with him. He wants to be seen as a hero. But he's just an imposter. A fraud."

His rant stopped suddenly. Charity gazed at him in astonishment. Aunt Bee, Jeremy, and Zach remained silent in the back seat as Jeff parked the car in the driveway and got out. As he strode to the front door, Charity said, "Come on, boys. It's been a long day."

They both lay awake in bed that night, lost in the events of the day.

Charity's thoughts, focused on Jeff and Papa all day, turned to the loss of her own father once again. Her father's funeral had been a blur; the most she remembered was sitting with Nadine and Kirkwood, Nadine's arm around her the whole time. Later, there were casseroles of food brought to the house by his coworkers at the grocery store, and many cards in the mailbox every day, considering people were still sending cards for her mom, and now for her dad. She didn't know what to do with them all, and just gave them to her sister. By the end of the month she had moved in with Nadine to finish high school in Akron.

Jeff reached his arm around Charity, who snuggled her head against his shoulder. "Thanks for keeping things calm at lunch today."

"Mm-hm."

"Antony . . . he just knows how to push my buttons."

She was glad he was opening up. The past few days she discovered he was better at conversation in the comfort and safety of bed, when he was a little tired, and the normal defense he put up weakened. Maybe this was the secret of communication.

She hoped to continue the exchange. "When you were growing up, was it like that? Were you two always at odds?"

He thought a moment. "As children, we did a lot of things together. And since we were two years apart, we walked to school and played on the playground together. I s'pose things changed in high school."

"What happened?"

"Antony played football and ran track. He was popular. I was on the speech team."

"I didn't know that." She gazed at him in surprise. "I can't see you saying that much to a roomful of strangers."

He grimaced. "I didn't last long. It was fine when we were giving speeches to one another. But at competitions I froze." He rolled over. "I don't want to talk about it."

"We don't have to." She wrapped her arm around him and pressed against the warm comfort of his back.

"Chair," Jeff said. He turned onto his back again.

"Hm?"

"I think that's why my dad and I had a better relationship. He was a quiet man, and liked fishing, reading, watching TV. I'm a lot like him, I guess."

"Besides the fishing."

"Yep. I s'pose I'm not exactly like him. But I hope he knew how much I—" his voice caught. "How much I loved him."

Charity smiled. "He knew. Even though he complained a lot, he loved when you visited. He would tell the whole staff you were coming and have them get out his nicer clothes. He didn't care that me or the boys came. He just wanted to see you."

Jeff cinched his eyes. "How do you know that?"

"The nurses from Northern Woods who came to the mercy luncheon told me when you were getting the car. They said they didn't even know he had two sons till today. It was just you he talked about."

He turned over and she snuggled against his back once again. "I'm sorry. I meant to tell you earlier."

"It's okay," he murmured. "I'm glad to know he felt that way."

After a few moments she felt her body relaxing when: "Chair."

"Hm?"

"I just . . . I just wanted to tell you that I think I understand now. About your mom and dad. It's like feeling all alone in the world. Even though there's still a 'history', those forebears, the ones who were with you when it was happening, are gone." He closed his eyes. "I'll never hear his old stories again."

"I'm sorry." She squeezed his arm.

"I should have been more sympathetic about that, toward you. I didn't really get it till now."

It was true, and was the reason she quit bringing it up. Talking about her mother's death during their vacation was the first time she had done so in a long time.

But tonight, Jeff's admission rang true.

"Thanks. That's sweet of you to say."

In the darkness, an understanding passed between them. An unspoken connection, through grieving, that bonded them.

After a moment, Jeff said, "I was switching channels on TV tonight, and a fishing show came on. It made me think of my father and actually brought a tear to my eyes."

"When?"

"When you were in the kitchen."

"My mom comes to mind unexpectedly, sometimes. It might be something at work that reminds me of the times she spent in the hospital. Or some decoration or painting that looks like something she might have made. I'm used to being without her, but at those times, I'm caught off guard, and that's when it's hard. Don't be surprised if it happens a lot at first."

He mumbled some response.

"I used to think I saw my dad at Andrews Groceries, where he worked, after he died, and had to start going to a different store."

He turned his head. "The one where we met? Value Foods?"

"Mm-hm."

She smiled at his nostalgic memory.

"You were such a young thing, with your hair in a ponytail. I started going every two or three days, hoping to see you."

"Really?"

"Yeah. I parked by your car to catch you coming out. Or I'd go in and watch you pick out produce."

"You watched me?"

He chuckled. "You took a long time, comparing lettuce or apples. The boys would get restless, and I would have to leave before you were done."

She nestled closer to his back. How nice to know he still remembered those early times when they fell in love.

After a moment she said, "I remember you leaving me that note."

"Mm-hm."

"I couldn't believe you wanted to see me."

He murmured something unintelligible, then, "You were such a young thing. So pretty."

She smiled in the darkness. Their bedtime talk revealed much about her husband—a thoughtful and sentimental side she had not seen much of. She felt filled up. Connected. This kind of communication was what she longed for.

The darkness and warmth echoed the comfortable feeling in her heart as her body relaxed and her mind stilled. Peace reigned. Sleep finally came.

~30~

Charity came back to work Monday night feeling a little foggy. She had been off for two weeks for vacation and the bereavement days. This put her off her sleep schedule, and her brain was starting to shut down for the night. Funny how easy it is to go back to a nighttime sleep routine, even after working nights for over a year.

She was glad to be working with Miranda and Teri, sure they would have her back as she readjusted to a night-shift routine. Having made it through to early morning, she had just finished placing an IV in her patient's hand when she heard a faint cry for help coming from outside the room.

She quickly secured the catheter, attached the IV solution, and stepped out of the room, hearing, "I need some help in here—" again. The voice, laced with panic, came from the other end of the unit.

Striding down the hall, Charity realized it was Teri's voice. Miranda must have also heard because she was making her way to patient room 8, as well.

Charity was unprepared for the sight she beheld when entering the room. There was Teri, leaning over her elderly male patient, holding him down with all her might. Covering his midsection with both her arms, she was making a valiant effort to hold his entire abdominal contents in place.

"What did you do?" Charity asked.

"He ruptured! I opened the binder—" was all Teri managed to get out. Donald Morgan shoved her hands out of the way and his intestines sprang from his abdominal cavity—glistening, moist, and bloody.

He had had bowel resection surgery that afternoon. A portion of diseased colon had been removed and the healthy intestine re-attached end-to-end to form a continuous length. It was this organ which was exposed.

Charity threw on a pair of gloves and grabbed his hands. Teri leaned over him and gathered the exposed bowel in her arms once again. Miranda shuffled through the door and to the bedside.

"Randi, hand me that folded sheet," Teri ordered, reaching for a slippery section of bowel that was getting away. "And go get a pack of sterile towels and a bottle of saline from the supply room."

Miranda snatched a folded top sheet from the pile of clean linens on the nightstand. She passed it to Teri, who pressed it over Mr. Morgan's bowels and incision.

Miranda headed toward the door, calling over her shoulder, "Hang on. I'll be back as soon as I can." Despite her enlarged pregnant belly, she hustled out of the room quickly.

Mr. Morgan redoubled his efforts at escape and Charity strengthened her grip on his large gnarly hands. "Hold still, Mr. Morgan!"

He slipped his left hand from her grasp and clenched down on Teri's shoulder.

"Get him off of me!" she said, shaking her head violently, loathe to release her hold on his abdomen.

Not wanting to let go of his right hand, Charity held it firmly while attempting to free Teri from Mr. Morgan's grasp.

He kept pushing Teri's shoulder, saying, "Let go of me, you stupid—"

Just then, Nikki appeared in the doorway, tugging at her blonde braids. "Randi sent me in here. Do you need *help*?" She approached, eyes wide.

"Yes! Put on some gloves and get his other hand," Charity said. "He ruptured because Teri opened his binder."

Without delay, Nikki wrested his left hand from Teri's shoulder. Teri flashed Charity a riled look at her remark to Nikki.

"Ow!" Nikki said. "Mr. Morgan, please don't grab my hair like that." She worked his fingers from around her braid. "He's really strong."

Mr. Morgan decided to try a different tack. Focusing on Nikki's hand, he opened his mouth, exposing a few irregular teeth, and aimed for it.

"Watch out!" Charity said.

"Mr. Morgan!" Nikki said, scuffing back a step. She shot him a look of indignation while grappling with his hand.

Teri repositioned her hold over his abdomen. Glancing at Charity, she said, "I opened the binder to check his incision and he started coughing. He coughed so hard his dressing flew off and the incision burst open. The staples just popped off, one by one, and he—ouch! Keep his hands out of the way."

"Sorry! He's still trying to bite me." Nikki grasped his left arm again and stepped aside until it was held straight out from the shoulder while Charity lay on his kicking legs and continued holding the other hand up and out of the way. Teri remained over his midsection, desperately holding the folded sheet in place. It was like a game of Twister.

"I called for help," Teri continued. "Didn't you guys hear me?"

"I was busy with another patient," Charity said. "I got here as soon as I could."

Miranda rushed back into the room bearing a bottle of saline, a pack of sterile towels, and wrist restraints.

"Pour the saline on the towels," Teri said.

Miranda drenched the towels and put on a pair of vinyl exam gloves while Teri gently eased the intestines back into the abdominal cavity. They didn't all fit, and some of the bowel and omentum remained piled on top of the opening.

"Pass me a wet towel," Teri said. She applied a saline-soaked towel directly to the exposed intestines and covered it with a clean bath towel. She and Miranda fastened the abdominal binder, holding Mr. Morgan together. By now he was subdued, spent from the physical exertion.

Wrist restraints were applied to keep him from injuring himself further, and Nikki was instructed to remain with him until he appeared calm enough to leave. The three nurses returned to the nurse's station where Teri placed a call to the surgery resident on duty.

When Dr. Chole called back she informed him of the incident, told him of the measures they had taken, and obtained the required order for wrist restraints. Dryly, he replied, "Keep him NPO. I'll be up to see him."

"How do you like that?" Teri said after replacing the phone. "He's too superior to get excited about something like this. All in a day's work. I tell you, when it was happening, I pictured Mr. Morgan stumbling to the doorway, trailing his colon after him. It reminds me of the time—did I ever tell you about my cousin going deep sea fishing and catching that huge eel?" She continued without waiting for a response. "It wasn't an electric eel, except, if it was he would have been killed, right? I mean, when you get electrocuted, like in a storm, most people don't live, unless you're wearing sneakers, or some other shoes with rubber soles, ya know what I mean?"

Charity shook her head slowly. She turned her office chair to face a computer and murmured, "Good thing Dr. Chole wasn't in the room when it happened. What were you thinking?"

"What did you say?"

Charity spun back. "That fresh anastomosis could have burst apart. And at the very least, he will probably get a bad infection from having his guts all exposed like that. Everyone knows that. Even a student nurse could tell you that."

Teri's eyes were steely. "I didn't know his incision would open up," she said evenly. "Like I told you, I just loosened the binder, and when he coughed it all started happening. And then he kept pushing my hands out the way and trying to get out of bed. I did the best I could."

"You better hope it's not classified a 'sentinel event'." Charity caught sight of Teri's alarmed look as she turned back to her computer.

Nikki appeared at the nurses' station just then. "He's resting quietly now. I just wondered, is that tube in his nose supposed to be connected to anything? It's dripping green stuff on the floor."

"Oh, no!" Teri said, "The suction machine. It must have become disconnected." Teri darted back to room 8 to re-connect the naso-gastric tube to the suction machine. Stomach contents and bile were drawn into the suction canister via a tube passed through his nose and down his esophagus, thus keeping Mr. Morgan's stomach from filling up until the intestinal tract was functioning properly again.

While Teri was attending to the suction tube, Charity said to Miranda, "She'll be lucky he doesn't go septic. Really—what a stupid thing to do."

Miranda looked up from her computer keyboard. "Hm?"

"Teri. She needs to slow down. She does stupid things sometimes."

"Really? Ya think?"

Charity nodded.

Miranda turned around to face her. "Well, I don't agree. She's actually pretty smart. Remember what she told me about eating ice? Turns out my iron was dangerously low and I had to start taking supplements. I wouldn't have known if she hadn't said anything."

"Well, maybe she is *book smart*."

"Didn't you learn during orientation to always check surgical incisions?"

Charity propped a hand on her hip. “I wouldn’t ever take a fresh surgical dressing off, though. That’s for the surgeon to do.”

“She didn’t take it off. She just loosened the binder, and it popped off when he started coughing. Didn’t you hear what she said?”

Unwilling to concede, Charity turned her back on Miranda and reached for her cold coffee. Maybe she was being unfair. What happened seemed to be something Teri had little control over. But Charity couldn’t forget that each of their patients depend on them for excellent care that would lead to recovery. Nurses were the advocates, they were responsible to recognize and address problems, provide skillful care, offer comfort and, most of all, “Do no harm”.

When her mother . . .

She squeezed her eyes shut and thought about it.

Her mother was in the hospital to have a feeding tube inserted during the last few months of her life. Two days later, just before being discharged home, the tube quit working. The nurse on duty said she irrigated it with water after instilling crushed medication through it, but it still became hopelessly clogged. The tube had to be replaced.

This involved going hungry that whole night and the next day, being transferred to a cold procedure room on an uncomfortable cart, waiting an hour on that cart for the surgeon to arrive, and undergoing the surgical procedure for the tube re-insertion. This also postponed her home-going by one day.

Charity remembered blaming that nurse for causing her mother more distress. She may have followed protocol in using the feeding tube, but it getting clogged didn’t ‘just happen’. It was *someone’s* fault.

She knew she wasn’t perfect, and neither were her coworkers. But should that absolve Teri of her actions that caused a patient additional suffering? She didn’t know.

Teri reentered the nurses' station several minutes later, just as Dr. Chole buzzed down the hall to room 8, his rumpled white coat flapping open.

When he returned, he approached the three nurses, all quietly seated before computers, doing last minute charting before the early morning rush of tasks.

"Who put him back together?" he asked.

Teri raised her hand timidly. "And they helped me," she said, indicating Charity and Miranda seated near her.

"Looks good. May as well get him ready for surgery. We'll take him first thing this morning. I'll enter an order for IV antibiotics to be given right away." He turned toward the doorway, then back again. "One more thing—call his daughter, Susan, and get phone permission to take him back in. She's his power of attorney."

Maybe he was human after all. He did give them a veiled compliment. A large man with ruddy skin and light, thinning hair, his demeanor was usually rushed and aloof, tossing verbal orders over the nurses' heads. He treated those under him disdainfully, shooting rapid-fire questions at them during rounds. He enjoyed seeing them falter, correcting wrong responses with a sneer. But tonight it was, "Looks good."

Teri administered the IV antibiotic to Mr. Morgan. Charity volunteered to call the daughter and obtain phone permission.

She dialed the mobile number listed in the chart. It was just past 5 AM—hopefully she's an early riser.

"Hello?" a brisk voice answered.

"Hi, is this Susan?" asked Charity.

"Speaking."

"This is Charity, I'm one of your father's nurses. He . . . what?"

Susan was interrupting in an authoritative tone: "What's wrong? Did the nurses give him his IV push pain meds on time? He has dementia and won't ask for it. But it should be given every four hours. And he must be repositioned every hour. He will not turn himself." She paused for half a second. "I want to speak to the surgeon as soon as he rounds, and to the nurse in charge first thing this morning."

Miranda, seated next to Charity, gave her a look of astonishment, eyebrows raised, at the loud commands coming through the phone—commands even she could hear well.

"Just a minute," Charity said. "Ex . . . ex . . . excuse me." She finally broke through Susan's remonstrations. "He's fine. Except that he needs another surgery. . . . What? I said another surgery."

If Susan would just stop talking she would be able to hear what Charity was saying. "His incision came apart . . . No! He didn't fall. Yes—he had a binder on . . . It's just . . ."

"If someone was watching him, this wouldn't have happened," Susan scolded. "Connect me to the charge nurse. Someone must know what's going on."

Charity held the phone away from her ear for a second. She sighed deeply and got back on the phone. Bracing herself, she said, "Miss Morgan," hoping to sound more firm by using Susan's last name.

"It's 'MS'," she hissed.

"Sorry. *MS* Morgan, I just need your permission to send your father back to surgery. I can have the charge nurse call you when she gets here at seven. But he needs to go to surgery now."

Charity was finally able to get phone permission, and had Miranda also speak to Susan to witness the surgery consent.

Nikki helped Teri give Mr. Morgan a quick sponge bath, place a clean gown on him, load him onto a cart, and transport him to surgery. It was all done by 5:25 AM.

Following the exciting events surrounding Mr. Morgan's rupture, Charity and her coworkers continued routine nursing duties. Teri shifted around Charity as they passed each other in the hall, avoiding contact.

An hour later, Charity was exiting the med room just as Dr. Neil Kennedy and his colleagues entered the double doors of the unit.

"Hey, Charity," Neil said, pausing in the hall. "Welcome back." He leaned over and lowered his voice. "So sorry about your father-in-law."

Her heart fluttered. "Thank you. Yeah . . . it was unexpected."

He nodded, his expression sympathetic.

"And thanks for the arrangement of foliage. It was very . . . artistic." She started walking away, juggling an armload of IV fluids.

She heard him say from behind her, "By the way, I hear y'all are heroes."

She turned and stepped closer. "What do you mean?"

He nodded toward his colleagues, walking ahead of him. "We heard how you patched Mr. Morgan back together. Nice job."

"Who told you?"

"Dr. Chole. He told us how y'all put his bowels back in and re-dressed his evisceration. He said you did good."

"Uh . . . That's great."

"Well, he's in surgery now." Neil said, taking a step away. "See you later?"

She glanced back at Miranda, who was just exiting a patient room doorway. "I promised Randi and Teri I'd have breakfast with them. We need to catch up."

He waited a second.

She wanted to tell him she couldn't have coffee with him anymore, like she had promised herself during her vacation, but just one more time wouldn't hurt. She would have to learn about anything new that happened while she was away, to be up to date. It would be a professional interchange. "How about tomorrow?"

"Sounds good," he said, moving quickly to catch up to the others.

"Thanks," Charity called out behind him.

At that moment, she heard a strident voice behind her. "Who's in charge here?"

She spun around to face the speaker, recognizing her. "Susan?" Charity said.

"Yes, I'm Susan Morgan. Where's your team leader?"

"Susan," Charity said again, a little incensed she wasn't taken for being in charge. "It's me—Charity."

"Charity."

"From Hill N Dale? Remember? I worked there last year, just after graduating . . . ."

"Hmph. I remember," Susan said, tossing her head. "So—this is where you landed." She took a quick look around the unit.

"Yes. But I am so grateful for all I learned at—"

"Never mind," Susan interrupted, and strode purposefully down the hall past the nurses' station.

Before Charity could catch up and warn Joyce Foster, Susan was at her office door. She just zoomed in and found it on instinct.

Later, Charity relayed the disconcerting encounter with Susan Morgan to her friends over breakfast. "I think she always held it against me that I left Hill 'n Dale."

"At least she wanted you to stay. That means she approved of the way you worked," Miranda said.

"More like she didn't want to train someone again." Charity sipped her coffee, thinking back to those days. "She's just . . . just . . . a zealot when it comes to patient care. I don't think she believes anyone is as good as her. She's a little like Theda that way."

"Ugh," Miranda said.

"And she *was* very good."

"But so are we," Teri said.

"That's right," Miranda said, laying her hand on Teri's. "I never saw you so much in charge. Good job."

Teri looked at Charity with a smirk. "Thank you," she said to Miranda. "I think we all did good, ya know what I mean? Otherwise Mr. High-and-Mighty would have told us."

"Apparently Dr. Chole bragged about what we did," Charity said with a sigh. The whole event was exhausting,

Teri raised her eyebrows. "How do you know?"

"Neil . . . Dr. Kennedy told me."

"Hmph! That drives me up a wall." Miranda said. "He's too important to give us lowly nurses a compliment personally. I'm just glad to know he has some appreciation for how we handled that."

"I hope Mr. Morgan's surgery will go well," Teri said.

Charity kept quiet and stirred her coffee listlessly.

"Hey," Miranda said, poking her in the arm. "What's wrong?"

Charity glanced up. "You think Susan Morgan will say anything bad? You know, to Joyce?"

"It's not my fault he came apart," Teri said, defensive again. "We're supposed to open the binder to check the incision, right?"

Charity rolled her eyes. She couldn't help herself, and said, "It's *someone's* fault he came apart. It didn't just happen."

Teri opened her mouth to say something when Miranda cut in and said, "You did the right thing, Teri. We all did. Our manager will stand behind us."

Joyce Foster was loyal to her staff. She would not let herself or her staff be bullied by obsessive Susan Morgan, someone who bulldozes right over your words and does not take time to listen. She would set her straight.

Charity came home to find Zach sitting at the kitchen table downing a sugar-laden bowl of cereal, up early for a Saturday. "Hi, mom," he said between crunchy bites. "I'm going to Damion's. We're gonna walk to school to play basketball."

School had just started that last week of August, and they let kids inside the gym on the weekends.

She set her purse and lunch bag on the table. “Don’t eat too much of that.”

“This is my first bowl,” he said through his chewing.

“Alrighty. I might still be sleeping when you get home, so be quiet, please.”

“We were gonna play video games at his house after, so I’ll be home for dinner.” Zach got up from the table and stepped to the kitchen side door, backpack in hand.

“Hold it,” Charity said, nodding toward the kitchen table.

Zach made a grumble. He turned back and placed his cereal bowl and spoon into the sink, then sped out the side door.

Charity peered through the kitchen window and watched him dart through the back yard to Damion’s house, his dark hair floppy and his broad shoulders easily supporting the weight of the backpack. Having just had his fifteenth birthday, he seemed to have shot up this past year. She observed the back door of Damion’s house open, and could barely see him, his dark skin blending with the shadows as he let Zach into the house.

Brewing a mug of herbal tea, she glanced up as Jeremy passed her, jingling his keys.

“Good morning, Jeremy. Is Aunt Bee up?”

Jeremy paused at the door. “I heard her take Sparky out, earlier. But I think she went back to bed.” Aunt Bee was getting accustomed to staying in the spare room. *Just visiting*, she made a point of saying.

Charity looked up at Jeremy, who had a puzzled look on his face. “What’s wrong?”

“Is Aunt Bee okay?” he said.

“Why?”

“She called me ‘Larry’ last night, and asked if I was going to the tire plant today.”

Like when she called Charity “Lilly” that night she came home from vacation.

"Hm. She's getting a little muddled," Charity said. "She used to have a boyfriend named Larry. They dated for a few years. Might have even lived together. The best thing to do is keep telling her you're Jeremy."

He nodded.

"Where are you off to?"

"I'm picking up McKayla. We're going to the mall."

She raised her eyebrows. "To the mall?" Apparently she was giving Jeremy another chance.

He nodded. "She needs shoes."

Charity smiled. McKayla always seemed to need shoes. In the few times she has seen the girl, she had on a different pair of shoes each time.

The mall was in Canton, a half hour drive away. "Have fun, but be home for dinner, okay?"

"Will do," Jeremy said as he dashed out the front door.

Dinner. As tired as she was, Charity wanted to have something planned for the one meal they ate together as a family. She opened the freezer and withdrew a packet of frozen meatballs and sauce; she had made a double portion before the vacation. Placing a box of penne pasta on the table next to the thawing meatballs, she picked up her tea and trod to the staircase.

Slowly stepping up, her mind returned to the incident with Donald Morgan early that morning. Why did she lash out at Teri, criticizing her about something over which she had little control? It could have happened to any of them. It could have happened to *her*. Indeed, there had been times she felt ineffective, even powerless, trying to work out a way to take care of someone or find a remedy for a tricky situation. She thought of Elise, eating less and less no matter what she tried.

And her father came to mind, as well. She had planned to make the pancake and sausage dinner that Sunday, a week and a half after they buried her mother, and purchased all the ingredients for the meal. Saturday morning she got up early to clean the house. Aunt Bee was away on a bus tour to Cleveland with a group of friends and couldn't come that day, as she usually did. Charity pulled the cleaning stuff from the closet as the phone rang.

It was her father's work, Andrews Groceries. He was late.

She hung up the phone with a sense of foreboding. His car was still in the garage, and she didn't hear movement from the basement. Maybe he just slept in. It would be the first time in forever, but maybe . . .

That's when she found him. Barely breathing, crumpled on the couch.

The next thing she remembered was that her sister came that evening, finding her hiding under her bed cover.

She said to her sister through tears, "I didn't take care of dad."

~31~

September arrived as a continuation of summer. The days were hot and dry, and crickets heralded the evenings, which were becoming cooler. Driving home in the mornings Charity was greeted with the deep blue skies and billowy clouds typical of autumn. Soon the leaves would change again, coloring the countryside a joyful array of red and gold.

Jeremy started his senior year and was still working weekends at Bargain Retail. Since Zach was in high school now, too, he usually rode to school with his brother. He was looking forward to getting his driver's permit in a month or so.

Now that the kids were in school, Charity and Josephine had time to get together at the Coffee Cave. After catching up on their kids' goings-on: Manuel and Maria had started the tenth and eleventh grade, respectively, and George had been offered a full time job as a driver for Country Springs. Natalie was entering the fifth grade, and continued to be integrated into regular school. She started piano lessons over the summer, and seemed to have a real gift for music.

"Did you know she would do well at the piano?" Charity asked.

"She loves playing the piano at church, ever since she was little. Pastor lets her play on it after service is over. I probably should have started her on lessons much sooner, but I'm just finally getting on top of bills." Josephine took a generous bite of a boston cream donut, the custard filling oozing out of the other end.

"Is she enjoying it?"

"Ha! The piano teacher says she's a prodigy. They often are, you know. Kids with Asperger's."

They sipped coffee in the refreshing atmosphere of the patio, Charity's mind on how all their kids were growing up and doing well.

"I never heard about your trip to the Outer Banks," said Josephine. "I figured you were too busy to talk after your father-in-law passed away."

"I was. We finally got the rest of his belongings from Northern Woods. He had a pile of fishing magazines Jeff insisted on going through, and we donated his better clothes to the facility."

Josephine shook her head. "I can't believe that happened. And right after your vacation. Probably ruined your good time."

Charity sighed. "We didn't really have a good time." She placed her coffee cup down in front of her. "I mean, it started out good. But Jeff . . . he just doesn't communicate well, and we got in a big argument about it on the beach, over something stupid he didn't tell me. And then he told me I always make him feel like he says the wrong thing. Can you believe it?"

Josephine shrugged. "Maybe you do."

"What? He *does* say the wrong thing. Lots of times. It's like he's not really concentrating on what I'm saying, or what I *really mean*, and just says the first thing that he thinks of."

"That's what you're doing wrong. Men can't be expected to know what we *mean*. We have to be more direct, say it in black and white. And you should try not to be too sensitive. If he's answering you at all, that's progress, right? It *is* communication, even if he doesn't always say what you think he should."

Charity took a minute to absorb Josephine's advice, and realized she knew how it was to feel like you were saying or doing the wrong thing. There were times her father made her feel like that. Like when they gave her mother the set of markers for Christmas, and she was unable to use them. Her father scolded her, making it seem like it was all *her* idea, even though they both chose the gift. She was left feeling the sting of giving the unsuitable present all by herself.

Breaking into her thoughts, Josephine continued, "What about when his father died? Was he able to talk about it?"

"Believe it or not, that actually opened a door for us to talk about *my* parent's deaths. He said he finally understood how it felt, losing someone so close. All these years he didn't get why it still bothered me. But now I think he does."

Josephine smiled. "That's definitely progress."

Another hour slipped by, the two discussing changes in both of their work places, and their children's plans for the school year. Charity got up and purchased a dozen donuts for the guys before taking leave of her friend. "Thanks for listening, and understanding," she said.

Josephine gave her a warm hug. "Any time. You've always been there for me."

Getting ready for work that night, Charity retrieved her lunch bag from the kitchen and stepped into the family room to say goodbye. As usual, Jeff was in his recliner. He had a book open, but appeared to be dosing.

She touched his arm, waking him gently. "Hey. I'm going to work. Why don't you go to bed?"

He closed his book and lowered the footrest of the recliner. "Will do. Thanks for waking me."

"Don't forget tomorrow night is Zach's open house. He wants us to come."

"That's okay. You can go."

"I know, but since it's his first year in high school, we should both go. Be glad he *wants* us to come."

Jeff chuckled. "That's true." He leaned in and kissed her cheek. "See you in the morning."

◆◆◆

Arriving on the unit, Charity stepped into the break room, to be joined by Teri, Nikki, and a float RN. Miranda was on her pregnancy leave, having delivered a robust baby girl with a thatch of dark hair the week before. Teri sat across from Charity and kept an invisible bubble around herself by sitting back in her chair and keeping her attention on her phone. She responded to Charity's greeting with a terse "hello".

The group listened to the recorded report highlighting the latest developments on their patients as well as a few particulars about two new admissions coming from the emergency room. Day-shift report was held at the patient's bedside, one nurse to another. At night it was done differently—recorded on a device by the evening-shift charge nurse to reduce interruptions of patients' sleep.

Charity's new patient was a gall bladder attack vs. ovarian cyst named Rebeccah Kennedy. Her surgical history included an appendectomy as a teen. She was transferred to the unit just as night-shift began.

Charity checked on her other patients briefly before reviewing Rebeccah's e-chart. It was quite revealing—she listed her first contact person as Neil Kennedy.

She entered the room and greeted Rebeccah in her usual fashion. "Hi, my name's Charity. I'll be your nurse tonight." She quickly took in what she saw of Rebeccah. Curled up beneath a cotton blanket was a pale, delicate young woman in her mid-twenties. Thin, damp hair clung to her neck. The drawn brow and squinted eyes were indications of pain.

"Hey," Rebeccah returned. "Do you know if my pain medication's come up yet? My side really hurts." She had a familiar southern accent.

"Let me check you first. Where does it hurt?"

Rebeccah reached for her right side. During the exam, Charity was able to note that her patient was 'guarding' her right flank region. She also complained of nausea and had an elevated heart rate, presumably from pain or anxiety, or both. Her body temperature was normal.

Charity used her stethoscope to listen to all lung fields and then placed it over the abdomen, listening for bowel sounds, being especially careful over the right side. She draped her stethoscope over her shoulders and examined radial and pedal pulses, checked skin turgor, and made sure the IV catheter looked patent. Lactated Ringers IV solution was infusing at the prescribed rate.

Completing the physical exam, Charity quickly noted her findings in the bedside computer. She made a brief trip to the blanket oven located in a cubby in the hall and tucked Rebeccah beneath two freshly warmed blankets.

Now that Charity had a complete picture of her physical condition, she addressed the issue of pain medication.

"What do you usually take for pain, Mrs. Kennedy?"

"It's Becky, please." She winced. "I usually take Tylenol, but they gave me a shot of morphine in the emergency room, and that really helped." Her hand stole to her painful right side.

She checked the medication administration record for the last dose of morphine. Clicking on Becky's home medication page, it was empty. "Do you take any pills at home, on a regular basis?"

"Sometimes I take Tums for heartburn. I was taking birth control pills till about two months ago."

"You don't take them anymore?"

"They're . . . they're real expensive. And we don't have a drug card." Becky changed her position in bed and tugged the blankets up around her shoulders.

"Do you take any other medications? Over the counter?"

"Jus' Tylenol. And the Tums."

"Anything else?"

She hesitated. "Not really."

"Alrighty . . . are you having pain anywhere else?"

"No. Jus' here," Becky said, indicating her right side again, and across her belly. "And I'm nauseous. And hungry, too. Do you have any of those turkey sandwiches?"

"Well, for now you're not allowed food—until we figure out what's wrong. And I'll bring you something for nausea and pain as soon as I can. I'll see if we can get you some more morphine," Charity said as she left the room.

She sat before a computer at the nurses' station to complete documenting the physical assessment, and check lab values—standard blood and urine tests done in the ER. A urine pregnancy test was done, routine procedure for any woman of child-bearing age. This was revealing—the pregnancy test was positive. That might explain the nausea.

Does she know? Does Neil know?

After a trip to the med room she returned to Rebeccah's bedside. She injected a syringe-full of medication slowly into the IV port. "This should help your nausea. And I brought you some ibuprofen. You can take it with a sip of water. I also ordered a heating pad for your tummy. Unfortunately, that's the safest thing I can give you right now."

She sat up and swallowed the pills. "What do you mean, 'safest'? Can't you give me morphine?" Her voice reached a higher pitch as she made the request.

Charity hesitated. "I'm probably not the person to be telling you this, Becky, but you really should know. Your pregnancy test came back positive."

Speechless for a moment, she leaned back into her pillows.

"Did you know you're pregnant?"

"No. And . . . and I don't think they did a pregnancy test. I . . . I don't remember." She squeezed her eyes shut.

Charity touched her hand. "They always do those tests on young women, Becky. Listen, it's better that you know, now, don't you think? They're ready to do a CT scan of your abdomen in the morning. That's a test using x-rays, which pregnant women shouldn't have. I'll check with your doctor and see if he can order a different diagnostic test."

"I jus' don't know what my husband will say. He just graduated college and we don't have much money. How am I gonna work?"

"You'll make it, Becky. Lots of couples find themselves in those circumstances. It might not be real easy, but if you work together, you'll get through this. And depending on what you do, you can still work, as long as you take care of yourself."

She placed a pillow under Becky's legs and raised the head of the bed slightly. "Try to rest. Call me if you need anything, okay?" Exiting the room, Charity felt annoyed at the whiny, faint-hearted woman, so helpless when faced with life's challenges. No wonder Neil sought intelligent socialization elsewhere.

Charity watched for Neil when the residents came to the floor that morning. Of course, he wasn't there. Probably was down in the ER with his wife till very late last night. Must have gone home to sleep.

She phoned Becky's attending physician that morning. "Dr. Henson? Hi, this is Charity, Rebeccah Kennedy's nurse. I wanted to let you know about her lab results."

Following her conversation with Dr. Henson, Charity cancelled the CT scan and ordered some more blood work to check liver and pancreatic function. If it is a gall bladder attack, and it settles down, Becky may be able to hold off on having surgery and control the problem with diet, for now. The right sided pain could also signal an ectopic pregnancy, so an OB-Gyn consult was ordered.

Charity checked on Becky before leaving that morning. She was just waking up and said that her pain had really subsided with the ibuprofen and heating pad. She didn't need another pain pill. She also said, "I'll try to tell my husband when I see him this morning. We did want young-uns, jus' not right now." She added quietly, "I don't know how I'm gonna tell him. I hope he doesn't get mad at me."

"Children are never convenient, believe me," Charity said. "We have two sons and when I started nursing school five years ago they were still young. It was hard, taking care of kids, with my husband working double shifts and me going to school. But we made it, somehow. You'll get through this." *Don't be so tragic,* she thought, but didn't say.

Becky gazed up at Charity, her eyes moist. "I hope you're right. Thanks for everything."

At change of shift Charity made her way to the locker room near the elevators. She opened her locker, withdrew her windbreaker and purse, and placed her pens and scissors among the rest of the detritus clogging the interior.

Pausing at the full-length mirror on the locker room wall, she peered at herself a moment, evaluating her appearance. She reached into her purse and withdrew strawberry lip gloss and smoothed it onto her lips. She combed her hair and fluffed it back from her forehead.

Who knows? She might encounter Neil in the hallway on her way home.

She faltered. *I have to stop this*.

There must be a way to shake off the feelings she still had for the medical resident. She's taking care of his wife, for goodness sake. It's just not ethical to still have a thing for him while also being his wife's nurse.

Despite having breakfast with him two or three times since her vacation, she intentionally kept, or tried to keep, conversation centered on hospital- or patient-related matters. It was when he brought up their similar interests in artwork, that she caved, and found herself in stimulating discussions about his photography, enamored by his ease in talking about this finer pursuit. He even invited her to go to the Museum of Fine Arts in Akron with him. She declined.

The fact that she unconsciously primped in front of a mirror with him in mind just now pointed to the truth that her crush was not over. And her condescending attitude toward Becky? Thinking she was superior to her in some way when it came to Neil? That just wasn't fair.

She really needed to end the cozy breakfasts and keep her relationship with him on a totally professional level. No giving in to those intense eyes, the way he gazed at her, asking when she could meet for coffee.

With an abrupt movement, she swiped the back of her hand across her mouth, removing the lip gloss. She gave her hair a shake and exited the locker room.

The elevator door opened and Neil strode out. He looked like he had been up all night judging from a day's growth of beard and tousled hair. He was dressed in faded jeans and a Football Hall of Fame tee-shirt, and sipped coffee as he moved toward the Four South double doors.

Charity's stomach did a tumble and she remained in the shadow of the locker room doorway for a moment. Uncertainly, she stepped into the light. "Hey, Neil."

He stopped at the Four South doorway and turned toward her. A hand on a hip, he said a throaty, "Hey."

She approached closer.

"I didn't make it in this morning. I was in the ER all night with my wife. I guess she's on this unit?"

"She was one of my patients. I figured she was your wife. Gall bladder problem?"

"That or ovarian cyst. They're still trying to determine. She had a number ten pain in her right side. Is that any better?"

"It is. I offered her some more ibuprofen this morning and she said she didn't need it. She had a few good hours of sleep, too."

Neil gave a nod. "Thanks for all you did for her. I'm glad you were her nurse." He turned back toward the Four South doorway. "See ya'll later."

Taking a step toward the elevator, Charity felt a surge of pride at giving good care to Neil's wife, and at his approval of her. She felt warm inside.

~32~

On his way out the door that morning, Jeff caught Charity in the driveway as she pulled in. "Rough night?" he asked.

Why? How bad do I look? Remembering not to take his comments the wrong way, she said instead, "Just the usual. Busy, but not crazy."

He nodded. "I wanted to ask you when we should go to dinner." They had been trying to plan their twelfth anniversary dinner date, but work schedules kept getting in the way.

"Maybe this Saturday. Are you off this weekend?"

He was, and she promised to make a reservation at Chef Mario's.

He pecked her on the cheek and got into his car to go to work. "And when is open house tonight?"

"Seven o'clock till about nine. We can go after dinner."

Jeff nodded and backed out of the driveway.

Charity woke up early in the afternoon. Automatically, she reached for her cell phone on the nightstand. She saw the text: "It's Neil. Call me." Her heart skipped a beat.

He picked up after the first ring.

"Hey, Neil, I got your text. What's up?"

"Did you tell Becky she's pregnant?"

"Well . . . yeah. The test in the ER was positive. Didn't you see it?"

"That's great. Just great." His voice was charged with irritation. "You know, that's really impossible."

"Well, I know you two haven't had a lot of time together, but she told me she was off her birth control pills, so . . . it's not really impossible."

"No, you don't understand. It really is impossible. When I was twelve, I had leukemia. I had chemotherapy. They said I would never be able to have children."

"Well, maybe they were wrong . . . have you been checked since then?"

"I had a, a . . . you know . . ." He hesitated. "Yeah—I was checked before I got married. The count was really low."

"Does Becky know?"

"Well, no. I didn't tell her. She might not have married me. I was gonna tell her eventually."

At that moment. Charity's admiration for Neil plummeted from a 10 to about a 3. How could he withhold such important information from his wife? Furthermore, he let her go on taking birth control pills. And now he had misgivings about her being pregnant? Serves him right.

Maintaining a neutral tone of voice, she said, "It seems you two have a lot to talk about. I think, though, the first thing you should do is get checked again. Who knows? Maybe something's changed."

"That was almost eight years ago. You're right. Maybe something has changed."

Back at work that night, Charity checked on Becky shortly after 11 PM. She found her in tears. "Hey, Becky. What's wrong?"

"Neil . . . Neil's mad at me. I don't think he's ready for a baby. I'm not, either." Becky announced amid more tears. She made an effort to calm down, holding her breath for a few seconds before exhaling through pursed lips. "How accurate is that blood test for pregnancy, anyway. I jus' don't feel pregnant."

"It's not a blood test. It's a urine test. The hospital saves money using those urine tests similar to what people use at home. It's cheaper than a blood test, and just as accurate. They still do the blood test if there's any question."

Becky looked up at Charity, eyes big. "A urine test?"

"Yeah, you gave a urine sample in the ER. They tested it for a bladder infection and pregnancy."

Becky became quiet and fidgeted with her blanket, folding the edge over and smoothing it with her hands. "I never gave them a urine sample," she mumbled.

"Well, you must have. There's test results to prove it. Maybe you don't remember."

She remained silent, concentrating on her blanket.

"Becky?"

Still gazing down, she said, "I . . . um . . . I gave the aide the cup and asked her to do it. The bathroom was right next to me in the ER."

Stunned, Charity waited.

"She didn't want to do it, so I gave her ten dollars . . ."

"—Why?"

She looked up with pleading eyes. "I thought they were doing a drug test. I jus' didn't want them to know I took some Xanax that morning. I didn't want my husband to know. He's a resident here and I thought he would check all my results. He doesn't know I sometimes take those pills. I'm really sorry. I didn't know it would cause all this trouble." Penitent, Becky suddenly seemed very small beneath the white blanket.

Collecting herself, Charity took a deep breath. She said, "I think you should tell your husband the truth. Maybe he'd be relieved to know you're probably not pregnant. We will have get another sample, too. From you. Just to be sure," Charity opened a cupboard in the bathroom. She left a receptacle in the toilet and placed the sterile specimen cup by the sink before turning to leave.

"Charity! Wait!" Becky called out. "How am I gonna tell him? What should I say?"

Charity turned back, mentally rolling her eyes. "You'll have to decide that yourself, but it's not good to keep things from each other. Open communication is always best. And, as your nurse, I have to say if you need to take something for your nerves, like Xanax, it's okay. Nothing to be ashamed of." She peered at Becky. "It is your prescription, right?"

Becky avoided her eyes. "Well . . . no. That's why I didn't want him to know. I work two mornings a week at a day-care, and someone at work gave them to me. I'm nervous being at home all by myself and I get lonely during the day. Why does he have to be at the hospital every day? And stay late every night? I mean, what kind of life do I have home alone all the time?"

Charity understood that. Despite having the evenings together with Jeff, she often felt lonely, too. There was little of the friendly banter, relaying amusing events of each other's days, that she envisioned other couples might enjoy. Just the usual—making plans for their dinner date, his work schedule, the things that needed purchased for their home or the boys' classes at school. At once she sympathized with Becky, a home-town girl who didn't sign up for an absent husband.

She touched Becky's arm. Gently, she said, "Talk to him. It's best to be honest and tell him how you feel. Don't hold things inside. Communication is important."

Charity made herself scarce when the surgeons and residents came in, not wanting to be in the middle of a confrontation between Neil and his wife. She didn't know if Becky would have the courage to tell him. After work, she went home immediately.

~33~

Charity had been anticipating their anniversary date all week. Saturday afternoon she withdrew a black lace thing from where it lived beneath her cotton underwear. She held it up, glad for the largely elastic nature of the thing. Hiding it in a drawer in their bathroom, she hoped to surprise Jeff with it tonight, if the mood struck.

Taking a few steps to her closet, she pulled out a delicate light blue sweater and pair of linen trousers. Trying them on, she was pleased they still fit, albeit a little snug over her hips. Maybe she would skip dessert tonight, even though Chef Mario's had a delicious cheesecake. A string of silver and royal blue beads was the perfect accent to her outfit.

She secretly hoped that, despite promising they wouldn't give each other gifts this anniversary, Jeff would have something for her. Even just a little something. After twelve years, small considerations can mean so much.

They were greeted in the tiny foyer of Chef Mario's by a host in a burgundy vest and seated at a table for two. The muted atmosphere, from the dim lighting, to the display of house wines on the dark wood wine rack behind the bar, to quietly playing light jazz, promised a serene meal, undisturbed by life's daily cares.

Empty wine bottles were repurposed as candle holders on linen-covered tables, complete with layers of dripping wax over the surface of the bottle. The flickering flame at each table played on the stucco walls, casting shadows of dining guests across the rough surface.

Ordering from the daily specials board, they each got a variation of pasta, with salad and Chef Mario's special crusty garlic bread, accompanied by a red wine selection.

Jeff ate in silence, occasionally glancing at her. He seemed remote, even for him, and took a minute to respond to her questions, like he had something else on his mind. Some of his answers didn't even make sense; when she asked if the Civil War club was meeting next Saturday, his answer was, "Zach likes leading the pledge of allegiance when we open the meeting."

When she finished her meal she opened her purse in search of something to doodle on to pass the time. Catching sight of her cell phone, she resisted the urge to take it out. She didn't want to be one of *those* couples—the few she saw as she glanced around, staring at screens, not talking to each other.

She pulled an old receipt out of her purse and started sketching the wine bottle candle holder. Maybe a good idea for her next watercolor venture.

A busboy appeared and cleared the dinner plates. The waiter brought coffee.

Dessert signaled a near end to their date, much to Charity's relief. She ordered the cheesecake after all. She didn't care about the extra calories—just wanted to feel better. Jeff's diffident behavior was getting annoying.

Once again attempting to have a conversation with him, she took a nibble of cheesecake and said, "Jo sent a nice sympathy card. It came in the mail yesterday."

Jeff nodded vacantly.

"What do you want me to do with all the cards?"

He paused and said, "Cards?"

"The sympathy cards. Are you saving them?"

"Oh. Um . . . you can throw them away."

"You sure? Some of them are really pretty."

He shrugged. “Then save them if you want.”

“It’s up to you.”

Jeff worked through his chocolate lava cake. Charity toyed with her dessert, unenthusiastically nibbling at tiny bites of graham cracker crust. This date, anticipated all week, couldn’t have been more disappointing. The few steps they had made toward better communication seem to have dwindled and they were back to cursory, meaningless conversation.

He glanced at her. “You don’t like your dessert?”

“It’s fine.”

“It looks good.”

“Mm-hm.”

“Chair.”

She looked across the table at her husband. “What?”

“What’s wrong?”

Charity sucked in a deep breath, then exhaled, her lips pressed together.

Jeff raised his eyebrows and shrugged a shoulder.

“It’s just . . .”

Should she open up? Risk further disappointment? She didn’t like feeling hostile toward her husband. And she knew he loved her, and she loved him. She tried to be a support to him in dealing with Papa’s death, and it seemed he was beginning to understand her struggle about her own parents’ deaths. But she still didn’t know what he was thinking most of the time. He was a puzzle box. Sometimes she knew the right combination to open him up, and other times no matter how she tried, he still remained closed.

There was a detachment between them. Maybe it was because, like Josephine said, she actually did discourage conversation by criticizing what he says, making him feel it’s the wrong thing. But should communication be so hard? Such work? When she and Neil talked . . .

Perhaps next time she was attracted to someone else, like with Neil, she just might pursue more than just a social relationship. Might try something exciting. Something new. And yet, what she had with Jeff—the stability and history—was worth fighting for. It was worth saving.

". . . you don't understand me. We don't talk about anything," Charity said.

He put his fork down. "I don't talk to anyone much."

"Not even your wife?"

Jeff sipped his coffee.

"I feel . . . disconnected." *And lonely.*

There was a long silence. Charity waited. He could make the next move.

After a few sips, he said, "Remember when we first started dating? I told you a little about Jen, the boys' mom. About her illness and . . . and death."

Charity nodded slowly. This wasn't what she expected.

He swallowed, then continued. "And, when she died, how . . . how the boys thought she was just asleep there, in the coffin."

"Mm-hm."

He sighed. "Well, what I didn't tell you was, at the end, before she died, she was staying at her parents' house. She wasn't living at home. With me and the boys."

Jeff's first wife's parents had never been in their lives. They moved to their condo in Florida permanently after Jen died and send Jeremy and Zach cards and gifts of money on their birthdays. This was the first time Jeff brought them up in conversation.

"Was it so her mother could take care of her while you were working?"

"It wasn't that." He centered his coffee cup on his empty dessert plate. "She had been seeing someone else."

There was a sudden pang of disbelief. "You never told me that."

"I know. I know. It's not something I like to talk about."

She couldn't help but ask, "Who was it?"

He looked into her eyes. "My brother."

"Antony?"

He nodded.

Charity tried to wrap her head around this revelation. So, Jeff's first wife dated Antony when she had cancer? She just couldn't see Antony being a sympathetic or capable caregiver. Was it before or after . . . ?

"So, she found out she had cancer, and left you to go with your brother?"

"No, not quite. I found out she was seeing him. I had stopped by the car repair shop he worked at back then. I needed an oil change, so I went there after work to make an appointment. Only thing is, Jen's car was there. It was there in the parking lot. And she was in the car. And Antony, too."

He stopped talking for a moment, his lips pressed together.

"I parked a few spots over. There were two cars between us, but I could watch them through the windows. I watched them talk . . . . And before he got out of the car, I watched them kiss.

"We had a fight about it that night. She said she was bored being married to me, and tired of keeping house and taking care of children. She wanted excitement, and Antony was exciting. I believed it. Antony was always the more outgoing one. You know how some people fill up a room, just by being there? That's how my brother was. And he still thinks he's like that—the life of the party."

"Only now he has a bad toupee and has put on about fifty pounds." Charity raised an eyebrow. "It's kind of a joke."

"It is."

"How long before, you know ?"

He looked up at the dark tin ceiling. "Hm. I think she was living with him for about six months or so when she found out she had cancer. It was lung cancer. And she never smoked a day in her life."

Being a nurse, Charity's curiosity naturally turned to diagnosis and treatment. She asked, "Did she have chemo? Was she ever in remission?"

"Yes and no. Chemo for four months. No remission. It was very . . . what do they call it, when it spreads fast?"

"Aggressive?"

"Yes. Aggressive. By the time she lost all her hair, she had moved into her mom's house. Antony couldn't cope with her illness, taking her to chemo, dealing with the after-effects. So she was living with her mom. One morning her mom couldn't get her out of bed to go to the cancer center. She had died in her sleep."

He reached across the table and clutched her hand.

"So, I wanted . . . I wanted to take you out tonight for our twelfth anniversary. But mostly to celebrate you sticking with me. Being faithful to me. Always being there for me."

Charity opened her mouth to speak. She closed it again. She didn't know what to say.

"And, I know I'm not good at making conversation. I guess I just figure you always know what I'm thinking anyway." He grinned. "But I'll try harder. I'll try to understand what you need from me."

Her heart tore within her. "You don't have to—" She didn't think about Neil. She didn't think about their breakfasts together, or her silly crush.

She only thought about this husband of hers, who, with more perception than she gave him credit for, identified what made her feel far away from him. He finally got it.

"I *do* have to," he continued. "I blame myself for Jen going after my brother. Back then, I was mad at her. I blamed her for our marriage breaking up. I thought she should love me no matter what. But I'm older now. I understand. You need something else in a marriage. It's not just enough to be there with each other. You have to be there *for* each other." He paused, thinking.

She kept quiet. His admission was real. It was honest. Cherishing this side of him, she let him continue.

"When my father died," he said, "you were so sympathetic, even though we had that argument on the beach. I know you were still upset about it, but you were there for me through the funeral and everything. You were there for me. And I want to be there for you."

Charity sat silently in her chair across from him. She had no words. She watched him pay the bill and stand up and put on his jacket. She wasn't sure how she ended up exiting the place with Jeff holding her hand.

They walked past the outdoor patio seating, now closed for the season, and got into the Blazer.

"Oh!" he said, grinning slyly. "I almost forgot." He reached into the glove compartment and withdrew a slender packet.

"Here." He thrust it into her hands.

"Jeff, we said—"

"I know. But it's not much."

She gently tore open the newspaper taped around the paperback book. "Love. By Leo Buscaglia."

"He's a priest."

"A priest?"

Charity leafed through the thin volume. It was obvious the book had been read before.

Jeff started the car and turned on the heat. "It was mine. I was in a youth group at a Catholic church when I was in high school."

She looked at him. "You were?"

He steered out of the parking lot. He turned his head toward her briefly. "And, we studied this book one summer."

"The Summer of Love," she said, laughing.

When they got home, Jeff went up to bed. Telling him she would be up in a few minutes, she reached into the kitchen cupboard for an open bottle of Rose` and poured herself a glass. The paperback beckoned to her, and she spent a few minutes with it, unwinding in the quiet of the family room, seated in the velvet chair by the front window. She opened it and riffled the pages. An underlined passage caught her eye: “One does not fall ‘in’ or ‘out’ of love. One grows in love.”

Her eyes misted. Despite twelve years of marriage, their love was still immature. She expected him to be something he wasn’t—gregarious, expressive, a ‘feelings’ person. And, unknowingly, she had been discouraging his efforts at communication by berating him when his words came out wrong.

But tonight she saw a different side of her husband. She saw a side that was willing to try. Willing to try to at least meet her halfway. Willing to work on communicating. And as she continued trying to open the puzzle box that was her husband, she would also work at accepting him as he is.

What was it he said? ‘It’s not enough to be there with each other. You have to be there *for* each other’.

She set the book on the table, retrieved a second wineglass from the kitchen cupboard, and carried the wine up to bed, where Jeff was waiting for her. She remembered the lace thing she hid in the bathroom drawer, and excused herself from Jeff for a moment, an enigmatic smile playing on her face.

~34~

After the dinner at Chef Mario's Charity resolved to forego any further one-on-one breakfasts with Neil. It was hard not to give in to those eyes, but she was working on a relationship that was much more important than the one with the medical resident. Besides, discovering the crack in his personality—a trait of selfishness—she realized her infatuation was more about being unsatisfied with Jeff, rather than being so enamored with this other man. Every man and every woman, *every person*, has their flaws. The question was not so much can I endure the imperfections, as can I live without that person in my life.

After a few excuses begging off breakfast, and the mention of Jeff's name once or twice, Neil seemed to understand.

It was several days later that Neil drew Charity aside as she was finishing her shift. They stood in the shadow of a doorway, the hall lights still dim as morning approached. Charity glanced down the hall of the unit, then back up at Neil. Being this close to him was still a little problematic. As usual she noticed the shadows of his face, accentuating his strong features, but was able to look him in the eye without feeling that flutter in her stomach.

"I wanted to thank you for taking care of Becky. It was just an ovarian cyst after all. The pain all but disappeared after a couple days."

She smiled up at him. "I'm glad she's feeling better."

His voice got quieter. “And she told me what you said. About being honest with each other.”

“It’s not really my business.”

“She’s coming to meet me here for breakfast this morning,” he said, eyes bright and one side of his mouth drawn up into almost a smile.

Charity was genuinely glad for him. “Good idea! Randi always says it’s the cheapest breakfast in town.”

Becky started coming to the hospital to join Neil for breakfast or lunch most days. He also took her to the annual Labor Day get-together hosted by the senior residents. It was traditionally held to introduce the new medical and surgery residents and get to know their families. Becky met the other wives. She appreciated learning she was not alone in feeling abandoned by her new-physician husband. The wives had formed an informal support group and welcomed Becky among them. All of a sudden she had a half dozen new friends.

~35~

Aunt Bee was sitting on the couch with Sparky, watching court TV, when Charity got home after a round of errands later that week. Her day-off tasks ended with a visit to her hair stylist for a cut.

Aunt Bee enjoyed having a working TV once again and hadn't mentioned moving back to her old house for a while. Hopefully, she gave it up. Jeff and Charity talked to her about moving, and Charity arranged to view a few retirement residences, trying to find something suitable and affordable for her aunt.

"Lilly? Is that you?" Aunt Bee said as Charity entered the room. She stood up and took a step away from the couch. Bright light from the setting sun through the front window flooded around Charity. Aunt Bee shaded her eyes, gazing at her. "Lilly?"

Charity moved away from the window. "It's me, Aunt Bee." She took a few steps forward and touched Aunt Bee's hand.

"Aunt Bee, It's me—Charity."

"Charity?"

She waited for Aunt Bee to work it out in her addled brain. Her confusion came and went, and was one more reason she was determined to get her settled in a senior apartment complex rather than allow her to live on her own again.

Aunt Bee's attention was caught by the court TV show and she turned to watch it for a moment. Sitting back on the couch next to Sparky, she said, "This young man left the apartment a *mess*, and now is trying to collect his *rental deposit*." She pointed at the TV.

Charity sat next to her aunt. "Aunt Bee," she said in a small voice.

"What's wrong, Charity?" Aunt Bee said.

Taking a big swallow, she said, "Nothing, Aunt Bee. Nothing's wrong. Did you have lunch?"

Charity went into the kitchen and made lunch for them—ham and cheese sandwiches with plenty of pickles. They ate in at the coffee table so they could finish watching the TV show.

Aunt Bee loved watching TV. She also loved taking in the mail. There was already a pile of unopened junk mail and old newspapers on her dresser. "I just have to make time to read that," she would say when Charity offered to throw it away.

As she loaded the breakfast and lunch dishes into the dishwasher, Charity struggled with Aunt Bee thinking she was her mother just now. Did she look that much like her at this age? It would make sense that her appearance was like her mother's, especially since she wore her hair in a similar short style. Puzzled, she finished her task and pressed the 'on' button.

Later that night, after cleaning up from dinner, Charity went up the stairs bearing two mugs of tea and tapped on Aunt Bee's door.

"Come in," she said cheerfully.

Stepping around Sparky, who had finally gotten used to her, Charity settled on Aunt Bee's neatly made bed, covered with a worn quilt. Scissors in hand, Aunt Bee was seated in an armchair sorting through newspapers, placing the crosswords and her favorite comics (Little Orphan Annie and Dick Tracy) in a pile on her dresser. She liked to work on a crossword puzzle before going to bed, and usually had a few going at once.

"I brought you a cup of tea." Charity set the mug on the dresser. She took a sip of her own.

"Thank you, Charity."

As they sipped tea, Charity noted the new look of the spare room since Aunt Bee moved in. Considering the room her painting space—it faced south, giving it an abundance of natural light—Charity gave it up for Aunt Bee. There was a comfortable bed and spacious dresser, as well as a sturdy armchair, which Sparky liked to sleep on. A few framed photos and knick-knacks had been brought over from Aunt Bee's house, as well as her old Amish-made quilt, to make it more homey for her.

After a moment, Aunt Bee lay a hand on Charity's knee. "What's wrong?"

It only took those two words. Charity's eyes brimmed with tears. She leaned forward to be embraced by Aunt Bee, who patted her back and made soothing noises. After a moment, Charity leaned back and took a deep breath. Aunt Bee pulled a tissue from her sleeve and handed it to her.

Dabbing at her eyes, Charity said, "Aunt Bee, can I ask you something?"

"Sure, sweetie. What's bothering you?"

"It's about my mother. I wanted to know . . . just . . . am I anything like her?"

"Is that what's wrong?" Aunt Bee sat back in her chair, quiet for a moment. "You do look like her, a little, when she was your age. You're in your thirties, right?"

Charity nodded.

"She used to wear her hair short, like yours. But I think you have your father's *smile*."

"Hm. So I don't look that much like her?"

"I didn't say that. In fact, there are some things you do that remind me of her. Like when you twirl your *hair*. You know, when you watch TV, you twirl your hair in your fingers. Your mother did that."

Charity smiled. "Anything else?"

Aunt Bee looked up to the ceiling for a second. "Well, your *paintings*. She was a good artist. In fact, she used to send me homemade birthday cards every year. *Handpainted* ones. I've saved them all."

Charity brightened. "You've saved them?" And for a moment her heart jumped into her throat. Nadine had already gone to Aunt Bee's old house to start cleaning. She had told Charity that she loaded up the curb for the past two weeks with bags of paper, old mail, and newspapers. Were Aunt Bee's birthday cards among the mail Nadine threw away? Could she have thoughtlessly disposed of something as precious as her mother's handpainted cards?

Hesitating, she said, "Do you have them?"

Aunt Bee got up. "Of course. They're right here, in my jewelry box." She turned the large wooden jewelry box around and slid a hidden drawer from the back, revealing a tight stack of envelopes, which she withdrew.

"Here—" She handed them to Charity. "I know there were more, somewhere, but these were the last ones she sent me."

A cursory examination revealed twelve envelopes with postmarks through 1992. Her mother ended that year in a wheelchair.

She glanced at Aunt Bee. "May I?"

"Sure, sweetie. Take them down with you. I'm going to do my crossword and go to bed."

"Thanks, Aunt Bee," Charity said, standing.

"Are you okay?"

She sighed. "I think so. Sometimes I just really miss her."

Aunt Bee nodded. "Me too." She moved toward her bed. "Thanks for the tea."

Charity kissed Aunt Bee's cheek and carefully closed the door against Sparky. She stepped down the stairs with her mug and the bundle of cards and sat in her chair in the front window. Looking out of the window, she glimpsed Laura walking briskly, sheltered from the cold in her gray coat and red beret. As usual, she turned and waved in Charity's direction. Charity returned the greeting.

Gazing at the envelopes on the table, she detected the struggle handwriting had been for her mother those last couple years. She must have hidden the disability well, as Charity didn't remember her having so much trouble with writing. How did that problem affect her ability to produce art?

Deciding to open the most recent card first, and go back in time, she pulled the 1992 card from a pale yellow envelope. It was a picture of the sunset—a simple array of oranges and reds surrounding a glowing sun setting over the sea. A good choice for her mother to paint, as it didn't require much detail with the watercolor brush. Charity appreciated the way the colors blended into each other, and the way the orange ran into the blue of the ocean, just like the rays of the sun bounce off water at sunset.

Reverently, she opened the card, feeling she should be wearing white cotton gloves, like archeologists wear when examining ancient documents. It felt that precious.

There was her mother's handwriting, the letters boxy and painstaking, unlike her usual fluid script. After the usual birthday greetings and a brief account of her and Nadine's activities, Charity read, "I am having a hard time walking, and have to sit down often during the day. I try to be up when the girls are at home—I don't want them to worry. But I fear this is getting worse at a quick pace. I'll be 40 this year, and I hope I live long enough to see them graduate and marry. The doctors don't know how long I will last. It's a waiting game, it seems. The joy of my heart, these days, is the times I spend with James and my daughters. They are my life."

"I just turned 40 this year" Charity re-read this line. In two years she would be 40. Would she have been able to cope with the burden of a debilitating illness, while also taking care of a home and family? How strong her mother was. How brave. Until she was wheelchair-bound, Charity didn't remember anything except business as usual in their home. Although the illness surely had wrought its effects on her mother's body before that stage, according to the words to Aunt Bee on the card, her

mother had toiled to hide them. Ever selfless, she thought only of the worry it would cause her and Nadine, and strove to take care of them and her father as usual.

Charity caught rare glimpses of a clumsy step by her mother, or difficulty using a kitchen utensil. She would shoo her of the kitchen when she was cooking; Charity realized now it was to hide her disability from her. She wished she had helped her mother more and not let her do everything herself.

They all should have pulled together and done more. But her father was always late home from work and Nadine was graduating high school that year—her life full of debate team and the many other clubs she was involved in. Their father had finally taught Charity to drive, and she was intoxicated with the freedom having a driver's license gave her, often taking long drives in the country, and coming home just as her mother was bringing dinner to the table.

Seeing the exhaustion her mother experienced at day's end, and the way she sometimes dozed at the dining table, fork dropping from her hand, she knew she was sick, but the illness didn't become real until the wheelchair.

How her mother must have grieved at her loss of function, unable to care for her family like she used to. Unable to be the wife she prided herself to be—creative, organized, a good cook. A companion and helper to her father. No wonder her last request was for someone to take care of him.

Charity sighed, and sat for several minutes with the card open in her lap. So many memories. So much regret. She rubbed a tear from her eye.

"Chair," she heard from the back of the living room. She had forgotten Jeff was there, in his recliner, reading. She had forgotten everything but the words on the card. The words her mother wrote. Possibly some of the last things she wrote. And it was about her family. The ones she loved.

Jeff was standing up. "I'm going to bed. They want us at work by six tomorrow for some kind of inspection."

Charity sniffled, and blew her nose on a tissue. “I’ll be there soon, too. I’m going to check out a couple retirement apartments in the morning for Aunt Bee.” She would open the other cards another time. It was something she should do mindfully, taking her time, uninterrupted by her family. Then she could really focus on her mother’s words, and the paintings. She placed the bundle of cards in the round table’s drawer and took her cup of tea up with her.

~36~

The last week of September Charity found an available retirement apartment. Aunt Bee, however, fought against it. She remarked that she felt claustrophobic, having only one room to herself, and claimed Sparky missed their house. She even began packing her clothes in her old suitcase in preparation to move back.

Charity tried several tactics to convince her to move into a safer environment. It would be an apartment all her own, with lots of rooms, and where pets would be welcome. There had been a few break-ins on Aunt Bee's street, and one arson. Her house needed a new roof and other repairs.

They argued about it at dinner.

"I'll be *fine*. Jeff can change the locks, and I have my *police scanner*. I always know what's going on in the neighborhood."

Charity had forgotten about the police scanner and couldn't remember how her aunt got hold of one. "That doesn't matter. It's not safe. You could be the next house targeted for a break-in. The police still haven't caught who's doing it."

Aunt Bee opened her mouth to make yet another point.

Jeff settled the problem handily. "Sorry, Aunt Bee. The city of Akron condemned your house. There's no running water and the roof is caving in. It's not worth fixing."

"No running—" Charity started, then caught the look in Jeff's eye, the look that said, "Don't ask."

"I had water," Aunt Bee said.

"Well, there was . . . there was a break in the main pipe under the house. The basement's flooded and the block walls are crumbling in. You can't move back."

Defeated, Aunt Bee rose from her half-eaten meal and trudged up the stairs, Sparky trotting behind her.

Charity raised an eyebrow at Jeff.

"Sorry," he said. "She can't move back. I had to say something."

"It's okay. I'm glad you did. Nadine has already started cleaning out her house." She scraped the last bite of mashed potatoes from her plate and took a final sip of iced tea. "The apartment I found for her will be ready in about a week. The previous tenant lived there for twenty or so years. The carpet needs changed, and they were going to update the kitchen and paint some walls."

"Will the house be ready to sell by then?"

Charity rose and began collecting dishes from the table. "I'm going to help my sister clear out all the junk next week. That house does need a lot of work, and it may be condemned in the end anyway."

◆◆◆

In preparation for selling Aunt Bee's old house Charity, Nadine, and Zach spent a long day clearing it of debris. Since Nadine began several weeks earlier by gathering piles of paper trash, they had a head start. They bagged the rest of the paper trash and sorted through several closets-full of clothes and shoes. Aunt Bee agreed to let them put the bags on the curb and donate the clothes to the rescue shelter. They threw away the three broken TV's; the larger appliances were hauled away by a scrap collector.

Aunt Bee insisted on keeping her knick-knacks and furniture, even though the family offered to buy her a new living room and bedroom set. It was a concession Charity was willing to make—her aunt would feel more comfortable having those things she was used to.

Packing the many framed photos and figurines into boxes, Zach hefted a large ceramic pitcher down from the mantle. It was full of coins.

"Hey, Mom. Come here and look at this," he said.

Charity entered the living room from the kitchen. She had been emptying the cupboards of outdated boxes of food and bulging cans of vegetables.

"Look! This is full of change," Zach said.

Charity approached closer and inspected Zach's find. It was indeed filled almost to the top with coins of all denominations. "Where did you find it?"

He pointed at the mantle. "Up there. Do you think Aunt Bee will let me keep it?"

"Maybe. She may have forgotten it was there. Bring it home and you can ask her."

When back at home, Zach asked Aunt Bee about the coins in the pitcher.

She looked up, puzzled. "I think . . . Larry used to throw all his change in it to save for a *vacation*."

"Vacation? Did you ever go?"

"No. And after he died I didn't want to *count* it all, so I just put it up there and forgot about it."

They were in the family room watching Jeopardy. Next to court TV it was Aunt Bee's favorite show. After a commercial break, Zach tentatively approached the subject again. "If I counted all the change, would you let me keep it?" He had already begun wrapping the quarters. So far he had eighty dollars, and he wasn't even half done.

"What? Sure. I don't want it. You can save it for when you start *courting*."

"Courting?"

She turned to him. "I guess you're too young for a girlfriend yet." She patted his leg. "Maybe when you're older."

"Sure . . . Thanks, Aunt Bee."

Charity came into the room bearing a large ziploc bag full of about ten pill vials. "Aunt Bee, do you still take all these pills? I found them in your house while we were cleaning today." She began placing them, one by one, on the coffee table.

Aunt Bee peered at them. She picked up a small amber vial and shook it. "This is my water pill."

Charity looked closely at the label. "HCTZ. It says you should take this daily."

Aunt Bee waved a hand. "I don't need to. Just when my *legs* swell."

"Who told you that?"

She sidestepped the question. "I don't like to have to go to the bathroom so many times. So I just take it 'as needed'."

Charity sighed. She held up a larger pill vial. "How about this? Percocet."

"I don't take that anymore. That was for when I broke my *wrist*."

Charity remembered her aunt had broken her wrist several years ago when tripping on a loose board on the porch. The expiration date on the vial was 2008. "I'll get rid of these. And check all these other pills—see if there's anything else you need to save. I can take the rest to work and dispose of them at the pharmacy."

There was a knock on the front door, and before Charity could answer, Nadine peeked through the doorway. "Can I come in?"

"Sis! Sure, come in," Charity greeted. Nadine set down a large shopping bag containing shoeboxes.

Aunt Bee gave Nadine a quick hug and returned to the game show, occasionally shouting out an answer.

"I meant to give these to you earlier, at Aunt Bee's house. These are from spring."

Charity removed the top box's lid. The dressy white sandals didn't look like they had ever been worn. "You sure?"

She shoved the bag away from herself with her foot. "Please! Take them. I'm running out of room in my closet." She glanced at the coffee table. "What are you doing, selling drugs?"

Zach snickered. "Good one, Aunt Nadine."

She reached out and ruffled his hair. He smoothed it down quickly.

"I brought these from Aunt Bee's house and I'm just going over what she's still taking. Apparently, not much. And some of these pills are really old. This Percocet is five years old."

"From when she broke her wrist. I remember." She picked up the vial. "It's the same thing Mom was on."

Charity looked up at Nadine. "I had forgotten about that."

"I don't think she took many of them."

She nodded slowly "You're right. That's about when her swallowing got worse, and we started using the morphine drops under her tongue instead."

Nadine picked up her purse and stepped to the entry. "What happened to those pills? Did you throw them away?"

"No. I think . . . I think maybe Dad used some of them for his arthritis."

"From all those delivery trucks. Up and down, up and down."

Charity was thoughtful. "Right. He ran out of aspirin . . ."

Nadine turned at the door. "Bye, Zach. Bye, Aunt Bee," she called.

"Thanks for the shoes," Charity said. "I'll see you later."

As Charity closed the door the memory of her mother and the Percocet nagged her.

Aunt Bee took Sparky out for a last bathroom trip after Jeopardy and then retired up to bed. Jeff and Zach went to the Civil War Enthusiast's meeting and Jeremy was still at out. He had gone to the auto parts store to purchase new wiper blades for the Century.

The house was quiet. Charity made a cup of tea and sat on the couch, focusing on the orderly row of pill vials on the coffee table, sorting them into groups of what to keep and what to dispose of.

She picked up the Percocet and peered at the label. They didn't agree with her mother, she recalled. The few times she took one she slept so hard, it was difficult to arouse her the next day. And they had to be crushed to mix in with pureed food, as her swallowing function was severely diminished by then.

Eventually, her respirations became so labored she had to be hospitalized and have a breathing tube inserted into her neck for ventilator hook-up, as the illness had by now affected the nerves and muscles needed for chest expansion. She also had the feeding tube placed in her stomach at that time to ensure better nutrition. It was easy to pour canned nourishment and water into the tube three or four times a day. Unable to speak with the breathing tube in, she began using the letter board and chopstick for communication.

When the hospice nurse came to teach Charity how to use the ventilator and feeding tube, she also recommended the morphine drops as a better alternative for pain control. It didn't have as lingering effects or cause confusion when used at that low dose.

Later that summer, as her father prepared to withdraw to the basement family room with his sandwich, he had asked her for the aspirin. She retrieved the aspirin bottle from the cupboard and shook it. It was empty. "We don't have any more," she said.

He began to berate her about not getting more when she went to the store. "You're supposed to make sure we have everything."

"Here—you can use this," She said, tossing him the bottle of Percocet.

He glanced at the label and said, "Doesn't Mom . . . ?"

Charity remembered the sudden flash of anger she felt just then. “Have you even seen her? She can’t swallow those. She can’t even eat. Why do you think she had the feeding tube put in? She’s been taking morphine drops for pain.”

Chastened, her father limped down the basement stairs, back to his solitary living quarters.

~37~

Charity checked on the apartment Aunt Bee would be occupying by the first of October, and determined which pieces of furniture she would need. The smell of fresh paint lingered in the rooms, and sunshine poured in through the numerous windows. It will be a perfect apartment for her aunt.

Now that Aunt Bee's house was cleaned out, all usable furniture and belongings were moved to their garage. She would be taking some of it with her when she moved, but a few pieces were quite large, and still in good condition, albeit old. There was an old fashioned floor model radio that still picked up a channel or two, several wooden end tables, and a dressing table complete with a heavy round mirror and padded stool. Charity figured they could sell them or donate them to a worthy cause.

She remembered the annual rummage sale at Hill 'n Dale, and called Josephine about it.

A young woman's voice answered. "Hello?"

She thought fast. "Is this Maria?"

"Yes?" the voice said, guarded.

"Maria! This is Charity, your mom's friend. Is she home?"

In a moment Josephine got on the phone. "Charity! I'm so glad to hear from you. How have you been?" They had been playing phone tag for the past few weeks. Working opposite shifts made it hard to connect.

"Doing okay. I've missed you."

"And . . . Jeff? How are things? Better?"

Charity smiled. "We're getting there. We had some good talks lately, and I think there's more understanding on both our parts."

"I told you, if you could get him to open up, you would learn a lot about him."

"It's the opening up that's hard. Did I ever tell you he's like a puzzle box?"

The other end of the phone was silent.

"Jo?"

"Sorry, before you called I was on the phone with Northern Woods, and I was still thinking about it. We had to put *mi mama* there, in the Alzheimer's unit—Memory Court."

"Geez. That's too bad. When was that?"

"Two weeks ago. She was becoming more argumentative, and didn't recognize any of us, which made it impossible to do anything with her. I couldn't get her washed, and she wouldn't eat anything or take her meds. The only way she ate is by rummaging in the kitchen after we all went to bed. During the day she would just hide under the covers of her bed and when the kids got near her she would scream at them. Jesus, Mary, and Joseph! It affected Natalie the most. She's just now starting to be able to leave the house."

"So sorry about that. Northern Woods is a good place. My father-in-law was there till he passed away."

"Yeah. She's doing good there. A couple of the nurses have really bonded with her. She treats them better than me or my sister, Rosa. We take turns visiting every other day, but we may as well not bother. She doesn't remember us at all. I don't even take the kids there anymore, it's just too upsetting. But at least she seems happy. And she's safe, and getting her medications, as long as those two nurses she likes gives them to her. They're both from Puerto Rico and speak Spanish to her." Changing subjects, she said, "Sorry, Charity. What did you call about anyway? Shouldn't you be sleeping?"

"Yes. I'm about to. Just wanted to know if Hill 'n Dale still has that annual rummage sale. I have some furniture I could donate."

"They still have it. In fact, it's next month, the Friday and Saturday after Thanksgiving, sort of a Black Friday thing. They only accept good, sellable items, so don't bring any junk."

Josephine offered to have George pick up the furniture for the rummage sale in his truck; there was space at Hill 'n Dale to store the furniture until the sale. Charity would let Josephine know when Jeremy was available so he could help load it. They also made plans to get together at the Coffee Cave the following week.

After ringing off, Charity lay down for a belated nap. She didn't fall asleep right away, however. Her friend's dilemma with her mother came to mind. As it was, Josephine's mother was already lost to her. Dementia, in all its forms, was a thief. It stole remembrances and relationships.

She was glad that, despite her mother's disabilities, especially at the end, her mind was still sharp and she retained the ability to communicate with her and know her. Those final conversations, though painstaking through use of the letter board, were precious.

In the final month of her mother's life, Charity had pulled up a chair next to the bed, spending time with her whenever she could. She felt sorry for her mother, trapped in her bedroom without any company, sometimes for hours. She mentioned it to her one evening, upset her father had once again secluded himself in the basement.

"I wish Dad would visit you more. I don't want you to be alone so much."

"Came yesterday," her mother spelled out on the letter board.

"For a minute. It's not enough."

"He grieves."

Charity lowered her head and placed her hand on the comforter. “It’s just . . . it’s hard to . . .”

Her mother began pointing with the chopstick. “U do it all. Thank u.”

“I don’t mind.”

“He cant.”

“He could help a little more.” Charity tried to keep her voice even.

Her mother sighed and closed her eyes. She was getting tired. Charity picked up a book she had begun reading to her—a teen coming-of-age novel from the library.

“Sorry, Mom. Let’s read for awhile.”

Her mouth formed a grimace in a laborious effort to smile.

Charity started reading: “Chapter ten—"

Aunt Bee was happy to donate the furniture to the Hill ‘n Dale rummage sale. She spent the weekend cleaning the end tables and dressing table, and rubbing the veneer on the old radio to a shine with Milsek. George and Jeremy moved the stuff to a pole building behind the retirement home, among many other items stored there for the Black Friday rummage sale.

Two weeks later, Charity visited Aunt Bee in her new apartment at Quarry Run’s retirement apartments, St. Thomas’s. Not quite assisted living, each apartment was equipped with an emergency alert system—a necklace ‘panic button’. Activating the alert system resulted in a phone call to the apartment by the sheriff dispatch office, or a visit by an ambulance.

Charity rode the elevator to the third floor. Bearing a yellow mum and a dish of tuna casserole, she knocked on Aunt Bee’s door. Aunt Bee let her in and showed her to the living room. She was watching a daytime court show on her new TV.

To her surprise, Sparky also welcomed her by jumping on her leg and yapping for attention. She reached down and scratched his head. “So, you do remember me, don’t you, boy?”

“He’s finally getting used to our new place. At first he was afraid to get on the *elevator*, but now he knows right where he’s going.”

Charity sat on the worn couch from the old house and admired the neat, efficient living space, noting, with amusement, a stack of unopened junk mail on the end table. She said, “Aunt Bee, this is a nice place you have here.”

Aunt Bee considered this and nodded. She rose from her overstuffed chair and stepped into the kitchenette. After a few moments, she returned with a bowl of pretzels, cans of soda, and three glasses full of ice, all on a tray, which she placed among the knick-knacks on the coffee table.

“This place is nice,” Aunt Bee said. “It’s warm. And all the outlets and faucets work. I’ve made a few friends here and even went to bingo a coupla times.” She then said something that convinced Charity that the decision to move her to this cloistered community was the right one.

Looking at the empty recliner across the room, Aunt Bee said, “You like it here, don’t you, Larry?” Then, to Charity, “He likes it here. He just doesn’t say much.” Continuing in a whisper, she said, “I’m so glad he decided to move back in with me. I’ve missed him so much!”

~38~

Driving through the streets of her neighborhood after her visit with Aunt Bee, Charity enjoyed viewing the Halloween decorations on many lawns—animatronic skeletons, large inflated jack-o-lanterns, and ghosts suspended from trees. She remembered the festivity around the holiday when growing up. Of course, her mother designed her and her sister's costumes every year. One year she was a princess, another year a Geisha girl, or a flapper from the roaring 20's. They started early in October deciding on the costume and collecting fabric and special items required by the pattern. Their father helped them carve jack-o-lanterns, good-naturedly trying to outdo his girls at carving the most creative design.

She parked in the garage and went through the side kitchen doorway. After making a mug of tea, she took it to her table in the front window. It was the last hour before the boys would arrive from school. The rest of the evening would be a bustle of activity, but she could take a few minutes of quiet time for herself now.

Thinking about her mother and the homemade costumes reminded her of her mother's paintings, and she thought about the hand-painted cards in the round table. She withdrew them from the little drawer. Handling them again, she felt her mother's presence in the intimate details of the painted cards and notes written to Aunt Bee. Here was a painting of a vase full of tulips and daffodils, and on another card a bowl of strawberries was portrayed. She smiled at some of the more whimsical depictions—two robins fighting over a worm, and a squirrel with a cheeky grin.

She felt a familiar tightness in her throat when she came to the card from 1992—the watercolor of the sunset and the last thing her mother wrote to Aunt Bee. Her mother always enunciated her words well when speaking, like a first-grade teacher, and Charity could hear her voice speaking those last sentences: "The joy of my heart, these days, is the times I spend with James and my daughters. They are my life."

There would be no more handmade birthday cards, no further expression of her mother's talents, as the illness robbed her of the ability to move her hands and arms and grasp anything in her fingers. How her mother must have been relieved when she could finally give herself over to death and the promise of a healthy hereafter.

The days after her mother's death had been a blur, a slow-motion of the activities of daily life: sleeping, dressing, eating, listening to her father move about in the basement, catching his occasional appearances in the kitchen.

She recalled something that happened on Friday, the day before her father died. Finishing her usual lunch of a peanut-butter and jelly sandwich, Charity had gone back into the kitchen to grab a few cookies to eat while watching a TV show. Closing the cupboard door she paused, hearing talking coming from the basement. Nudging the kitchen door ajar, she could hear her father's voice coming up the stairs, his strained voice saying, "Lilly—", and the sound of crying—great convulsive sobs—as he wept alone in the dark.

She began crying, then, too. Hearing her father's grieving, her heart broke for him, and for herself. Closing the basement door, she leaned against it, her whole body wracked with an immense, silent sorrow as she wrapped her arms around herself, giving in to grief. After crying all her tears, she dried her face on a kitchen towel and felt wrung out from the release of emotion. She thought to reach out to her father and talk about their shared heartache. It would feel good to comfort one another in a long embrace, perhaps cry any tears that were left. She cracked the door again, listening. Hearing a loud belch and the snap and hiss of a beer can, she thought better of it. Closing the door again, she retreated to watch TV.

She thought being a nurse would absolve her of the feeling of responsibility surrounding her father's death, but so far she hadn't learned anything that may have caused it. And lately it was all she thought about—how her mother charged her with taking care of him, and how she neglected him that first week. She let him languish in the basement, full of sorrow, unaware of whatever sickness he had that claimed his life.

She needed someone to talk to. She needed to gain some resolution around her parents' deaths. Her over-sensitivity at Jeff on the anniversary of her mother's death proved she still had a lot to deal with. The anger she felt after the Don Morgan incident, which reminded her of how her mother suffered, still lingered in her heart. And remembering her father's grief just now, and her own, and how they never talked about it, and how she found him barely breathing in the basement, too late to help him—she would have to settle these issues and the sense of responsibility that came with them.

Perhaps Jeff?

They were making baby steps in communicating. Foregoing her compunction to clean the kitchen right after dinner, she sat with Jeff at the table, nursing a mug of herbal tea, as they leisurely talked about their day. Going to bed a little earlier gave them time to talk, as well. It usually started with Charity bringing up open-ended topics, such as plans for the boys' college days or whether to attend a function at church. She learned Jeff needed time to think and respond, as he typically had something to say, but she had unknowingly been discouraging his input by talking over him or misunderstanding his responses.

Last week they sat together on the back patio on a mild night, watching the harvest moon rise over the neighbors' houses. She asked him about his Civil War club meeting of that evening. In response, he spent about thirty seconds outlining the meeting's agenda. With gentle prodding, and some leading questions, they talked another hour about the club's activities and some funny anecdotes surrounding Zach's involvement. Once he got going, Jeff spoke with ease on his favorite subject, the Civil War, regaling her with facts about Lincoln and the union and confederate armies. She was still unsure which side was which, but it was nice to listen to Jeff talk about something without having to pull every word from him.

But talking about her parents' deaths? Jeff wasn't good with bereavement, or death, and was still dealing with his own father's recent passing. No. She would have to find another avenue, another way to deal with those events, and the feeling of blame that plagued her. It was *someone's* fault her father died. Was it hers?

~39~

A few days later Charity joined Teri in the break room before the night shift. She poured coffee for both of them and added cream to hers and cream and sugar to Teri's. She continued to feel Teri's indignation toward her since the Don Morgan incident in the way Teri kept to herself, sitting apart from her in the nurses' station, and avoiding her in the corridors of the unit. Charity sought for a way to win her back.

Teri looked up and accepted the coffee. She turned back to a texting conversation on her phone. Her new hairstyle consisted of braids close to her head in a swirly pattern, and she was dressed, as usual, in a stylish, well-fitting scrub set, this one sporting accents in lime green, matching her nails.

Miranda, back from pregnancy leave, stepped into the room and cleared her throat.

"What?" Charity said. Teri looked up from her phone.

"Our census is down, and we're overstaffed," Miranda said with a grim expression.

Charity and Teri let out a united groan, knowing what came next.

"One of us has to float," Miranda continued. She glanced at Teri. "Sorry, the house manager says it's your turn."

Teri rolled her eyes and started gathering her belongings.

Charity placed a hand on her arm. "Wait. I'll go."

"What?"

"I'll go. I don't mind."

Teri shot her a look of confusion, eyebrows drawn together. Everyone hated floating—working with unfamiliar staff in an unfamiliar setting.

"Look," Charity said. "I was unfair to you that day, with Mr. Morgan. I want to make it up to you."

Teri shrugged and sat back down, smoothing her report paper on the table. Charity exited the break room, ambiguous as to whether her gesture of apology had been accepted.

She took the elevator to Three North, the orthopedic unit. Total knee replacements, hip surgeries, and broken bones were the usual maladies on this floor. On the night-shift pain management and antibiotics were the priority. The staff also assisted all patients to get out of bed and be seated in sturdy bedside chairs for breakfast, served by 6 AM.

Stepping onto the ortho unit, Charity realized she had been there one other time. It was during orientation when she was introduced to staff members on all the different units. Almost a year ago, she still remembered the many ambulatory devices—walkers, crutches, and wheelchairs—stored in a large alcove on one end of the unit. For a while her mother's room looked a little like that, assistive devices cluttering one side of the room, impotently, as her mother remained bedridden.

She took a seat with the other nurses and HCAs to get report.

One of the other RNs was a tall guy named Adrian. The white tee shirt he wore beneath his uniform looked pristine against his dark brown skin. His scrub top was tight across his chest and shoulders—he obviously worked out. The other nurse, an older woman with a smiling skull tattoo on her wrist, was the team leader for the night. She gave Charity a fair assignment which consisted of two patients with knee replacements, a hip fracture, and a young car accident victim with a fractured collarbone and a couple broken ribs.

Charity began the night by administering pain medication to the two patients with knee replacements and setting the CPM (continuous passive motion) machines in place. These bulky devices gently move the affected leg back and forth at a prescribed angle to improve mobility.

Looking in on the car accident patient, she saw he was sleeping soundly. The young man would probably be discharged tomorrow as there wasn't much more to be done with his injuries.

She next attended to the hip fracture patient, who was bundled up to her chin beneath blankets, lying on her back. A large foam wedge was between her legs, keeping her ankles apart.

Turning on the switch for the night-light, Charity approached with the post-op dose of antibiotics. Logging onto the computer, she clicked on the chart for 'Laura Gilbert' and scanned the piggyback IV bag. She gently reached for her patient's arm to verify her name by scanning the armband.

Laura Gilbert woke and turned her head. It was then Charity recognized her. "Laura? It's me, Charity. From Poplar."

She lifted her hand and touched Charity's. "How are you doing?" she said in a sleepy voice. "I didn't know you worked on this floor."

"I don't usually. I was pulled."

"It's nice to see a familiar face."

"Same here. I don't even know the other nurses on this floor." She hung the antibiotic. Automatically, she began a quick physical assessment. "Are you in pain?"

"Not too much. As long as I don't move." She reached for the large foam wedge. "Can we get rid of this thing?"

"I'm sorry—that's important the first few days after your hip surgery. It helps keep the hip joint in place until it tightens up."

Charity poured fresh ice water and elevated Laura's heels off the bed with pillows. She brought warmed blankets and tucked them around her slender frame. Turning out the light, she promised to look in on her every hour. She would have liked to talk to her neighbor a little more, but knew it was important to let her sleep, if she was able. Maybe in the morning.

During the quiet of the night, Charity took a place at a computer in a hallway alcove to complete charting her physical assessments and make a list of the morning's medications. She felt a presence behind her and looked back to see Adrian smiling down at her.

"Hi," she said, turning her chair to face him.

"Don't you usually work on Four South?"

She nodded.

"With Teri Green?"

"Mm-hm. Why?"

He shrugged. "Do you know if she's seeing anyone?"

"I don't think so, why?"

"I was gonna . . . you know . . ."

She smiled. "You should ask her out. She's a lot of fun. And really smart."

"I tried talking to her in the cafeteria last week when I was on break. She just wanted to talk about a marathon she was running this fall. She seemed really preoccupied."

"That must be the one on Halloween weekend. She's been training for it all season. Maybe go to the marathon to cheer her on."

Adrian pointed both forefingers at her in a jaunty gesture. "Hey! Good idea." He skipped away with a smile.

Later that morning, Charity made last rounds to assist her patients into chairs to be ready for breakfast. One of the knee replacements, an elderly woman with the tell-tale finger deformity of rheumatoid arthritis, was having too much pain to get up. "Just give me my pain pill, nurse. I'll feel good enough to get up in about a half hour," she said.

Charity administered the medication and helped her into a sitting position in bed, her tiny build surrounded by several pillows for support. She placed the over-bed table so she could reach her meal when it arrived and continued to her last patient, Laura.

One of the HCAs was already in Laura's room, facing her as she sat on the side of the bed. Bracing her knees with his own, he wrapped his arms around her lower back and, on the count of three, helped her to a standing position. Whisking a walker in front of her, he instructed her on how to make the few steps to the chair.

"You really know what you're doing," Laura said to him. "I thought getting up would be much harder."

"I've been on this floor for a lot of years. We're taught how to assist with basic transfers by the physical therapy department. You'll learn a lot more with them today." He reached for the foam wedge, still in the bed.

"I can get that," Charity said, picking it up.

"You sure?"

She squatted in front of Laura and fit it between her legs, strapping it carefully in place.

"Nice job," the HCA said. "Sure you don't want to work on this floor?"

"I'm good. I don't mind floating once in a while, but I like my floor." As he left, Charity sat on the edge of the bed to spend a few minutes with Laura. "How does your leg feel? Do you want me to bring you a pain pill?"

"It's a little painful. Maybe after breakfast."

"Don't be afraid to take them—you will be able to move better and do your PT exercises if your pain is controlled."

"Thank you. I won't forget."

"So . . . what happened? How did you break your hip?"

Laura chuckled. "It was Whiskers. That darn cat was trying to get in the house."

"Your cat?"

"Oh no. Not my cat. More like the neighborhood cat. But I leave food out there for him sometimes. I guess the bowl was empty, so he tried to get in. I tripped over him and fell on the outside walk."

"Geez! How did you get help?"

"I have one of those panic buttons I wear around my neck. The ambulance was there in no time."

"Did Whiskers get in?"

"Ha! He sure did. I think he was laughing at me through the front window."

The meal hostess arrived and stepped into the room with breakfast. Charity placed the tray before Laura and arranged the containers so she could reach everything.

Laura touched her hand. "You are so kind. I can tell you love being a nurse." She picked up her fork and took a delicate bite of scrambled eggs.

Caught off-guard by Laura's words, Charity sat back on the bed as she continued eating. Laura nailed it. She identified the desire of her heart. As cliché as it sounded, she truly just wanted to help people.

"Thank you. I do love it." She paused. "My mother . . . it was her wish that I become a nurse."

"She must be proud of you."

Charity traced the pattern on the coverlet with her finger. "She died when I was young. Still in high school. She had ALS, and I took care of her for two years before she died."

Laura paused in her meal and shook her head. "It's a terrible disease. Usually affects the young, I believe. You were very brave to take that on."

"I don't know. It's just what I had to do. My father . . . my father couldn't help. He was in a deep depression. And then he died two weeks later."

"How awful for you."

Charity wasn't sure of the ethics of unloading her personal baggage on this patient, but once she started, the floodgates opened. With her gentle eyes and quiet manner, she found Laura easy to talk to. Plus, she was a neighbor, a friend. "It *was* awful. I found him passed out on the basement couch, barely breathing. I called 911 and the ambulance came and got him. He died two days later."

Laura shook her head, her lips pressed together.

"The worst thing is that it was my fault he died. I neglected him after mom passed away. Something was wrong. He was sick, or something, and I didn't take care of him."

"No. You can't look at it that way." Laura reached for Charity's hand. "You had just lost your mother. You aren't to blame for what happened."

"I don't know," Charity said, shaking her head. She swiped a tear from her cheek.

Adrian appeared in the doorway. "Charity. We're having report. You done? Or do you need help finishing?"

Keeping her head down, she said, "I'll be right there. Thanks." She took a deep breath and blew out through pursed lips. "I'm sorry to unload on you," she said to Laura. "You have enough to worry about." She inclined her head toward Laura's repaired hip.

"Don't worry. It's good to talk about things that bother us." Laura squeezed her hand.

"I'll come visit you again tomorrow," Charity said as she left the room.

Charity finished her shift feeling a little of the weight she had been carrying lifted. It was a balm to the soul to talk about it, to unburden herself to this kind woman, who did not judge, but expressed understanding. It was the kind of conversation she needed.

After work she took the long way home and drove Rt. 21 north, through wooded land, the trees sending shadows across the road in the early morning sun, like a UPC code. She hopped onto the interstate. Freeway driving was always soothing, and she found her breathing and heartbeat slowing in the rhythm of keeping a steady 65 MPH among others traveling her way.

Windows kept partially open filled the car with fresh air, keeping the post-work lethargy at bay.

Driving across bridges over country roads, she glimpsed the occasional Amish buggy trotting those roads alongside farm fields, much slower than her freeway pace. Frenetic living, such as she experienced, with work, and homemaking, and keeping up with her family's activities, was draining. How nice it would be to live at a slower pace. It would lend more time for talking, for really understanding one another. Like the time she just spent with Laura, who, though recovering from surgery, had time and patience for a meaningful conversation.

After fifteen minutes of freeway driving, she turned back toward home, her mood lightened and her heart calm.

~40~

Charity set her alarm for noon. She was off work that night, and wanted to make use of the time to run errands before the boys came home from school. She got home too late to see them off for the day, since she spent time talking to Laura and driving the long way home.

Most mornings, lately, she was able to eat with the guys. Jeff even learned to make a decent fried egg, and enjoyed serving breakfast. Handing her a mug of coffee as she dragged herself through the kitchen door, he usually had eggs, toast, and sometimes bacon on the menu. Jeremy had gotten used to packing his own lunch, which inspired Charity to give him the responsibility of making Zach's, as well. In these small ways, she tried to adhere to Josephine's advice to get her family to help her more, instead of doing everything herself.

After grocery shopping she stopped in at Bargain Retail to purchase a picture frame for her latest work—a still life of fruit in a bright red bowl. The celebration of color was meant as a birthday gift for Aunt Bee, who was coming for dinner the following week.

The next day was Saturday, and Charity did some meal prep and deep-cleaned the house. She prevailed on Jeremy to vacuum the upstairs hall, bedrooms, and stairs, since he was off work that day.

"But, Mom," he whined. "It's my day off."

She placed a hand on her hip and responded, "Mine too," and returned to cleaning the bathroom.

"Just so I have tomorrow night free. McKayla and I are going to the church youth group hayride."

"Before a school night?"

"Monday is Columbus Day. No school."

"Nice. Make sure you wear a warm coat. It's been chilly at night."

"Will do," he said, returning to vacuuming.

Several moments later, Zach burst through the kitchen door and raced up the stairs, followed by Damion.

"Hey!" Jeremy said. "I just cleaned there."

"Sorry," Zach said. He and Damion picked up the few errant leaves they had left in their wake, grabbed his duffle bag and basketball from his room, and headed back down. Damion hefted the basketball expertly, bumping it off his wrist and catching it again.

Charity peered out of the bathroom. "When are you coming home?"

"When am I coming home?" Zach looked at Damion, who shrugged. "In time for dinner, I guess."

"You want to come over for dinner tonight?" Charity asked Damion.

He thought a moment. "My mom . . . she needs me back later. She goes to bed early and I have to help her up the stairs. My dad's working late."

"Well, you're welcome any time," she said. Watching them leave, she felt a pang in her heart at Damion's words about helping his mom up the stairs. It was something she had done many times when her mother was still able to take showers in the upstairs bathroom. You never know who else is burdened with similar problems.

Zach came back home in mid-afternoon and stepped into the family room.

"You okay?" Charity said. She was watching a cooking show on TV, her knitting in her lap.

"My belly hurts. I had to leave basketball early." He cradled his abdomen with his arms.

"Well, take one of your pills and lay down for a while. It's probably something you ate."

"I hope I feel better. I'm going to the hayride tomorrow."

"You too? With Jeremy?"

"He's gonna let me drive," Zach said with a wide grin. He had gotten his driver's permit a week ago and was itching to spend more time behind the wheel. "Damion's coming too."

"If you don't feel better, you should stay home."

"Stay home?" He paused, and shifted his feet. "I really don't want to. I'm meeting Thankful there. The hayride is at her dad's farm. He uses real horses and everything."

"Thankful?"

"She comes to our youth group. They're Men . . . Men—"

"Mennonite."

"Yeah. Mennonite."

Charity remembered the family. The girls were all copies of each other and had names like Hope, Grace, and Thankful. The only son was named Earnest. Thankful was the oldest, a lovely girl with long brown hair.

"So . . . Thankful is going to sit with you."

"Yeah. Maybe. I don't know. She said she might." He began for the stairs.

"I'll check on you later," she called after him. Smiling to herself, she realized he was growing up, too. Driving already, and a first crush. How cute.

She returned to her knitting, and thought about having dinner early that night, as soon as Jeff came from work. She wanted to have time to visit Laura before her shift started.

Arriving at the hospital at 10:15 PM gave Charity a decent amount of time to visit Laura. She was still awake, lying in bed with the foam wedge between her legs.

Laura pressed the button on the bedrail and raised her head. "Charity, how nice of you to visit."

Charity placed a bag of snacks and box of Puffs tissues on her table and smiled sheepishly. "I'm sorry I didn't come last night. I forgot I was off work."

Laura waved a hand airily. "I know you're busy taking care of your family. It's okay. I was doing PT all day and was really tired last night." She pulled a tissue out and wiped her nose. "These are much softer than the sandpaper the hospital supplies. Thank you."

Charity smiled and nodded. "Did you have therapy today, too?"

"Just this morning. Weekends they let you take it easy, though I am anxious to get walking again. I miss my daily walks around the neighborhood."

"And we miss seeing you. Yesterday at dinner Jeff mentioned he hadn't seen you walking in a few days. I hope you don't mind I told him about you breaking your hip."

"That's ok."

"He felt really bad, and sends his wishes for a quick recovery."

"How nice of him. He's a good man." Laura reached for the snack bag and withdrew a cello wrapped cupcake. "What a treat! They don't give us junk food here."

After a few minutes of chatting, Charity said, "Is there anything else you need? Pain med? Warm blankets?"

Laura looked around. "I had a Norco about an hour ago, but I could use a fresh blanket." Charity arranged two warmed blankets around Laura and positioned the items on the overbed table so everything was within reach. Giving Laura a quick hug, she stepped toward the door, promising to check on her again soon.

As Charity strode along the corridor of the orthopedic unit, she bumped into a nurse hurrying out of the med room, carrying a heavy load of IV fluid bags. She dropped them all over the floor.

"Here, let me help," Charity said as she bent down to pick them up. Standing up, she gasped. She'd recognize that nurse cap anywhere.

It was Theda.

"I'll take those, if you don't mind." She snatched the IV bags from Charity's hands.

Charity watched, stunned, as Theda marched away, her cap askew on her head.

Despite the interchange with Theda, the night progressed peacefully. Charity and Teri had only five patients each, usually unheard of. Miranda passed meds on three of each of their patients. The entire hospital census was still low, flu season not being in full swing yet.

Nikki was training a new HCA that night, so there was extra help with vital signs and baths, as well. Charity and Miranda had some down time to catch up with each other in the small hours of the night.

Sipping contraband drinks at the nurses' station, Charity reached over and touched Miranda's hair. It was copper penny red again, and she had let it grow all the same length, ending at her earlobes. The bangs were blunt cut above her eyes. "I like it best this way," Charity said.

Miranda swung her head from side to side playfully. "It grows fast. My gyne said it's because of the pre-natal vitamins. Since I'm nursing, I'm still on them."

"How's the baby?"

Miranda pulled her cell phone from her pocket. She scrolled to a photo of the baby with Mitch, both with the same shock of black hair, and held it out for Charity.

"So cute! And look at that hair!"

"Mitch's grandmother has some old black and white pictures of him when he was a baby. Little Justine looks just like him."

"She's precious." Charity handed back the phone. "How's Mitch doing?"

"Hmph. He was laid off a week ago. That's why I had to come back to work early."

"Too bad."

"Yep. The road department let all the low seniority employees go."

"So he's watching the baby?"

Miranda nodded. "If you want to call it that. I still have to feed her in the morning, and give her a bath. And get Olivia ready for school. *And* do all the cleaning and cooking. I'm also picking up extra shifts. Gotta pay the rent. And before you know it Christmas will be here. It drives me crazy."

Charity didn't know what to say, and hoped to demonstrate her support by a nod and an understanding smile.

"Maybe I should quit my job. Maybe we could go on assistance. I'm just worn out and I never get to see the baby." She took a sip of her drink. Voice quieter, she said, "She smiled for the first time last night. Mitch told me. He texted me a picture of her with this big goofy grin, looking straight at him. I missed it because I was at work."

Charity reached for her hand. "It's hard to miss those milestones."

"Olivia missed her speech therapy appointment earlier this week. I was sleeping and he was supposed to take her, but forgot. It drives me up a wall! How am I supposed to take care of everything?"

Charity sighed. "You can't." She had to tread lightly, not wanting to offend. "He can help you more now that he's off work. He *should* help you more. You have to talk to him. Communicate. Tell him how you feel. Men can't figure those things out on their own. Jeff and I had some issues earlier this year, and we're finally talking about it. Things still aren't perfect, but he is trying. And so am I."

"I'm not good with confrontation."

"Don't confront. Make it something he can do for you. Like, 'I really need you to get the girls bathed before bed while I clean up the kitchen.' If you give him specifics, he'll know what to do."

Miranda smiled. "Good thinking. That might work better that me doing everything, and then us fighting about it later. I have to stop holding it all inside."

"I'm working on that, too," Charity said with a grimace.

Miranda gave her a puzzled look.

"I ran into Theda tonight. Literally. I ran into her and made her drop a bunch of IV bags. She gave me a snarky remark after I helped her pick them up, then took off without a word of thanks."

Miranda laughed. "Only you. Where did you see her?"

Charity explained about visiting Laura on Three South and seeing Theda as she was leaving.

"So, you see I have to work on speaking my mind, too, and not let people like her bully me," Charity said.

Miranda held up her cup, and Charity tapped it with hers. "Here's to communication."

Teri approached with her coffee au lait and dropped into an office chair. "Did you tell Adrian I would go out with him?" she asked Charity, her eyes steely.

Charity's eyes got wide. "I . . . I told him I work with you. And he asked me if you're seeing anyone."

"He wants to watch me at the Jack-o-lantern Run. To 'cheer me on' he said. How did he know I was even involved?"

There was a pause, and Teri made a pointed gesture toward Charity with raised eyebrows, awaiting her response.

"I might have mentioned it," Charity murmured.

"Why?"

Charity sighed. “I got to know him when we worked together the other night. He’s sweet. And really nice looking. Why not go out with him?”

Teri huffed and got up from her chair. “I just don’t have time.” She stomped away, then whirled back. “And stay out of my business.”

Charity grimaced as she looked back to Miranda, who suppressed a grin. “Don’t worry about her,” Miranda said.

“She’s still mad at me, I guess.” Just then, the call bell system on the desk sounded. Charity looked down to see it was one of her post-op patients ringing. “I better go. He needs his pain meds.”

~41~

Charity arrived home that morning to her family at the breakfast table. The boys were having an argument, and Jeff was trying to referee.

"Mom or I can drive you, pal, what's the problem?" he said to Zach.

Charity hung her jacket on a kitchen chair and poured coffee. She sat down at the table. "What's going on?"

"Jeremy promised he'd take me to the hayride tonight," Zach said. "He was gonna let me drive. And now—"

"—I have to drive McKayla. It will be too crowded," Jeremy said.

Charity held out a hand. "Wait. Can't you take Zach and Damion, too? They can sit in the back."

"I just—McKayla might have a friend coming. There won't be room."

There had been an escalating objection to getting rides to things with parents since Zach got his permit. Having his brother take him, or even walking, was cooler than having his mom or dad drop him off. Plus, there was this girl . . .

"I'll take you," Jeff said firmly, placing a hand on Zach's shoulder. "What time is it?"

"Never mind," Zach huffed, shrugging away Jeff's hand. Shoving the chair back, he sprang up, then suddenly doubled over and grasped at his belly.

"Zach!" Charity said, rushing to him.

He dropped down on the chair, remaining bent over. “Ow! This hurts!”

She sighed. “What did you eat?”

“Just cereal with chocolate milk.”

“Did you feel okay last night?”

“Last night?” He slid his eyes to her. “Yeah . . . I felt fine.”

Reaching for the kitchen cupboard where medications were kept, she brought out the bottle of Spaz-no and handed it to Zach. “You better take this. Don’t go to church this morning, and maybe lay down for a bit.”

“Hope you feel better, pal,” Jeff said as Zach got up and stepped carefully up the stairs. “Come on, Jeremy. You’d better get dressed for church.” Jeff placed the few dirty dishes into the sink and waited for Jeremy to get ready.

Turning to Charity, Jeff said, “I have to go in to work later today. We have a big shipment tomorrow and they need the extra help.”

“Okay, when?”

“I told them I could come at one. Jeremy and I can get carry-out after church, and then I’ll go in.”

“I did plan to cook something when I got up, but we can have it tomorrow. Get me and Zach something, too, okay?”

“Will do.”

Charity dragged herself upstairs and stopped in Zach’s bedroom. “Stay in bed till you feel better, Zachy. And don’t eat anything till I get up.” She made sure he was comfortable and stepped across the hall to her room. Closing the blinds against the bright sun, she switched on the electric fan for the white noise and crawled under the covers. Thirty seconds and she was asleep.

Charity woke up to a knock on the door. A glance at her cell phone showed the time as 2:35 PM. Her brain was still a little foggy. Another insistent knock on the door roused her. Donning her bathrobe and stepping across the darkened room, she opened the door to Jeremy. His face was drawn.

"What's wrong with Zach?" Jeremy said.

"He had a bellyache, remember? Why? Is he still sleeping?"

"He's still in bed, but he doesn't look good."

She drew her robe around herself and said, "What do you mean?"

"He's pale."

Alarmed, she strode into Zach's bedroom and turned on the overhead light. Zach stirred. He opened his eyes and whispered, "Mom."

His skin was pale. And sweaty. And cool. Charity took his temperature and it was subnormal. By then he was sleeping again.

The alarm bells sounded loud and clear in her mind. "Zach!" She shook him awake. He looked at her without focusing. "Zach, does your belly still hurt?"

"Hm?"

"Your belly. Does it hurt here?" She gently pressed his left abdomen. Then slid her hand to beneath his ribcage. Then the right side, just above his groin.

He shoved her hand away. "Ow! Don't!" His face blanched whiter than before, and beads of moisture popped out on his forehead.

Charity sprang up. "Jeremy! We have to get him to the hospital. He may have appendicitis." She raced down the hall to her room and threw on some clothes. Back in Zach's room, Jeremy was trying to get him up.

"Come on, pal," Jeremy was saying. He lifted him by his shoulders, but Zach's head lolled back like a ragdoll.

Jeremy looked at Charity. "He won't wake up."

She raked her hand through her hair. "He's got a bad infection. We have to get him in the car." She sat on his bed and called his name. Pressing her fingers to his inner wrist, she was barely able to detect a pulse. It was thready and racing. And now his skin was cold and dry. She could not wake him.

She shot up from the bed and shouted to Jeremy, “Go get my phone!”

Punching at the numbers 9-1-1, she quickly got through, and said, “I need an ambulance now! Here, to my house! . . . What? . . . I said to my house!”

Jeremy wrested the phone from Charity and said, “Hello? The address is 345 Poplar. . . . It’s my little brother. He’s really sick. Passed out. What? . . . He’s fifteen years old.”

The ambulance siren pierced through her heart as it got louder and closer. Jeremy let the EMT workers into the house as Charity sat with Zach. She had wrapped him in a blanket and kept him lying flat in bed with his legs on a pillow. She was unable to rouse him—all she could do now was hold his hand and pray.

She described Zach’s symptoms through tears to the paramedics who came to his bedside.

The buff paramedic looked at his partner and said, simply, “Appendicitis.”

“Please save him! Don’t let him die. I didn’t know how sick he was.”

Watching them work, Charity’s heart broke and she reproached herself for not recognizing the signs, taking his abdominal pain simply for another spell of IBS. How could she be so obtuse? So unobservant? Priding herself in giving ‘excellent care’ to all her patients, she allowed her son to develop a life threatening infection under her watch. She let it happen. She didn’t recongnize what was going on. It was her fault. If he died it would be her fault.

She paced around the room to avoid hovering over the paramedics and getting in the way. She felt nauseous and her heart raced.

By the time Zach was hoisted onto a gurney and into the ambulance, he had two IV drips pouring fluid and antibiotics into him, as well as an oxygen mask and heated blanket as supportive therapies. He moaned a little as the gurney bumped in the doorway of the ambulance, that little sign of life giving hope to Charity. She and Jeremy followed the ambulance to the hospital.

Charity and Jeremy sat in the hospital waiting area while ER personelle attended to Zach. Charity tried to reach Jeff several times on her cell, and finally left a text message to call right away.

After an eternity, Dr. Amala Doshi approached her in the waiting room. "Your son is very sick," she said in her crisp accent. "He has appendicitis, as you suspected, but in addition to that, the CT scan shows the appendix has burst. He is full of peritonitis."

"What is peri—?" Jeremy said.

"His abdominal cavity is full of poisons that are starting to attack the body organs," the doctor said.

Again, Charity felt a wave of nausea. She closed her eyes and filled her lungs, blowing the air out through pursed lips. She looked at Dr. Doshi. "Can I talk to him?"

"Mrs. Cristy, he is intubated. His oxygen saturation was very low and so was his blood pressure. His heart rate is still nearly two hundred. There is no urine output at this point. If we can't control this infection, he may have damage to his kidneys." Charity gasped.

"As soon as the helicopter arrives we will transfer him to Akron Children's. They are better equipped to handle his sepsis." Jeremy held up the cell phone for Charity to see. It was vibrating.

"It's Dad."

Dr. Doshi pressed Charity's arm. "Talk to your husband, and then you can come in and see him." She turned and walked through the entry to the Emergency unit.

"Jeff? Oh, Jeff! It's Zach!" Charity said, and told him everything.

~42~

Charity took a leave from work to stay with Zach at Akron Childrens. He was kept intubated and on paralytics for two more days, while his body conserved energy to fight the infection, and his cells were nourished with oxygen and IV fluid. Powerful IV antibiotics were given, and frequent blood testing performed to monitor the white blood cell count.

Charity was barely aware of the passing of hours as she sat beside Zach and watched for each breath. She swept his long bangs out of his eyes and cradled his head, murmuring prayers over and over again. Her thoughts went to his childhood, and the many loving gestures this youngest step-son, who never really knew his biological mother, had made to her—handmade mother's day cards and Sunday school crafts. Unashamedly giving hugs. It was different with Jeremy. The older one, he was more distant, responsible, grown up, even as a child. Like his father, he often had to be drawn out.

Zach was the emotional one, and the one she felt closer to. She could not lose him.

During the night, as she kept vigil, her in-and-out dreams returned to her mother, whose breathing had been sustained by a ventilator, like Zach's. She envisioned herself turning off the ventilator machine at her mother's bedside, the morning she found her having died. The dream switched to her leaning over Zach, her finger poised on the 'off' switch. She lurched awake in the recliner, focusing frantically on Zach's body in the dark, relief flooding her as she saw him taking regular breaths, assisted by the machine.

On Monday, a thin tube was inserted into Zach's side in the x-ray department to allow the purulent material from the infection to drain out of his body into a small bag, which was emptied by the nurse each shift.

The sedative was discontinued Tuesday evening, and Jeff and Charity both sat with Zach, holding his hands, observing as he gradually roused and began gnawing the breathing tube. The ventilator was disconnected, allowing him to breathe on his own through the tube for several minutes. Since his oxygen saturation remaind in the high nineties, the pulmonologist removed the plastic halter from his face and, as Jeff and Charity held his hands out of the way, gently slid the tube from between his lips. They watched as Zach glanced around with sleepy brown eyes, and took in plentious breaths.

"Hey, pal," Jeff said, squeezing his hand. Zach turned his head and gave a little grin as he recognized his father.

Charity wiped his mouth with a tissue. "Mom," he said in a hoarse whisper.

She finally let out the breath she was holding. Full of gratitude and relief, she wanted to give in to the flood of emotions just then, and allow them to come pouring out as tears. Observing how feeble and pale he looked, however, she knew she would have to be strong, and not give way to her feelings—feelings of anxiety coupled with the guilt lurking deep in her heart. This wasn't about her. And she hoped her strength, or at least the portrayal of strength, would help her son recover.

Now, as Zach continued to arouse, and the pulmonologist felt it was safe to leave the room, she gazed at Jeff, holding their son's hand.

He looked at her, his eyebrows raised. "You think he's through the worst of it?"

She nodded. "I believe so."

"Why don't you go home tonight. I can take time off work and stay."

"No. I can't. I can't leave him." She glanced down at Zach, sleeping now, the monitor on the wall exhibiting vital signs all in normal limits. "Maybe tomorrow."

An hour later, Jeff went home as Charity remained at Zach's bedside. He was offered a clear liquid meal—popsicles, jello, and broth. He ate a few bites of green jello and most of a popsicle. Tired, he lay back on his pillow. Charity rang for the nurse to remove his tray and bring a warmed blanket. Tonight she was the parent. The mother. She could not be the nurse, and depended on his team of caregivers to meet his needs.

This setback, this blunder of hers, had her doubting her ability as a nurse, anyway, blaming herself for missing important signs of Zach's infection. Perhaps she really *was* an imposter—playing nurse, remonstrating her coworkers, like Teri, when they failed to perform like seasoned RNs—but actually having no more skills than when she was a teen, letting her father languish and die in the basement when she should have been taking care of him. A sham. That's what she was.

Full of self-doubt, all she wanted to do was take care of Zach and be there when he needed her. Concerned texts from her friends went unanswered. She placed her cell phone in her purse and concentrated on her son.

Her attempts at conversation with Zach were met with him responding in sleepy phrases, often dozing in the middle of a sentence. Keeping busy, she helped him into a clean gown and changed the pillowcase and topsheet. She washed his face and brushed his hair.

When the nurse came to empty the urine catheter bag close to midnight, she asked when it could be removed.

"Probably tomorrow morning. It shouldn't be in any longer than needed."

"Can we get him up then," she peered at his name badge. "Eric?"

He squatted down on stout legs and emptied the bag. Getting up with difficulty, he said, "I'm here till 7 AM. If he's awake, I'll help him get up in the chair for breakfast. He's ordered a full diet starting tomorrow."

"Thank you," Charity said, relieved to have such an accomodating nurse take care of her son.

Eric changed the IV bag and hung a piggyback IV of antiboitics as well. He made some notes in the e-chart and signed off. Zach was awake by then, watching Eric at work.

"Hey, sport," Eric said. "How are you feeling?"

"How am I feeling?" Zach mumbled. "Okay. Sleepy."

"To be expected. Any pain?"

Zach struggled to reach to his side with his right hand. "Just here." He reached for the tube.

Eric gently worked his fingers from the tube. "Don't touch that. That tube is draining all the poison from inside you."

"Cool," he said, with a drowsy grin.

Eric chuckled. "We'll take it out in a few days."

Eric made sure Charity was comfortable in the recliner and fetched a few extra blankets to have on hand in case she got cold at night. He filled Zach's ice water and placed two jello cups on his over-bed tray to snack on overnight. "Call me if either of you need anything," he said as he departed.

Charity got Zach to eat half of a jello cup before he started dropping off to sleep again. She got comfortable in the recliner and switched channels on the TV, keeping the volume low. She answered Josephine and Miranda's text messages with a brief report of Zach's progress. Wishing she had a cup of tea, she shot a quick text to Jeff to bring her a mug and some tea bags to have on hand. He responded with, "Will do. C U tomorrow after work. Jeff." Then, as an afterthought, another text came from him, "XXOO. Jeff"

She grinned. *Jeff. Who else would it be?* His handwritten notes had recently been replaced by cell phone texts, which she cherished, and made sure not to erase. Was there a way to print them so they wouldn't be inadvertantly lost? She would have to check on that. These were her thoughts as she dozed, snuggled in warmed blankets, lulled by the hum of the IV machine, the rhythmic bloop of the heart monitor, and the barely audible voices on the TV.

She woke to Eric entering the room in the early morning light.

"Morning, sport," he said to Zach, who was already awake.

Charity got up and stroked Zach's hair. "How are you?"

He smiled at her. "Hungry."

"That's a good sign," Eric said. "His breakfast tray should be here soon. You like chocolate milk?"

Zach nodded, smiling.

After completing his assessment and documentation, Eric assisted Zach into the bedside chair and tucked a blanket around him. It was slow going, and his weakness and pale appearance troubled Charity. His appetite was good, however, and he ate half of his meal with gusto.

When Eric returned to remove the tray, he helped Zach back to bed and prepared to take out the urine catheter.

"Isn't your shift over?" Charity asked. It was 8 AM.

"More or less. I wanted to make sure this got done." Turning to Zach, he said, "Okay, sport, on the count of three—one, two—" and he slid the urine catheter out.

"Hey," Zach exclaimed. "What happened to 'three'?"

"It's better this way, believe me. Does it feel okay?"

Zach peered beneath the cover, and shot a sidelong glance at Charity. He looked at Eric. "Yeah. Can I go to the bathroom now?"

"Drink lots of water. Or juice. Wait an hour and ring for the HCA to take you to the bathroom."

"Can't you take me?"

"I'll be back tonight, okay?" He cleared the overbed table, leaving the extra juice containers from the breakfast tray, and said goodbye, promising to check on them as soon as he got there that night.

The rest of the morning was busy with visits from the pulmonologist and pediatric surgeon.

A well-dressed doctor in a pressed white coat visited in the afternoon. Entering the room, he immediately launched into: "The sepsis has been well controlled by the infusion of intravenous anti-infective agents, namely, ceftriaxone and metronidazole. We will contine this course of treatment, barring any further complication in the renal or hepatic systems."

Watching him as he spoke, he reminded Charity of a soap opera doctor, and she briefly wondered who did his eyebrows. He lost her halfway through his diatribe, however. When he finished, she stepped forward. "I'm sorry, but you are . . . ?"

Not quite looking at her, he said, "Dr. Paxos. Infectious disease."

"How many more days will he be here?"

"Five more days."

"Do you think he is progressing well?"

"That depends. How long has he been sick?"

"He got sick on Sunday, so" she ticked the days off on her fingers "four days, including today."

"He wasn't sick before Sunday?"

"No. He—"

Zach, who had been moving his head back and forth during the conversation like someone at a tennis match, spoke up. "I had a bellyache on Saturday."

"So it started *five* days ago. A day prior to you bringing him to the emergency department."

"Well . . . not technically," Charity said, trying to hold her own. "It was IBS. Or so I thought, originally."

He shifted his gaze to her forehead. “And what do you know about infective processes? Do you have the capability to diagnose whether this was irritable bowel syndrome or infectious peritonitis triggered by a ruptured appendix?”

“I *am* a nurse. And I—"

“Even more inexcusable to have waited.” He pronounced, then turned on a heel and exited the room.

Defeated, she slumped back in her chair.

After a few minutes, Zach said, “Mom.”

She looked up, still stunned at the scolding she was given by the ID doctor. “It’s okay, Zachy. We didn’t know.”

“But I—”

She approached his bedside. “Shhh. Don’t get upset. He should know about your IBS. It’s in your chart. You didn’t do anything wrong.”

Looking miserable, Zach slid beneath the covers. She stroked his bangs, trying not to let him see how much the accusation hurt.

But it did hurt. It brought all the regret and guilt back again. Once again she pictured her boy with the breathing tube protruding from dry lips, his skin pale and his eyes closed. Despite responding well to the treatment, he *could* have died. *Almost* died. The remorse swelled up in her like a tidal wave, crashing down on what was left of her self-confidence.

Jeff was required to work a double shift that day due to report-offs by other employees. Jeremy had plans with McKayla since several weeks prior—a Halloween party at her sister’s house. She expected him to coordinate with her mermaid costume as Triton, god of the sea, and he didn’t want to disappoint her, especially since they didn’t make the hayride earlier that week.

Miserable, Charity kept her texted answers to them short, trying to keep her mind occupied with sit-com reruns as Zach dozed.

After dinner, Eric entered the room to remove the meal tray.

"You're here early," Charity said.

"Twelve hour shift tonight. We have to do two a month to staff the unit adequately."

"So I have you all night?" Zach said with a smile.

"Sure do, sport." He scanned the IV antibiotic bag and got it running. "I brought you something." From his back pocket, Eric produced a copy of the current month's *Game Informer*. Zach reached for it eagerly.

"This is great!" He flipped through the pages. "Thanks, Eric."

Eric looked up at Charity. "How was your day?"

She turned her head and squeezed her eyes shut. A tear escaped.

"Hey," Eric said, coming nearer. "What's wrong?" He sat beside her on the marble windowsill.

She sniffled and gave a sad laugh. "Just a little fragile tonight, I guess."

"Hey. It's to be expected. It's not easy to see your child sick."

"You're right. But . . . I also had visit from Dr. Paxos. He—"

Eric pressed his lips together. "What did he say?"

She took a cleansing breath, and exhaled deeply. Glancing at Zach, she saw he was deep in his gaming magazine. Quietly, she said, "He said I should have brought my son to the ER earlier. Last Saturday I thought he was having one of his spells of IBS, and Dr. Paxos said I should have had him checked then. He practically blamed me for Zach getting so sick. But what he doesn't realize, is, I already blame myself. I almost lost him. And it would have been my fault."

Eric lay a hand tenderly on her arm. "Dr. Paxos is . . . He's a good doctor. That is, he knows what he is doing when it comes to infection. His patients respond well to his treatments, even those with weird, unusual germs." He paused, looking up to the ceiling. "Problem is, his bedside manner is in the toilet."

Charity nodded.

"Ever notice how he doesn't look directly at you? We have a running theory here on the unit that he is somewhere on the spectrum, because you can't get him to look you in the eye." He shifted on the windowsill. "Look. All parents, or at least *good* parents, blame themselves when their children get sick. I see it all the time. They think they should have magically known something was brewing, or that their child was going to get sick. But sometimes it's no one's fault. Kids get sick. Kids get appendicitis. It's very common. And often there is no warning." He stood up to silence the IV pump that was beeping, disconnecting the empty IV bag. "You can't blame yourself. You have been a terrific mother."

"Thank you, Eric," Charity said.

Eric nodded, the kindness in his eyes almost causing her to tear up again. "I'll check on you two in about an hour." Turning to Zach, he said, "How about a walk around the unit when I come back? Time you stop being lazy and start getting some exercise."

Zach grinned at him. "Exercise? Sounds like a plan."

~43~

Jeff and Jeremy visited Zach the next two days. On Friday they brought pizza from Chef Mario's to eat in his room, and a dozen donuts for the staff. Jeff tried to convince Charity to go home for a break, but she remained stubbornly at Zach's side.

The next day was Saturday, and the drainage tube was removed. Finally, Zach's abdominal pain abated. He enjoyed the attention of Eric and the other staff members over the weekend, who spent extra time walking him around the halls and into the common room which contained the latest in video game equipment. Eric was a whiz at Warrior Kings.

Jeff brought Damion to visit on Sunday, and the two spent a few hours playing video games in the common room. While they played, Charity and Jeff had time to talk.

Seated in Zach's room, Charity drank a mug of tea while Jeff updated her on neighborhood happenings. "That Laura called. She wanted you to know she was at Hill 'n Dale for rehab."

"My old stomping grounds," she said with a smile.

"She'll be there for about a week."

"I feel bad I couldn't visit her again," she said. "I hope you told her what happened."

"I did."

"What did you tell her?"

"About Zach."

Charity gazed at Jeff, her mug aloft, waiting.

Jeff caught her look and said, "I . . . I told her about Zach having appendicitis, and being here, at Akron Childrens."

"Thank you."

"She said she hoped he got better soon."

"I'll have to call her. And Josephine. I have to call her, too. I won't see her in church tomorrow." She paused. "When you go to church, don't forget to put Zach on the prayer list."

He nodded, and gazed out of the window a few moments. The trees were nearly bare, and there was even a few smatterings of snow in the air. "It's really cold out today."

Being there with Jeff, and not having to focus on Zach, Charity's thoughts went back to the beginning of this nightmare. To her failure. Her incompetence. Quietly, she said, "I'm so sorry, Jeff. I didn't know how sick he was, back then."

He turned to her. "Hm?"

"I thought it was his IBS. The stomach pain. I thought his IBS was flaring up. And the infection doctor told me I should have brought him to the ER sooner. He said since I'm a nurse I should have known better." She choked back a sob.

Startled, Jeff got up and knelt before her. "You *didn't* know."

"But I should have," she said, leaning on his shoulder, clutching onto his flannel shirt. "He's right. I should have known."

Jeff got up and sat back in his chair. Leaning with his elbows on his knees, he grasped her hand. "Look, you can't blame yourself. You did everything to save him once you realized how sick he was."

She shook her head, miserable in her self-reproach.

"Chair."

She kept looking down.

"Chair," Jeff said again, reaching for her chin, lifting her head. He looked into her eyes. "You are a great nurse. And a great mother. This thing . . . this could happen to anyone." He sighed. "*I* don't blame you. And Jeremy said you were awesome, that you knew just what to do. He said we have you to thank for Zach surviving."

"He said that?"

At that moment, Zach and Damion came back to the room, followed by an aide with a meal tray.

"Cool! Mac-n-cheese," Zach said, getting into bed.

Damion approached Jeff. "Mr. Cristy, I have to get home soon. My mom texted me. She has to go up to bed."

"Of course, Damion," Charity said. "He was just getting ready to leave."

Jeff kissed Zach on his forehead. "Get better soon, pal."

"I'll text you tomorrow," Damion said as he left with Jeff.

As evening fell, Charity prepared for another night sleeping with Zach. Familiar with the layout by now, she fetched warmed blankets, made herself a mug of tea in the family refreshment area, and brought Zach a couple chocolate pudding cups from the fridge.

He finished the pudding and snuggled down beneath the blankets. Charity reached for her knitting bag; Jeff brought it to her a few days ago.

Quietly, she heard, "Mom?"

She looked up.

Zach's eyes were drawn together as he gazed at her. "I'm . . . I'm sorry."

"For what?"

"When I got sick . . . I should have—"

"Zachy," she said, getting up. "You couldn't help it." The last thing she wanted was for him to bear a sense of guilt for getting sick. She stroked his hair. "*I'm* sorry. I didn't know how sick you were. I should have seen how bad your bellyache was, and realized there was something wrong."

He sat up in bed. "No—listen. I heard what you said to Dad. Me and Damion were in the hall and I heard what you said. But it wasn't you. I should have told you. My belly kept hurting all Saturday, after basketball. And Sunday morning." He looked down at his blanket. "I took my pill, but it never got better."

Her heart jumped.

"I just didn't . . . I didn't want to miss the hayride. Thankful wanted me to come."

"Oh, Zachy." What to say? She wasn't mad. Not even a little. How could she be, after walking this journey, this last week together with him. Praying, hoping, watching him recover. Reaching out, she embraced him, and felt the strength of the return hug from her younger son as they held each other for a moment.

As they released each other he reached for a tissue and wiped his eyes and blew his nose.

Charity pressed her lips together in a smile. "Oh, Zachy." She shook her head. "Well, son. It's almost over. Your angel is looking after you, and is making sure you get well." She pulled the cover up to his chin and kissed him as he snuggled down again.

Getting comfortable beneath a blanket on the recliner, her feelings ranged from relief that Zach was eating well and gaining weight, still some contrition for missing the warning signs of his severe belly-ache, although, apparently, he hid it from her, and gratitude to God for bringing her son from the brink of death and to recovery. She also felt compassion for her son who was at that awkward age between boy and man, and having his first crush.

Thankful would still be there when he got back, and would probably be even more enamoured with him having endured a life-threatening illness. She would tell him how brave he was. Perhaps.

~44~

The homecoming party two days later included Nadine and her family, Aunt Bee, and Damion. Nadine brought a dozen donuts from the Coffee Cave, each specially decorated for Halloween. Jeff picked up pizza and they all sat around the fire pit on the back patio, congratulating Zach on his recovery. Jeremy covered Zach with a blanket and brought him slices of pizza.

That night, Charity overheard the boys talking in Zach's room as she passed the partially open door.

"If you're up to it, I can take you driving this Saturday. It's my weekend off work," Jeremy said.

There was a murmured reply.

"It's all right. McKayla can wait." Jeremy walked away a few steps, then turned and went back. He reached into his pocket. "Hey, I forgot I was supposed to give you this."

He handed Zach a small envelope. "Thankful gave it to me at church."

Charity peered into the room to observe Jeremy fluff Zach's pillow and tuck the comforter around him. She slid away hurriedly so he wouldn't see her watching, her face lit up in a grin.

Later, she checked on the boys, as she always did before bed. Zach was sleeping that deep sleep of the recovering, his hand clutching the envelope. Charity slid it from his fingers and unfolded the note inside. It said, "Sorry you missed the hayride. It was fun, but I wish you were there. Get well soon. Thankful." She placed it back into the envelope, sliding it beneath Zach's pillow.

Charity requested her leave from work be extended for the rest of the week. She spent the time making nutritous food for her family, mainly thinking of Zach, trying to be sure to include plenty of protien and green leafy things in the meals. She also caught up on cleaning, laundry, and errands.

Jeremy helped Zach with his homework and spent time watching TV with him one or two evenings. Sometimes it takes the threat of losing someone to make you realize how much they mean to you.

On Wednesday Charity and Jeff took Zach to his appointment with the infectious disease specialist, Dr. Paxos. A blood sample was drawn when he first arrived, and a half hour later they were all ushered into an exam room.

Dr. Paxos' back was turned as he tapped at a computer and asked questions. "Is there any pain?"

Zach looked to Charity, who nodded her head toward Dr. Paxos, seated in an office chair, still with his back turned.

"Any pain? Just when I cough. Or take a deep breath," Zach said. He took a deep breath to demonstrate, his hand stealing to his right side.

Dr. Paxos tapped at the keyboard. "How is the appetite?"

"I'm eating good."

Dr. Paxos scribbled something with a pen, spun around in the chair, and held out a script. Charity reached for it.

"This course of antibiotics must be completed. Then check back in two weeks." He turned back to the computer, the appointment presumably over.

"Excuse me." It was Jeff.

Dr. Paxos turned again and focused over Jeff's shoulder. "What is it?"

"You didn't say why he needs more antibiotics."

Dr. Paxos sighed. He glanced in Charity's direction. "Your wife said she's a nurse. Ask her."

Charity's eyes got wide as Jeff took a step forward. "But she's not Zach's nurse. And you're his doctor."

He raised a well-manicured eyebrow. "Okay. His bloodwork from today shows elevated leukocytes. The antibiotics will take care of any lingering infection." Looking toward Charity, he said, with a smirk, "Do you concur?"

Jeff's nostrils flared and he pressed his lips together. "Dr. Paxos. You may not speak to my wife like that." Taking Charity's arm, he said, "Let's go."

They left the exam room rapidly, Zach following them. Charity quickly scribbled a check and thrust it across the counter at the receptionist. She made it to the parking lot behind the guys before bursting into laughter. "I thought you were going to slug him."

Jeff groaned. "I felt like it. The pompous jerk." He slammed his door shut and drove the car out of the lot somewhat rapidly.

Zach spoke up from the back seat. "I wanted to ask Dr. Paxos a question."

Charity turned around. "Sorry. We had to get out of there before Dad got into a fight with him. What did you want to ask?"

"When am I having surgery?"

"Not yet. Maybe not ever. The surgeon who saw you at Akron Childrens said the primary goal is to heal the infection. They don't remove appendixes all the time, like they used to. We'll ask Dr. Stoudt when you have your follow-up appointment."

She sat back in her seat. Stealing a glance at Jeff. She felt pride grow in her heart for her husband standing up to that bully of a doctor. She touched his hand. "Thanks for sticking up for me. You said the right thing."

Jeff answered her with a wide grin.

◆◆◆

Charity and Josephine met for a coffee date the next day. Charity relayed the whole story of Zach's illness. She ended with, "I thank God my mistake didn't cost Zach his life."

"You shouldn't feel bad," Josephine said. "My Manny is like that sometimes, complains of this or that ache or pain. I never know when it is really something serious. Once he fell from his bike and fussed about his wrist hurting. It's sprained, I told him, and wrapped it in an ace bandage. Later that week the school nurse sent him home with a note about his wrist, so I had to take him to get it checked and x-rayed. Jesus, Mary, and Joseph! Here—it was actually broken."

Charity grinned.

"He had it in a cast for six weeks." She took a bite of bagel and chewed noisily.

"You always make me feel better. It's all such a blur to me now, but it's hard not to feel in some way responsible."

Josephine reached for Charity's hand. "Listen. You can't control everything. The good Lord worked it all out, and that's what you should focus on."

~45~

Saturday afternoon Charity drove to the little brick house on Dogwood Lane, the next street over from Poplar. Laura was expected home from home Hill 'n Dale rehab, and Charity offered to help her get settled. Despite having two brothers, and a few nieces and nephews, Laura was far too independent to look to them for help. Charity insisted, however, so Laura agreed to let her come, joking about her being her private duty nurse.

Charity and the ambulette driver helped Laura up the two steps to the front stoop, and into the entry.

"Watch him!" Laura called out, looking back through the doorway.

Charity glanced back and saw an orange cat with a stubby tail sidling up to the entry. She closed the door against him.

"Whiskers?"

Laura nodded. Stepping into her walker, she moved slowly to a high-backed chair. Charity reached for her arm to help her get seated.

Laura held up a hand. "Have to be able to do this myself." Using small steps, she rotated her body till the backs of her legs touched the seat. Releasing the walker, she reached for the arms of the chair and lowered herself into it. Once settled, she raised her hands in a triumphant gesture.

Charity clapped. "Good job. You learned a lot in rehab."

"When you live alone, you can only depend on yourself."

Charity sat in an adjoining chair. She touched Laura's arm. "True. But I hope you would call me if you need help. I'm only a few minutes away."

"Thank you. But I know you're busy taking care of your boy."

"I am. But he's nearly recovered. He's going back to school this week."

"Well, fortunately, everything I need is on the first floor. I don't go upstairs much, since I had a full bath installed there, next to my bedroom." She pointed toward a hall leading from the right.

Charity observed the small kitchen and dinette were accessible through the front room archway. Everything was in easy reach. The décor was clean and clutter-free, so different from Aunt Bee's old place. The rooms and furnishings were all in hues of tan, white, and slate blue. It reminded her of the sea.

"Your house is lovely," she said. "The colors are so restful."

"When I first moved away, I spent a lot of years in Jersey, on the coast. I miss the ocean—the sand and the waves. So I had the interior painted in those colors."

"What made you move back?"

"Five years ago my sister, Lucy, was diagnosed with leukemia. The acute form. She didn't really have anyone—her husband died when they were young, and she lived by herself in a small apartment since then. My brothers . . . well . . . they were just too busy. So I bought this house and she moved in with me. I took her back and forth to Pittsburgh or Columbus—special cancer hospitals." She adjusted herself in her chair and stretched out her legs.

"How did she do?"

Laura waved a hand, "Well—let's not talk about that." She pointed at her carry-on, still near the front door. "Can you please put that in my bedroom before you leave? I think I'm going to lie down for a half hour."

Charity rose to her feet. “Do you need anything? How about groceries?”

“I still have some things in the freezer, and the social worker at Hill ‘n Dale set up Home Helpers to come tomorrow morning, in case I need anything. I figure I could send them to the store and then they would leave me alone.”

“I used to work for them, years ago.”

“Kind of a ‘rent-a-friend’ agency, isn’t it?”

Charity retrieved the carry-on and stood near Laura in her chair. “I guess so. Some people really need that, though. At least they can help you till you are able to drive again.”

Laura nodded. “True. I didn’t mean it that way. I just don’t like to be dependent on anyone.”

“What are you doing about physical therapy? Did they arrange for that, too?”

“Yes. So much bother. All those exercises: ‘move your foot, up-down-up-down’.” She demonstrated by moving her foot in that manner. “It doesn’t really do anything. What I really need is the chance to go on my walks again. That would help me recover more than anything.”

Charity had a thought. “Why don’t I come a couple days a week, and we can walk together. At least till you can go by yourself. I could use the exercise, too.”

Laura looked up to her. “That’s something I would like. You wouldn’t mind?”

“Of course not. I work nights, as you know, so it would be in the afternoon.”

“No problem. I’m not an early riser, anyway.” She stood up with effort and reached for Charity’s arm. “I would like that.”

Charity smiled. “I’ll call you in a few days and see if you are up to it.” She pulled the carry-on down the hall and into the bedroom, and returned. “In the mean time, call me if you need anything, okay?”

“I will.” Laura propelled the walker to the entry and grasped the doorknob. She peered out the small window. “Just be careful of Whiskers. I don’t see him, but he’s sneaky, that one.”

“I’ll watch for him,” Charity said with a grin.

She left with a promise to call Laura soon.

~46~

Monday was Halloween. Zach, though recovering well, opted not to go door-to-door with Damion and their friends, all dressed as ghouls or the undead. "It's probably your last year to go, are you sure?" Charity asked him.

"Am I sure? Yeah. I'm just not into it. I'll hand out candy."

"That will help me. I have to work tonight. If you pass out the candy I can get my nap early."

Jeff strolled through the kitchen as they prepared the treats, cutting open bags of tiny-sized candy bars and pouring them into a large bowl. He reached in and snatched one, grinning.

"Zach's handing out the candy this year," Charity said.

"Want me to help you with that, pal? We could wear our union soldier uniforms and sit outside together."

Zach glanced at his father, nearly the same height, now. "Um . . . Maybe not. I'll be fine by myself." He grabbed the bowl and withdrew before Jeff could protest.

"He loves going to the club meetings," he said to Charity. "I figured he would want to dress up."

Charity gathered the candy bags and tossed them in the trash. "It's not that. You remember what it was like at his age, don't you?"

"I s'pose."

"And your father—did you try to get out of doing things with him?"

Jeff thought a moment. "I remember he wanted me to go fishing with him every Saturday. But the speech team would meet that day, and we always went somewhere to eat after." He unwrapped a candy bar and popped it into his mouth. "I'd go fishing with him in summer, sometimes. He'd make me go."

"It's good you have those memories with him."

"You're right. It's the first thing I think of when he comes to mind. Him in his waders with a fly-fishing pole. I always ended up enjoying myself, too."

"Same with Zach. Just keep taking him to the club meetings. He'll always have those memories." She moved to the refrigerator and looked inside for inspiration. There was a covered dish of leftover lasagna. She withdrew it, placed it in the oven, and set the temp for 350.

Jeff began for the family room, then turned. "I wanted to tell you, Laura called and left a message. She said she's ready for your walks. Do you know that that means?"

Charity smiled. "I told her I'd walk with her in the neighborhood a couple days a week, to help her hip heal faster."

"Good idea." Jeff got comfortable in his recliner and opened the paper. Charity continued preparing dinner.

The next day, Charity drove to Laura's house for their first walk. They arranged to go on Tuesdays and Fridays, for now. Home physical therapy was scheduled on the other weekdays. After two weeks, Laura was able to walk with just an aluminum cane. The bracing air encouraged a brisk pace while they walked and talked together.

Sometimes their talks included stories of Laura's growing up years, or her experiences living on the East coast, running a B & B in Cape May with long-time boyfriend, Henri. Charity found herself bringing up problems at home, with the boys, or quarrels with Jeff, and taking in Laura's wisdom and advice ("After Henri and I parted ways," she said one day, "I was very lonely.

Somehow all those little annoying things he used to do just didn't matter. I just missed *him*.").

Charity also reminisced about life as a youngster in Quarry Run—family vacations to the lake and special outings with Aunt Bee. "You would like her," she said. "I'll have to bring her for a visit one day, when you feel up to it."

"I'd like that. I get tired of the same old faces around here."

"She lives at St. Thomas' with her little dog, Sparky. He would enjoy a walk around the neighborhood, too."

"Maybe he could scare Whiskers away," Laura said. They enjoyed a laugh together.

◆◆◆

On rainy days Charity had started bringing the old Scrabble game to play with Laura. Setting it up and handling the wooden tiles gave her a warm feeling, remembering that her mother's hands had touched these pieces. Visiting with Laura, Charity started to feel a mother's touch when Laura greeted her with a quick hug. She could imagine her mother's voice discussing the events of the day and giving advice in the way Laura talked. Gradually, her relationship with Laura filled a void in Charity's life, left there when her mother passed, and she could feel the sting of grieving diminish.

Her father's death remained a mystery, however, and she continued to feel the pang of guilt when it came to mind.

It came up in conversation during a game of Scrabble. Though usually keeping those events buried, Laura's practical manner made it easy for her to talk about it.

"I felt guilty for a long time, but that first day when I saw you in the hospital, you said something. You said I wasn't to blame for what happened. That helped." She reached into the velvet bag and withdrew six letter tiles to replace those she used for the word: SIGNED.

Laura smiled. "It's the truth. You weren't to blame." She placed the letters: VEXE on the D.

"Good one," Charity said. "And Double Word, too!" She played the word: TAXI.

The game progressed rapidly, ending with a score of 239 for Charity, and 244 for Laura.

"So close," she said, patting Charity's hand.

The rain had let up and they decided on one turn around the neighborhood before Charity went home. As they walked, they talked about Zach getting sick that summer. "I just wouldn't have been able to forgive myself if he had died." Now that he had recovered so well, she was able to talk about it without tearing up. "As it is, I blame myself for not realizing he was so sick. Thank God Jeremy woke me up when he did, and alerted me to his condition."

Laura nodded. "True. A higher power was definitely at work there. But you . . . you can't keep blaming yourself for everything. You aren't responsible for the bad things that happened to your son. Or your father."

A silence stretched between them. Charity sniffled and dug into her coat pocket for a tissue.

Laura took Charity's arm as they strolled, having left her cane at home. "Why don't you tell my what happened? You told me he moved to the basement and drank a lot. Was he on any medication that maybe ran out? Or was he taking anything new?"

It came to her immediately. "Percocet."

"Percocet?"

"It was my mom's leftover pills. Dad had arthritis and ran out of his aspirin."

As Laura asked questions, Charity dug deep into her memory, making herself think about that day it happened—when she went downstairs to check on her father, and found him sunken down into the couch cushions, barely breathing, his face pale as her mother's when she died. Her words to Laura came spilling out as she started remembering everything.

She was afraid she was too late. She shook him by the shoulders, crying and screaming his name. When she realized he was still breathing, she dialed 911 and remained at his side till the ambulance whisked him away.

Wallowing in worry and guilt, she worked off some nervous energy by cleaning the basement family room. She collected all the empty beer cans, bottles, and fast food containers. There were also several larger glass bottles. She sniffed them—the strong smell of whiskey lingered. Lugging the filled trash bag up the stairs she turned back and noticed one more beer bottle under the couch. When she retrieved it she also found the empty vial of Percocet.

The empty vial.

There was something about that vial. It was larger than a standard pill vial, and as she rounded a corner with Laura, she described how she stood by the couch holding it, reading the label—the label that said #90. Which would have been correct. It was originally prescribed to be given three times a day to her mother, and was a month's worth of medicine. Only a few had been used for her mother.

She had given the pills to her father a week before her mother passed away, and he died two weeks later.

In a period of three weeks her father had taken nearly ninety Percocet.

The emotional strength it took for Charity to relay this account to Laura had her spent. She took a break on one of the benches the village had installed along walks, her mind still a jumble of recollections.

Laura sat next to her, tugging her red beret over her ears in the cool air. "You were so young—what could you have known about the dangers of mixing alcohol with narcotics?"

It was the pain pills. The narcotics. Deadly when taken with alcohol.

She pictured the pill vial in slow motion, arcing through the air as she tossed it to her father. Him catching it and turning to the basement steps.

"But, Laura, *I* gave them to him." She felt her throat close as Guilt tried for one more thrust.

Laura parried. "Yes, but *he* should have known better. You weren't responsible for what he did." She got up and reached for Charity's hand. "Let's go inside. I want to tell you something."

They walked the remainder of the block and entered the warmth of Laura's house. She made tea for them both—it had become a ritual during their visits.

Sitting down in her chair, Laura sipped tea silently for a few minutes, collecting her thoughts. "When my sister Lucy went into remission from acute leukemia and had the bone marrow transplant, we figured we would live out our days here together—two old spinsters. We celebrated each others' birthdays and the holidays. Took turns cooking. It was nice, having someone with me again."

Charity stirred a spoonful of honey into her tea and tasted it.

"Two years ago Lucy . . . she drove the car to one of those Amish farm markets they have out in the country. We liked to support local businesses, and they have the best produce around, not to mention their jams and cider."

Charity smiled and nodded, a quick memory of her family doing that very thing when she was young came to mind.

"Lucy was walking across the parking lot by the farm market with a bag of apples and jug of cider when a car pulled in and plowed right into her. Just turned off the street and ran her over. Didn't even see her, they claimed."

Charity's eyes got big. "I'm so sorry. What a terrible thing."

"It bothered me for a long time, because, you see, she wanted me to go with her that day. It was a sunny fall day and she loved driving around to see how the leaves had changed. I should have gone. But I was in the middle of cleaning the bathrooms—Lucy wasn't much for cleaning, so it fell on me—and I told her to go without me." Laura pressed her lips together and shook her head. "If I had gone, she may not have died."

"You can't know that," Charity said quietly.

"You're right. And, believe it or not, for a while I blamed her. If she had not been so stubborn and have to go to the farm market that very day, she would still be here. I was angry with her."

"The stages of grief include anger," Charity said, quietly. "Denial. Anger. Bargaining. Depression. Acceptance. We learned that in nursing school."

"That sounds about right. I finally made my peace with it and realized it was out of my hands."

Charity remained quiet, thinking. She, too, had been angry with her father—for neglecting the care of her mother, for retreating and isolating himself, and also for dying in the way he did. A way that left many unanswered questions and no real closure for her, making her live with guilt and self-reproach. And it was still there, the anger and unforgiveness. She hadn't moved on.

Laura reached for Charity's hand. "Same with you. You aren't responsible for your father dying. You were young. He was dealing with things you couldn't understand and in his despair did something you never expected. It wasn't your fault."

It wasn't my fault.

She squeezed Laura's hand.

It wasn't my fault.

Charity held her breath a few seconds, then blew it out in a deep sigh. "All my life . . . all my life I needed to hear those words. I never really knew how he died. My mother told me to take care of him, but I was young, and grieving, too. And for a long time I didn't remember anything past finding him there, and then my sister coming over at night. It was all a blur. But what you say makes sense."

Laura nodded.

Charity sipped on her tea, her thoughts on Laura's comforting words. Laura picked up a magazine and thumbed through it. The sound of increased traffic was heard as neighbors drove home from work. The living room clock chimed 5:30.

Charity looked at the clock and got up to place her mug in the kitchen sink. She put the Scrabble game together and placed it on a shelf in the dining area. Turning, she said, "I'd better go. Jeremy's bringing his girlfriend over, and I'm making tacos." She put on her down vest and wrapped her scarf around her neck. Laura joined her at the door.

"Thank you," Charity said, pressing her arm. "Thank you for helping me deal with my father's death." Her voice caught.

Laura waved away the emotional moment. Then, seeing the tears brimming in her eyes, she reached out for a quick hug. Charity clung to her for a moment, then broke away.

"Are you okay?"

"Yes," Charity said. "Better than ever."

"Come back on Friday?"

Charity pulled on her gloves and smiled. "Sure." She stepped along the walk and turned for one last little wave before getting into her car.

Charity left the neighborhood and went for a quick drive out to the country, her mind still processing deeply buried memories that finally surfaced, and what Laura said about them, releasing her of guilt. She no longer had to feel responsible for her father's passing, no longer had to feel she let her mother down, did not do enough to help him. Her father's own unhealthy choices caused his death, and she could not have saved him.

The resentment she felt toward her father was beginning to ease, being replaced by compassion. How desperate he must have felt that that was the only way out of his misery.

Finding her way from blame she once again thought of Laura's words, " It wasn't your fault."

She made two right turns on country lanes and headed back to town, her thoughts still on the conversation with Laura, thinking about her words, and how they brought restoration. She breathed in the scents of mown hay and cow pasture, and exhaled deeply, freedom flooding her soul.

~47~

Amidst the chilly late autumn days, Quarry Gen celebrated its golden anniversary—November 20. Starting out fifty years ago as a clinic serving the region's farmsteads, the hospital grew with the village into the four-story structure it now was, becoming part of the NEOHOS system and benefiting several surrounding communities.

Every employee received a key fob in the form of a golden chunk of limestone with a tag that said "Quarry Run General Hospital: fifty years of serving people", and a $10 gift card donated by Mr. Speedy.

Several activities were planned to commemorate the milestone, and the TV news station came early that morning to film a helicopter landing on the new helipad out front.

As the news crew assembled, all available nurses, aides, housekeepers, doctors, and other workers were asked to gather in front of the hospital for a photo.

Charity, Teri, and Miranda stayed after their shift and joined the group on the walkway outside for the photo opportunity. Adrian approached from behind and placed his hands on Teri's shoulders.

Teri spun to face him. "Oh. It's you. What do you think you're doing, scaring me like that?" She batted at him with her hand. Despite her scolding words, she looked pleased he was there.

Charity heard a voice calling, "Charity! Over here!"

She looked around for the owner of the voice. It was familiar. Could it be?

When she turned back she beheld Josephine standing before her in a new navy blue scrub set. "Didn't you hear me calling?"

"Jo! Jo! It's you!" She wrapped her arms around her old friend, her face split with a wide smile.

Miranda approached. "Hey, I know you. Weren't you at her father-in-law's funeral?"

Josephine opened her mouth to speak, but Charity beat her to it. "Randi, this is my friend Jo, from where I used to work, at Hill 'n Dale." She grasped Josephine's arm as she introduced her to Teri and Adrian, as well.

"Are you working here now?" Teri said.

"Got hired a few days ago. There was an opening in telemetry, on days. I beat out seventeen other applicants."

"I believe it," Charity said, "How did Susan take it?"

"Like you'd expect—not good."

"We know about Susan," Teri said. "Her father was a patient on our floor. She reminded me of my cousin Leyla. So superior. I wonder anyone could work with her, ya know what I mean?"

At that moment, an announcement was made: ALL STAFF MEMBERS WHO WISH TO BE IN THE GOLDEN ANNIVERSARY PHOTO COME TO THE HELIPAD.

The friends joined all the other employees and were posed by a professional photographer, shortest in front, tallest in back. Charity and Miranda were the same height, so stood together, with Josephine in front of them. Teri stood at Miranda's other side with Adrian behind her, his hand on her shoulder. The photographer gave instructions for all to remain still as he framed the photo to fit the entire group of workers as well as the helicopter, with the hospital in the background.

Charity used the moment to gaze around, and focused on the helicopter, remembering when Zach was taken up in it. Too bad he was too sick to enjoy the thrilling ride. She looked to see who else was there. Across the throng she could see Neil Kennedy bringing up the back row with Dr. Chole and a few other residents. Nikki, her hair glowing in the sun, was present out in front, next to Joyce Foster, resplendent in her white jacket.

Just before the photo was snapped, a strident voice was heard.

"I never! Can't even wait for me. I've been here since just about the day this hospital opened. Least ways you could wait for me to get here."

It was Theda. She wormed her way into the group and ended up in front of Teri. Josephine, at her side, gave her a disapproving glance.

The group was instructed to count down and then say 'Quarry': "Three—two—one—QUARRY!"

In the seconds the group counted down, Adrian reached over Teri's shoulder and flicked Theda's nurse cap with his finger, shifting it over her forehead. She instinctively grabbed for it. Teri gave a snicker.

SNAP! The picture was taken.

A week later, the group photo was displayed on the wall of the hospital lobby, large as a big-screen TV. Charity purchased a 5 x 7 copy of it and placed it on a bookshelf at home.

Jeff peered at it when she put it up. "You look tired."

"I worked all night," she said, a little miffed.

He turned to her with a sheepish grin. "I know. But you don't want to look like it, right?"

She nudged him in the shoulder. "Right!"

Looking back at the photo, he said, "Who's that?", pointing at Theda.

Charity groaned and said, "Theda. My nemesis." She was amused to see the photo caught Theda with her hand on her hat and that vexed expression on her face, as well as Teri's bemused grin and Adrian at his prank, his hand a blur over Teri's shoulder.

"Don't be afraid of her," Jeff said. He moved to the recliner and sat down. "Look at all you've learned, and the friends you made. Be proud of yourself." He picked up a newspaper and added, "I sure am."

Meet the Author

A voracious reader all her life, Silke Chambers' childhood favorites were *all* the Oz books by L. Frank Baum, and The Little Prince by Antoine de Saint-Exupéry.

Her love for reading grew into a love of writing, and she has won awards and published short stories related to her work as a nurse through Writers' Digest and local journals.

Her debut novel, "Among the Ruins—the Story of David" was published in 2020.

She lives in northeast Ohio, where nothing happens, with her family, and writing buddy, a cockatiel named Jesse.

Visit her website at www.silkechambers.com for more stories, or contact her at silkechambers20@gmail.com.

Thank you!

My life as a homemaker and nurse would not have been nearly as possible without the support and love of my friends, Faye, Deb, and Karen. These women lived the life of the night-shift nurse along with me, making it more bearable, and even, sometimes, great fun. Remember all those New Year's Eve parties in the social worker's room? Looking out over Youngstown at the fireworks downtown? Such good times.

I am also indebted to McKayla Rockwell, my editor and creative writing coach. Thank you, again, for your patience and all the hours you put into helping me with this novel.

Lastly, I would like to express my gratitude to friends who tolerated my endless babble about 'my book', reading early copies of it, and giving practical advice. Alison, Anne, Kim, and my co-workers in the endoscopy department—a big Thank You!

SC
stories that inspire
1
www.silkechambers.com

Made in the USA
Middletown, DE
28 February 2022